This book should be returned to any branch of the Lancashire County Library on or before the date shown

11 JUL 2019

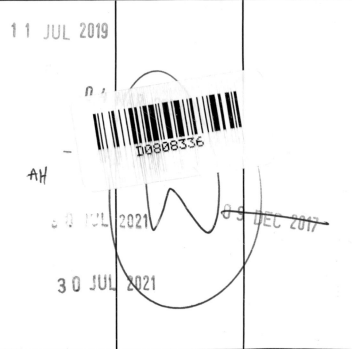

AH

30 JUL 2021

30 JUL 2021

0 5 DEC 2017

D0808336

"Where are you taking me?" Abby asked from the passenger seat of the pickup.

He could tell that each word hurt her to speak. He would have brought the Suburban so she could lie down in the back but he hadn't known how badly she was hurt.

"To the hospital," he said.

"No!" She tried to sit up straight but cried out in pain and held her rib cage. "That's the first place he'll look for me."

"Abby, you need medical attention."

"Please."

He quickly relented. He couldn't let Wade near this woman, which meant no hospital. At least for now.

"I'll take you to the ranch and call our family doctor. But, Abby, if he says you have to go to the hospital—"

"Then I'll go." She lay back and closed her eyes. "I didn't want you involved."

"I've always been involved, because I've always loved you."

She said nothing. He could tell that she was in a lot of p... find Wac...

DEAD RINGER

BY
B.J. DANIELS

First Published in Great Britain 2017
By Mills & Boon, an imprint of HarperCollins*Publishers*
1 London Bridge Street, London, SE1 9GF

© 2017 Barbara Heinlein

ISBN: 978-0-263-92914-0

46-0917

Our policy is to use papers that are natural, renewable and recyclable products and made from wood grown in sustainable forests. The logging and manufacturing processes conform to the legal environmental regulations of the country of origin.

Printed and bound in Spain
by CPI, Barcelona

B.J. Daniels is a *New York Times* and *USA TODAY* bestselling author. She wrote her first book after a career as an award-winning newspaper journalist and author of thirty-seven published short stories. She lives in Montana with her husband, Parker, and three springer spaniels. When not writing, she quilts, boats and plays tennis. Contact her at www.bjdaniels.com, on Facebook or on Twitter, @bjdanielsauthor.

This book is dedicated to JoAnn Hammond, who was one of the first in Whitewater to read one of my books :) So glad we got to know each other—and share a love for quilting and reading.

Chapter One

Abby Pierce opened her eyes and quickly closed them against the bright sunlight. She hurt all over. As she tried to sit up, a hand gently pushed on her shoulder to keep her flat on the bed.

"Don't sit up too fast," her husband said. "You're okay. You're in the hospital. You took a nasty fall."

Fall? Hospital? Her mouth felt dry as dust. She licked her lips. "Can you close the drapes?"

"Sure," Wade said and hurried over to the window.

She listened as he drew the drapes together and felt the room darken before she opened her eyes all the way.

The first thing she saw was her husband silhouetted against the curtains. He was a big imposing man with a boyish face and a blond crew cut. He was wearing his sheriff's deputy uniform, she noted as he moved back to the bed to take her hand.

She'd known Wade for years. She'd married him three years ago. That was why when she saw the sheepish look in his brown eyes, she knew at once that he was hiding something.

Abby frowned. "What was I doing that I fell?"

"You don't remember?" He cleared his throat, shifting on his feet. "You asked me to bring up some canning jars from the garage? I'm so sorry I didn't. If I had you wouldn't have been on that ladder..." He looked at her as if expecting... Expecting what?

"Canning jars?" she repeated and touched her bandaged temple. "I hit my head?"

He nodded, and taking her hand, he squeezed it a little too hard. "I'm so sorry, Abby." He sounded close to tears.

"It's not your fault," she said automatically, but couldn't help but wonder if there was more to the story. There often was with Wade and his family. She frowned, trying to understand why she would have wanted canning jars and saying as much.

"You said something about putting up peach jam."

"Really? I wonder where I planned to get peaches this time of year."

He said nothing, avoiding her gaze. All the other times she'd seen him like this it had been after he'd hurt her. It had started a year into their marriage and begun with angry accusations that led to him grabbing her, shaking her, pushing her and even slapping her.

Each time he'd stopped before it had gone too far. Each time he'd been horrified by what he'd done. He'd cried in her arms, begging her to forgive him, telling her that he couldn't live without her, saying he would kill himself if she ever left him. And then promising he'd never do it again.

She touched her bandaged head with her free hand. The movement brought a groan out of her as she realized her ribs were either bruised or maybe even broken. Looking down, she saw the bruises on her wrists and knew he was lying. Had he pushed her this time?

"Why can't I remember what happened?" she asked.

"You can't remember *anything*?" He sounded hopeful, fueling her worst fears that one of these days he would go too far and kill her. Wasn't that what her former boyfriend kept telling her? She pushed the thought of Ledger McGraw away as she often had to do. He didn't understand that she'd promised to love, honor and obey when she'd married Wade— even through the rough spots. And this she feared was one of them.

At the sound of someone entering the room, they both turned to see the doctor come in.

"How are we doing?" he asked as he moved to the foot of her bed to look at her chart. He glanced at Wade, then quickly looked away. Wade let go of her hand and moved to the window to part the drapes and peer out.

Abby closed her eyes at the shaft of sunlight he let in. "My head hurts," she told the doctor.

"I would imagine it does. When your husband brought you in, you were in and out of consciousness."

Wade had brought her in? He didn't call an ambulance?

"Also I can't seem to remember what happened," she added and, out of the corner of her eye, saw her husband glance back at her.

The doctor nodded. "Very common in your type of head injury."

"Will she get her memory back?" Wade asked from the window, sounding worried that she would.

"Possibly. Often not. I'm going to prescribe something for your headache. Your ribs are badly bruised and you have some other abrasions. I'd like to keep you overnight."

"Is that really necessary?" Wade asked, letting the drapes drop back into place.

"With a concussion, it's best," the doctor said without looking at him. "Don't worry. We'll take good care of her."

"We can talk about it," Wade said. "But I think she'd be more comfortable in her own home. Isn't that right, Abby?"

"On this, I think I know best," the doctor interrupted.

But she could see that Wade *was* worried. He apparently wanted to get her out of here and quickly. What was he worried about? That she would remember what happened?

If only she could. Unfortunately, the harder she tried, the more she couldn't. The past twenty-four hours were blank, leaving her with the terrifying feeling that her life depended on her remembering.

Chapter Two

When the phone rang at the Sundown Stallion Station late that afternoon, Ledger McGraw took the call since both his brothers were gone from the ranch and his father was resting upstairs. They had been forced to get an unlisted number after all the media coverage. After twenty-five years, there'd finally been a break in the McGraw twins kidnapping case.

"I need to talk to Travers," Jim Waters said without preamble. "Tell him it is of utmost importance."

Ledger groaned inwardly since he knew his father had almost fired the family attorney recently. "He's resting." Travers McGraw, sixty, had suffered a heart attack a few months ago. He hadn't been well before that. At the time, they hadn't known what was making him so sick. His family had assumed it was the stress of losing his two youngest children to kidnappers twenty-five years before and his determination to find them. His father was convinced that they were still alive.

"Do you really think I would be calling if it wasn't

urgent?" Waters demanded. The fiftysomething attorney had been like one of the family almost from the beginning—until a few months ago, when he and Travers had gotten into a disagreement.

"Jim, if this is about legal business—"

The attorney swore. "It's about the kidnapping. You might recall that we originally used my number to screen the calls about the twins. Well, I am apparently still on the list. I was contacted." He paused, no doubt for effect. "I have reason to believe that Oakley has been found."

"Found?" Ledger asked, his heart in his throat. The twenty-fifth anniversary of the crime had come and gone, but after their father had hired a true-crime writer to investigate and write a book about it, new evidence had turned up.

That new evidence had led them all to believe that his father's gut instinct was right. The twins were alive—and probably adopted out to good families, though illegally. The McGraw twins had been just six months old when they were stolen from their cribs. The ransom money had never been spent and had only recently turned up—with the body of one of the kidnappers. That left whoever had helped him take the babies still at large.

Ledger was thankful that he'd been the one to answer the phone. His father didn't need this kind of aggravation. "All those calls are now being vetted by the sheriff's department. I suggest you have this person contact Sheriff McCall Crawford. If she thinks—"

"He has the stuffed toy horse," Waters interrupted. "I've seen it. It's Oakley's."

Ledger felt a shock wave move through him. The stuffed toy horse was a critical piece of information that hadn't originally been released to the public. Was it possible his little brother really had turned up? "Are you sure? There must have been thousands of those produced."

"Not with a certain ribbon tied around its neck." The information about the missing stuffed animal was recently released to the press—sans anything about the ribbon and other things about this specific toy. "Oakley's stuffed horse had a black saddle and a small tear where the stitching had been missed when it was made, right?"

He nodded to himself before saying, *"You say you've seen it?"* It was that small detail that no one would know unless they had Oakley's horse, which had been taken out of his crib along with him that night twenty-five years ago. "Have you met him?"

"I have. He sent me a photo of the stuffed horse. When I recognized it, I drove down to talk to him. Ledger, he swears he's had the stuffed horse since he was a baby."

Letting out a breath, he dropped into a nearby chair. A few months ago they'd learned that the babies might have been left with a member of the Whitehorse Sewing Circle, a group of older women quilters who placed unwanted babies with families desperate for a child. The quilting group had been operating illegally for decades.

Not that the twins had been unwanted. But the kidnapper had been led to believe that was the case. The hope had been that the babies had been well taken care of and that they were still alive, the theory being that they had no idea they'd been kidnapped. His father had made the decision to release more information about what had been taken along with the babies in the hopes that the twins would see it and come forward.

And now it had happened.

"What's his name?" Ledger asked as he gave himself a few minutes to take this all in and decide what to do. He didn't want to bother his father with this unless he was sure it wasn't a hoax.

"He goes by Vance Elliot. He's in Whitehorse. He wants to see your father."

"ABBY DOESN'T REMEMBER ANYTHING," Wade said as he walked past his father straight into the kitchen to pull a can of beer out of the refrigerator.

He popped the top, took a long swig and turned to find his father standing in the kitchen doorway frowning at him.

"I'll pay you back," he said, thinking the look was because he was drinking his old man's beer.

"What do you mean she doesn't remember *anything*?"

"I was skeptical at first, too," he said, drawing out a chair and spinning it around so he could straddle it backward at the table. "But when I told her she fell off a ladder in the garage, she bought it. She couldn't remember why she would have been on a ladder in the garage. I told her she was going to get jars to put up some peach jam."

Huck Pierce wagged his head. "Where in the hell would she get peaches this time of year?"

"How should I know? It doesn't matter. She's not putting up any jam. Nor is she saying a word about anything."

"You are one lucky son of a gun, then," Huck said.

"Don't I know it? So everything is cool, right?"

"Seems so. But I want you to stay by your wife's side. Keep everything as normal as possible. Stick to your story. If she starts to remember…" He shrugged. "We'll deal with it if we have to."

Wade downed the rest of his beer, needing it even though he was technically on duty at the sheriff's department. He didn't want his father to see how relieved he was. Or how worried about what would happen if Abby remembered what had really happened to her.

"Great, so I get to hang out at the hospital until my shift starts. That place gives me the creeps."

"You're the one who screwed everything up. You knew what was at stake," his father said angrily.

"Exactly." Wade knew he couldn't win in an argument with his father, but that didn't stop him. "So what was I supposed to do when she confronted me? I tried to reason with her, but you know how she is. She was threatening to call the sheriff. Or go running to her old boyfriend Ledger McGraw. I didn't have a choice but to try to stop her."

"What you're saying is that you can't handle your wife. At least you don't have some snot-nosed mouthy kid like I did."

"Yeah, thanks," he said, crushing the beer can in his hand. "I've heard all about how hard it was raising me." He reached in the refrigerator for another beer, knowing he shouldn't, but needing the buzz badly.

Before he could pull one out, his father slammed the refrigerator door, almost crushing his hand. "Get some gum. You can't have beer on your breath when you go back to the hospital, let alone come to work later. Remember, you're the worried husband, you damned fool."

LEDGER HAD JUST hung up with the attorney when he got the call from his friend who worked at the hospital.

"I shouldn't be calling you, but thought you'd want to know," she said, keeping her voice down. "Abby was brought in."

"That son of a—"

"He swears she fell off a ladder."

"Sure she did. I'll be right there. Is Wade—"

"He just left to go work his shift at the sheriff's department. The doctor is keeping Abby overnight."

"Is she okay?"

"She's pretty beat up, but she's going to be fine."

He breathed a sigh of relief as he hung up. When it rained it poured, he thought as he saw his father coming down the stairs toward him. Travers McGraw was still weak from his heart attack, but it was the systematic poisoning that had really almost killed him. Fortunately, his would-be killer was now behind bars awaiting trial.

But realizing that his second wife was trying to kill him had taken a toll on his father. It was bad enough that his first wife, Ledger's mother, was in a mental hospital. After the twins were kidnapped, Marianne McGraw had a complete breakdown. For twenty-five years, it was believed that she and the ranch's horse trainer, Nate Corwin, had been behind the kidnapping. Only recently had Nate's name been cleared.

"I heard the phone," Travers said now. He'd recovered, but was still weak. He'd lost too much weight. It would be a while until he was his old self. If ever.

That was why Ledger wasn't sure how his father would take the news Waters had called with earlier—especially if it led to yet another disappointment. And yet Ledger couldn't keep the attorney's call from him. If there was even the slightest chance that this Vance Elliot was Oakley...

"You should sit down."

His father didn't argue as he moved to a chair and sat. He seemed to brace himself. "What's happened?"

"Jim Waters called."

Travers began to shake his head. "Now what?"

"He's still apparently the contact person for the family on some of the old publicity," Ledger said.

His father knew at once. "Oakley or Jesse Rose?"

"Oakley. Jim says the young man has the stuffed horse that was taken along with Oakley from his crib the night of the kidnapping. He says he's seen the toy and that it is definitely Oakley's."

His father's eyes filled to overflowing. "Thank God. I knew they were alive. I've…felt it all these years."

"Dad, this Vance Elliot might not be Oakley. We have to keep that in mind."

"He has Oakley's stuffed horse."

"But we don't know how he got it or if it was with Oakley when he was given to the woman at the Whitehorse Sewing Circle," Ledger reminded him.

"When can I see him?" his father asked, getting to his feet.

"He's in town. Waters wants to bring him over this evening. I said it would be fine. I hope that was all right. If it goes well, I thought you might want him to stay for dinner. I can tell the cook." Their cook for as far back as Ledger could remember had recently been killed. They'd been through several cooks since then. He couldn't remember the name of the latest one right now and felt bad about it. "Let's just keep our fingers crossed that it really is Oakley."

His father smiled and stepped closer to him to place a hand on his shoulder. "I am so blessed to have such good sons. Speaking of sons, where are Cull and Boone?"

"Cull and Nikki are checking into some of the adoptions through the Whitehorse Sewing Circle." Nikki St. James was the crime writer who'd helped unlock some of the kidnapping mystery—and stolen Cull's heart.

"I doubt the twins' adoptions were recorded anywhere, and with the Cavanaugh woman dying not long after the twins were kidnapped... You haven't heard anything yet?"

Ledger shook his head. "They said that clues to what happened to some of the babies were found stitched on their baby blankets. But the twins wouldn't have quilted blankets made for them because of the circumstances." Pearl Cavanaugh had been led to believe that the twins were in danger, so she would have made very private adoptions for Oakley and Jesse Rose.

"And Boone?"

"He went to check on that horse you were interested in, remember?"

Travers nodded, frowning. Loss of memory was part of the effects of arsenic poisoning. "Maybe I'll just rest until dinner."

Ledger watched his father go back up the stairs before he headed for his pickup and the hospital.

"You shouldn't be here," Abby said the moment she opened her eyes and saw Ledger standing at the end of her bed. Her heart had taken off like a wild stallion at just the sight of him. It always did. "Wade could come back at any time."

Ledger had been her first love. He'd left an ache in her that she'd hoped would fade, if not eventually go away. But if anything, the ache had grown stronger. He'd broken her heart. It was why she'd married Wade. But ever since then, he'd been coming around, confusing her and making being married to Wade even harder. He seemed to think he had to save her from her husband.

It didn't help that Ledger McGraw had breakfast on the mornings that she waitressed at the Whitehorse Café. She'd done nothing to encourage him, although Wade didn't believe that.

Fortunately, Wade had only come down to the restaurant one time threatening to kill Ledger. Ledger had called him on it, saying they should step outside and finish it like men.

"Or do you only hit defenseless women?" Ledger had demanded of him.

Wade lost his temper and charged him. Ledger had stepped aside, nailing Wade on the back of his neck as he lumbered past. Abby had screamed as Wade slammed headfirst into a table. He'd missed two weeks' work because of his neck and threatened to sue the McGraws for his pain and suffering.

She knew his neck wasn't hurt that badly, but he'd milked it, telling everyone that Ledger had blind-sided him.

Wade's jealousy had gotten worse after that. Even when she'd reminded him again and again, "But you're the one I married."

"Only because you couldn't have McGraw," he would snap.

Ledger's name was never spoken in their house— at least not by her. Wade blamed him for everything that was wrong with their marriage—especially the fact that she hadn't given him a son.

They'd tried to get pregnant when they'd first married. Since he'd joined the sheriff's department and changed, she'd gone back on the pill in secret, hating that she kept it from him. She told herself that when things changed back to what she thought of as normal, she would go off the pill again.

Now she couldn't even remember what normal was anymore.

Ledger took a step toward her. He looked both worried and furious. It scared her that he and Wade might get into another altercation because of her.

"I didn't come until I was sure Wade wasn't here," Ledger said as he came around the side of her bed. "When I heard, I had to see you. *You fell off a lad-der?*"

She nodded even though it hurt her head to do so.

"Clumsy." She avoided his gaze because she knew he wouldn't believe it any more than she did.

"What were you doing on a ladder?"

"Apparently I was getting down some canning jars to put up peach jam."

Ledger looked at her hard. "*Apparently?* You don't remember?"

"I seem to have lost the past twenty-four hours."

"Oh, Abby."

She could tell that he thought she was covering for Wade. It almost made her laugh since she'd covered for him enough times. This just wasn't one of them. She really couldn't remember *anything*.

Ledger started to reach for her hand, but must have thought better of it. She tucked her hand under the sheet so he wouldn't be tempted again. She couldn't have Wade walking in on that. It would be bad enough Ledger just being here.

"It was a stupid accident. I probably wasn't paying attention. I'm fine."

He made a face that said he didn't believe it as he reached out to brush the dark hair back from her forehead.

She flinched at his touch and he quickly pulled back his fingers. "Sorry," he said quickly. "Did I hurt you?"

Abby shook her head. His touch had always sparked desire in her, but she wasn't about to admit that. "My head hurts, is all."

She looked toward the door, worried that Wade

might stop by. When he'd left, she could tell that he hadn't liked leaving her. Even though he was supposed to be on duty as a sheriff's deputy, he could swing by if he was worried about her, especially since he was determined to take her home.

Ledger followed her gaze as if he knew what was making her so nervous. "I'll go," he said. "But if I find out that Wade had anything to do with this—"

"I fell off a ladder." She knew it was a lie, and from the look in Ledger's eyes, he did, too. But she had to at least try to convince him that Wade was innocent. This time. "That's all it was."

She met his gaze and felt her heart break as it always did. "Thank you for stopping by," she said even though there was so much more she wanted to say to him. But she was Wade's *wife*. As her mother always said, she'd made her bed and now she had to lie in it for better or worse.

Not that her mother didn't always remind her that Ledger hadn't wanted her.

"I'm here for you, Abby. If you ever need me..."

She felt tears burn her eyes. If only that had been true before she'd married Wade. "I can't." Her heart broke as she dragged her gaze away from his.

As if resigned, she watched out of the corner of her eye as he put on his Stetson, tipped it to her and walked out.

ATTORNEY JIM WATERS looked at the young man sitting in the passenger seat of his car as he drove toward the ranch later that evening. Vance Elliot. Here was Waters's ticket back into the McGraws' good graces.

He'd bet on the wrong horse, so to speak. Travers's second wife, Patricia McGraw, had been a good bet at the time. Pretty, sexy, almost twenty years younger than her husband. She'd convinced him Travers wasn't himself. That she needed a man she could count on. She'd let him believe that he might be living in that big house soon with her because Travers had some incurable ailment that only she and Travers knew about.

He'd bought into it hook, line and sinker. And why wouldn't he? Travers had been sick—anyone could see that. Also the man had seemed distracted, often forgetful and vague as if he was losing his mind. He'd been convinced that Travers wasn't long with this world and that Patricia would be taking over the ranch.

Little did he know that she was *poisoning* her husband.

As it turned out, Patricia was now behind bars awaiting trial. Since he had stupidly sided with her, things had gone downhill from there. He was hanging on to his job with Travers by the skin of his teeth.

But this was going to make it all right again, he told himself. He couldn't let a paycheck like McGraw get away. His retainer alone would keep him nicely for years to come. He just needed to get Travers's trust back. He saw a lot more legal work on the horizon for the McGraws. If this young man was Oakley, he would be back in the McGraw fold.

His cell phone rang. Patricia McGraw again. Travers's young wife wouldn't quit calling even though he'd told her he wasn't going to help her, let alone defend her.

Nor did he need to hear any of her threats. Fortunately, no one believed anything she said. Since Travers McGraw was idolized in this county, people saw her as the gold digger who'd married him—and then systematically tried to kill him. She got no sympathy. In fact, he doubted she could get even a fair trial.

"I'm innocent, you bastard," she'd screamed the last time he'd taken her call. "You did this. You framed me for this. Once I tell the sheriff—"

He'd laughed. "Like anyone will believe you."

"I'll take you down with me!"

He'd hung up and the next time his phone had rung it had been Vance Elliot.

Waters slowed to turn into the lane that led up to the main house. He shot the man next to him a glance. Vance looked more like a teenager than a twenty-five-year-old.

The man who might be Oakley stared at the house, a little openmouthed. Waters remembered the first time he'd driven out here and seen it. The house was impressive. So were the miles of white wooden fence, the expensive quarter horses in the pasture and the section after section of land that ran to the Little Rockies.

He couldn't imagine what it would be like to learn that he was part of this even at his age—let alone twenty-five. If Vance Elliot really was the long-ago kidnapped McGraw twin, then he was one lucky son of a gun.

"You all right?" he asked Vance as they drove toward the house.

The man nodded. Waters tried to read him. He had to be scared to face Travers McGraw, not to mention his three older sons. But he didn't look it. He looked determined.

Waters felt his stomach roil. This had better be real. If this wasn't Oakley McGraw he was bringing to Travers...

He didn't want to think about how badly this could go for him.

Chapter Three

Sheriff McCall Crawford happened to be standing at the window as Huck and Wade Pierce had come into work. Wade looked wrung out. She'd heard that his wife was in the hospital with a concussion after falling off a ladder.

McCall watched the two men. She'd inherited Huck when she'd become sheriff. Before that, she'd worked with him as a deputy. He'd made it clear that he thought a woman's place was in the home and not carrying a badge and gun. Huck hadn't been any more impressed when he'd been passed over and she'd become sheriff.

He was a good old boy, the kind who smiled in your face and stabbed you in the back the first chance he got. She didn't trust him, but she couldn't fire him without cause. So far, he'd done nothing to warrant it, but she kept her eye on him—and his son, Wade. The minute she caught him stepping over the line, he was gone. As for his son... She'd had hopes for him when he'd hired on, seeing something in him that could go a different way than his father. Lately, though…

Both looked up as if sensing her watching them from the window. She raised her coffee mug in a salute to them. Their expressions turned solemn as they entered the building.

Neither man was stupid. Both were hanging on by a thread, and if the rumors about Wade mistreating his wife could ever be proved, he would be gone soon. But in a small community like this, it was hard to prove there was a problem unless the wife came forward. So far, Abby hadn't. But now she was in the hospital after allegedly falling off a ladder. Maybe this would be the straw that broke the camel's back.

McCall's cell phone rang. She stepped to her desk and picked up, seeing that it was her grandmother. It felt strange having a relationship with her after all those years of never even laying eyes on the woman.

"Good evening," she said into the phone.

"What are you still doing at work this late?" Pepper demanded.

"I was just about to leave," McCall said. The day had gotten away from her after she dropped her daughter off at day care and came in to deal with all the paperwork that tended to stack up on her desk. Most of the time, she and Luke could work out a schedule where one—if not both of them—was home with Tracey.

But several days a week, her daughter had to go to a day care near the sheriff's office in downtown

Whitehorse. McCall had checked it out carefully and found no problems with the two women who ran it. Tracey seemed to love going because she was around other children. For a working mother, it was the best McCall could do.

"So is there any truth to it?" her grandmother demanded in her no-nonsense normal tone of voice. "Has one of the McGraw twins been found?"

The question took McCall by surprise. For twenty-five years there had been no news on the fraternal twins who'd been kidnapped. Then a few months ago a true-crime writer had shown up at the Mc-Graw ranch and all hell had broken loose. While some pieces of the puzzle had been found, the twins hadn't been yet.

Now was it possible one of them had been located?

"I heard it's the boy, Oakley," her grandmother was saying. "Apparently your theory about who might have adopted out the children was correct. It was the Whitehorse Sewing Circle. That bunch of old hens. You should arrest them all." Most of the women involved in the illegal kidnappings were dead now. "On top of that, that crazy daughter of Arlene Evans almost escaped from the loony bin last night."

McCall hadn't heard about that, either. It amazed her that Pepper often knew what was going on in town before the sheriff did—even though the Winchester Ranch was miles south of Whitehorse.

"Thank you for all the information. Is that it? Or was the bank robbed?"

Pepper laughed. "You should hire me since I know more of what is going on than you do." It was an old refrain, one McCall almost enjoyed. Almost.

"Well, let me know when you find out something worth hearing about," Pepper said. "I'm having lunch with the rest of your family tomorrow. Maybe sometime you can come out." With that, her grandmother was gone, leaving McCall to smile before she dialed Travers McGraw's number.

VANCE ELLIOT WATCHED the landscape blur past and wiped his sweaty palms on his jeans.

"You all right?" the attorney asked from behind the wheel of the SUV. The fiftysomething man wore a dark suit, reminding Vance of an undertaker. No one wore a suit like that, not around these parts, anyway. So Jim Waters must be some highfalutin lawyer who made a lot of money. But then, he worked for Travers McGraw, Vance thought as he saw the huge ranch ahead. Travers McGraw probably paid him well.

"I'm a little nervous," he admitted in answer to the lawyer's question. He was about to come face-to-face with Travers McGraw and his three sons. He'd heard enough about them to be anxious. Plus, the attorney had already warned him.

"They aren't going to believe you, but don't let that rattle you," Waters said. "They've had a lot of people pretend to be the missing twins, so naturally they're going to be suspicious. But having the stuffed horse will help. Then there is the DNA test. You're ready for that, right?"

Right. That alone scared the daylights out of him, but he simply nodded to the attorney's question.

He watched the ranch house come into view. He couldn't imagine growing up on a place like this. Couldn't imagine having that much land or that much money. Nor could he deny the appeal of being a Mc-Graw with all the privileges that came with it.

He knew he was getting ahead of himself. There were a lot of hoops he had to jump through before they would accept that he was Oakley, the missing twin. But at least he could admire the house until then. It was huge with several wings that trailed off from the two-story center.

He'd heard stories about lavish parties where senators and even the governor had attended. That was before the twins were kidnapped, though, before the first Mrs. McGraw went to the loony bin and the second one went to jail.

But the house and grounds were still beautiful, and the horses… A half dozen raced through a nearby pasture as beautiful as any horseflesh he'd ever seen. Horses were in his blood, he thought with a silent laugh. And as Waters turned into the long lane leading to the house, he thought maybe horses were in his future.

"There is nothing to be afraid of," the attorney said. "Just tell them what you told me."

"I will." He swallowed the lump in his throat. Just stick to the story. The attorney had believed him. So Travers McGraw should, too, right? The stuffed horse had opened the door. The DNA test would cinch it.

As Waters brought the SUV to a stop in front of the house, Vance picked up the paper bag next to him and held it like a suit of armor to his chest.

"Try to relax," the attorney said. "You look like you're going to jump out of your skin."

He took a deep breath and thought of his run-ins with the law as a horse thief. He'd talked his way out of those. He could handle this.

Think about the payoff, he reminded himself. This place could be his one day.

"DAD, I DON'T want you getting upset," Boone McGraw said as they waited in Travers's office. "You know what the doctor said."

"I had a heart attack," his father said impatiently. "Given the state of my health and why it was so bad, I'm fine now. Even the doctor is amazed how quickly I've bounced back."

Ledger stood by the office fireplace, as anxious as the rest of his family. They all knew that their father had bounced back because even before this phone call, Travers McGraw was determined the twins were alive and that he would see them again.

And now, after releasing more information to the press, maybe one of the twins had come forward.

Ledger couldn't help being skeptical. They'd been here before. Except this time, this one had Oakley's stuffed horse, which had been in his crib the night he was kidnapped. Would his father finally be able to find some peace?

Or, after twenty-five years, had too much time passed? Oakley would be a grown man, no longer that cute six-month-old baby who'd been stolen. He would have lived a good portion of his life as someone else, with other parents. He would have his own life and the McGraws would all be strangers to him.

Ledger feared this wasn't going to be the homecoming his father was hoping for as he heard a vehicle pull up out front. He looked from his father to his brother and then went to answer the door. Better him than Boone, who already looked as if he could chew nails. It was going to take a lot to convince Boone that whoever was headed for the door was the lost twin.

Unable to wait for a knock, Ledger opened the door. Attorney Jim Waters and the young man, who might or might not be his brother, were at the bottom of the porch steps. His gaze went right to the young man, who looked dressed in all new clothing from the button-down shirt to the jeans and Western boots. He was tall, broad-shouldered and slim hipped like all the McGraw men.

At the sound of the front door opening, Vance Elliot looked up, his thick dark hair falling over his forehead. Ledger saw the blue eyes and felt a shiver.

This might really be his brother.

"Vance Elliot, this is Ledger McGraw," Waters said by introduction.

"Please, come in," he said, unable to take his eyes off the young man. "My father and brother are in his office."

LEDGER LED THE two men into his father's office and closed the door. The new cook, a woman by the name of Louise, he'd made a point of learning, was in the kitchen making dinner. Cull and Nikki should be back soon. Unless they decided to stay in Whitehorse and go out to dinner. He still couldn't believe how hard his brother had fallen for the true-crime writer.

"Please sit down," Travers said, getting to his feet to shake hands with Vance. He waited until everyone was sitting before he asked, "So you think you might be my son Oakley. Why don't you start by telling us something about you?"

Vance shifted in his chair. He held a large paper bag on his lap, the top turned under. Ledger assumed the stuffed toy horse was inside. He would have thought his father would want to see it right away.

"I don't know exactly where to begin. I was raised in Bear Creek, south of Billings, on a small farm. My parents told me when I was about five that I was adopted."

"Did you have other siblings?" Travers asked.

Vance shook his head. "Just me." He shrugged. "I had a fine childhood. We didn't have much but it was enough. I went to college in Billings for a while before getting a job on a ranch outside of Belfry. That's about it."

"And how did you become aware that you might be one of the missing McGraw twins?" his father asked.

"I heard about it on television. When they mentioned the small stuffed horse and showed a photo of what it might look like, I couldn't believe it. I'd had one just like it as far back as I could remember."

"Is that what's in the bag?" Boone asked.

Vance nodded and stood to place the bag on the desk in front of Travers. He took a step back, bumped into the chair and sat again.

The room had gone deathly quiet. Ledger could hear nothing but his own heart pounding as his father pulled the bag closer, unfolded the top and looked inside.

A small gasp escaped his father's lips as he pulled the toy stuffed horse from the bag. Ledger saw the worn blue ribbon around the horse's neck and swung his gaze to Vance. If he was telling the truth, then this man was Oakley, all grown up.

WATERS COULDN'T HELP the self-satisfied feeling he had when he saw Travers McGraw's expression. He'd felt the same way when he'd seen the toy stuffed horse. It was Oakley's; there was no doubt about that.

Of course, this wouldn't be a done deal until after the DNA tests were run, but he was on the home stretch.

"Would the two of you like to stay for dinner?"

Travers asked, putting the toy back into the sack and rising to his feet. "I'd like to hear more about your childhood, Vance." It was clear he was fighting calling the young man by that name.

He'd also seen Travers's face when the two of them had walked into the office. The horse rancher had looked shocked by how much the young man resembled Travers's own sons.

Waters looked to Vance before he said, "We'd love to stay for dinner. If you're sure it isn't an inconvenience." He thought of the years he'd sat at the big dining room table and eaten under this roof. If this went the way he expected it to, he'd be a regular guest again.

"Wonderful," Travers said as he came around his desk. Putting an arm around Vance, he steered him toward the dining room at the back of the house. "Where are you staying?"

Vance cleared his voice. "I spent last night at a motel in town."

"You can stay here on the ranch if you'd like," Travers said. "I don't want to pressure you. Give it some thought. We can discuss it after dinner."

Waters smiled to himself. This couldn't have gone any better. Vance was in—at least until the DNA test. But if he passed that…

His cell phone vibrated in his pocket. He checked caller ID. Patricia, the soon-to-be former wife of Travers McGraw. He was sure his boss would ask him to handle the divorce. It would be his pleasure.

Chapter Four

Abby was dressed and sitting in the wheelchair waiting when her husband came into her hospital room the next afternoon. She felt fine, except for a headache and no memory of what had happened to her. But hospital policy required her to be "driven" down to the exit by wheelchair after her doctor came in.

Wade stopped in the doorway. She gave him a smile to reassure him that she was all right. He'd been so worried. She'd never seen him like that before.

He tried to smile back, but his expression crumbled. He burst into tears, dropping to his knees in front of her wheelchair.

"Oh, babe, I'm so sorry."

"Wade, this wasn't your fault. You have to quit blaming yourself," Abby said, wishing it was true, as he squeezed her hand with what felt like desperation.

"I just don't know what I would do if I lost you," he was saying. "When I thought you were dead…

Abby, I love you so much. Sometimes I do stupid things. I lose my temper or—"

"Well, fortunately, you didn't lose her," his father said from behind him in the doorway. Neither of them had heard Huck, so she didn't know how long he'd been standing there.

Her husband surreptitiously wiped at his tears but didn't get up. Nor did he let go of the one hand he held of hers too tightly.

"In fact, son, she looks like she feels much better," Huck said as he entered the hospital room. "But you should have gotten those jars from the garage when she asked you to. I'm sure you won't make that mistake again."

Wade squeezed her hand even tighter. "No, I won't," he said, his voice sounding strained. "I swear."

"Then let's get this woman home. Can't let crime run rampant because of peach jam," Huck said with a laugh.

Wade got up slowly as if he had a terrible weight on his shoulders. Abby watched him use the wheelchair arms to support himself as he lumbered to his feet.

She'd blamed his job at the sheriff's office for the change in her husband, but as she felt the tension between Wade and his father, she wondered how much of the change in him was Huck's doing. Her father-in-law often talked about making his son a man. It was no secret that he thought Wade wasn't "tough" enough.

The doctor came in then to talk to her about her recovery. He still questioned whether she should be going home. She could tell that he was worried about her—and suspicious of her accident.

But Abby found herself paying more attention to what was going on out in the hallway. Huck had drawn Wade out into the hall. She couldn't hear what they were saying, but just from her husband's hunched shoulders, she knew that Huck was berating him. Talk about the kettle calling the skillet black, she thought.

"Stop your damned blubbering," Huck said, taking Wade's arm and halfway dragging him down the corridor. "You didn't do anything wrong, remember? So quit apologizing."

"Easy for you to say," Wade said under his breath.

"You need to be more careful. If the doctor had overheard you…" His father shook his head as if Wade was more stupid than he'd even originally thought. "On top of that, the nurse said that Ledger McGraw stopped by to see your wife after you left," Huck said.

Wade swore and kicked at a chair in the hallway. It skittered across the floor, before Huck caught it and brought it to a stop with a look that told him to cool it. Wade wanted to put his fist through the wall. "He just won't stay away from my wife."

"So what are you going to do about it?" Huck asked, sounding as angry as Wade felt.

"I'm going to find the son of a bitch and kill him." He smacked the wall hard with his open palm. The pain helped a little.

"This is your problem—you go off half-cocked and just screw things up," his father said. "Listen to me. You want to get rid of him? I'll help you, but we won't be doing it when you're out of control. We'll plan it. As a matter of fact, I have a way we can be rid of Ledger McGraw and the rest of them, as well."

Wade stared at his father. "What are you saying?" He narrowed his eyes. "This is about the long-standing grudge you hold against Travers McGraw."

"What if it is? I don't just whine and cry. I take care of business."

He shook his head at his father. "I know you said you used to date Marianne before she married Travers, but—"

"But nothing." Huck wiped a hand over his face, anger making his eyes look hard as obsidian. "She was *mine* and then he had to go and marry her, and look how that turned out."

"You might be crazier than she is," Wade muttered under his breath, only to have his father cuff him in the back of the head as they headed back to Abby's room.

ABBY LISTENED TO the rain on the roof for a moment before she realized that she was alone. She rolled over to find the bed empty. More and more Wade was having trouble sleeping at night.

He'd said little after bringing her home from the hospital. Once at the house, he'd insisted she go to bed. He'd brought her a bowl of heated canned soup. She'd smelled beer on his breath, but had said nothing.

"I'll let you get some rest," he'd said after taking her soup tray away.

Sometime during the night she'd felt him crawl into bed next to her. She'd smelled his beery breath and rolled over only to wake later to find his side of the bed empty.

Now she found him sitting outside on the covered porch. He teetered on the edge of the chair, elbows on his knees, head down as if struggling with the weight of the world on his shoulders.

Abby approached him slowly, half-afraid that she might startle him. His volatile mood swings had her walking on eggshells around him. The floorboards creaked under her feet.

Wade rose and swung around, making her flinch. "What are you doing?" he demanded gruffly.

"I woke up and you weren't in bed. Is everything all right?"

"I just needed a little fresh air. You don't have to be sneaking up on me."

Abby desperately wanted to reach out to him, to comfort him, to plead with him to tell her what was making him so miserably unhappy. She blamed herself. They'd been good together once. Hadn't they?

But clearly he was in no mood for the third degree.

Also she'd learned to keep her distance when he was drinking. But she knew he was hurting. Because of her fall? Or because of something else?

It was raining harder now. She hugged herself, the damp seeping through her thin nightgown. There'd been a time when he would have noticed just how thin the fabric was, how it clung to her rounded breasts and hips. Back then he would have pulled her to him, his breath warm against her neck. That husky sound in his voice as he told her how much he wanted her, needed her. How he couldn't live without her.

Wade didn't give her another look as he sat down again, turning his back to her. "You should go to bed."

She felt tears burn her eyes. Wade kept pushing her away, then losing his temper because he thought some other man might want her.

"I saw Ledger McGraw looking at you when you came out of the grocery store," Wade would say. "I'm going to kill that son of a—"

"You can't kill every man who looks at me," she would say.

"You like it when he looks at you."

She would say nothing, hoping to avoid a fight, but Wade would never let it go.

"He wants you. He isn't going to give up until he tears us apart. Not that he would ever marry you. He had that chance already, remember? Remember how he lied to you, cheated on you—"

There was nothing she could say to calm him down. She knew because she'd tried. "Wade, don't be ridiculous."

"Right, I'm ridiculous. I'm no McGraw, am I?"

"I married *you*."

"Only because you couldn't have Ledger."

She would try to hug him and he would shove her away, balling his hands into fists. "You never got over him. That's what's wrong with our marriage. You're still yearning for him. I can see it in your eyes."

He would shove her or grab her, wrenching her arm. It would always end with him hurting her and then being sorry. He would berate himself, loathing that he was now like his father. He would promise never to do it again, beg her forgiveness. Plead with her not to leave him.

And each time, she would forgive him, blaming herself for setting him off. Then they would make love and it would be good between them for a while.

At least, that was the way it used to be. Lately, it took nothing to set Wade off. And there was no pleading for forgiveness or any making up afterward.

"It isn't like anyone else wanted to marry you," her mother told her when she'd seen Abby wince from one of Wade's beatings. Her mother loved to rub salt in the wounds. "It's plain to see that you aren't making him happy. You'd better do whatever it takes or he's going to dump you for a woman who will. Then where are you going to be? Divorced. Left like a bus at the Greyhound bus station. No man will want you then."

Abby had bit her lip and said nothing. She'd made her bed and now she had to lie in it. That was her mother's mantra.

"And stay clear of that McGraw," her mother had warned. "Men always want you when you're with someone else. But the minute they get you, they lose interest. So don't be thinkin' the grass is greener with him. You already know you can't trust him. Look how he broke your heart. Just be glad Wade was willing to marry you since you weren't exactly white-wedding-dress material, now, were you?"

Now she stared at the back of her husband's head for a moment, then padded barefoot back to bed. If only she could remember how she'd gotten hurt. She had a feeling that would have answered all of her questions about what was happening with her husband.

"ABBY'S STARTING TO REMEMBER," Wade told his father the next day. He'd been relieved that he had to work. The last thing he wanted to do was sit around with her. He felt as if he was going to come unraveled at the seams as it was. She knew she hadn't fallen off a ladder. He saw it in her eyes and said as much to Huck.

"So what? It isn't like she's going to tell anyone," his father said. "If she was going to do that, she would have done it a long time ago."

"She's going to leave me."

Huck swore. "She would have done that a long time ago, too. She's fine. It's you I'm worried about."

"*Everyone* knows." As he'd wheeled Abby out to his patrol car parked at the emergency entrance, he'd seen the way the nurses were looking at him. Everyone knew now that he was his father's son—a bastard who mistreated his wife. He was thankful he and Abby hadn't had a kid. What if he took his anger inside him out on his *own* son?

"Snap out of it!" his father barked as they stood talking by their patrol cars. "You're in the clear."

Wade shook his head. "I'm afraid she's going to remember why we fought. If she remembers what she overheard you and me talking about…"

"I thought you said she didn't remember *anything*?"

He shrugged. "She says she doesn't, but the way she looks at me… She's going to start putting it together. I can see it in her eyes."

"Bull. If she remembered, she'd either go to the sheriff or she'd be in your face. What she needs to do is get back to work, keep her mind off…everything. In the meantime, you need to stay calm. You can't mess up again."

"I'll treat her real good," he said more to himself than his father. "I'll make up for everything."

"That alone will make her suspicious. Do what you normally do."

"Get drunk and stay out half the night?" Wade

asked his father in disbelief. "And you think that will help how?"

"It won't make you seem so desperate. Stop saying you're sorry. It was her damned fool self who climbed up that ladder to get those canning jars."

Wade stared at him. He'd always known that his father bought into his own lies, but this was over the top. "She's not *stupid*. She knows damned well she didn't fall from a ladder." He felt a sob deep in his chest begging to get out. He wasn't sure how much longer he could hold it together. "You don't live with her. You have no idea what it's like. She knows she can do better than me. She's always known. If she ever finds out that we lied to her about Ledger McGraw and that girl at college—"

Huck swore a blue streak. "Stop feeling sorry for yourself, you miserable little miscreant. It's our word against McGraw's. He swore nothing was going on, but if she didn't believe him then, she sure isn't going to now. She isn't going to find out unless you confess everything. She married *you*. Don't blow this. If she remembers what we were talking about when she overheard, then we'll deal with it. In the meantime, go get drunk, get laid, stop worrying."

ABBY COULDN'T SIT STILL. The doctor had told her to rest, but she felt too antsy. Not being able to remember nagged at her. She got up and turned on the television.

Standing, she flipped through the channels, but found nothing of interest and turned it off.

Out of the corner of her eye, she saw a book lying open on the floor next to her chair. As she bent to pick it up, she winced at the pain in her ribs. Dizzy, she had to grab hold of the chair arm for a moment.

She stared at the book, trying to remember. Had she been reading? It bugged Wade when she read instead of watched television with him. He took offense as if her reading made him feel dumb. It made no sense. No more sense than what had happened to her. Why would she have been reading if she was going to get canning jars down to make peach jam?

Marking her place, she put the book down and walked into the kitchen to open the refrigerator. Of course there were no peaches in there. Had she really thought there would be this time of year? Her ribs hurt worse as she breathed hard to fight back the nausea. She hadn't fallen off a ladder. Why did she keep trying to make Wade's story plausible?

She turned to look at her house, seeing her life in the worn furniture, in the sad-looking cheap artwork on the walls, in the creak of the old floorboards under her feet.

Her gaze went to the floor as she caught a whiff of pine. Someone had cleaned the kitchen floor—but not with the cleaner she always used. Wade? Why would he clean unless...

Heart beating hard, she noticed that he'd missed

a spot. She didn't need to lean any closer to know what it was. Dried blood. *Her* blood.

ABBY REALIZED SHE had nowhere to go. But she desperately needed to talk to someone. Even her mother.

She knew she shouldn't be driving, but her house wasn't that far from her mother's. Once behind the wheel she felt more in control. Seeing the blood, she'd quit lying to herself. She hadn't fallen off a ladder. Wade had hurt her. Again. Bad enough for her to end up in the hospital.

Only she had no idea why, which terrified her.

Too upset to just sit around waiting for Wade to get off his night shift, she'd finally decided she had to do something. If only she could remember what they'd fought about. A vague memory teased at her, just enough to make her even more anxious. It hadn't been one of their usual disagreements. It hadn't even been Wade drunk and belligerent. No, this time it had been serious.

As she turned down the road, she saw the beam of a flashlight moving from behind her mother's house toward the old root cellar. Abby frowned as her mother and the light disappeared from view.

Why would her mother be going down there this time of the night? She pulled up in front of the house and got out. As she neared the back of the house, she saw that her mother had strung an extension cord so she would have light down in the root cellar. It would be just like her mother to get it into her head to clean it out now, of all crazy possible times.

Abby had spent years trying to please her mother, but she felt she'd always fallen short. She almost changed her mind about trying to talk to her tonight. Her mother would be furious with her for not believing her husband—even though it was clear he was lying. Nan Lawrence was a hard woman to get close to. The closest they'd been was when her mother had pushed her to marry Wade after her breakup with Ledger McGraw. Not that it had taken a whole lot of pushing since she had been so heartbroken.

She'd just reached the back of the house and was about to start down the path to the root cellar when she heard a vehicle. A set of headlights flashed out as the car stopped in the stand of cottonwoods nearby. Someone had just parked out there.

Her first thought was Wade. He'd stopped by the house to check on her, found her gone and figured she'd run to her mother.

Hanging back in the deep shadow of the house, she watched a figure come out of the woods. It was too dark without the moon tonight to see who it was, but it was definitely a man, given his size. Wade? He stopped for a moment at the opening to the root cellar before lifting the door and disappearing inside, leaving the door ajar.

Although she couldn't make out his face, she caught the gleam of a badge on a uniform. Abby almost turned back. She wasn't even sure she wanted to see her mother now that she was here. She definitely didn't want to see her mother and Wade. They would gang up on her like they often did, confuse her, make her feel guilty for not being a better wife. Make her believe that all of it was her fault.

And yet she was tired of running away from the truth. Wade had almost killed her. There couldn't be another time. Not unless she had a death wish.

She moved toward the open door of the root cellar. Wade had left it open. A shaft of light rose up out of the earth as she walked toward it. Her head ached and she told herself now wasn't the time to have it out with her husband.

But her feet kept moving, like a woman headed for the gallows.

The moon was still hidden well behind the cloud cover. She made her way across the yard until she reached the gaping hole of the root cellar.

The room belowground was larger than most root cellars. Having lived in Kansas as a child, her mother was terrified of tornadoes. No amount of talking had convinced her that tornadoes were rare, if not unheard of, in this part of Montana. She'd insisted that her husband build it large enough that if she had to spend much time down there, she wouldn't feel cramped. So he had. He'd have done anything for her. No wonder he'd died young after holding down at least two jobs all of his life.

Abby braced herself on the open door and took the first step, then another. The steps were solid. Also she could hear voices below her that would drown out any noise she made. They wouldn't hear her coming. She thought she might hear them arguing, but as she got closer, she realized there was only a low murmur rising up to meet her as if they were speaking in a conversational tone.

That alone should have warned her.

It wasn't until she reached the bottom step that she saw she'd been wrong about a lot of things. The man with her mother wasn't Wade. Nor was her mother down here cleaning.

Abby froze as she took in the sight. Black lights hung from makeshift frames along the earth ceiling. Under them green plants grew as far back into the root cellar as she could see.

Her mother and her visitor had frozen when they'd seen her. Deputy Sheriff Huck Pierce had a plastic bag filled with what looked like dried plants in his hand. Her mother had a wad of cash. Both quickly hid what was in their hands.

"What are you doing here?" her mother demanded. "You never stop by and tonight you decide to pay me a visit?"

Realization was like a bright white noise that buzzed in her aching brain. She stood stock-still. This, she realized, was why her mother had pushed her to marry Wade. It had nothing to do with him being her best choice. No, it was all about his father and the drug business her mother had been secretly running in her root cellar.

"Abby," Huck said casually. "I thought you'd be home in bed."

"I'm sure you did," she said and looked to her mother.

A mix of emotions crossed Nan's face before ending with resignation. "So now you know," she said.

Yes, now she knew why her mother had berated her for not being a better wife to Wade. Even when Abby had told her how Wade hurt her, she hadn't said, "Leave the bastard." No, she'd told Abby that it was her fault. That she needed to treat him better. That she needed to put up with it. Otherwise, she would be a divorcée, and look how that had turned out for her mother after Abby's father had died and she'd quickly remarried twice more and was now divorced again.

"I'll let you handle this," Huck said as he moved to leave. He tipped his hat as he edged past Abby as if she was a rattlesnake that couldn't be trusted not to strike.

But it wasn't Huck who she wanted to sink her venom into. It was her mother. All she'd wanted was her mother's love, she realized now. But the woman was incapable of real love. Why hadn't she seen that before?

"Don't be giving me that look," her mother snapped as she put away the empty jar that had held the dried marijuana the deputy had just bought. "I have to make a living. That's all this is. You have no idea what it's like being a single woman at my age.

Anyway, it should be legal in this state. Will be one day and then I'll be out of business. But until then…"

She thought of all the things she wanted to say to her mother and was surprised when the only words that came out were "I'm divorcing Wade."

"You don't want to do that."

"*You* don't want me to do that, you mean. Or is it Huck who wants me to stay with his son?"

"Huck and I agree that the two of you need to work some things out. You two married just keeps things…simple."

"Simple for you since you're apparently in business with his father."

Her mother took a step toward her. "I won't hear any more about this. What are you doin' here, anyway? You should be home waiting for your husband. No wonder he has to take a hand to you."

Abby heard herself laugh, an odd sound down in the root cellar. "It's not going to work, Mother. All I've ever wanted was you to like me if not love me. I tried to do what you asked of me, thinking that one day…" She shook her head. "Don't worry. I'm not going to turn in your little…operation or snitch on the deputy. Knowing Huck, he'd wiggle out of it and let you fry. But as for you and me?" She shook her head again and turned to leave.

"You're making a huge mistake. You leave Wade and things will only get worse for you. I'll tell you what. Quit your waitressing job and come into business with me. I'll cut you in and—"

"Save your breath," she said over her shoulder. "You and I are finished."

"I'm your *mother*. You listen to me," Nan yelled after her.

"I'm through listening to you." Abby topped the stairs and stumbled out. She took huge gulps of fresh air and fought tears. All this time she'd been trying to do the right thing according to her mother. It had all been to keep a drug dealer happy? Her mother had never cared what happened to her. It hadn't been about her marriage vows at all.

She staggered through the dark to her car, her ribs hurting as she took each ragged breath. She half expected Huck to be at the edge of the darkness, waiting to leap out at her. But apparently he'd left, believing that her mother could handle her. Look how well she'd done so far.

The moon peeked out from behind a cloud, startling her. Abby held her breath until she was behind the wheel of her car, the doors locked. She sat for a moment, gasping between sobs, the pain deeper than even her bruised ribs.

She started the car, desperately needing to leave here. Looking behind her, she saw her mother come out of the root cellar and stand, hands on her hips in the dim moonlight, scowling as she watched Abby drive away.

Chapter Five

"I didn't expect you to be back to work already," Ledger said, eyeing Abby a week later. "Are you feeling all right?"

"I'm fine," she said, handing him a menu and placing a glass of ice water in front of him. The familiarity of it after all this time had a nice resonance. She realized that if he ever quit coming in, she would miss him terribly.

That thought made her feel guilty. She knew what Wade would make of it.

Since the night she went to her mother's, Wade had been an adoring husband. Abby was sure his father must have said something to him about what she'd seen in the root cellar. Was that why he was being so attentive? Because he was afraid she would tell?

But tell what? She hadn't been able to remember anything from her lost twenty-four hours. She'd wondered if it hadn't had something to do with Wade's father's illegal business with her mother. Was that what she and Wade had argued about?

She didn't think so. All her instincts told her it was more serious than that. It nagged at her. She feared it was something worse, but couldn't imagine what that would be.

Seeing Ledger made her forget for a moment about that part of her life. He had always brightened her days. She'd often regretted jumping into marriage with Wade, but had been determined to stick it out no matter what. She'd taken her marriage vows seriously—even without her mother's nagging.

"What would you like this morning?" she asked as Ledger picked up the menu. He had to have it memorized as often as he came in and the menu hadn't changed in fifty years except for the prices.

"Abby," he said, lowering his voice.

She fought the impulse to lean in closer. Close enough she could smell his distinct male scent, something that was branded on her memory. The soft sweetness of it was a painful reminder of when they'd been together. Ledger had been her first, something that Wade had never let her forget.

"I spoke to the nurse on your floor at the hospital. She told me that your injuries weren't consistent with a fall off a ladder."

"Ledger." The word came out a plea. He wasn't telling her anything she didn't already know. He couldn't keep doing this. It was killing her.

"I thought you should know. Wade lied to you."

Tears burned her eyes. She'd known Wade was lying to her the moment she'd seen his face. It wasn't the first time nor did she suspect it would be the last. But he was trying, something he hadn't done since becoming a deputy sheriff.

"He's going to kill you one of these days and then I'm going to prison for the rest of my life because I am going to tear him limb from limb." He said it so matter-of-factly that his words were like an arrow through her heart.

"Ledger. No."

"Why, Abby? Why have you stayed with him?" The pain in Ledger's voice made tears blur her eyes. She hadn't just been putting *herself* through this.

She shook her head. All her reasons for staying no longer mattered. She took a step back, then another, bumping into a table before she got turned and rushed back to the kitchen.

"Get control of yourself," her elderly boss snapped as she rushed into the kitchen in tears.

"I can't do this anymore," Abby cried.

Ella took a step toward her. "If you're quitting, you aren't quitting in the middle of a shift."

"I'm not quitting." She lowered herself to a stool by the back door, her face in her hands. "I can't keep going back and forth, even in my mind."

Ella stepped to her and placed an arm around her shoulders. "Honey, this has been coming for a long time. You can't be that surprised."

"I'm a *married* woman."

Ella snorted. "And Wade is a married man. You think that means much to him? Now wipe your face."

She handed her a paper towel. "Honey, it's time to fish or cut bait. You're going to have to make a decision, and from where I'm sitting, it's pretty damned clear. You going to let Wade keep knocking you around? Or are you going to put a stop to it?"

She looked up, surprised, although she knew she shouldn't be. Of course her boss knew. "I've told him—"

"*Telling* him don't mean squat. Anything short of shooting him won't do any good if you don't leave him. I've held my tongue, but I can't anymore. Stop being a damned fool."

"But—"

"No buts. And stop listening to your mother. She doesn't have the sense God gave a goose. I'm telling you straight. Dump that man and get on with your life before you don't have a life. Now get back to work."

Abby went into the restroom and wiped her face. She'd cried enough over her situation. She looked as she came out to see that Ledger had left.

"I told him to get on out of here and to quit crowding you," Ella said. "You need to cut him loose if you don't have the sense to end your marriage. Now do what women have always done—buck up and get back to work."

VANCE COULDN'T BELIEVE IT. He looked around the bedroom thinking he had to be dreaming. He'd downplayed how poor his adoptive family had been or how hard he'd had to work or how much debt he had from college.

As he walked to the window to look out, he felt a stab of jealousy for Cull, Ledger and Boone. They'd grown up here. They'd had all this and more.

But now you're one of them.

"Not yet." There was the DNA test. He'd managed to put it off as long as he could, knowing it was just a matter of time before he'd be forced to take it.

In the middle of dinner tonight Cull McGraw and his girlfriend had shown up. Both had looked at him like he was a bug under a microscope as if searching for his fatal flaw—just as they had the first night he'd met them. The girlfriend, Nikki St. James, the true-crime writer, had wanted to see the stuffed toy horse that night. He had watched her inspect it and seen that the horse had definitely been the ticket in.

But it would all come down to the DNA test.

"When is the DNA test scheduled?" Cull had asked his father tonight.

Travers had seemed taken aback by his son's abruptness.

"No reason to put it off any longer, right?" Ledger had interjected.

Vance had met Travers's gaze. "They're right. No reason not to schedule it," he'd said with more confidence than he felt. One more major hurdle and then he was home free, so to speak.

But he remembered that first night well. "So

what have you been doing since college?" Nikki had asked.

"You can interview him for the book some other time," Travers had said with an embarrassed laugh.

"Sorry, questioning goes with the occupation," she'd said, but he had known he'd have to answer a lot more questions before this was over.

That was why he'd answered it that first night. "I've been working on some ranches in southern Montana. I'm apparently good with horses." That had pleased Travers—just as he knew it would. Vance had smiled to himself as he'd finished his meal.

Now over a week later and alone in his room, he tried to relax and enjoy how far he'd come. This was definitely an upgrade from how he'd been living, but, he reminded himself, it was temporary.

"How are you settling in?" asked a voice from the doorway.

He swung around to find the attorney smiling at him. "This place is beautiful."

Waters agreed as he stepped into the room and walked to the window to look out on the swimming pool, pool house and horse barns. Past them, the Mc-Graw ranch stretched to the Little Rockies. "Dinner went well again tonight, don't you think?"

"I guess."

The attorney shot him a look. "Is there a problem?"

"No, but I think it's time I took the DNA test. Until I do…"

Waters nodded. "I don't see any rush, but it's up

to you. Travers has accepted you. You seem to fit this place and this family."

He wasn't so sure about that. He might have won Travers over, but he wasn't so sure about the others.

"Now it is only a matter of tying up the loose ends," Waters said.

He wondered if the attorney was referring to the DNA test or the five-hundred-thousand-dollar reward. "I was wondering... The reward money? The friend who pointed out that I might be Oakley... I want him to have it."

The attorney studied him for a moment. "Minus my ten percent, you mean. I'm sure that can be arranged. Do you want me to speak to Travers?"

"No, not until after the DNA test." He swallowed back the bile that rose in his throat. "Once there is no question that I'm Oakley..."

LEDGER CORNERED HIS brother Cull.

"What do you want me to say?" Cull demanded after listening to what his brother told him.

"He lied about Abby falling off a ladder," Ledger repeated with more force.

"Wade Pierce lied? Hell, stop the presses. What should we do? I know—let's go over to his house and beat the crap out of him. Is that what you want me to say?"

"That would be a good start. Not that I need your help."

"Yep, you should go alone, that way I'll be able to

get you out of jail on bail after you've gotten the hell kicked out of you by both Wade and his worthless father, who is also a deputy. Good plan."

"What am I supposed to do?" Ledger demanded.

"Do I have to remind you that Abby isn't your wife, not your responsibility, not even your business?"

"I'm just supposed to let him keep hurting her?"

Cull sighed. "She chose him. I know that's hard for you to accept but—"

"You don't know her. She sticks with whatever she promises to do. She promised to love him until death they do part."

"Then that's probably what's going to happen."

"I'll kill him."

"Oh, damn," Cull said and dropped his head into his hands for a moment. "Okay, what do you want me to do?"

Ledger looked at a loss for words. "We have to save her."

His brother nodded. "Okay, I reckon we could kidnap her."

"Kidnap who?" Boone had come into the room but stopped at his words and looked at him as if he'd lost his mind.

"Abby," Cull said. "We could wait outside the restaurant about the time she got off work and just grab her and—"

"And go to prison for kidnapping?" Boone demanded.

"Wait, this isn't such a bad idea," Ledger said. "Once we get her away from him, she will come to her senses and—" He stopped, seeing their disbelieving looks, and realized Cull had been kidding.

"Haven't you been trying to convince her to leave him?" Cull asked. "Has it done any good?"

"It's…complicated."

"Isn't it, though? I hate to tell you this, little brother," Cull said. "But as hard as it is, you need to step off."

Ledger flopped down in a chair. "I can't do that."

"What choice do you have?" Boone asked. "She doesn't want you."

"That's blunt enough, thanks, Boone," Cull said sarcastically. "Where are you going?" he asked as Ledger got to his feet and headed for the door.

"I'm going to find Wade," he said as he approached the door.

"He's going to end up in jail," he heard Boone say behind him. "Or worse if Huck and Wade tag team him. You ought to stop him."

"I suppose we could hog-tie him in the barn, but eventually we would have to let him go and then what?" Cull said.

Ledger let the door slam behind him as he headed for his pickup.

"Where have you been?" Abby asked when Wade finally showed up at home later that night.

He jumped, startled to find her waiting in the dark corner of the porch. "You scared the devil out of me."

Somehow she doubted that.

"I asked where you've been."

"You'd better change your tone and right now," he said, but it wasn't with the same meanness in his voice. She really *had* scared him. The last thing he'd expected was to see her sitting in the dark waiting on him.

He reached in and turned on the porch light, blinked and then studied her as if trying to gauge what was going on.

"I'm still waiting," she said calmly.

"I was working," he said, starting to get belligerent. She could smell the beer on his breath from where she was sitting. But that wasn't the only scent she picked up on him. The cheap perfume turned her stomach.

She also noticed that he seemed to be swaying a little as if fairly drunk. Normally she wouldn't confront him. But tonight it was as if something had snapped in her. He'd been so good for weeks, but she'd known in her heart it wouldn't last.

"Don't bother to lie," she said, getting to her feet. "I know where you've been and what you've been doing." She started past him.

He grabbed her arm, spinning her around to face him. This was when she would normally hurriedly apologize, look at the floor, take whatever belittling he threw at her and then try to get away as quickly as possible.

Tonight she looked him in the eye with a fire she hadn't known she possessed. He seemed startled, his grip on her loosening a little.

Her gaze went to where his fingers clutched her arm. "Get your hands off me."

Amazingly, he let go. "You're getting some kind of mouth on you," he blustered. "You keep that up and I'll—"

"No, you won't," Abby said. She kept her voice calm but with an edge to it he'd never heard before because she'd never dared talk to him like this. "If you ever touch me again, you and I are done." She pushed past him, half expecting him to grab her from behind and backhand her.

But he didn't touch her. He let her go into the bedroom where she closed the door, the sound of the lock deafening in the house at this late hour.

Her heart was pounding like a war drum. She quickly moved away from the door, afraid he would charge it using his body like a battering ram and knock it down. The lock was fairly flimsy. It wouldn't take much.

But beyond the door she heard the shuffle of his heavy boots. He knocked over a lamp and cussed as it hit the floor. She heard him say, "I should bust down that door and teach that bitch what's what."

But with relief, she knew he wasn't going to do anything but pass out. She moved to the bed as she heard him collapse on the couch. Would he wake up in the middle of the night having sobered up just enough to be furious that she'd locked him out of his bedroom?

She climbed into bed, feeling the cold aluminum of the baseball bat she'd purchased in town. It lay next to her. She'd bought it on impulse today after work because as good as Wade had been, she'd known in her heart it wouldn't last.

Abby took hold of the bat. If he busted down the door and came in all raging fists and angry threats, he would get another surprise.

For a long time, she lay propped against the pillows, clutching the bat and waiting. Ella was right. She had to take control of her life. This was a start.

If she could save her marriage, she had to try. Ella was right about that. She was also right about Ledger. She needed to cut him loose.

Chapter Six

Last night Ledger had driven around Whitehorse, looking for Wade's pickup. The deputy hadn't been at work. He also hadn't been at any of the local bars.

While he'd thought about driving out to Abby's house, he had enough sense not to. The more he drove through the sleepy little Western town, the more he realized something had to change. He'd been carrying this torch for Abby since high school. If he'd married her when he'd had the chance, none of this would be happening.

But they'd been too young and he'd promised his father that he'd finish college before they married. Unfortunately, Abby hadn't been able to wait. He'd heard that she was pregnant with Wade's baby, but that hadn't been true. Instead, he suspected the rushed marriage had been Abby's mother's doing. That woman just wanted to get her daughter married off—didn't matter to whom, apparently.

He'd finally driven toward home, telling himself he had to stop going by the café on the mornings

Abby worked. He upset her too much. He had to back off. His brothers were right, as hard as that was to admit.

Feeling as if his heart was breaking all over again, he drove home. As he got out of his pickup, he saw that his brother Cull was sitting on the porch as if he'd been waiting for him.

"You don't have to get me out of jail," he said as he climbed the porch steps.

"Glad to hear it. Not that I was waiting up for you," Cull lied.

Ledger smiled at him as he took a step next to him. "I drove around looking for Wade for a while."

"Must not have found him."

"Nope, but I did do some thinking. You're right. Abby knows how I feel. It's in her court now."

Cull reached over and clasped his shoulder to give it a squeeze. "I know how hard this must be for you. But you've done all you can at this point."

He nodded. "I love her."

"I know." Cull was quiet for a moment. "So you think this Vance Elliot is our brother?"

Ledger shrugged. "He looks like us."

"He does that. Says he's good with horses." Cull chuckled. "I was thinking we'd put him on that new stallion."

Ledger actually smiled at that. "I'd pay money to see it."

Cull got to his feet. "It's late. Guess we'll know for sure when the DNA test results come back. I would imagine Dad will talk the lab into putting a rush on them. Or maybe not. I think he's enjoying the idea of Oakley being home. You going to be okay?"

"Don't have a lot of choice."

ABBY WOKE THE next morning, only her and the baseball bat in the bed. No Wade. He hadn't awakened in the night. Or if he had, he'd thought better about breaking down their bedroom door.

She realized that she felt better. Her ribs were still sore. She still had a dull ache in her head, but even it was better.

Rising, she dressed, and moving to the door, she slowly unlocked it. She had no idea what to expect. The wear and tear of living in a relationship where she had to walk on eggshells had taken a toll on her. She felt jumpy, unsure, afraid as she slowly opened the bedroom door, the doorknob in one hand, the baseball bat in the other.

The couch was empty. She stood listening before taking another step. Was he waiting for her in the hallway off the bedroom, planning to jump her the moment she came out?

With the bat in both hands, she started down the hallway. She took a few steps and stopped to listen. The house creaked and groaned, but there was no sound of Wade.

She could see the indentation in the couch where Wade must have slept at least part of the night. One of the couch pillows was on the floor.

Cautiously she moved down the hallway toward the kitchen. The floor creaked under her step. She froze and listened again.

Just a few more feet and she would be able to see into the kitchen. He would have had time to think about what she'd said to him last night.

She prayed that he would know she meant it this time and that if he didn't change she would leave him. But she knew that her ultimatum might just as easily set him off and make things worse between them.

If what Ledger had told her was true about people at the hospital knowing she hadn't fallen off a ladder? Word would spread fast and everyone in the county would know the truth about her and Wade. Shame burned her cheeks. They'd know her terrible secret. All her lies had been for nothing. Because this time Wade had hit her hard enough that he'd had to take her to the hospital.

That story about her climbing the ladder in the garage for jars to make peach jam had been just that— a ridiculous story that he'd cooked up.

She shuddered as she realized that Wade hadn't come up with that on his own. His father's fingerprints were all over it. Wade would have panicked when he couldn't wake her up. He would have called Huck to ask him what to do.

Abby felt sick because all of it sounded so much more believable than the jam jar story. Yet she had wanted to believe it. Worse, she'd wanted Ledger to believe it.

What was wrong with her? She'd let her husband hurt her, telling herself that he was under a lot of pressure because he'd lost his job or because he wanted to make good at the sheriff's department or because he'd had a rough day at work. Like she'd never had one of those.

When he'd lost his temper and hit her, she'd told herself it was her fault. She'd promised to try harder to please him—just as her mother had said.

A wave of disgust washed over her as she moved to the doorway to the kitchen and stopped.

Wade was sitting at the table, elbows on the tabletop, his head resting in his hands. A floorboard must have creaked, because he suddenly lifted his head and turned it in her direction.

His eyes were red and shiny. Hungover? Or crying? She couldn't tell. Either, though, could change in a heartbeat and turn violent.

Those eyes focused on her, shifting from her face to the bat in her hands. His expression went from sorrowful to surprised, then deeply hurt. She realized he'd been crying. It was what he always did after he hurt her. She'd never doubted that he was sorry or that he didn't want to hurt her again. Until the next time.

"Abby?" His voice sounded lost.

She shifted the bat to one hand and let it rest against her leg.

"You don't need that," he said, still sounding shocked that she would either think that she needed a bat to protect herself or that she would consider hitting him with it.

She felt the irony of that soul-deep.

Yesterday she'd been determined to save her marriage. But looking at him sitting there, she knew that she no longer wanted to. The last few months had been so much worse than any she could have imagined. Him putting her in the hospital because of his temper… It was the last straw.

"I want you to pack your things and move out," she said, surprised how calm she sounded. Her heart was pounding in her chest.

"Abby, you can't mean—"

"I do, Wade. I can't live like this." He had started to get up, but her words stopped him. He settled back in the chair and put his head in his hands again.

"Don't do this, Abby. I'll change. I swear I will. In fact, things are going to get better."

The familiar words had no effect on her. She stared at her husband and wondered how long it had been over. She'd left him once. That night, running for her life, she'd made the mistake of going to her mother's.

"Don't you ever darken my door again. Your place is with your husband."

"You don't understand. He's going to kill me." She had pleaded with her mother.

"What did you do?"

She'd stared at her mother in disbelief. "I didn't do anything."

Her mother sneered. "You did somethin' to make him mad."

"He came home drunk, smelling of some other woman—"

"Grow up, Abby. He's a man. He has to let off a little steam. Be glad he took some of it out on that other woman before he got home. You want to be a good wife? Don't make him mad. Now get out of here. He finds out you came here…"

She'd left, walking home in the dark and realizing she had no other place to go than back to Wade.

Now she felt a sadness deep in the pit of her stomach. She hadn't been strong enough to leave Wade then, but she was now. "It's over, Wade."

"You can't throw me out of my own house," he said belligerently. But he didn't make a move toward her.

She felt the weight of the bat. "If you don't leave, I'll call the sheriff. I don't think you want that."

He fisted his hands at his waist, glaring at her. Then knocking over the chair, he jumped up and stormed out. She listened to the sound of his pickup engine dying off in the distance before she went to the door, locked it and pushed the fallen chair under the knob.

But all her instincts told her he wouldn't be back. At least not until tonight.

WATERS SHOWED UP the next morning to see if Vance needed a ride to the lab for his DNA test.

"This really isn't necessary," Travers said when he opened the door to see his attorney standing there.

"I'm representing Vance through this," Waters said, surprising his old boss. "He asked me to on his behalf. I hope you don't mind."

"I guess I can understand how he might feel alone in this, though if this test comes back like I think it will, he'll now have family to take care of things. I hope, after all these years, that you won't be involved in any litigation with my son."

"I was the one who brought him to you," Waters reminded him. "I promised to look after his interests even though I've spent years looking after yours. But I'm sure once we confirm he's your son that he will have everything he needs."

Travers nodded.

"Since I am only on a retainer with you, I thought you'd appreciate me taking care of things on his behalf."

"You know I do." The horse rancher turned as Vance came down the stairs.

Just moments before, Waters was feeling good. Travers did appreciate what he was doing. He thought they might actually be able to patch things up. He was about to breathe a sigh of relief when he saw Vance's expression.

Worry wormed through him. The kid looked petrified. Maybe he hated needles. Waters could only hope that was all that was going on with Vance. Surely he wouldn't be so stupid as to think he could pass a DNA test if he knew he wasn't Oakley McGraw.

Then again, maybe Vance thought the toy stuffed horse would be enough.

He tried to relax. The kid had the horse. Unless he'd picked it up at a garage sale, he was Oakley McGraw, right?

"I thought you and I would ride together to the lab," the attorney said to him. He promised to see Travers and his sons at the lab and quickly steered the would-be Oakley outside.

Once the two of them were in the car, he buckled up and looked over at the kid. "If there is some reason you think you might not pass this DNA test, then you need to tell me now."

ABBY WONDERED WHAT had made her think she could stay in this house. Everywhere she looked there were too many bad memories. Her first thought this morning was simply getting away from Wade. She didn't think her body could take another run-in.

But once she realized she didn't want to stay here, she knew she had to find a place of her own. Something small. Something she could afford by herself.

They'd been paying on this house for the past couple of years. If there was any equity in it, Wade could have it. She just wanted out.

That decided, she couldn't wait to pack up and leave. It wouldn't take much packing. She hadn't accumulated hardly anything she cared about over these few years of marriage.

When she looked around, she thought she could pack all of her possessions into the two suitcases out in the garage. She walked through the kitchen, opened the door from the house to the garage and froze.

A memory tugged at her the moment she saw the ladder lying on the garage floor. Was it possible she *had* fallen—just as Wade had said? She shook her head. No, the blood was in the kitchen. But there was something about the garage and the ladder.

Standing there, she tried hard to remember. Closing her eyes, she felt another nudge. Wade and his father. She frowned. They'd both been in the garage. She'd come to the door and heard them talking.

A shudder moved through her. Why had they been talking in the garage? Because they hadn't wanted her to hear. But she *had* heard. Had she let them know it?

Apparently not at once since she'd found her dried blood on the kitchen floor. Had she confronted Wade about what she'd heard and the argument had gone from the garage to the kitchen?

She squeezed her eyes closed tighter. They'd argued, but she'd already suspected that. But not in the garage. No, it had been in the kitchen. The two of them alone. But what had it been about?

Something important. Had Wade found out that she'd gone back on the pill and had been keeping it from him? She shook her head and tried to concentrate on what she'd seen and heard in the garage.

She could almost see Wade and Huck with their heads together, talking in grave tones in the garage. Almost hear… She opened her eyes with a groan, the memory just out of her grasp. But whatever it was, it was serious.

WATERS HAD FOUND a local lab to do the DNA test so they didn't have to travel out of town.

"Won't you need to get DNA from Mother?" Ledger asked. Once they'd seen that Jim Waters would be taking Vance to the lab, he and his brothers had insisted on driving their father.

"At this point, all they need is mine," Travers said after lecturing them about babying him. "It should be conclusive enough. If needed, we can get your mother's."

As they walked in, Ledger wondered how long it would be before the news was all over town. He'd already heard the rumor going around that one of the twins had been found. Waters's doing? Or Vance's?

Vance had spent his first night in a motel in town. If Waters had checked him in, that could have been enough to get tongues wagging.

At the lab, his father walked up to the reception desk and was told that he could come on back. As he disappeared down a short hallway, Ledger looked around. The building was small. His brothers had taken seats in the waiting area, but he was too antsy, so he'd moved where he could see down the corridor.

There were a series of small rooms off the hall. His father had gone into one of those with the lab tech. He wondered where Vance was. At the sound of a familiar voice, he saw Deputy Sheriff Huck Pierce step out of one of the rooms with one of the lab techs, this one a redhead. She was laughing at something the deputy had said.

Ledger turned away, but not before he'd seen the lab tech move to open the door of one of the rooms. He got a glimpse of Vance sitting nervously on a gurney, waiting to have the test done. He didn't look like a man who believed he was Oakley McGraw.

"Good thing Dad is smart enough to demand a lab test," Ledger said when he joined his brothers. "I just saw Vance. He looks scared to death. What if he's lying?"

"Then we'll know soon enough," Boone said. "DNA doesn't lie."

"He had the toy stuffed horse." Cull shook his head. "What I want to know is what happens if he *is* Oakley."

Chapter Seven

Ledger let a few days go by before he stopped in the Whitehorse Café. He halted at the door to scan the room as he always did. Today, he would tell Abby why he hadn't been back. He would apologize for making things worse for her. He would step off.

But as always, there was that moment of expectation, that sense of hope, then concern when he looked around for her. If he didn't see Abby, there was always a painful disappointment that ruined his appetite. But he was too polite to turn around and leave on those days when she'd traded shifts. He would have a little something to eat even though the other waitress could tell there was only one reason he'd come in and it wasn't for the food.

"Abby took the day off," her friend Tammy said as she swung by on her way to a table with two plates full of biscuits and gravy. She didn't give him a chance to comment.

Abby never took a day off unless something was

wrong. He waited until Tammy came back to ask, "Is she all right?"

Tammy slowed to a stop even though he could tell that she was really busy this morning. He saw her hesitate. He knew she didn't like telling something that Abby might not want him to know.

"It's okay," he said, not wanting to put her on the spot. "She needs loyal friends."

"She's looking for an apartment," Tammy said and gave him an encouraging smile.

"An apartment?"

"A studio," she said pointedly and then took off as she had another order come up.

A studio apartment. Did that mean what he hoped it did? That she'd finally left Wade? He tried to keep from getting too excited about the prospect, not knowing what it meant. There was always the chance she would change her mind. Or worse, that Wade would stop her.

He couldn't possibly eat a thing. He left and walked to his pickup, his step lighter than it had been in three years.

He'd just climbed into the ranch pickup when his cell rang. He thought for a moment that it would be Abby calling with the good news. He reminded himself that he wasn't part of the equation. He hadn't been since she married Wade. Just because she was getting an apartment—

Ledger quickly dug out his phone, still hoping.

"Hello?" he said without checking to see who was calling.

"You need to get home," his brother Cull said without preamble. "Dad just got the DNA test results. He wants us all there."

"That quick?" Ledger asked in disbelief.

"They did just a preliminary one that should tell us if Vance Elliot has any of our blood running through his veins."

"I'm on my way." He disconnected and sat staring out over the steering wheel. It was the moment of truth.

He started the truck and drove as quickly as he could toward the ranch, his thoughts straying radically from what was waiting for him at home to what Abby was doing right now.

He wanted to call her, but he resisted. He'd promised himself he would give her space. Ledger chuckled to himself, thinking about the times he'd wanted to pull some crazy romantic stunt like he'd seen in the movies. He'd ride into the café on his horse, scoop Abby up and ride off into the sunset with her. He'd save her from herself, from Wade, from her horrible mother.

Ahead the ranch came into view, the Little Rockies in the distance. He slowed the pickup to turn down the road past the bright white wooden fence that lined both sides of the road. A half dozen horses had taken off in the wind, their manes flying back as they ran.

The sight always made him smile. He loved this ranch, loved raising horses. He'd always thought that he would bring Abby here after he saved her.

Waters's car was parked in front of the house along with an older-model pickup he didn't recognize. Vance Elliot's?

Both trepidation and excitement filled him. For twenty-five years his father had searched for the twins. Was it possible the DNA test would prove that one of them had finally made his way home?

ABBY FELT STRONGER every day both physically and emotionally. She'd made a point of ignoring the pleading messages her mother left on her phone as well as the angry, threatening ones.

To her surprise, Wade had stayed away, as well. Each night she had expected him to get a snoot full of beer and come banging on her door. When she woke each morning to realize he hadn't, she felt like a woman in the eye of the hurricane. She didn't kid herself that it would be this easy to get her freedom from him.

Now she braced herself. The last couple of days had been nice not having to confront him. Unfortunately, she had to talk to him. She found Wade as he was getting off his shift. From the look in his eyes, his father had already told him everything, including that Abby now knew about the marijuana business.

"We should talk about all this at home," Wade said once he was close enough to whisper.

"I don't have that much to say and I don't want to

be alone in the house with you." She saw the sharp ache of pain in Wade's eyes. The other times, she'd weakened. "I moved out of the house today. You can keep it or sell it, whatever you want. I don't want anything from you."

"You don't mean that. You're just angry and upset. Once you calm down—"

"No, Wade. I do mean it and I'm not going to change my mind. It's over between us."

A muscle jumped in his jaw. He got that familiar look in his eyes. If they hadn't been standing on the street in front of the sheriff's office, he would have lost his temper and they both knew what happened then.

"I saw a lawyer today and filed separation papers. There is a waiting period, but once it's over, if you sign the divorce papers, you won't have to pay for a lawyer of your own. Up to you, but dragging this out will only cost us both money."

He stared at her as if he couldn't believe the words out of her mouth. "You just hold up a minute. You didn't say nothin' about no divorce."

"I told you I was done."

"That ain't the same as a divorce," he said, taking off his Stetson to rake his fingers through his hair. "I just thought you needed some time to cool off."

"No, Wade. I can't be married to you anymore. Please don't put up a fight. It's over and I'm not going to change my mind."

He put his hat back on, looking like he was going to cry. "I'll change. You have to give me another chance."

"I've given you too many chances," she said, looking away from him.

His voice broke and, when she looked at him, fury was back in his gaze. "It's McGraw. Ledger McGraw."

"Believe what you want because you will anyway, but this is only about you and me." She started to walk back toward her car, hoping he wouldn't come after her.

But, of course, he did. "Abby, I know I've messed up..."

"Please stop," she said, continuing to walk. "I don't want to rehash this. You know exactly why I'm divorcing you. I won't tell anyone about how you physically abused me unless you fight the divorce."

She heard the breath come out of him in a whoosh. Clearly, he hadn't thought about that. Not that people didn't know already. Ledger had always known. But it was clear that Wade liked to think it was still their secret.

"It's my word against yours," he said, grabbing her arm and spinning her around to face him.

She jerked her arm free. "People saw the bruises on me, Wade. They'll testify in court. The doctor at the hospital is already suspicious after my...accident."

He looked furious but also scared. If it became public knowledge, he could lose his job. He grabbed her arm again.

"You're hurting me," she said, keeping her voice down. He released her arm and stepped back as if he didn't trust himself. "Just let me go. It's for the best. And, Wade? Don't let your father make you do something stupid."

"What does that mean?"

"My mother and your father have their own self-ish reasons for wanting us together. I wouldn't take their advice." With that, she opened her car door and climbed in to roll down the window. "My lawyer will have the paperwork to you soon. Just sign it and let's part amicably, okay?"

She didn't give him a chance to answer as she turned the key in the ignition and drove away. He was still standing there looking after her when she pulled onto the street. They would never be *amicable*. She would be lucky if he gave her the divorce, let alone left her alone. No, she thought, fighting tears. She'd be lucky to get out of this alive.

LEDGER WATCHED THE celebration feeling strangely outside it. After twenty-five years, one of the twins was back. It was more than surreal. He glanced at his father. Travers looked so happy it made his heart ache with joy. But he was the only one, Ledger thought as he surveyed the family. They all looked as stunned as he felt.

He saw Nikki watching Vance. Or did they now start calling him Oakley? Nikki was sharp; that was what made her such an excellent true-crime writer. She saw things that other people missed. And she knew people. Look how much she'd uncovered in a very short time recently.

She was frowning as she studied Vance. Ledger wasn't sure he could call him Oakley, even if the twenty-five-year-old would answer to it after all this time.

His father was suggesting another bottle of champagne as he put an arm around his long-lost son. Vance just looked uncomfortable in his new role.

Ledger moved closer to Nikki in time to hear her whisper to Cull, "Something's wrong."

His brother sighed. "He has the toy," Cull said quietly. "He has our blue eyes. He looks like us. But more to the point, he passed the preliminary DNA test with flying colors. So what are you saying?"

Nikki shook her head and looked to Ledger. "You feel it, don't you?"

He nodded. "It just feels..."

"Wrong," Boone said, joining them at the edge of the party.

Just then their father called them over so he could fill their champagne glasses.

"Whatever it is all of you think you know, keep it to yourself," Cull warned them. "Look at Dad. He's happy. So I'm happy. It will take some time, but let's make the best of this."

MEMORY IS A *funny thing*, Abby thought. One minute her mind nagged at her to remember what had happened that night in the garage and later in the kitchen. The next, she would get a flash. Just enough to make her stop what she was doing to try to hang on to it before it disappeared again.

She'd realized that she was missing one of her favorite earrings. Knowing that Wade should be working and away from the house, she'd driven out to look for the earring.

It was while down on her hands feeling around under the bed for the earring, when her fingers closed on it, that she had her strongest flash yet. She froze as the memory came to her like the trailer of a movie. She saw Wade and his father in the garage, their heads together in serious conversation. But this time, she heard what they were talking about.

At the sound of a vehicle pulling up in the yard, Abby jerked up, banging her head on the bed frame as she drew back, the earring biting into her fingers. Her head swam for a moment from the pain, from the memory, from the sound of a car door closing and heavy footfalls on the porch steps.

She rose and looked out the bedroom door toward the front of the house. At the sound of a key in the lock, she knew it had to be Wade. He would have seen her car parked out front.

Abby looked around as if for a way to escape. But the bedroom window was painted shut and she'd never be able to get down the hallway to the back door without being seen. If Wade saw her trying to get away from him, it would only make it worse.

Indecision froze her to the spot. She felt sick to her

stomach from what she'd remembered. She wished she'd never remembered. Just as she wished she had forgotten about the earring. She should never have come back here.

But she realized that knowing what she now did, she would have to go to the sheriff. She had no choice. Wade wasn't a good husband. He had a miserable temper and he often struck out when he was hurt or mad or drunk, which was often. But she'd never thought he was a bad man. She'd often felt sorry for him, knowing how he was brought up by his father.

But after what she'd heard Wade and his father discussing in the garage… Once she went to the sheriff, she would never be safe. If Wade didn't get her, his father would. She would be just as good as dead. Her only other option would be to stop Wade before he and his father went any further—as if anything she could say would convince her husband to go against his father.

She'd forgotten all about her earring until she heard it hit the floor. She hadn't even realized it was still in her hand until she'd dropped it. Bending down, she felt around for it in the dim light of the bedroom. She'd just recovered it when she heard a floorboard creak behind her.

"Abby?"

She hadn't heard him come down the hallway. Now he was standing in the bedroom doorway.

He saw the look on her face and swore. "You remembered."

Now she really was trapped.

Chapter Eight

Abby backed away from her husband. She'd never seen such fear and fury in his eyes before.

"You are going to keep your mouth shut. Is that understood?" he demanded as he advanced on her, matching each of her steps with one of his own until he backed her into a corner.

"Wade, I'm begging you not to do this," she said, trying to keep the tremor out of her voice and failing.

"Begging?" He laughed. "I like the sound of that."

"I'm serious. I've gone along with a lot since we married, but this—"

"This is our ticket out of this hellhole. Come on, don't pretend that you wouldn't like a nice big house like the McGraws'." He snickered. "Just the mention of that name and your eyes sparkle, but it's not the house you crave, is it?"

"Please, don't start on that."

"Don't even want to hear Ledger McGraw's name on my lips, do you?"

She bumped hard against the wall. He had her

trapped and he knew it. She'd put up with so much from him in the time they'd been married. At first he'd been so sweet, so understanding. He'd put her on a pedestal, but then he'd been fired at his feedlot job. His father had gotten him on as a sheriff's deputy and Wade had changed. He'd become more like the father he'd told her he despised.

He was close enough now that she could see the fire burning in his dark eyes. He desperately wanted to hit her.

Why had she tried to reason with him the night before he'd put her in the hospital? Why hadn't she gone straight to the sheriff when she'd found out what he and his father were up to?

Too late now. If only she could reach the gentle man who often cried in her arms after hurting her.

"Ledger McGraw," he repeated, his mouth twisting in an angry sneer. "I think my saying his name hurts you more than if I was to knock you into next week."

"Wade, this isn't about Ledger. This thing you're planning is cruel and illegal."

"Illegal?" He guffawed. "Honey, did you forget who you're married to? I'm a frigging deputy sheriff. There ain't nothing illegal when I'm carrying my badge and gun."

She feared he believed that. It would explain the change in him since becoming a deputy. She'd been a fool to provoke him by trying to change his mind.

Even if she backed down, she had his ire up. He was going to hurt her.

And then what? Suddenly she wasn't sure how far he'd go to keep her from telling what she'd overheard him and his father planning.

"I NEED YOU to come right over," Wade said into the phone, his voice breaking.

His father swore. *"What did you do?"*

He glanced over the body lying on the floor. "It wasn't my fault but I might have hit her too hard."

His father swore again. "Don't do anything, you dumbass. Just stay there. I'll be right over," he said before slamming down the phone.

Wade hung up and rubbed a hand over his face. Then pulled it away, shuddering as he saw it was covered in blood. He quickly wiped it on his pants.

"Stupid, stupid, stupid," he said, hitting his forehead with his palm. Why did he let it go so far? Why didn't he just walk away before it got so bad? Maybe he could have talked some sense into her. Why did he have to take it out on her?

"Because I'm my father's son," he said in disgust.

Walking over to Abby, he squatted down beside her. She didn't look that bad. His old man had taught him not to hit a woman in the face. Didn't want the neighbors talking or, worse, someone down at the sheriff's department being forced to call him on the carpet because everyone in town had seen his wife's black eye.

But he must have hit her in the face this time because her nose was bleeding and after her concussion...

His back door banged open. Angry footfalls marched down the hallway. He turned as his father came storming into the room.

"She still alive?" Huck asked.

"I don't know."

"You didn't check?" He let out an angry snort and, shoving Wade out of the way, squatted down to check her pulse. "You lucked out, you worthless little prick. She's still breathing. How long has she been out?"

Wade looked around as if the answer was in the room. "I don't know."

His father rose and glared at him. "What are you doing beating on her again?"

"You mean like you used to hit me and Mom?"

"Watch your mouth, smart boy," he said, stepping to him. Huck grabbed him by the front of his shirt and slammed him against the wall. "Why pick a fight with her today, of all days? Do I have to remind you that we have too much at stake for you to be calling attention to yourself with the authorities again because of some petty argument with your old lady? What were you thinking?"

"It wasn't petty," he gasped out. His father was choking him with the balled-up shirt at his throat. "She *knows*." He wiped a hand over his face, smelled her blood on him still and rubbed his palm against his jeans.

Huck let go of him and took a step back. "How?"

He shook his head. "I don't know. She must have just remembered. She'll tell."

Huck swore and turned to look at the woman on the floor. "We don't have any choice, then. We can't take her back to the hospital. I know someone who's an EMT. We can take her to him. He'll cover for you, and if she's smart, she'll keep her mouth shut and go along with it."

Wade bit at his cheek. He hated to tell his father but he didn't think Abby would be going along with anything anymore.

"It may take more than that," he said quietly.

Huck turned to look at him. "What are you saying?"

"I don't think she's going to keep this to herself. Not this time."

His father took a step toward him. Wade raised his arms to protect his head and waited for the force of Huck's punch to knock him to his knees.

Abby moaned.

Wade peeked from under his arms, surprised his father hadn't struck him.

"We'd better decide what to do with her," Huck said. "But first, you have any whiskey? I could use a drink."

ABBY DIDN'T KNOW how long she'd been lying on the floor bleeding. She groaned and tried to sit up. Her ribs protested violently and she had to lean back against the side of the bed. The room began to spin and she thought she might throw up. She closed her eyes, fighting the nausea. She could hear Wade and his father in the kitchen. From the clink of ice in the glasses, it sounded as if they were having a drink.

How was that possible with her lying in here on the floor, fading in and out of consciousness? Or had, this time, Wade thought he'd killed her?

They had lowered their voices, but she could make out most of what they were saying since this house was so poorly insulated. Her head ached. She had to concentrate hard to understand the words.

"…get rid of her body…have to do it tonight… can't just dump it anywhere."

Fear spiked through her. They couldn't be talking about getting rid of her. Getting rid of her for good. But even as she thought it, she knew it was true. Wade had gone too far this time. He thought he'd killed her.

She realized that he couldn't take her back to the hospital or questions would be asked. He might lose his job. He loved being a sheriff's deputy. He'd never give that up just because this time he'd hit his wife too hard.

Abby caught hold of the edge of the bed and pulled herself up. She realized she'd left a bloody handprint on the spread. For a moment, she stared at it, thinking the spread would have to be soaked to get that out.

A noise in the other room brought her back to the

pain in her body, the ache in her head. She felt dizzy standing and wasn't sure how much longer she could stay upright.

Get out before it's too late, a voice screamed in her head.

She worked her way to the door and looked out. She could still hear Wade and his father in the kitchen. They were talking in very low tones now. She only heard the occasional clink of a glass or an ice cube.

They would be coming back for her soon.

She looked toward the back door. It seemed too far away to reach given how dizzy she felt, but she started for it, moving at a snail's pace as she used the wall for support.

She felt dazed, not even sure she was awake as she reached the door and tried the lock. Unlocked. It felt slick in her hand as she turned the knob and the door swung open.

A cool breeze hit her in the face, and from some survival instinct older than time, Abby knew she had to run for the trees now. If the men in the kitchen felt this breeze, they'd know she'd opened the back door. They would know that she was trying to get away.

She ran, the first step jarring her ribs and making her hurt all over. She ran bent over, her arms wrapped around her middle as if she could hold herself together. She didn't look back. She didn't dare. She had to believe she could reach the trees. She didn't think past that.

Abby stumbled on a tree root, lost her balance and went down hard. The fall knocked the air out of her and hurt her already aching ribs. She rolled over on her back and lay there, gasping like a fish out of water.

Over her head, stars glittered, making her think she was blacking out again. Her vision cleared as she caught her breath. She lay there listening, expecting Wade and Huck to find her and that her painful run for safety had only been a waste of time and effort.

Hearing nothing, she was suddenly aware of the weight of her cell phone in her pocket. She pulled it out, but for a moment, she couldn't think who to call.

Not her mother. Not her friends. She couldn't drag them into this. Wade had already warned her what he would do to them. As she held the phone, she felt a sob rise in her chest.

There was only one person she could call. She got up and stumbled deeper into the woods. She thought for a moment that she wouldn't be able to remember his number. But it was right there when she touched the keypad. She prayed he hadn't changed his cell number as she waited for it to ring.

The first ring filled her ear, making a sob escape. She held her breath as it rang a second time. "Please answer. Please."

She had no one else to turn to. She couldn't call the sheriff where Wade and Huck were both deputies. They would talk their way out of it even if she were believed.

It rang again. He wasn't going to answer. She gripped the phone tighter, feeling all hope slipping away.

She was just about to give up when Ledger answered on the fourth ring.

She began to cry so hard with such relief that she couldn't speak.

"Abby?"

She managed to get out two words. "Help me."

He didn't hesitate. "Just tell me where you are."

"SHE'S GONE!" WADE CRIED as he rushed back into the kitchen, where his father was finishing off the last drop of whiskey in the bottle. Fortifying himself for what had to be done.

"What do you mean, she's gone?" Huck demanded, slamming down his glass.

"She's not lying in there where we left her. There's blood on the spread and on the wall outside the room…"

"Come on, she can't have gotten far in her condition."

Wade returned to the bedroom, checked the bathroom and even looked under the bed.

"This way, you fool," his father snapped.

As he stepped out of the bedroom, he saw the handprints along the hallway. They led straight to the back door, which was standing open.

"What are we going to do?" Wade cried. He'd had just enough whiskey that he felt warm inside, but his head felt fuzzy. Everything about this felt surreal.

"She can't get far on foot," Huck said after checking to make sure she hadn't taken one of the cars. "We would have heard her start up the engine, if she had."

Wade headed for the stand of cottonwoods along the creek behind the house. It was a straight shot from the back door and seemed the obvious place to try to hide.

He hadn't gone far, though, when he found her shoe. It lay on its side next to the creek. He whistled for his father to join him as he looked deeper into the dark shadows of the trees.

I'm going to find her out here dead. That thought immobilized him until he heard his father's heavy footfalls behind him.

"There's her shoe," Wade said, pointing at it.

"Pick it up. She must be close around here." Huck started to step past him.

"I don't think so," Wade said, holding him back with his free arm. He shone his flashlight on the tracks past the shoe. "They look fresh," he said of the tracks.

Huck bent down. "Someone picked her up and carried her." He glanced past the creek and the cottonwoods to the dirt road on the other side. "She have her phone with her?"

Wade swore under his breath. "You can damn well bet who she called. Ledger McGraw."

Huck rose right in front of his son. "You screwed

this up royally. I could…" He reared back, but Wade blocked the punch.

"I'm not that boy you used to knock around," he said through clenched teeth. "You can call me a fool, you can say whatever you like, but if you lay another hand on me, I'm coming after you."

Huck scowled at him. "You think you can take me? You punk."

"Don't know but I'm going to try."

Huck laughed. "Tonight isn't the time to find out. If she goes to the sheriff—"

"She won't. She's gone to Ledger McGraw. If anyone comes looking for me, it will be him and I'll be ready."

Chapter Nine

Ledger could think of only one thing. Take Abby to the hospital and then find Wade. He'd never been violent, but seeing what Wade had done to Abby had him to the point where he thought he could take the man's life. Wade had to be stopped and if it meant ending him…

"Where are you taking me?" Abby asked from the passenger seat of the pickup. He could tell that each word hurt her to speak. He would have brought the Suburban so she could lie down in the back but he hadn't known how badly she was hurt.

"To the hospital," he said.

"No!" She tried to sit up straight but cried out in pain and held her rib cage. "That's the first place he'll look for me."

"Abby, you need medical attention."

"Please."

He quickly relented. He couldn't let Wade near this woman, which meant no hospital. At least for now.

"I'll take you to the ranch and call our family

doctor. But, Abby, if he says you have to go to the hospital—"

"Then I'll go." She lay back and closed her eyes. "I didn't want you involved."

"I've always been involved because I've always loved you."

She said nothing. He could tell that she was in a lot of pain. It had him boiling inside. If he could have found Wade right now...

He slowed to turn into the ranch and called Dr. Johns. His service answered. Ledger quickly told the woman what had happened. "We need him to come out to the McGraw ranch." She put the call through. Doc asked a few questions about her condition.

Ledger answered best he could.

"I think you should take her to the hospital. I can meet you there."

"She doesn't want to go to the hospital because her husband can find her there. I'm taking her to the ranch."

"Then I'll meet you there."

Ledger pulled up in front of the house. He saw that she was looking at it, tears in her eyes.

"This is not the way I ever wanted to come back here," she said.

"I know. But right now the only thing that matters is that you're here and safe."

"Promise me you won't go after Wade." When he didn't answer right away, she cried, "Ledger, please. I can't bear the thought of losing you."

"I promise," he said, although they were the hardest words he'd ever had to say.

ABBY REMEMBERED LITTLE of the ride to the ranch or Ledger and his brothers helping her to a bed upstairs. The doctor had apparently told Ledger not to let her sleep because he stayed with her, asking her about everything but what had happened until the doctor got there.

It wasn't until the next morning, when the doctor told her she could sleep now, that Ledger asked, "Do you want me to call your mother?"

"No!" She'd looked so stricken that he hadn't pushed it as the doctor left.

"Is there anyone else I can call?"

She shook her head, tears filling her eyes. "He's already told me what he'll do to my friends if I involve them."

Ledger gritted his teeth, his anger a rolling boil inside him. What the man had done to Abby... But when he spoke, he sounded calm. "Okay, you just rest. Everything is going to be all right." As he started to turn from the bed, she grabbed his hand.

"You can't do anything to Wade. You can't let him know where I am. If you do anything... You promised."

He nodded as if he'd already figured that out for himself, but she could tell he wasn't happy about it. "Don't worry. He won't know where you are."

"Oh, he'll know," she said. "But he wouldn't dare

come out here." Wade didn't operate that way. He would wait until she left here. He would wait until he could catch her alone.

And when that happened, she had no doubt that he would kill her. She'd done the unforgivable in his eyes. She'd gone to Ledger McGraw.

MCCALL TOOK ONE look at Abby and wanted to take a two-by-four to Wade Pierce. Locking him behind bars wasn't enough.

"How are you feeling?" the sheriff asked as she took the chair next to the woman's bed.

The changes going on at the house had surprised her. She'd heard that there had been quite a lot of renovation since Patricia was arrested and never coming back.

But McCall knew that wasn't all there was to it. With one kidnapper identified and now dead, the money recovered and news that the twins had been adopted out to eager families through a member of the Whitehorse Sewing Circle, Travers seemed to have a new lease on life.

For twenty-five years, he'd kept the children's rooms and the entire wing of the house just as they were the night of the kidnapping. As if freed of some of the past pain, he was opening up the rooms and redecorating them.

The room where Abby was staying looked as if everything in it was brand-new. The walls had a fresh coat of a pale yellow. The curtains billowing in the faint breeze were light and airy. It was as if the room had been decorated just for her.

"I'm feeling better."

McCall could tell that it was going to be hard for her to open up and talk about what had been going on. Abby had tried to keep the secret, no doubt out of shame. McCall had run into this before. Often an abused woman never wanted anyone to know, blaming herself as her husband also did.

"Do you remember what happened?"

Abby shook her head and seemed to realize that McCall would think she was covering for Wade. "The doctor said having another concussion so close after the first one has caused even more memory loss."

"The first one? The fall from the ladder?"

Abby looked away. "That's what Wade told me."

"I spoke with your doctor. You need to know that he reported the incident as physical abuse. This time I think you realize that something has to change, right?"

Tears filled the young woman's eyes as she nodded. "I had left Wade, moved into an apartment in town and filed for a separation, the first step in the divorce proceedings. I remember going out to the house to get something." She frowned. "Wade must have come home early." She shook her head. "I'd told him earlier in the day that he would be getting divorce papers and to please sign them."

McCall nodded. "Abby, do you remember calling 9-1-1 and telling the operator it was urgent that you speak to me?"

She felt her eyes widen. Had she called 9-1-1 as a threat to Wade if he came near her? "I don't remember calling."

"The operator said you told her that you'd discovered something horrible that your husband and his father were doing."

She shook her head as she thought of her mother's marijuana operation. Surely she wouldn't have called the sheriff on her own mother. It was something Wade and his father were up to? She had a glimmer of a memory but it only made her head hurt worse. "I'm sorry. I don't remember calling and I can't imagine what I was calling about."

McCall nodded. "I think it's time you filed a complaint against Wade. Will you do that?" When Abby hesitated, the sheriff added, "And I wish you'd also take out a restraining order against him. True, it isn't worth the paper it's printed on if Wade ignores it and comes after you, but the order will tell him you mean business—especially if you call 9-1-1 the moment he breaks it." Both of them knew he would break it.

Abby closed her eyes for a moment. "I'll do it. The complaint and the restraining order." She opened her eyes and met McCall's worried gaze. "He'll lose his job, won't he?"

"Not right away, but once he breaks the restraining order, yes. When Wade first got on at the department he seemed to have so much potential. He was really excited about the job. I'd had hopes for him. This is his wake-up call. I hope he takes it. In the meantime, I just want to keep you alive."

Abby chewed at her lip. "Wade's just so angry right now about me leaving him."

"It's even more dangerous now. The operator heard Wade in the background before you disconnected. She heard him say something like, 'You'd get me sent to prison? Your own husband?' Whatever you tried to tell me about Wade and his father, it sounds serious. If they thought you might remember..."

THE SHERIFF DIDN'T need to tell Abby how much trouble she was in. Wade had almost killed her. She vaguely remembered hearing him and his father in the kitchen, their heads together. They'd been talking about what to do with her body.

She shivered at the thought, suddenly restless. The room where Ledger had brought her was beautiful, but she couldn't stay here forever. Then what?

Even with the restraining order McCall had her sign, she knew Wade would come after her. He'd told her that if she ever left him, he'd kill her and then himself. She'd never doubted that. But he'd also told her that if she ever went to Ledger, he'd kill him, as well.

Her heart pounded at the thought of what she'd done by calling him. But last night there'd been no one else. She knew Ledger would come and get her.

She knew he would take care of her. If she had hoped to survive, she had to get away from Wade and his father last night. Otherwise...

Climbing out of the bed, she felt a little dizzy for a moment but needed to move. She felt anxious and afraid. Ledger had promised he wouldn't go after Wade. She had seen how hard it was for him to do that. She trusted that he would keep his promise.

But Wade coming after Ledger... Not that Wade would come out to the ranch. He wasn't that stupid. No, he'd wait until he could get Ledger alone.

She felt a memory pull at her. Something about the garage. It slipped past, refusing to let her grasp it long enough to make any sense of it. Wade and his father had been up to something that would send them both to prison if caught?

Abby felt sick to her stomach. What had the two gotten involved in? Something that apparently they would kill to keep quiet, she thought, remembering them whispering in the kitchen. The hair stood up on the back of her neck. If she hadn't gotten out of the house last night when she did, she'd be dead and buried out in the middle of the prairie.

McCALL TOOK NO pleasure in calling Wade Pierce into her office. When she'd hired him, she'd hoped he would make a better deputy than his father. He had seemed to have that potential. But maybe his upbringing was harder to overcome than she'd hoped.

He tapped at the door and stuck his head in when

she said, "Come in, Wade. Please have a seat." Not surprisingly, he looked nervous. He had to know what this was about.

"I wanted to give you a heads-up," she said once he was seated. "Your wife has filed a domestic abuse complaint against you—" She held up her hand, seeing that he was about to argue the point. "As well as a restraining order."

The man looked dumbstruck. He really hadn't expected she would do that. Then he looked furious.

"I want to make something perfectly clear. Right now I'm suspending you for two weeks without pay so you can think about your life and any changes you might want to make. However," she said quickly as again he was half out of his seat, mouth open and ready to argue. "However, if you break the restraining order or if there is another call from your wife, you will be dismissed."

"But it's a lie." He wasn't very convincing and she could see that he knew it.

"I don't take these kinds of charges at face value. I spoke with her doctor at the hospital. After that, I advised your wife to take these steps not just for her sake but for yours."

Wade shifted his gaze to look down at his boots. "So two weeks."

"This is serious, Wade. You can end up behind bars. If there is no trouble between now and then, I'm willing to give you another chance here. Anyone else I would have let go. Tell me that my faith in you isn't misplaced."

He looked up and swallowed, his Adam's apple bobbing up and down for a moment. "There won't be any trouble."

"Good. I'm glad to hear that. Wade, get some help." She slid a pamphlet across the desk to him.

"Anger management?" He let out a nervous laugh.

She saw his father in him then and knew she was probably wasting her breath. "Often this problem is generational. But it can be stopped."

"Generational," he repeated and frowned. He looked again at his boots. "Right."

"That's all."

He got up slowly, his hat in his hand. She could see that he was fighting all of this, going from embarrassment to anger and back. She feared anger would win.

"You know this will get all over town," he said quietly.

"Wade, everyone already knows what's been going on. Now's your chance to show them what kind of man you are."

He nodded slowly. "Two weeks." And walked out, closing the door a little too hard behind him.

Chapter Ten

"I thought you said she'd never go to the sheriff," Huck Pierce demanded when Wade found him at his house and told him the news.

"She didn't. Apparently the sheriff went to her. It's that doctor at the hospital. The sheriff said he suspected physical abuse and reported it."

"So much for patient privacy," his father snapped.

"Isn't he required by law to report it? Maybe that's what happened."

"Or maybe your wife's boyfriend is behind all of this."

Wade ground his teeth. "As far as I know, she's still out there."

"Well, she can't stay there forever. I asked around. I found out where the apartment is that she rented."

"The sheriff was real clear. I can't go near her or I'll be fired."

"Well, there's no restraining order against me, but you're right. Now isn't the time to be worrying about this. We have bigger fish to fry." He winked at Wade. "Our plan went off without a hitch. Now it's just a matter of waiting for the money to roll in. Once you don't need this job anymore, you can get your wife back—if that's what you want."

"I'd rather die than see her with McGraw."

His father smiled. "That's what I thought. Believe me, she won't be for long."

LEDGER COULDN'T BELIEVE how different the house felt with Patricia and Kitten gone. But it was even better now, he thought, that Abby was free of Wade.

The biggest change in the mood at the McGraw ranch, though, was one of the twins being found. Vance had settled in upstairs in the wing where he'd once lived as a baby.

It had surprised Ledger when his father had announced that the wing would be remodeled. No longer would it be a shrine to the kidnapped children. Instead, it would be made into quarters for Vance— and eventually Jesse Rose, once she was found.

"You do realize that Jesse Rose might have a life she doesn't want to leave," Boone had pointed out. "She'll be twenty-five years old. She might not want to move back into the house where she was kidnapped."

It seemed odd to the three older brothers that Vance would move in. But he apparently had little going on in his own life and this had been his home.

"I'm aware of that," his father had said with a laugh. "But I want them to feel at home here on the ranch. I want them to have a place. Oakley might not end up staying, but he will at least know that he has a room here."

"Oakley?" Cull had asked. "Is he going to change his name?"

"We're discussing it. Of course, it would be an adjustment for him," Travers had said.

Ledger thought Vance would be up for whatever his father wanted. He seemed to have adjusted quite well to living on the ranch. Earlier, he'd seen him at breakfast putting away any and everything set before him. Later he was down at the pool swimming and napping in the sun.

"He said he had a way with horses," Boone pointed out. "When is he going to start working?"

Their father sent his son a disapproving look. "He's just getting used to being Oakley McGraw."

"Oh, I think he's gotten used to it quite well," Boone said, getting to his feet. "If you want me, I'll be in the horse barn. Working."

Cull rose, as well. "He has a point, Dad. Maybe you should discuss with Vance… Oakley what is expected of him." With that, he left.

Travers looked to Ledger. "Aren't you going to give me your two cents' worth, as well?"

"I think they pretty much covered it. I'm going into town to get a few things from Abby's apartment for her. You don't mind her staying on for a while, do you?"

"Of course not. Just be careful. Putting yourself

in the middle of these kinds of things is very dangerous, especially with Wade Pierce."

Ledger nodded. "I'm not going to do anything stupid."

"But I don't think you can depend on Wade Pierce not to."

He smiled at his father. "I'll be careful."

As he started to leave, his father said, "I want to just enjoy having my son back for a while. But I don't want the rest of you resenting him. Am I wrong?"

Ledger turned at the door. "It's an adjustment for all of us. You just got him back. I don't think you need rush it."

His father smiled. "I could say the same about you and Abby."

He laughed. "Yes, you could, but you'd be wasting your breath. I'm going to marry that woman just as soon as she's free."

WATERS LISTENED TO Patricia McGraw's latest threat and realized he would have to go to the jail and have this out in person. It wasn't something he was looking forward to. He hadn't seen her since her arrest. He probably could have gone the rest of his life without seeing her. But she wasn't having any of that and somehow she'd hired herself a fairly good lawyer.

As Patricia was brought in, he picked up the phone. From the look in her eye, he was glad to have the thick, scarred Plexiglas between them. She sat down, glaring at him for a moment, before she picked up her own phone.

"You bastard," she said into the receiver.

"Nice to see you, too, Patricia. I'm a busy man, so if you have something to say, please do it."

She sneered. "I heard you're buttering up Travers so you don't lose your job. Good luck with that." He smiled and saw steam come out of her ears. "He's just stupid enough to keep you on. And what's this about Oakley being found?" she demanded.

He shrugged. "Seems that way."

She heard the suspicion in his answer and he could have kicked himself. "You think he's a fraud?"

"No. He looks like his mother, has the McGraws' blue eyes and dark hair."

Patricia made a face. She never liked the mention of Travers's first wife. "But?"

"No buts. He passed the preliminary DNA test. Travers is convinced and Vance seems to have settled into your house just fine."

She let out a growl. "Vance?"

"Oakley. I think he'll be changing his name soon. So we have a happy ending."

"Maybe you do. Listen to me. I'm not going down alone, you hear me? I promised my lawyer that you will be helping finance my defense."

"You what?"

"You're in this up to your neck. Unless you pony up some money…" She smiled, no doubt seeing how uncomfortable he was with what she was saying.

"You can't drag me into this."

"Jim, darlin', I have dates and times. I have phone messages. I have phone calls. I have enough that my lawyer assures me you will go down as an accessory—if not the person who actually bought the poison and administered it. You were there almost every meal. Did you really think you could frame me for this?"

"I didn't frame you. This is all you."

"I don't think so, Jimmy." She hung up the phone and stood, smirking down at him as if she thought she had him by his private parts.

What killed him was that he feared she did.

ABBY COULDN'T HELP being nervous. Ledger hadn't returned from town. He'd taken one of the ranch hands with him to drive his pickup back after getting what she needed from her apartment and picking up her car at the sheriff's department.

"I want someone with you in case—"

He'd stopped her. "Wade is in a lot of trouble. He's not going to do anything that would get him thrown in jail."

She wasn't so sure about that. The sheriff had called to let her know that Wade had been warned—and that the restraining order would be served within the hour. On top of that, Wade had been suspended for two weeks without pay.

Abby couldn't even imagine how furious he was.

It would only get worse when the restraining order was served—and he told his father.

"He's going to want to kill me—and you," she'd told Ledger before he left. "I shouldn't have involved you in this. I'm so sorry."

"Hey," he'd said, lifting her chin with his warm fingers until their gazes met. "I've been involved since the day I fell in love with you all those years ago. I couldn't let go. I know I should have but once I saw how he was treating you…"

"That's why you need to be careful. Give him time to cool down."

She had smiled at the man she'd loved for as far back as she could remember. So many times she'd regretted her hasty marriage to Wade. She knew now that Ledger would never have cheated on her. But back then she had her mother and Wade telling her different. She'd been afraid that the reason Ledger had put off marriage was because he didn't love her enough.

When she'd seen the photos of Ledger with some other woman at college…

She knew now that Ledger and the woman had just been friends. Her mother had wanted her with Wade for her own selfish reasons.

"I've made such a mess of things," she'd said, hating that she sounded near tears. She'd cried way too long over Wade and the mistake she'd made.

Ledger had cupped her cheek. "It's nothing that can't be rectified. I just want you to be sure of what you want to do now. I don't want to talk you into anything. Whatever you do, it has to be your decision. So maybe you should take this time to—"

"I've already filed papers to begin divorcing Wade. He knows it's over. I'd kicked him out of the house and I had packed up my things and moved them into the apartment in town. I guess I'd gone back to the house for something. I didn't expect him to be there..."

"That's all behind you, then." He'd leaned down and given her a gentle kiss. She'd wanted to pull him to her and kiss him the way she'd often dreamed—and felt guilty about. But it was too soon.

She'd jumped into a bad marriage. If she and Ledger had a future... Well, they could take it slow.

"As I was saying, I really think you should stay here for a while longer. I could go to your apartment and get you whatever you needed."

"My car is out at the house. I don't want you going out there."

"Why don't you call the sheriff and have someone bring your car into town for you," Ledger had suggested.

She'd agreed and made the call. McCall had said that was smart not to send Ledger out to get it, or worse, go herself.

"I'll have the keys here at the sheriff's office."

"Ledger will be picking it up," she'd told McCall.

"This afternoon would be good since Huck isn't working."

Yes, she didn't want Ledger running into Wade's father, either.

"Thank you for doing this," she'd said to Ledger as she'd hung up.

"Don't you realize by now that I would do anything for you?"

She'd smiled. "I do."

But he wasn't back yet and all she could think was that he'd run into Wade. Maybe even Wade and his father.

She got up, too nervous to stay in the room any longer.

OAKLEY MCGRAW. "OAKLEY MCGRAW." Down the hallway from Abby's room, Vance stood in front of the mirror and tried out the name. His new name. When Travers had asked him if he had considered changing his name to his birth name legally, he hadn't known what to say. Maybe because he never thought it would get this far.

"Oakley McGraw." He was Oakley McGraw. He wanted to pinch himself. Two weeks ago he was Vance Elliot, ranch hand. All of his belongings were in his beat-up, rusted-out pickup. He barely had a job let alone a nickel to his name.

Now he was Oakley McGraw, son of Travers McGraw, heir to all of this. Along with three brothers, he reminded himself. Three brothers who he could tell didn't like him. As if he cared. Their father adored him.

That was why he was going to tell him he wanted to have his name changed to Oakley McGraw legally. Then there would be no question, would there. He would be the missing son. Travers was even thinking about throwing a party to introduce him to his friends. His friends were powerful people in this town, in this state.

Vance couldn't believe his luck. He looked out his window at the swimming pool shimmering in the sun. Maybe he would go sit down there in the shade after he helped himself to a beer from the refrigerator in the kitchen. That he had the run of this place was unbelievable. He thought he could live like this without any trouble.

As he started down the hallway, a door opened at the other end and a young woman stepped out. The cook had mentioned that there was a friend of Ledger's staying in the house. Apparently the friend had her meals brought to her, though, since he hadn't seen her before. He'd thought she must be a "special" friend.

He let out a silent whistle when he saw her. Even from a distance, she was real pretty. She hadn't seen him yet, so it gave him time to study her. As she drew closer, her gaze on the floor at her feet as if distracted by her thoughts, he saw that she had a black eye and other bruises.

Also she was walking as if in some kind of pain. Clearly, something had happened to her. A car accident? A mugging? An assault? This explained why she'd been eating in her room—and Ledger eating with her.

He hadn't realized that he'd stopped just short of the stairs to stare at her. She must have sensed him, because her gaze came up quickly and he got his first good look at her. With a shock he realized that he recognized her. Wade Pierce's wife.

Worse, she recognized him. Her blue eyes widened in alarm. She stumbled a little, but caught herself. "I'm sorry. You startled me."

"Sorry." He waited, heart in his throat, expecting her to say more.

But she only stared at him, recognition in her eyes and yet... He realized that she was trying to place where she knew him from.

"Please, you go first," he said, motioning to the stairs.

She shook her head. "I wasn't going down. I was just stretching my legs." She took a step backward and another, before she turned and went back down the hall the way she'd come.

He watched her, knowing it was just a matter of time before she remembered where she'd seen him. All he could think was that when she did, she was going to take all of this away from him.

Chapter Eleven

Wade was surprised to see Abby's car gone when he drove out to the house. Had she come out to get it? Or had that bastard Ledger McGraw retrieved it for her?

He pulled up in front of the house, threw the car into Park and sat just staring at where her car had been. He should go out to the McGraw ranch and drag Abby out by her hair. Frustration had him shaking all over. He couldn't do that any more than he could get her back. His dad was right. He'd have to bide his time if he wanted any satisfaction. Look what the woman had done to him. He wouldn't be able to hold his head up in this town ever again.

He turned off the engine and started to get out when he remembered the restraining order. He couldn't come any closer than fifty feet? Seriously, in a town the size of Whitehorse with only one grocery store, one post office, one damned theater?

Grabbing up the paperwork, he tore it into a hundred pieces and threw it in the air like confetti. He felt a little better.

His cell phone rang. For just an instant, he thought it might be Abby calling to say she'd changed her mind. All the other times they'd had problems she'd come back.

But it was only his father calling. He swore and picked up. "What?"

"I see your mood hasn't improved."

"Her car is gone. You think she came out and picked it up?"

"The sheriff sent two deputies out to bring it back to the office, where Ledger McGraw picked it up with one of his ranch hands."

Wade let out a string of curses. "I want to get out of this damned town."

"Oh, come on, don't you want a little retribution first? Have you forgotten? We have an ace in the hole, remember? We're in the catbird seat, son. Soon we will be calling the shots."

When his father had come to him with his plan, he'd thought the old man had lost his mind.

"You're going to get us both sent to prison. This can't possibly work."

His father had winked at him. "These years as a deputy, I've made a few...friends. Leave it to me. We can pull this off."

Wade had been skeptical at best. But to his amazement, the plan seemed to actually be working.

"So knock off the 'poor me' routine," Huck said.

"Soon you will have the money to go anywhere you want. And we'll have gotten some retribution along the way."

"I HAVE GOOD NEWS," Travers said when he saw Vance.

He could use some good news. "How is that?"

"I'm calling a press conference tomorrow to introduce you to the world and announce that my son has been found."

This was not what he'd consider good news. Especially when Abby Pierce was upstairs, no doubt racking her brain to remember where she'd last seen him. "Do we have to?"

Travers put a hand on his shoulder. Vance tried not to flinch. He'd known all of this would feel... strange. A father he'd never known. A family he'd never met. A new name. He wondered if he was up to it. The money, the name that carried weight, the ranch and all the expensive horses, all that he could get used to. But the rest...

"Son, I want to introduce you to the world as a McGraw. I've waited twenty-five years. Can you indulge an old man?"

How could he not? "I understand, but I've never been good at getting up in front of people like that."

"It will be fine. You won't be required to say but a few words. Or none if you aren't comfortable."

Just stand there and smile into the cameras and let everyone speculate on me, he thought. "You're planning to tell the circumstances of how I was adopted."

Travers nodded. "I hope you don't mind. I think it might also help bring back our Jesse Rose."

Jesse Rose. His fraternal twin sister. He'd almost forgotten about her. Why not? Pretty soon they would be just one big happy family. Right, he thought.

"If I can help bring her home, of course I'll do it," Vance said, knowing he had no choice. He was Oakley McGraw. He needed to start acting like him.

For a moment, he forgot about Abby Pierce. "There is one thing, though," he said as Travers started to step away. "What do I wear for this…press conference?"

"I'm sorry. I should have thought of that. You'll want to pick up a few things. We can go into town—"

"Would you mind if I did this alone? I feel enough like a kid as it is."

"Of course you do. How foolish of me. Take one of the ranch pickups. There are keys on the board by the back door. I'll call the clothing store in town and tell them to put it on my account. Get whatever you need." He smiled. "Treat yourself, please. Head to toe. You're Oakley McGraw. Nothing is out of your reach." He started to turn away. "There is one more thing. Your mother. You know she hasn't been well. But she is doing much better. In fact, she wants to see you."

All Vance could do was nod as he thought, *Holy crap! Just when I think it can't get any worse.*

LEDGER TOOK THE stairs two at a time, anxious to see Abby. He'd picked up what she'd asked for from her apartment. It wasn't much. He'd been shocked to see how little she owned.

He tapped at her bedroom door. No answer. He tapped again and tried the knob. She stood at the window, her back to him, hugging herself as if cold.

"Abby?"

Startled, she turned from the window, looking scared.

"I knocked. You didn't hear. What is it?" he asked as she quickly rushed to him and threw herself into his arms.

"I was so worried about you," she said into his chest. "I thought—"

"I'm sorry. I hurried as fast as I could." He stared at her. "You're as white as a ghost. Are you feeling worse?"

She lifted her head to look up at him. "I don't know." He could see the fear still in her eyes. "I think I might be losing my mind."

"Why? What happened? Wade hasn't come here, has he?" He held her at arm's length to look into her beautiful face. It was still bruised. Every time he saw it, he felt anger boil up inside him. It was all he could do not to go after Wade.

Abby shook her head. "I saw someone in the hallway." He frowned. "A man. He came out of a room down the hall. When I saw him—" She shuddered and he pulled her close again.

"Are you talking about Vance? Vance Elliot. He's staying here. Abby, I'm sorry. There's been so much going on. I thought you knew. My brother, the one who was kidnapped... He's been found."

Her eyes were wide with horror. "*He's* the missing twin? He can't be your brother." She sounded as scared as she looked.

He drew even farther back to look at her. "Why would you say that?"

She pulled away to pace the floor. "When I saw him, I recognized him. And he recognized me. I had this jolt of memory, nothing I could recall, really, just this frightened feeling."

Ledger didn't know what to say at first. "You say you recognized him? Could it be from the café in town?"

Abby shook her head. "It wasn't in that context. It was...a bad memory. I know that doesn't make any sense. It's just this...feeling more than a memory. But I know I've seen him before, and wherever it was, it wasn't...good."

"Okay," he said, wondering what to make of this. "And you say he recognized you? Did he call you by name?"

"No. He seemed as shocked to see me here as I was him. I made him nervous."

Ledger took this all in.

"I know I sound crazy," she said, stopping her pacing to step to him again. "I'm trying to remember where I saw him. So much of the past is a blank because of the concussions. I'm afraid I won't remember."

He held her, drawing her close and kissing the top of her head. "It's going to be all right. You're here." But so was Vance Elliot—soon to be Oakley McGraw, if his father had anything to do with it. He wondered how much he should worry. Wade had scrambled Abby's brain. Could he trust this feeling she had? Could he *not* trust it?

ABBY LEANED INTO Ledger's hard body. Breathing in his scent, she felt safe and loved in his warm, strong embrace. With his arms around her, she believed anything was possible. Even the two of them having a happy ending. She never wanted him to let her go.

But she couldn't shake off the bad feeling she'd had the moment she'd seen Vance Elliot in the hallway. Something was terribly wrong. If only she could remember where she'd seen him.

"Maybe I really am crazy."

"You're not crazy," he said, a smile in his voice. "You're going to be fine."

In his arms, she believed it. But when she was alone with her black hole of a memory... "I don't know." She stepped away to move to the window overlooking the ranch. She loved this view. It was so peaceful, unlike her mind right now. "Maybe my head is so jumbled up that I might never straighten it out again."

"The doctor said to give it time. You've been

through so much," he said, stepping to her and clasping both shoulders in his big hands. His fingers tightened as if he was thinking of Wade. "Trying too hard to remember is only going to make your headache worse."

She nodded. "Thank you for not going after Wade."

His smile was tight. "You don't know what you're asking. You realize that, don't you?"

"Yes. I don't want you to lower yourself to his level."

Ledger let go of her. His laugh held no humor. "Oh, Abby, you don't realize how much pleasure it would give me to beat that man to within an inch of his life. I want to give him some of his own medicine." He smiled. "But for you, I won't go after him. All bets are off, though, if he shows up here."

She smiled and nodded through fresh tears. "Once this is over," she whispered as he took her in his arms. "Once this is over." But would it ever be over?

VANCE COULDN'T BELIEVE it as he sat behind the wheel of the ranch truck and looked at the fancy clothing-store bags and boxes piled high on the other side of the pickup.

"Treat yourself. From head to toe." That was what Travers—his father—had said. That meant Stetsons to boots. Any other time, he would have been over-the-moon excited. The truck smelled like good leather and expensive fabrics. It smelled better than anything he could remember.

As he looked down at his boots, he felt for the first time like Oakley McGraw. He'd never owned a good pair of boots before. Somehow it made him feel better about himself. At least temporarily.

He pulled out the burner cell phone, sick at heart that he had to make this call now, of all times. But he didn't know when he was going to be able to get back into Whitehorse alone.

It rang three times before a male voice answered with "You done good, boy."

"Yeah," he said, loving the feel of the fine leather on his feet as much as the new gray Stetson perched on his head. For a moment, he thought about hanging up, starting the engine and seeing how far he could get away before someone came after him.

He didn't want to give any of this up, let alone have it snatched from him. He liked being Oakley McGraw, but it would be hard to get rid of Vance Elliot after twenty-five years of him living in the man's body. As Vance, he'd made his share of mistakes that were bound to come out.

But he had a more immediate problem. "The thing is—"

"What's wrong?"

"Abby Pierce. I crossed paths with her in the house today. She recognized me, but I could tell she was having trouble remembering where she'd seen me. But I have to tell you, that look she got in her eyes... It won't take her long to put it together."

"Where are you?"

"In town. Travers treated me to some clothing. He's planning on a big press conference tomorrow to tell the world that I am his son. But if she remembers before that—"

"Meet me at the Sleeping Buffalo rocks. Fifteen minutes."

"I'M GOING TO see your mother," Travers said when Ledger came downstairs. "I was hoping you and your brothers would come, as well."

"Sure." He'd been once when he was younger. He hated seeing his mother like that, and his father had said that he didn't want his sons going if it upset them. Cull was the only son who continued to visit her—not that she'd noticed.

"I heard she's doing better," Boone said as they started toward the front door for the drive to the mental hospital.

"She is," their father said, smiling. He looked so much happier now. His prayers had been answered. Now, if Jesse Rose would turn up... "She asked about each of you the last time I saw her."

"She's talking?" Ledger said.

"She is. Not a lot, but she's improved so much I have hope, and so do the doctors, that she could make a full recovery," Travers said.

On the drive to the hospital, they talked about the ranch, the horses and finally Vance.

"Is this press conference really necessary?" Boone asked. "Yesterday, I was out in the pasture and a drone flew over low with a video camera attached to it. Is it ever going to stop?"

"Not for a while," Travers said as Cull drove. "When Jesse Rose is found, we'll have to go through it all over again, but eventually we'll be old news."

"That day can't come soon enough," Ledger agreed.

"If it ever does," Cull said. "Whenever our name comes up, it's in connection with the kidnapping."

"And Nikki's book on it isn't going to help," Boone said.

Cull shook his head. "I disagree. We're in the public eye. People want the inside scoop. Well, they will get it in the book. After that there won't be anything to add."

"I hope you're right," Ledger said. "I want to marry Abby, but I don't want to bring her into all this."

"Patricia still has to go to trial," Boone said. "Who knows how long it could take to find Jesse Rose, if ever. I can't see this ending for years, so unless you want to make the mistake of putting off your marriage again—"

"Abby isn't even divorced from her current husband," Cull pointed out. "I think we should just be glad that Oakley has been found."

"Yes," their father said. "Let's count our blessings. After the press conference tomorrow, I have a good feeling about Jesse Rose being found, as well."

Chapter Twelve

"Well, would you look at this dude," Deputy Huck Pierce said as Vance Elliot climbed out of the Mc-Graw ranch pickup. "Oakley McGraw, all duded out. How ya likin' livin' in luxury?"

All the way out to the Sleeping Buffalo rocks, Vance had been thinking he should just take off. It wasn't like he'd left anything he wanted back at the ranch. And he knew Travers McGraw would never send the cops after him. Not his own son. He could just keep going.

The problem was that he would eventually run out of gas. He didn't have a dime to his name. But as Oakley McGraw, he could have it all. It meant staying, though, and taking his chances with Abby remembering where she'd seen him. It also meant dealing with Huck and his son, Wade, he thought with a groan as he glanced past the two deputies to the rocks.

"So what's this?" he asked, motioning to two brown boulders, a large one and a smaller one, under a roofed-over enclosure beside Highway 2. He was stalling for time and he knew it. As he stepped closer to the rocks, he saw that they appeared to be covered with tobacco and some loose cigarettes that had been broken and spread over the larger of the rocks.

"You ain't heard the story of the sleeping buffalo?" Huck asked. "These rocks are sacred. Indians—excuse me—Native Americans believe it has spiritual power. You see, the Native Americans were looking for buffalo, hadn't seen any and were worried. Then they saw what they believed was the leader of a herd perched high atop a windswept ridge overlooking Cree Crossing on the Milk River not far from here. It turned out just to be these rocks. But past it was a herd of buffalo. So they believe these rocks led them to the buffalo and that the rocks have some kind of special powers. That's why they leave tobacco on the rocks to honor the spirits."

"And you believe that?" Vance asked.

"You might, too, if you knew what happened back in the 1930s when the rocks were moved into town," Wade said. "Town folk swore that the rocks changed positions and bellowed in the night. So they hurried up and brought them back out here."

"No kidding?" Vance said, staring at the rocks. The larger one was way too huge for even a group of men in town to move by hand each night in order to scare people. He thought maybe there was something to the story since apparently a lot of the Native Americans believed in these rocks.

He wished he believed in something right now as he saw Huck fidgeting. He had something on his mind and Vance feared he wasn't going to like it.

"There's a hot springs up the road here, if you ever get out this way again," Wade was saying.

"Are we through shooting the breeze, because I want to know how things are going out at the ranch," Huck said impatiently.

Vance took a breath. He thought of his beautiful accommodations. He was now living in the lap of luxury—just as Huck had said—and he loved it. He'd never thought it would go this far. But now that he was so close to legally being Oakley McGraw, he didn't want it to end.

"There could be a problem," he said, turning away from the rocks. The sun beat down on him. Standing here, he could see the prairie stretched out in front of him for miles. This country was so open. He thought a man could get lost in it and thought he might have to before this was over.

"A *problem*?" Huck repeated, already looking angry.

He glanced at Wade. "It's your wife. I didn't realize that she was at the ranch because she's been holed up in a room down the hall. Well, I saw her today. And she saw me. I think she recognized me from that first night we met."

WATERS LOOKED AT the messages on his phone. Patricia. One of them caught his eye.

Travers came by to visit me.

He stared at the screen and swore. The last thing he wanted was for Travers to be talking to Patricia. Who knew what lies she'd tell him. She was determined to take Waters down with her. He didn't know how to stop her. Surely the sheriff and Travers knew that she was a liar.

But some things would have a ring of truth in them. He'd been so sure everything would be blamed on Patricia's conspirator, Blake Ryan. Blake had been the former ranch manager, an old family friend and one of Patricia's lovers. He would have done anything for Patty—and did.

Now, though, there seemed to be fallout around the case and Waters knew he was directly in the line of fire if Patricia kept shooting off her mouth. Plus, she said she had evidence in emails and texts.

He paced around his small apartment, telling himself that now would be the perfect time to leave the country. Except that what money he'd managed to put away over the years was in stocks and bonds and not that easy to liquidate. Also it was the worst possible time.

But if he could get his hands on some money…

"Calm down." He stopped pacing, tried to stop panicking. Vance Elliot was Oakley. He'd brought him to Travers. Everything was fine. Travers wouldn't take Patricia's word over his. If he could just hang in…

A thought struck him. If he could find Jesse Rose, Travers would be indebted to him forever. He thought about the strange call he'd gotten from that private investigator in Butte. Probably a dead end. But maybe he should mention it to Travers. Maybe make more out of it than it had been.

"WHAT THE HELL are you talking about?" Huck demanded. "I know Abby can't hardly remember her own name. That's right—not only do I have friends at the lab in town, but also I have friends at the doctor's office and in other places. She doesn't remember *anything.*"

"Maybe," Vance said skeptically. "But if you had seen the way she looked at me."

Huck waved it off. "You're just being paranoid. Suck it up. So how are things going with Travers McGraw?"

"Like I told you, he's scheduled a press conference tomorrow to announce to the world that I am Oakley McGraw. After that, he wants me to change my name legally."

Huck burst out a huge laugh and pounded Vance on the back. "Nice work. I can see that you're enjoying the fruits of our labor. The accommodations up to your standards?"

"It's nice living out there."

Wade snorted. "I'll just bet. Abby eating it up?"

"She doesn't look good. I mean, she's still hurt pretty bad," Vance said. "She's kind of limping, holding her ribs, and there's bruises." He could see that this pleased both men. What had he gotten himself involved in? As if he hadn't known right from the get-go.

"So you stand up there tomorrow at the press conference," Huck said. "You tell the world how happy you are to be back in the bosom of your family and you start going by Oakley."

"What about the reward money? You said I'd get my share."

Huck's gaze narrowed. "You wouldn't be thinking about taking off once you got a little money in your pocket, would you?"

Vance looked away.

"Listen to me," the deputy said, closing the space between them. "This is for the long haul, not for a measly five hundred grand. You'll get your share but not until you are settled in and Daddy's put you in his will."

He blinked. "Why would you care about the will?"

"You let me worry about that," Huck said, patting him heavily on the shoulder. "I'll let you know when we're through doing business. In the meantime, stay clear of Abby. She's probably picking up on your nervousness. We're home free."

Vance could see now how this was going to go. At first it had been about the reward money. They were to split it and then part ways. But Huck was getting greedy. Which meant the deputies would bleed him dry for years if Vance let them.

LEDGER WAS STILL shaken from seeing his mother. He hadn't seen her since he was a boy. It had been shocking then. It was still shocking. Cull had gone to visit her at the mental institution over the years, but he and Boone had gone only once when she'd first been admitted.

He'd asked about her, though, when Cull had returned from a visit. "She's still catatonic. In other words, she doesn't know anyone, doesn't talk, doesn't respond to anyone around her," Cull had said. "She just sits in a rocking chair and...rocks."

Ledger had kept the rumors going around school about her over the years to himself. He didn't want his brothers or his father to know what the kids were saying about his mother.

"She's crazy scary. The nurses are all afraid of her."

"Her hair turned white overnight. She turned into a witch and puts spells on people."

"She sits and rocks and holds two old dirty dolls. She thinks they're the twins she kidnapped."

That was the hardest part, everyone believing his mother had helped kidnap her own children. Unfortunately, none of them still knew who inside the house had handed out the twins to the kidnapper on the ladder outside the window. The ladder had been found leaning against the house—one of the rungs broken halfway down. That had led the FBI and sheriff at the time to speculate that the kidnapper could have fallen with the twins and that the six-month-old babies had died.

Fortunately, they'd found out that that wasn't true.

Now Ledger stared at the white-haired woman in the rocking chair on the criminally insane wing of the mental hospital and wondered what *was* true. The woman in the rocker looked much older than fifty-seven—until he looked into her green eyes. There was intelligence there—and a whole lot of pain.

"Ledger," she said and held out her arms.

He stepped into them, kneeling down so she could hug him, and felt his heart break for all that she'd lost. Twenty-five years. Gone. Worse, only one of the twins had been found. If Vance really was the lost twin.

Ledger couldn't help thinking about what Abby had told him. Maybe it was just wires crossed in her brain. Or maybe not.

Worse, his mother was still a suspect in the kidnapping. But he didn't want to believe it. This woman who'd suffered so much… She couldn't have been responsible for helping the kidnapper take her own children.

"I want to see Oakley," his mother said as she looked at Travers. "Will you bring him to visit me soon?"

Travers promised he would. "He seems to have taken after you."

WADE WATCHED VANCE drive away. "We can't trust him."

Huck laughed. "You're smarter than you look. He's not going anywhere until he gets money."

"What if Travers gives him some?"

"He won't for a while. McGraw is no fool. He can see that Vance isn't comfortable in Oakley's clothes." Huck scratched his jaw, laughing at his own joke. "McGraw will spoon it out slowly to him so as not to scare him. Anyone can see that Vance has never had much. He won't want to overwhelm his son."

Wade had to hand it to his father. That night when he'd shown up with this crazy plan, Wade had been outside the garage putting new spark plugs in his old pickup. The moment he'd seen his father's face, he'd known something was up. He knew about the marijuana deal the old man had going on with Abby's mother, but he wanted nothing to do with it.

"Abby gets wind of this and she'll flip out," Wade had warned his father. "You're going to screw up my marriage."

"On the contrary, I'm helping you out. She'd never rat out her mother. This way we have leverage. One day, maybe you'll be as smart as me—probably not, but keep trying." He'd cuffed him and then changed the subject.

So that night when he'd seen the smug look on Huck's face, he'd thought, *Oh, hell, now what*.

"Somethin' I wanna show ya," his father had said. Wade had caught the smell of beer on the old man's breath even though he was still in uniform. Often he worried that Huck would get them both fired.

That was when he noticed the paper sack his father was carrying. Huck motioned for him to step into the garage. "Where's your wife?"

"In the kitchen making supper. Why?"

"Look at this." His father had opened the top of the large paper sack.

"What's that?" Wade asked after getting a glimpse of what appeared to be a stuffed toy horse.

"That is money, son." Huck had gone on to explain how he'd been one of the first law officers called out to the McGraw ranch the night of the kidnapping and how he'd found the stuffed animal lying on the ground and picked it up. "I was thinking eBay. People will pay a bunch of money for something from a crime scene."

Wade had interrupted to tell him what a dumb idea that was. "They'd have traced it back to you. They'd fire you, charge you with…tampering with evidence at a crime scene and who knows what else."

"Settle down," his father had said. "I put it away, all right, and forgot about it until I ran into this guy at the bar down in Billings. It was his blue eyes. Dark hair, too. I thought, hell, that kid could be the missing McGraw twin." Huck had started laughing. "We got to talking and…" He'd motioned to his pickup parked behind Wade's. The passenger side door had opened and out stepped Vance Elliot.

Wade had argued that it would never work. "They'll want a DNA test."

"Already got that covered. There's this cute little red-headed lab tech…" Huck had winked. "It gets better. Vance is adopted. No kidding. Tell me this couldn't be more perfect. And he's about the right age."

"But won't there be paperwork?" Wade had argued.

"Falsified to cover up the fact that his parents had knowingly adopted the son from what is now a famous kidnapping."

"But what if the real Oakley comes forward?"

"Who will believe him once our boy is in the big house on the ranch?" Huck had scoffed that things could go very wrong. "Five-hundred-thousand-dollar reward. Vance here gets a cut, but he will have the McGraw horse ranch."

"Along with his three brothers and his sister, if she turns up," Wade had pointed out.

"Stop looking for trouble," his father had said irritably. "This is going to work. Trust your old man."

That was when Wade had heard a sound from behind him. He'd turned in time to see the door to the kitchen close quietly.

Chapter Thirteen

Waters couldn't help looking at his watch. Vance was late for dinner. He saw that Travers looked worried.

"Where is Vance?" Boone asked as Travers finally told the cook she could go ahead and serve the meal.

"He went into town to get a few things to wear," Travers said. "I wanted him to look nice for the press conference tomorrow."

"You're really going through with this," Boone said.

"Of course. He's my son. I want the world to know."

"Also it won't hurt to get the kind of publicity we need for Jesse Rose to see it and possibly come forward," Waters interjected.

Travers actually shot him a smile. "Exactly. I have faith that both of the twins will have been found by the end of the year."

Louise was serving the salads when Vance hurried in.

"Sorry I'm late. Getting clothing took longer than I thought."

Travers seemed to light up as the young man came into the dining room. Waters saw that his other sons noticed. Nothing like sibling rivalry. But he wondered how long it would be before the new rubbed off Vance and Travers wasn't quite so enamored with his long-lost now-found son.

"Did it go well?" Travers wanted to know.

"I took your advice and let the clerk help me," Vance said, taking his usual seat next to his father. "I hope she didn't go overboard."

Travers laughed. "Not to worry. I just want you to have what you need."

Waters had been watching Vance and now saw him look around the table—and start. His gaze had fallen on Abby Pierce. She paled as the two met gazes across the expanse of the table.

"This is Abby," Ledger said as he, too, had noticed the exchange between his girlfriend and Vance. "Abby, I don't think you have officially met my... brother Vance. Or is it Oakley now?"

"Vance for now." The words seemed to get caught in his throat.

"But soon to be Oakley," Travers said, sounding pleased. "Unless you've changed your mind."

Vance looked again in his direction. "No, of course not. It will just take a little getting used to."

Waters noticed that Abby was still staring at the man as if trying to place him. He fought back the bad feeling that now knocked around in his chest. Things had been going so well. Except for Patricia. He and Travers had talked and now he would be handling some of the family affairs again. And he'd been invited to dinner almost every night since finding Vance.

He had his foot in the door. The last thing he wanted was for a problem to come up involving the soon-to-be Oakley. And yet, as he picked up his salad fork, he realized he'd been waiting for the other shoe to drop as if he was afraid to trust his good luck in Oakley turning up.

VANCE DIDN'T THINK he could eat a bite. He was still shaken from his meeting with the deputies. Huck scared him since he seemed to be carrying a grudge against the McGraws. His son, Wade, had mentioned something once about Huck having dated Travers's first wife, Marianne.

It must have been a long time ago since the woman had been locked up in a mental ward for the past twenty-five years.

"I think after dinner, Oakley and I are going to go out and visit his mother."

Vance didn't realize Travers meant him until he felt all eyes at the table on him. "Tonight?" His voice had risen too high.

"There's nothing to be concerned about," Travers said. "I'm sure you've heard stories, but Marianne is doing well now and she is very anxious to see you."

There was no way he was going to get out of seeing his mother. Not gracefully, anyway. So he smiled and nodded and took a bite of his salad. He could have been eating wood chips, for all he tasted.

With each bite, he could feel Abby's gaze on him, burning a hole in him headed straight for his soul. If he had one.

He hadn't taken Huck Pierce seriously the first time he'd met him in a bar down by Billings.

"I'm telling you, you're the spitting image of the McGraw boys," Huck had said, fueled by the half dozen beers he'd consumed. "I think you might be Oakley McGraw."

He hadn't known who Oakley McGraw was and said as much.

"It's the most famous kidnapping in the state of Montana. Where you been living, under a barrel?"

He hadn't taken offense because Huck had been paying for the drinks, so he'd listened as the man had filled him in. Two missing babies, a boy and a girl.

"They think they were adopted by well-meaning parents who kept it quiet," Huck had said.

Vance had felt a strange stir inside him. "*I* was adopted." He'd always been told that it was some teenager who couldn't raise him. But years later he'd heard that it was an aunt who'd dumped him off when he was a baby and his parents had finally had to adopt him.

His old man hadn't minded having a son around to help with the work on the dirt farm they had. Vance couldn't wait until he was eighteen to escape it. He'd taken off at sixteen and hadn't looked back. He'd heard, though, that both his parents had died in a gas leak at the house. The place had been mortgaged up to the rafters along with the land, so he hadn't gotten anything. He'd let the county bury them. They'd never liked him, anyway.

"Here's what I'm proposing," Huck had said that night at the bar. He'd spelled it out. Vance had said he'd have to think about it. "Doesn't look to me like you have much for prospects. Don't be a fool. This is too easy since I have something that was taken with the male twin the night of the kidnapping. Oh, don't give me that look. I didn't kidnap the kid. I was one of the first deputy sheriffs at the scene."

"You're a deputy sheriff?"

Huck had laughed. "You bet your sweet ass I am. You think about it. You call me tomorrow or forget it."

Vance hadn't been able to sleep that night. He'd looked up the kidnapping online. Huck had failed to mention that the McGraws raised horses. Vance had been making his living as a horse thief. He'd started to laugh until he saw something else Huck had failed to mention. The McGraws were rich.

He'd called the number the deputy sheriff had given him early the next morning. "This is crazy, but I'm in."

Huck had laughed. "You won't be sorry."

Now the meal ended too quickly. Travers got to his feet. "Let's go see your mother."

Vance rose. He shot a guarded look at Abby. She

was putting the pieces together. He could see it in her eyes. How long before she figured it out and blew the whistle on the whole damned thing?

As he started to leave the dining room, he just wished she would do it now and save him the trip to the mental hospital to see his "mother."

"You okay?" Ledger asked Abby as he led her back to her bedroom. She looked pale and he could tell she was still a little unsteady on her feet.

"I know you don't want to hear this, but I've definitely seen Vance before. There's something wrong."

"Wrong how?" he asked as they reached her room.

"You're sure he's Oakley?"

"He had the stuffed toy horse that belonged to Oakley. Also he passed the DNA test. It came back that he's Dad's son."

Abby sighed as she took a chair near the window. He took the other chair in the room. "I can't trust my memory or my instincts or..." She met his gaze. "But the feeling is *so* strong. I know him from somewhere and it's worrisome."

"It will come to you," he assured her even though he wasn't convinced. "Let your brain heal. I can tell you have a headache. Can I get you something?"

"No. When I take the pills the doctor prescribed I feel even more fuzzy. But I'm all right."

"You're telling me that you don't trust Vance," Ledger said.

"No."

"That's good enough for me. I'll keep an eye on him. In the meantime, I'm going to move into the bedroom next door. I don't like you being on this wing with him in case your...instincts are right." Ledger had been staying at his cabin on the ranch. She knew he'd been trying to give her space. As they both knew, she was still married to Wade.

She looked relieved, though, that he would be close at hand. It wasn't just that she didn't trust Vance. She was a little scared of him, as well.

"Thank you. I hope I'm wrong. Your father seems so happy to have him here. I hate to think what it will do to him if Vance isn't the person he believes him to be."

"That's just it. We know very little about him. Jim Waters did some checking and swears there is nothing to worry about. But I have my reservations, too. I do wonder how it will go with Mother."

THE SMELL HIT him first, then the noise of the mental hospital. Vance halted just inside the door, telling himself he couldn't do this.

"It's okay, son," Travers said. "Give it a minute. I'm sure this is hard for you, seeing your mother."

Vance wanted to laugh hysterically. The man had no idea. "There was this neighbor girl. She had to be...restrained. She ended up in a place like this. I visited her only once. I couldn't bear going there." He shuddered at the memory. Crazy Cathy—that was what the kids at school called her when they'd get a glimpse of her from the school bus. She would be tied up to the clothesline and she would run, her face stretched in a lopsided smile because she loved Vance—almost to death. She finally got sent away after she'd tried to kill him with a butcher knife one night after seeing him with another girl.

"I'm so sorry," Travers said. "This must be even more difficult for you. If you'd rather not right now…"

"No." He just wanted to get it over with. Trying to block out the sounds, the smells, the tension that sparked in the air like heat lightning, he walked down the hallway to be let into the violent wing. The sounds down here were worse—the crying, the screaming, the tormented shrieks that made goose bumps ripple across his skin.

A nurse opened the gate for them and led them down the hallway. Vance didn't look into the barred windows. He stared at the floor at his feet, telling himself he could do this, but feeling the weakness run like water through his veins.

His mother used to say that he wasn't strong. "We just need to toughen him up." Then she'd give him the worst chores she could find on the farm. The calluses he got were heart-deep and still rubbed him raw some days. He knew he wouldn't be here now if it wasn't for his childhood and that made him angry. His adoptive mother was right. He wasn't strong.

The nurse stopped at a door, used her key to open

it and then told Travers she would be right outside the door if he needed her.

Heart in his throat, Vance followed him into the room and stopped dead.

The woman sitting in the rocking chair had lightning-white hair that hung around her shoulders like a shroud. But it was the face that froze his feet to the floor.

"Oakley?" the woman asked with a voice that cracked. She motioned for him to come closer.

It took every ounce of his courage to take that first step, let alone the second one, until he stood before her.

"Oakley?" she repeated, her green eyes narrowing.

He couldn't speak, could barely breathe. He swallowed, trying hard not to look into those eyes as if he might be looking into his own hell.

She reached for him before he could move. Her wrinkled hand caught his and held it like a vise as she dragged him closer. The green eyes widened in alarm and he felt a chill rocket through him.

Then the woman shoved him away and began to scream.

ABBY HADN'T BEEN able to sleep last night. Her mind had been alive with strange flashes that could be memory or could be her losing her sanity. Knowing that Ledger was in the next room hadn't helped. Several times she'd almost gotten up and gone to him.

But she'd known what would happen. She was still married. It didn't matter that it was a bad marriage. It didn't matter what Wade had done. She couldn't go to Ledger. Just the thought of him lying in his bed...

This morning she'd felt a little better.

"Stop trying so hard to remember," the doctor had said when he dropped by to check on her. "You will make yourself crazy. If your memory is going to come back, it will, and when you least expect it. Relax. Enjoy this beautiful place. In fact, I think you should get out of this room. Maybe sit by the pool."

Abby couldn't help herself. She could feel the memories just at the edge of her consciousness and she had the horrible feeling that it was imperative that she remember. And soon.

"I'll see that she takes it easy," Ledger had told the doctor after thanking him for driving out.

Abby had tried to relax as she and Ledger went out by the pool after breakfast. She'd been glad that breakfast was more casual, with everyone eating on their own in the large, warm kitchen. Boone and Cull had already gone to work in the barns and Travers was in his office, so she and Ledger had the kitchen to themselves since the cook had gone into town for more groceries.

She was glad that Ledger didn't mention marriage again. Right now, she couldn't think of the future. There was so much of the past missing in her memory. She had to deal with it first. Or maybe she was just afraid of rushing into another marriage for the wrong reasons. She knew Ledger wanted to save her from Wade. For so long, he'd been trying to get her to leave Wade. But was that enough to build a marriage on? Once she was divorced, would Ledger still want to marry her?

Her head hurt even thinking about it. She had too much to worry about, she realized.

Ledger seemed content to sit with her by the pool and talk about the horses and his family's plans for the ranch. She found herself smiling at him. He was a man with dreams. And she loved him so much it hurt.

"See that land on the mountainside over there?" He pointed toward a pine-studded hollow below a rock ridge. "That's mine. That's where I will build the house someday." His gaze shifted to hers and she saw so much promise in his eyes that she wanted to cry.

"It's beautiful."

"Like you," he said and reached over to take her hand.

She closed her eyes and told herself that everything was going to be all right. But deep inside she felt afraid. Wade and his father were up to something. Something she'd apparently overheard. They wouldn't trust that she might never remember. This wasn't over. Once she left here…

"Abby?" Ledger looked concerned.

She opened her eyes, realizing she'd been gripping his hand too hard. "I'm scared," she admitted. "I can't think about the future until I know what in my past has me so terrified."

Something moved past Ledger and she looked in that direction to see Vance. He saw her and quickly disappeared from view. The bad feeling washed over her, threatening to take her under.

Ledger followed her gaze. "You still think something is wrong, don't you?"

She nodded.

"My father said that the visit with our mother didn't go well. When she got a good look at him, she screamed. They had to sedate her. He's worried that this might have set her back. He can't bear that she might revert back into a catatonic state again."

Abby shivered at the news. "She must have sensed what I do about him."

"A BOOK?" WATERS COULDN'T believe what he was hearing as he stared through the scarred Plexiglas at Patricia. "You do realize that Nikki St. James is doing a book on the kidnapping."

"Nikki St. James wasn't there that night. I was," Patricia said into the phone at the jail. She gave him a smug look. "They're giving me enough money that it will pay for my decent lawyer. That's right. I'm going to get off, and when I do, they are going to start looking around for the person who really poisoned my husband."

He knew what she would be selling. The dirt on the McGraw family. The dirt on him, as well. "What is it you want?"

"*Now* you want to deal?" she asked, sweet enough to give him a toothache.

"Patty."

"Don't call me that."

"You don't want to hang out all your dirty laundry."

"Don't you mean your dirty laundry, Jimmy?"

"Think of Kitten."

"Oh, now you're going to show an interest in her?" Patricia snapped angrily.

She'd told him that Kitten was his, but he'd never been sure it was true given the way the woman lied. He had a feeling that she'd also told Blake Ryan, the former ranch manager, that Kitten was his. It would explain why Blake had done her bidding.

He lowered his voice. "You know why we had to keep this a secret."

"To protect your relationship with Travers. But look how that turned out. Unless you've managed to get back into his good graces." Her eyes lit. "Oh, you have! You…stinker you. You always land on your feet, don't you?" Her eyes narrowed. "Well, hang on for the ride of your life. I'm about to bring down your world and Travers's, too." With that, she slammed down the phone, rose and motioned to the guard that she was ready to go back to her cell.

Vᴀɴᴄᴇ ᴄᴏᴜʟᴅɴ'ᴛ ʜᴇʟᴘ being rattled.

Travers had apologized at length for taking him to see his so-called mother. "I should never have taken you to see her so soon," he'd said on the ride home. "Marianne is just now recovering after all this time. This is all my fault. I'm so sorry."

"It's all right," he'd said. "Maybe I scared her." He hadn't scared her. He'd seen the look in the woman's eyes. She *knew*. Somehow she knew he wasn't her son.

"I think she was expecting to see you as a baby," Travers had said. "Or maybe it was just too much for her."

But Vance knew better and he feared Travers Mc-Graw was having his doubts. Just not enough doubts to stop all this craziness.

The press conference was a blur. He'd blinked into the flash of cameras, stepped up to the microphone to say how glad he was to have found his birth family and had then been ushered to the ranch Suburban as reporters shoved microphones at him and yelled questions.

He managed to escape after lunch, telling Travers he wanted to go for a ride and just digest everything that had been happening. He'd used the burner phone to call Huck, who'd been in a great mood.

"Saw you on the news! You looked real smart in those new clothes. Next step, legally becoming Oakley McGraw."

"We need to meet and talk."

Huck's good mood had evaporated in a snap of the fingers.

"Okay," Huck said when the three of them met,

this time out by Nelson Reservoir in a stand of trees. "So Marianne freaked last night when Travers took you to see her. How did McGraw react?"

"He felt bad about taking me there, made excuses for Marianne, but I could tell he was shocked and taken aback. He has to be thinking she saw something he hadn't."

Huck waved a hand through the air. "It wasn't like she cried, 'This isn't my son!' Even if she had, she's…*sick*. So forget about it. You're still good as gold. McGraw wouldn't have gone through with the press conference if he had any doubts."

Vance raked a hand through his hair, his Stetson hanging from the fingers of his other hand. It was hot, but a breeze came off the water, and in the shade of the trees it wasn't too bad. But still he was sweating.

"I saw Abby looking at me again. Now she's got Ledger looking at me the same way."

Wade swore and kicked a rock into the water at the mention of Ledger's name.

"It's just a matter of time. I see her trying so hard to remember," Vance said, hating that he was whining. "She remembers just enough that she doesn't like me, doesn't trust me, and she's been bending Ledger's ear about me. How long before he goes to his father with this?"

"You just borrow trouble, don't you?" Huck demanded angrily. "She *hasn't* remembered. She isn't going to. What you need to do is dig in. Stop acting like a guest at the ranch. You need to go to work in the barns with your brothers."

Vance stared at him. How did he know…? "The cook? *Louise is spying on me?*"

Huck smiled. "I told you. I make friends easily. I know what is going on out there."

"I think Vance is right." Wade spoke up. "You know Abby. Once she gets her teeth into something…"

Huck swore.

"What are we going to do?" Wade cried. "Let me go get her. Once we have her back—"

"Don't be a fool."

But Vance could see that Huck was more worried than he let on.

"Okay, maybe it's time to take care of Abby." Huck turned to Vance. "Make it look like an accident."

"What?" He'd hoped he'd heard wrong, but one look at the deputy's face and he knew he hadn't. He took a step back. "I didn't sign on for murder."

Huck quickly closed the distance between them and got right into his face. "You signed on for whatever I tell you or you'll be meeting with your own accident. Is that understood?"

Vance's blood ran cold at the look in Huck's eyes. There was something bitter and heartless in that gaze. The deputy wasn't joking. Worse, he thought Huck was right about the places where he had "friends."

He wouldn't look at the cook the same now that he knew Huck had her in his pocket.

"You are Oakley McGraw," Huck said, looking less dangerous even though Vance knew he wasn't. "You will have a great life if you don't weaken now, you understand? Abby *can't* remember who you are because that will raise suspicion and involve Wade and me. So take care of it."

"But that still leaves Marianne," he said, hoping to find a way out of this.

Huck laid a hand on his shoulder and squeezed just hard enough to make his point. "Marianne is mentally unstable. We aren't worried about her, okay? Don't make me worry about you. You're in this up to your neck. Just remember this. You double-cross me and you won't live long enough to see prison."

Go to the sheriff. Confess everything. But even as he thought it, he knew Huck was right. The deputy had friends everywhere. Look how he'd managed to get the lab tests to appear that Vance was a McGraw. He must have gotten someone to get him DNA from one of the real sons. Or maybe the lab already had something of the twins from the kidnapping.

It didn't matter how Huck had pulled this fraud off. He had. And now he'd painted Vance into a corner. When had it gone from simply pretending to be Oakley McGraw to murder, though? Broke and now involved in fraud with a psychopath, he didn't see any way out of this but one. He had to kill Abby Pierce.

Chapter Fourteen

"You think he'll do it?" Wade asked after Vance had driven away.

"Nope," his father said. "He has it in him, but he's too gutless."

Wade shot his father a look. "But you made it sound as if you believed he would." He wasn't about to admit the sense of relief he'd felt. He still loved Abby. He figured he always would.

But that love came with such a sense of guilt over how he'd mistreated her it had turned into something hard as flint. In order to be rid of it, he had to be rid of Abby. Not that he wanted anyone else to have her.

"Son, if there is one thing I'm good at, it's reading people. Vance…well, he's damaged, no doubt about it. That's one reason why I knew he'd jump at the chance to be Oakley McGraw. But he's weak. I knew he'd never be able to go the distance."

"What the devil was the whole point of this, then?"

His father smiled. "Because we don't need it to.

I've contacted Waters through a friend. He's taking care of getting us the reward money."

"But once they find out that Vance isn't Oakley—"

"That is never going to happen," Huck said with so much confidence that Wade wondered if the man had a screw loose. "By then anyone who could hurt us will be dead."

He stared at his father. "How—"

"You don't worry about that end of it. I have it all figured out. But first, we need to stop out by that rattlesnake nest in the Larb Hills." Huck grinned. "I brought along a couple of burlap bags. That wife of yours? You're not going to have to worry about her much longer. Neither is Vance."

WATERS COULD SEE his world exploding in front of his eyes. Patricia was the missile coming in hard and fast. He had to do damage control before she hit. But that meant telling Travers the truth. Well, at least enough of the truth to cover his behind. All he had going for him was the fact that Patricia didn't believe he would tell.

He found Travers in his office. "Do you have a minute?"

The older man looked up and waved him in. "Boone tells me that you've had another inquiry that sounds like it might be legitimate."

Waters had forgotten about the call from the private investigator in Butte. "Yes, there was something about the call. I mentioned it to Boone."

"Did you get any specifics?"

"Not exactly, but by the questions the PI asked, I think he might have information about Jesse Rose."

Travers leaned back into his chair and motioned Waters to sit. "This is great news. We should get on this right away. I'll talk to Boone about following up on it."

"The PI was called out of town. He said he'd be back in a week or so. I was planning to go myself."

"I'd rather have Boone go," Travers said.

Waters figured the lead would take Boone nowhere. But he had to look as if he was trying to help find Jesse Rose. "There was something else." He stopped. His role in this house was tenuous at best after he'd sided with Patricia. Now he wasn't sure how his confession would go down. Travers could fire him and that would be that. He hesitated.

"Yes?"

"I need to tell you something. I should have a long time ago, but Patricia begged me not to and I foolishly listened to her."

"If you're going to tell me that you're possibly her daughter's father, it isn't necessary. I've known all along."

Waters stared at him. "How—"

"I knew about the two of you before the kidnapping." Travers's gaze hardened. "I also knew about the two of you after I married Patty."

He didn't know what to say. *I'm sorry* didn't quite cut it. "I don't understand."

"Oh, I think you do. That old expression, keep your enemies close."

"You see me as your enemy?" That shocked him. He'd always thought that Travers trusted him, maybe even liked him. "If you knew, why didn't you say something?"

"I like to see how things play out. I was fine with you and Patty because I saw that she was using you the same way she was me. A leopard really can't change its spots."

He wasn't sure if Travers was referring to Patricia or to him. "She's doing a tell-all book to help pay for her lawyer's fees."

Travers nodded. "I heard."

"I can try to get an injunction to stop the book from ever being published if you—"

"Not necessary."

Waters couldn't help feeling confused. "But the bad press…"

Travers laughed. "Did you really think that would bother me? Jim, I believe you're the one who doesn't want to see Patty's book published. But I figure by then her trial will be over and the truth will have come out."

"The truth?" he asked.

Travers only smiled and said, "If that's all, please

make sure Boone has all the information about this private investigator in Butte. I want him down there as soon as the man returns."

VANCE HAD NO idea how he was going to kill Abby and make it look like an accident. All the way back to the ranch, he cursed his luck. If he hadn't been in that bar in Billings, if he'd never met Huck Pierce, if he'd never gone along with this crazy idea for money...

Money was the root of all evil. If he had some right now, he'd be gone. He'd just disappear. Maybe go to South America. All he would need was a fake ID, and he'd heard that you could buy those if you knew the right people.

Except he didn't have money and he didn't know the right people. But Huck did. All this time, the cook had probably been watching him, reporting to the deputy that Vance was down at the pool or lying around the house.

Who knew how many other spies the man had at the ranch, he thought, reminded of the ranch hands he occasionally saw when he was down at the pool. It wasn't like Huck to show all of his hand, so Vance figured there were others watching him—not to mention Travers and his sons. He felt like someone was always watching him, looking for a crack in the story he'd built, waiting for him to unravel and admit he wasn't Oakley McGraw.

The house was unusually quiet when he entered. He looked around. Travers's office was empty. He thought he heard the clatter of pots and pans in the kitchen, but no voices. Happy not to be forced to make polite conversation with anyone, he took the stairs two at a time, wanting only to get to his room and hide out for a while.

He was almost to the top of the stairs when suddenly Abby appeared. Seeing her when she was so much on his mind, he reared back in surprise. Her eyes widened in alarm as he lost his balance.

Vance groped for the handrail, but it was slick and he wasn't close enough to get a grip on the highly varnished wood. He teetered and then felt himself start to fall backward. The irony of it didn't escape him as his arms windmilled wildly to no avail.

SHOCKED BY WHAT was happening, Abby rushed down a couple of steps to reach for the man. His hand closed on her wrist. He flailed, still off balance. But he held tight as she tried to keep her balance.

In those frantic moments, she realized he was so much heavier than her that she wasn't going to be able to keep him from falling. And with his hand clutching her wrist, he was going to take her with him.

She felt her heels lift off the step. Her free hand grabbed the railing, but Vance's pull was too strong. She felt herself falling toward him.

Abby let out a cry as Vance jerked her arm hard, then let go. She was thrown toward the center of the stairway as his body was pushed toward the railing. Her gaze tumbled down the long stairway to the marble floor below. She waited for her life to pass before her eyes as she felt herself falling through nothing but air.

Below her, the front door opened and Ledger stepped through. Their eyes met, his rounding in horror. He shot forward as if he thought he'd be able to catch her before she hit the bottom and the hard unforgiving marble.

She closed her eyes as a scream escaped her lips. She'd come so close to being with Ledger, but now fate had stepped in to keep them apart forever.

LEDGER'S CRY OF alarm mixed with Abby's scream as she began to fall. He rushed toward the stairs, his gaze locked on Abby. He'd only reached the bottom step when Vance's free arm shot out, the other looped over the handrail in a death grip. He grabbed Abby at the last minute.

For a moment, it looked as if Vance couldn't hold them both on the stairway. Ledger saw the pain in his face, the exertion as he looped his free arm around her waist and pulled.

He hadn't known he was holding his breath until he saw Abby find footing on the stairs. Vance let go of the railing and sat down hard on the steps. All the color had drained from his face, and even from where he stood, Ledger could see that the man was sweating profusely.

Abby had sat down, too. She was crying softly and holding her ribs after her close call. If Vance hadn't grabbed her when he did... But what were the two of them doing on the stairs together?

"Are you all right?" Ledger said when he reached Abby. He fell to his knees in front of her.

"Vance saved my life," she said between sobs.

His gaze went to the man.

"It wasn't like that," Vance said. "I was coming up the stairs not paying attention."

"I startled him. He started to fall backward," Abby filled in as they both seemed to be trying to catch their breaths.

"She grabbed me, but I was so off balance..." Vance finished with a look of such regret as he rubbed his shoulder. "I could have killed her."

"But you didn't," Ledger said. "You saved her. Is your shoulder hurt?"

"I think I might have pulled something," Vance said.

"I'll call the doctor to look at it." Ledger touched Abby's face, pushed back a fallen lock of her hair and wiped away a tear. "I'll have him take a look at both of you. I thought we agreed you'd stay off the stairs?" he said to her, smiling with such gratitude that she was all right. When he'd first seen her... If Vance hadn't grabbed for her at his own peril...

"Believe me, I'll take the elevator from now on," she said and let him enclose her in his arms. Past her, Ledger studied Vance.

"You're a hero," he said to his brother. "Thank you."

Vance shook his head. "I'm far from a hero."

VANCE'S HEROISM WAS the talk of the dinner table that evening. He'd pulled a muscle in his shoulder and had to ice it. Abby's ribs were even more sore from his saving her, but now when she looked at him, it was with gratitude as if her earlier suspicions were gone.

He tried to breathe, but his shoulder hurt like hell, and all this talk of how amazing he was hurt even worse. He'd had a chance to let Abby tumble down the stairs and instead he'd saved her—after she'd tried to save him.

"Maybe you should both stay off those stairs," Travers joked. "Seriously, I've given all my other sons a piece of land for them to build on one day, if they can be talked into staying on the ranch."

The table had gone deathly silent.

A piece of land? Vance swallowed.

"We can look at a map of the ranch later if you'd like and you can pick out a section you might want," Travers was saying.

"That is very kind of you."

"Kind?" The man laughed. "Son, this is your birthright."

His birthright. He hung his head, muttering, "Thank you."

"Here's to your future," Travers said, lifting his wineglass. "May it be everything you've ever hoped for."

When he looked up to lift his glass, he saw the cook standing in the kitchen doorway looking right at him. His heart took off at a gallop. She would report all of this to Huck.

Vance took a sip of his wine and felt it instantly curdle in his stomach. His future was anything but bright.

Chapter Fifteen

Abby stood at the window looking out over the ranch. "I can't stay here," she said, more to herself than to Ledger as she shifted her gaze to him. She could see that he wanted to argue the point.

"You can't go back to your apartment. Not alone," he said.

She had a feeling that if she went back to her apartment—back to town—more of her memory would return. Travers was getting more attached to Vance. She'd heard Travers offer him a piece of land on the ranch. She knew that was a mistake. She just didn't know why.

"Wade doesn't know where my apartment is and there's the restraining order…"

Ledger cursed under his breath. "You aren't that naive. He's just waiting for you. And if you think a restraining order is going to stop him…"

"What about my job?"

"You don't have to work there anymore."

She shook her head. "Ledger, I enjoy my work.

I miss the people. I miss feeling like there is a little normal in my life."

He sighed deeply, pain in his eyes. "What is it you're running from? Is it me?"

Abby quickly shook her head as she turned to him. "Never you. But I'm still married to Wade. I can't move on until I put that behind me."

He nodded. "You need time. I understand that."

"What will people think, my staying here with you?"

"Is that what you're worried about? What people will think?"

The moment she said it, she realized she sounded like her mother. The same mother who was growing pot in her root cellar, the same one who guilt-tripped her into staying in a bad marriage because it was to her benefit—not her daughter's.

Abby touched his cheek. "I want a fresh start."

"With me?" Ledger asked.

She smiled. "Oh, yes, with you. But I jumped into one marriage. I won't jump into another even with you."

He dragged her to him and kissed her. "I want you so badly."

"I feel the same way. It's been awful knowing you are just in the next room. I can't tell you how I have fought the need to come to you."

He let her go as if he felt the chemistry that arced between them as strongly as she did. "I'll wait as long as it takes." He grinned. "I've waited this long."

She had to smile.

"But you have to know Wade isn't finished with you. A man like him? His pride will be hurt. He'll take it out on you and this time he'll probably kill you."

"I know." She hated that she sounded close to tears. She'd cried so much over all this. "How do I get him out of my life?"

Ledger shook his head. "I don't know. But I wish you would stay here until the divorce is finalized. Maybe by then he will have realized it's really over. Maybe he will move on."

She nodded, but she knew neither of them believed that. He reached for her again. The memory hit her so hard, she cried out, jerking back.

Ledger looked alarmed as if he thought he'd hurt her.

"I saw them!" The memory hung before her, crystal clear, before it flickered and died away as she tried to see more. *"I know where I've seen Vance. It was at the house. He was with Wade and Huck."*

LEDGER DIDN'T KNOW what to make of what Abby had told him. He found his brother Cull downstairs and pulled him aside.

"Since the first time Abby saw Vance, she felt she'd seen him before, and wherever it was, it wasn't good."

Cull lifted a brow. "In other words, she just had a feeling about him."

"Something like that, only just now she remembered where she'd seen him. He'd been at her house talking with Wade and Huck."

"What?" Cull rubbed a hand over his face. "Okay, if this is true—"

"Why are you questioning it?"

"Because Abby's had two concussions in a row. Her memory isn't the most reliable. After what happened earlier today on the stairs… Then add to that, the garage at the house is supposedly where she fell and got her first concussion…"

Ledger could see his point. "What if it's a true memory, though? What would Vance have been doing with Wade and Huck Pierce?"

Cull frowned. "Nothing good. We were led to believe that he didn't know anyone around here."

"Exactly. You think we should tell Dad?" Ledger asked.

"No," his brother said quickly. "It will just upset him. And after everything that's happened, including Vance saving Abby yesterday on the stairs, I wouldn't suggest it. Anyway, if it's true and Vance denies it, it would be his word against Abby's."

Ledger nodded. "It could put her in danger if I'm right and the three of them are up to something other than the obvious."

"The obvious being that Vance isn't our brother," Cull finished for him. "Then how do you explain the DNA test?"

He felt a shiver race up his spine. "The day Vance

was tested, Huck Pierce was in the lab. He was flirting with one of the techs."

"Interesting, but certainly not conclusive. We could do another test with another lab, I suppose," Cull said. "It would mean getting DNA from Vance. That shouldn't be too hard. We could have him tested against one of us."

Ledger smiled at his brother. He knew he could depend on Cull. Boone would have stormed upstairs and tried to throttle the truth out of Vance.

"This shouldn't be too hard," Cull said. "Let me handle it. In the meantime…"

"Right, just be cool."

WADE WATCHED HIS father storm up and down the floor, half expecting the floorboards to crack.

"He saved Abby! Saved her!" Huck roared. "Came out looking like a damned hero."

"Maybe that works to our benefit," Wade said when his father had calmed down a little.

Huck spun on him. *"What?"*

"When something happens to Abby, Vance will look innocent."

His father stopped pacing and stared at him. "You really aren't as stupid as you look."

"Thanks." Wade realized how sick he was of his father's belittling. He would be glad when they got the reward money. He was leaving town, putting all of this behind him for good. But then he thought of

Abby. Did he really want her dead? No. Could he stop his father? It was too late for that, he feared.

Huck was muttering to himself as he paced again. "I think we need to step up the ending to all this."

Wade had no intention of being around to see whatever his father had planned. "When do we get the reward money?"

"My friend talked to the attorney. He offered to cut a check today, but my friend insisted it be cash, saying he wasn't alone in finding Oakley, that the others want to remain anonymous. Jim Waters doesn't care. He said he'd get the money. Won't be long now," Huck said, smiling broadly.

His mood could go from happy to furious in less than a heartbeat. Wade realized his own wasn't much better. The sheriff had the gall to suggest he go to something called anger management. He'd been insulted at the time, but maybe once he was gone from here, he'd check into it.

"So what happens now?" Wade asked, not sure he wanted to know.

WATERS LOOKED AT the stack of bills inside his briefcase. Five hundred thousand dollars. Travers had been adamant about going ahead and paying the reward.

"Are you sure you don't want to wait a little longer?" Waters had asked. "Maybe run another DNA test." He knew it was the wrong thing to say. Voicing his suspicions wasn't doing him any good.

But he was still shaken. Travers had known about him and Patricia all along. He'd known and not said anything. As he'd said, he'd wanted to see how it all played out.

The only thing the man hadn't known was that he was being systematically poisoned.

"Just pay the reward, Jim. Oakley is home. Boone will check out this lead on Jesse Rose. I feel good about it. So I suppose we should discuss your...retirement."

That had been plain enough. But at least he could continue billing the bastard until then. And he would, he thought as he slammed the briefcase. First he would get rid of this money. He felt as if Travers was throwing it away, but what did he care?

Vance wasn't Oakley. Waters would bet his stock portfolio on it. He had no proof, just a gut feeling. The same gut feeling that told him Patricia was going to take him down with her.

He looked at the briefcase again. His passport was up to date. All he had to do was book a flight to anywhere there was no extradition. He could live comfortably on what was in that case—even if he couldn't get his money out of his retirement.

Waters let out a laugh. He didn't even think Travers would turn him in to the sheriff. Instead, he'd pony up another five hundred grand to pay the reward and keep his mouth shut.

With a start, Waters realized this was exactly what

the cagey old fool hoped he would do. This was "kiss off" money. Travers expected him to run.

LEDGER FOUND HIS father in his office, but one look at him and he felt his heart break for him. "What's wrong?"

Travers looked up in surprise as if he hadn't heard his son come in. For a moment, he seemed at a loss for words. "It's your mother. She's doing...worse. I blame myself. I should never have taken Oakley out to see her. Of course she expected a six-month-old baby—not a grown man. The doctor said she's trapped in that night twenty-five years ago."

"It isn't your fault. She asked to see him. You couldn't keep him from her."

His father laid his head into his hands, elbows on his desk. This was the most distraught he'd seen him. For so long, the man had lived on hope that his kidnapped children would be found. Ledger suspected it wasn't going quite like he'd hoped.

"I'm sorry," Travers said, lifting his head. "You wanted to talk about something?"

Now that he was here, Ledger almost changed his mind. "I want to marry Abby."

His father chuckled. "Son, that's not news."

"I know. I never got over her."

"I blame myself for that, as well. I should have let you marry her when you wanted to. I can't believe what she's been through."

Ledger nodded. "But your advice was good. Abby

had a lot of pressure from her mother and Wade. Also she was lied to. I don't blame her for doubting me. I didn't handle things well."

"All water under the bridge."

"Yes. That's why I hope you don't mind her staying here a little longer."

"You know I don't. I just worry. She's still married to Wade."

"Yes, but not for long. She's filed for a separation. Unfortunately, she has to wait six months in Montana before she can file for the divorce. At least here at the ranch, she's safe. But I can't keep her locked up here for six months."

VANCE HELD THE phone away from his ear and looked toward the big house. He didn't think he could be seen from the shade of the trees where he stood. Nor did he think anyone was home. But Abby.

"Are you a complete idiot?" Huck demanded.

He didn't bother to answer.

"You could have finished it right there on the stairs."

"She saved my life. I would have fallen if she hadn't grabbed me."

The deputy let out a string of curses. "You sound like my addled son. Now you have a soft spot for the woman, too?"

"No." Actually, he was scared of her. He kept watching her, thinking she was going to remember. While she seemed less standoffish since their incident on the stairs, she still had that memory lodged somewhere in that head of hers. Once it came out…

He heard a vehicle coming up the road to the ranch. "I should go." He was hoping it was Travers back from town. His "father" had gone in to set up a bank account for him.

"I should have thought of it before," Travers had apologized. "A man needs a little spending money."

Vance wondered what his father thought was a little spending money. Hopefully enough so he could take off in one of the ranch trucks and never look back.

"Any word on the reward money?" he asked now into the phone.

"Not yet," Huck said.

A lie. Travers had told him that the reward was being paid today by special messenger. That had surprised him. He'd thought the lawyer, Waters, would be handling it and said as much to the man.

"Jim Waters is no longer in my employ," Travers had said.

That had surprised him even more. "I thought he was like family." At least, that was what Waters had told him once.

"Family," Travers had repeated. "It's odd what makes a family, don't you think? It isn't always blood. But even blood sometimes can't hold a family together. I think it's trust and love." The man had smiled. "One day my sons will all marry and our family will grow. I hope to see grandchildren before I die."

Vance had thought of Cull and Nikki. "I would think you'll be hearing wedding bells before you know it."

"Yes. I hope Jesse Rose is here to see it. This family won't be whole again until she's home. And her mother, too." Travers had brightened. "At least you're home."

"You still there?" Huck asked over the phone, sounding even more irritated.

"I'm here." Right here at home.

"Just do your job."

Vance disconnected and headed for the house. Once Travers handed him that checkbook… And yet as he walked up the back steps, he felt a pang. If only he truly was Oakley McGraw. Surprisingly it wasn't the ranch or the money or name that pulled at him. It was the idea of having a father like Travers McGraw.

Chapter Sixteen

"Here, let me help you with that," Ledger said as he saw the cook struggling with a large box. He'd been busy making him and Abby a picnic lunch. He planned to surprise her with a ride around the ranch.

The fiftysomething matronly woman had just come into the back door with the box and seemed anxious to put it down. But when he tried to take it, the cook turned away from him. "I have it," she said, sounding as if out of breath. "But thank you." She set it down carefully.

He noticed that the top had been taped closed and wondered idly what was inside that so much tape had been used. Live lobsters?

She turned, looking nervous, and he realized he was making her so. "Did you need something?"

"No—sorry." He tried to remember her name. Louise? Elise? Eloise? He couldn't be sure. They'd had the same cook from as far back as he could remember. It was hard since they'd gone through a few before they'd gotten this one. Also he had the feeling that, like the others, she wouldn't be staying long. His family was a little too infamous and Patricia's arrest hadn't helped.

Ledger had forgotten why he'd come into the kitchen. His mind was on Abby, as usual. He'd realized that he couldn't keep her here like a prisoner. And yet he couldn't let her move back into town—not with Wade on the loose.

Now that she'd thought she remembered seeing Vance with Wade and Huck Pierce, he was all the more worried about her. He'd been so sure she was safe while in this house. But with Vance here, too...

Through the kitchen window, he saw Vance coming out of the trees at the back of the house. That was odd. He appeared to be pocketing a phone. Ledger realized he'd never seen Vance with a cell phone before. Who had he been calling that he hadn't wanted to make the call in the house?

"If you'll excuse me, I have work to do," the cook said.

"Yes, of course," Ledger told her distractedly and put the box she'd left on the counter out of his mind as he heard the elevator. Abby.

"Vance!"

He'd practically run into Travers as he'd come in the back door of the house.

"This is for you."

He took the envelope and glanced inside. The paperwork from the bank—along with what looked like a savings account bankbook and a checkbook. He wanted to see how much was in his account. The waiting was going to kill him.

"You need to sign some forms in there and return them to the bank," Travers was saying. "But you should be all set."

"Thank you so much," Vance said sincerely.

"You're my son."

He felt the warm, large hand on his shoulder and swallowed.

"But we do need to talk about getting your name changed legally—if that's still what you want. Also I hope you've been thinking about what section of land on the ranch you would like. I've hired a new attorney. I'd like to get this taken care of right away."

Vance could only nod.

"There is one other thing, though."

He froze. Why did he always expect the worst?

"I want you to pick out a horse. A man should have his own horse." Travers chuckled. "There's a few out there. You do ride, right?"

"Yes. As a matter of fact, I'd been wanting to saddle up and take a ride. I wasn't sure if that was all right."

Travers looked sorry again. "Son, this is your ranch, too. I want you to enjoy it. I also hope that you might be interested in working it with your brothers."

He'd known that was coming. "Absolutely. I just need to learn the ropes."

The man looked delighted. "I'll tell Cull. He'll

get you started. Tomorrow is soon enough. You're settling in here all right?"

"I am."

"I know it will take a while for it to feel like home."

Vance held the manila envelope with the bank papers in it to his chest. "Yes, this is all so new for me." He couldn't wait to leave the room, feeling as if he'd won the lottery. Except he didn't know how much he'd won. Or worse, how long it would last.

LEDGER MET THE elevator as it came down, anxious to see Abby. Her injuries were healing and he knew it wouldn't be long and he'd have to let her go. That scared him in a way that nothing on this earth did. She would never be safe as long as Wade Pierce was out there.

As the door opened and he saw her, his heart did a vault in his chest. He never saw her or heard her voice that it didn't send a thrill through him. He loved this woman. He'd never been able to let go because of it.

"Hey," he said, feeling like he'd been injected with helium.

She smiled broadly. She was almost her old self again. He could see it in her eyes. There was no reason for her to stay here—other than the fact that her husband was out there somewhere planning who knew what.

"I thought you might want to go for a ride. You've

been cooped up too long. What do you say? Want to see my favorite parts of the ranch?"

"I'd love that, assuming you don't mean on a horse."

He laughed. "I'm not sure your ribs could take that. I've packed us a picnic."

"You think of everything," she said and squeezed his arm.

He wished he did think of everything. Otherwise, he would have better understood why Abby married Wade. If he'd known about the lies… As his father had said, "Water under the bridge." But still it was hard not to want to rewrite history and save them both a lot of pain.

As they started through the living room, he heard a vehicle pull up out front, engine revved. Through the window, he saw nothing but a cloud of dust. Someone was in a hurry. His father and Cull came out of the office, both having heard the vehicle.

The knock at the door sounded urgent. Or angry. Just like the thunder of the boot heels did on the porch.

"I'll get it," Ledger said and then turned to Abby. "Wait here." He moved to the door, expecting it would be Wade.

Opening the door, he found a cowboy he'd never seen before standing there. He wore worn dirty jeans, a Western shirt with holes at the elbows and a belt with a rodeo buckle. The cowboy reached to take off his straw cowboy hat at the sound of the door opening.

Sans the hat, his dark hair caught the sunlight like a raven's wing. The young man brushed back a lock as he turned to look at him. Ledger found himself gazing into intense green eyes the same shade as his mother's. For a startled moment, Ledger thought he was seeing a male version of his mother.

"Can I help you?" he asked the man, his voice sounding calmer than he felt. There was something about this cowboy...

"No, but I can help you," the young man said, still standing in the doorway. "I heard there's someone here claiming to be Oakley McGraw."

That didn't surprise Ledger after the press conference had gone viral. What did surprise him was that this cowboy had not just gotten onto the ranch, he was standing at their front door.

"And what does that have to do with you?" he asked.

"The name's Tough Crandall. Before you ask, my father rodeoed and so did his father, thus the name."

"Well, Mr. Crandall, I'm not sure what that has to do with my brother Oakley—"

"I've been out of state. I just happened to see on the news that the McGraw kidnapping son had been found. I'm here to tell you that Vance Elliot is not your brother."

"How would you know that?" Ledger demanded.

"What's the problem?" his father said, moving from where he and Cull had stopped just outside his office doorway.

"Mr. McGraw," Tough said to Travers, hat in his

hand. "I heard you'd been sickly. I'm sorry to hear that. I didn't want to bother you, but I can't let you be tricked. The man staying with you pretending to be your son is a fraud."

"I think you'd better step inside," Ledger heard his father say. He could tell by Travers's shocked look that he'd seen the cowboy's green eyes and dark hair.

Once inside the office, his father asked Tough Crandall to sit down. The cowboy looked around at the expensive furniture and said, "I'd prefer to keep standing if you don't mind. I picked up a couple of horses over in Minot earlier today. I would have waited and come after I'd cleaned up, but I was afraid it couldn't keep. Anyway, this won't take long."

"Mr. Crandall…" Travers began.

"Please, call me Tough."

"All right, Tough. Why is it you think Vance isn't Oakley?"

Tough looked down at his straw hat for a moment before glancing up again. Ledger saw the effect those green eyes had on not just his father but his brothers, as well. Even Boone, who had quietly joined them, was staring at the man.

"Because, sir, I'm your biological son."

Travers cocked his head. "And what makes you think that?"

"My mother told me all about my adoption. I've known since I was five."

"Then why didn't you come forward before this?" Cull demanded.

Tough chewed at his cheek for a moment. "Beg your pardon, but I had no good reason to. I have parents who raised me just fine and I didn't want to bring that kind of trouble down on them. They are good people who believed they were doing the best for me. I agree with them."

"Are you saying you didn't want to be a Mc-Graw?" Boone asked, sounding as if it wouldn't take much more to make him mad.

"No offense," Tough said quickly.

"Who did your mother say brought you to her when you were six months old?" Travers asked.

"Pearl Cavanaugh from the Whitehorse Sewing Circle. She, too, meant no harm. God rest her soul."

"Do you have any proof?" Boone asked.

"No, other than me standing here telling you what I know."

"But you'd be willing to take a DNA test?" Ledger asked.

"I didn't come here looking to be adopted into the family. I just thought you ought to know that Vance Elliot is an impostor."

"Vance passed the DNA test," Boone challenged.

Tough nodded as he seemed to study the lot of them. "Then you've got more vipers among you than even I thought." He took a step back. "I've done what I came to do. Believe me or not, doesn't matter to me. I just couldn't have this on my conscience without speaking up." He turned toward the door.

"Just a minute," Travers said. "My youngest son was taken from his crib with two items—"

"I saw that on the news," Tough said with a sigh. "I don't know anything about a stuffed toy horse. But I had a baby blanket with tiny horses on it. It was blue. The horses weren't quarter horses like you raise. They were Arabians. My mother gave me the blanket before she died. She told me to do with it what I wanted. I burned it."

A gasp came up from the room. "Why in the hell would you do that?" Boone demanded.

"Because I had no interest in doing what I'm doing right now," Tough snapped. "I won't be grilled. I won't be tested. I won't be looked at under a magnifying glass. I sure as hell don't want any press conference for the world to know. I *know* who I am, who my 'real' parents are, and I'm fine with that."

"But if you're Oakley—"

Tough cut Travers off. "Please, sir, don't make me sorry I came here. I couldn't let you be defrauded. But if you want to go on believing Vance Elliot is your son, that's fine with me. Please don't take offense, but I want no part of this family or what comes with it." He stuffed his straw hat onto his thick head of dark hair and lit out the door, leaving behind a stunned silence.

VANCE HAD WATCHED the whole thing from the doorway of the kitchen. After Abby had come down in the elevator, he'd gone into the kitchen and, finding it empty, had gotten himself a snack before opening the envelope.

Now he stepped back so no one saw him.

He heard a sound behind him and turned to see the cook. She had her phone in her hand. All the color had drained from her face.

She must have heard what was going on, as well. She was looking scared, no doubt because she'd been snitching to Huck about him. She was probably afraid she'd get drawn into all this.

"Please tell Mr. Travers that I'm not feeling well and have to go. I'm sorry about dinner." She headed for the door. He saw her glance at a large box sitting on the counter and she seemed to avoid it, increasing her speed as she went out the door. He noticed that some of the tape had been removed from the top of the box. There was a pair of kitchen shears next to it.

Whatever the cook had been getting out of the box, she seemed to have lost interest. Vance had the feeling that they wouldn't be seeing her again.

He wanted to run, too. He'd opened the envelope with his new bank account information but had seen right away that until he signed the necessary forms, he couldn't withdraw any of the ten grand Travers had put in his account. Ten grand. He'd had to count the numbers since he couldn't believe it. There was also a note in the envelope that read, "Thought you might want to buy yourself a vehicle. Let me know and I will see that the money is put into your account."

He'd groaned when he'd seen that. If he stayed, he got to buy himself a brand-new pickup. It was all too much. Worse, it was all a lie.

Had he really thought this was going to last? He couldn't stay. Even before that cowboy had shown up, he'd known that. But he also couldn't hide in the kitchen like the phony he was.

Vance walked into the living room, feeling the tension thick as fog. "The cook just told me to tell you that she isn't feeling well. She's sorry about dinner." He knew he couldn't ignore that tension. Or the way they all looked at him. "What's going on?"

"Some cowboy just stopped by claiming to be Oakley McGraw," Boone said. He was the most suspicious of the brothers. Vance couldn't tell who he thought was lying. Maybe both him and the cowboy.

"Well, he's too late, isn't he?" Cull went to the bar and poured himself a drink. The others joined him, all except Travers. "You passed the DNA test. You're Oakley, right?"

Vance swallowed, his throat too dry to speak. Anyway, what would he have said?

"That was disturbing," Travers said as he looked at his sons, his gaze finally taking in Vance.

He thought of how much he'd wanted this man to be his father. More than he'd wanted the money and the name. He felt an apology working its way up from deep in his chest.

His cell phone rang. He cursed silently. He'd stupidly forgotten to turn the darn thing off after his call to Huck. Pulling out the phone with trembling fingers, he looked at caller ID. *Huck.* It was marked Urgent.

He saw he'd missed an earlier text from Huck. It read: Unless you want to die, get out of the house. Now!

"I should take this." Quickly turning, he headed for the back door, wondering what this could be about.

Chapter Seventeen

"Did any of you know he had a cell phone?" Ledger asked the moment Vance was gone. Abby had sat down with the others. He joined her. She looked as shocked as he felt.

"Everyone in the civilized world has a cell phone," Boone snapped. "What is your point?"

"I just wonder who's calling him."

"You think he didn't have a life before he came here? Friends? People who care about him?" Travers asked as if he'd wondered the same thing.

They all looked after Vance for a moment before Cull spoke. "This Tough Crandall. He described the baby blanket perfectly. The type of horse on the blanket was never released."

"But he didn't have the toy stuffed horse," Ledger said.

"Vance did," their father said.

"For the sake of argument, let's say Tough Crandall is Oakley," Cull said reasonably. "How is it he had the blanket but not the stuffed horse?"

Boone brought his drink over to the couch and sat down. "The stuffed toy was taken the night of the kidnapping along with Oakley and his blanket, right?"

"Maybe the kidnapper dropped it when the ladder rung broke," Cull said.

"And the kidnapper's accomplice picked it up?" Boone said.

Ledger felt a chill. "Or whoever was the first person on the scene."

"Like maybe one of the deputy sheriffs?" Abby said.

Travers sighed. "All this is just speculation. Vance's DNA matched."

"Dad, there's something I need to tell you," Cull said and looked at Ledger. "I've taken DNA from Vance's room and some of mine. I've had another test done at a different lab."

"Why would you do that?" His father sounded angry.

"Because Abby remembered something," Ledger said, looking at her. She nodded and he continued, "She remembered seeing Wade and his father with Vance. It was at her house."

"What?" Travers shook his head. "When was this?"

"Before he showed up at our door claiming to be Oakley. That's not all," Ledger continued. "When we were at the lab getting Vance's DNA test done,

I saw Deputy Sheriff Huck Pierce talking to one of the lab techs."

The room went deathly quiet again.

"Let's all take it down a notch here," Travers said, but Ledger saw that he looked worried. "You realize what you're accusing Vance of being involved in."

"Fraud," Boone said, putting down his drink and getting to his feet. "I think someone should go check on Vance."

Ledger reached for Abby's hand. "We're going on a picnic. Hope you get it all worked out before we get back."

They'd barely reached the pickup when the back of the house exploded.

VANCE HAD REACHED the trees past the pool house and was about to put in a call to Huck when the world behind him went up in flames.

He spun around in horror as he looked at the back of the house. The kitchen wing looked leveled while the rest of the house was quickly catching fire.

For a moment he couldn't move. Two ranch hands came running from the direction of the barns. Out of the smoke at the back of the house, he saw Boone. He'd been knocked to the ground but was now running back toward the burning house.

Vance's cell phone rang. Still in shock, he took the call.

"Did you get out in time?" Huck laughed.

"You did this?" he demanded.

"And just imagine what I will do if you cross me," the deputy said. "Now get rid of this phone. I'll find you when I need to talk to you again."

LEDGER GRABBED ABBY, not sure at first what had happened as glass showered over the porch as the front windows of the house were blown out.

The front door burst open. Cull and his father came stumbling out. "Call the fire department," Cull was yelling.

Ledger fumbled out his phone. Through the door he could see smoke billowing into the living room from what had been the kitchen.

He dialed 9-1-1 as he drew Abby farther away from the burning house.

"Are you all right?" he heard Cull ask his father. He noticed that the older man was holding his left shoulder.

"I'm fine. Go!" his father said as he stumbled toward one of the pickups parked out front.

Cull was running for their water truck parked next to one of the barns.

The 9-1-1 operator answered. Ledger quickly gave her the information, his mind reeling. What had happened?

"There was an explosion. The house is on fire."

"Is everyone all right?"

"I don't know," he said, suddenly terrified. Boone had started out the back door to go find Vance. The barns were far enough away that the ranch hands and the horses should be fine. But Boone…

"One of my brothers… I don't know where he is." And Vance. Ledger realized he'd never thought the man was his brother. "And another man."

"I'll send an ambulance, as well," the operator was saying. "The fire department is on its way."

HUCK HAD HEARD the call come over the radio and smiled. It just didn't get any better than this.

He drove partway out of town so he could see in the direction of the McGraw ranch. Black smoke billowed up into a cloudless blue sky.

With luck, Travers McGraw and at least some of his sons were dead, Abby along with them. If that damned cook had done her job, the box with the explosives in it would have been left under the front stairs, where it would have done the most damage.

Not that he'd told the woman what was in the box. He'd just told her to handle it with care and not say anything to anyone. It was a surprise.

Idly, he wondered if she'd been surprised.

You're a coldhearted bastard. He heard the last thing his ex-wife had said to him. "Yes, I am. Life made me that way."

And now he was getting back at everyone who'd wronged him. He had the five hundred thousand dollars from the reward coming. He'd give some of it to Wade and then he was gone. There was an island somewhere calling his name. Vance was now a Mc-

Graw. He'd be fine. And if he didn't like getting ripped off on the reward money, what could he do about it, Huck thought with a laugh.

For a moment, he watched the smoke rising higher in the sky as flames consumed more of the McGraw house. Things would have been so different if Marianne had married him and not McGraw. He would have done anything for her. Hell, he had that scholarship to the university. He was going to be an engineer, maybe build dams or skyscrapers; he hadn't decided.

But when she'd married McGraw, he'd lost his drive. Nothing mattered. He'd married Wade's mother on the rebound and his life had gone downhill from there.

An ambulance had been sent out to the ranch since they were unsure how many people had been injured. Huck waited patiently for the news, telling himself even if McGraw wasn't dead, his house would be gone. He would have been hit where it hurt the most. The house McGraw had built for Marianne? Gone. Just as Marianne was gone in every sense of the word.

He thought about the twins. They, too, were gone. In the months since more information had come to light about what had been taken from the house the night of the kidnapping, Vance was the only one to come forward.

McGraw had lost Oakley and Jesse Rose. He'd lost

Marianne. And now he'd lost his house and hopefully his life.

"Got you," Huck whispered as he watched the cloud of smoke grow larger and larger against the skyline.

VANCE STEPPED BACK into the trees as Boone yelled at the ranch hands to let all the horses out. The two headed for the barns, while Boone raced back into the burning house.

A few minutes later, horses came running out, wild-eyed in terror and headed out across the pasture away from the burning house.

Vance was too shocked to do more than stare at the flames licking wildly at the large house and try to make sense out of what had happened. What would happen now? Who had been killed? Would they think he had done this?

Since this was Huck's doing, Vance was in it up to his eyeballs. No one would believe he hadn't had something to do with this, even if they couldn't prove it.

Was that the way Huck had planned it? Was he going to let him take the fall for this? Was that why he'd texted him to get out?

Had the deputy already gotten the five-hundred-thousand-dollar reward money?

There was also the possibility that Huck warned him about the explosion hoping he would be the only one to survive and all this would be his so Huck could blackmail him right into his old age.

But what to do now?

If he was a real son, he'd be helping with the horses or running to the house to see if he could help whoever was still inside.

But he wasn't and Tough Crandall's visit had raised enough doubt that this would soon be over. The sheriff would be investigating. More DNA testing would be done and when he failed...

Vance began to run in the direction of the house only to swerve at the last moment and race toward the front of the house and the pickups parked out there. If one of them had a key in it...

"HERE, TAKE MY father to my cabin up the road," Ledger said to Abby. "I have to help my brothers fight the fire until the rural fire department gets here." She started toward her rental car, but he handed her the keys to his pickup. "Take my truck. The road is rough. I'll have the EMTs come down there to look at his shoulder."

"I'm fine," Travers said. "We need to find your brother."

"Dad, I don't want to have to worry about you. Go with Abby. I'll do what I can here."

Abby could tell he didn't want his father watching the house he'd loved burn to the ground. She couldn't see how they could save it the way it had gone up in flames.

She was happy to help. Getting into the pickup, they started up the road when she had to pull over and let the fire trucks go by. She just prayed that Boone had gotten out.

Travers was looking back, tears in his eyes. "Still no word on Boone?" he asked. "Or... Vance?" She noticed he hadn't called him Oakley.

She shook her head. "I'm sure Ledger will call the minute he knows something."

Travers nodded and closed his eyes.

LEDGER WAS JUST about to go back inside to look for Boone when his brother came bursting out the front door in a cloud of smoke.

"Where is Dad?" Boone cried.

"He and Cull got out. Cull's gone to get the water truck. Abby and Dad are fine. I've sent them to my cabin. I didn't want Dad to see this. He's been through enough."

"What the hell happened?"

Ledger shook his head and called Abby to give her the news as his brother ran toward the second water truck. Cull was already watering down the closest barn. Clearly, he could see that it would be impossible to save the house without more resources.

At the sound of sirens, Ledger turned to see the fire trucks and ambulance in the distance.

VANCE CAME AROUND the side of the house as Ledger went to join his brothers to water down the barns.

He rushed through the dark smoke toward the closest pickup. All he could think about was getting out of there. Let them think he died in the fire. It would be days before they realized his body wasn't in the ashes. Meanwhile, he would have put miles between him and this place.

No keys in the first pickup. Or the second. He swore. The smoke was starting to get to him. He spotted Abby's car and raced toward it. Behind him, the flames cracked and popped. Sparks flew into the air. The heat of the blaze felt as if it was frying his skin.

He could hear sirens and see the trucks coming up the road. He had to get out of there. If he stayed, he was looking at prison for a crime he didn't commit. He reached Abby's car, threw open the door and reached around the steering wheel, praying that the keys would be there.

They were!

His luck had changed. His mind was working again. If Huck had the reward money, he would get his share or blow the whistle on the deputy. Two could play at blackmail.

He dropped into the seat, reached for the key, turned it. The car engine caught and started. Vance glanced at the house, thinking what a waste and wondering who might still be inside.

He threw the car into Reverse, not letting his mind go there. He braked and looked again at the house, his senses warning him not to run. He would look even guiltier if he did. Maybe he could turn state's evidence on Wade and Huck. Maybe he could get out of this with a little honor.

He put the car in Park and turned off the engine, thinking about Travers McGraw and wishing with all his heart that he really had been his son. How different his life could have been.

Did he really think there was hope for him, that he could change? He told himself he needed to help water down the barns. He needed to be a different man, the kind of man Travers McGraw thought he'd welcomed into his family.

He reached for his door handle when he heard a noise. At first, it didn't register. A buzzing sound that he could barely hear over the roar of the fire.

Vance looked down at the floorboard, shocked to see what was coiled there. Two rattlesnakes intertwined, both of their ugly heads raised and looking right at him.

He jerked the door handle in that instant before the first one struck. He threw himself out of the car as the second one caught him in the neck. Its fangs going so deep that the snake was still clinging to him as he fell screaming from the car. He tore the snake from his neck.

Over the roar of the blaze, he heard the sirens. Looking up, he saw the first fire trucks pull up. He ran toward them, screaming for someone to help him as venom raced like flames through his veins.

WADE STARED AT his father, then at the cloud of smoke in the distance. "What did you do?"

"Instead of merely whining, I took care of your wife and her boyfriend," Huck snapped. "You should be thanking me. Hell, if it wasn't for me and Abby's mother, you would have never had Abby as long as you did."

"What are you talking about?" Wade demanded, his voice breaking.

"McGraw never had another girlfriend. He was in love with Abby and planning to marry her after college. And he would have if we hadn't tricked Abby into believing he was cheating on her. Why do you think she rushed into the marriage with you? You would never have stood a chance with her otherwise."

"You lousy son of a—" Filled with rage, he took a swing at his father. Huck easily stepped aside and hit him in the back of the neck. Wade staggered, turning to look back at his father. Lies, all lies. He felt as if his entire world had imploded.

He shook his head. He wanted to blame his father for all of it, but he couldn't. He'd gone along with this stupid plan. He could have walked away. He could have gotten help. He could have been a decent husband.

"Where do you think you're going?" his father demanded as Wade turned and walked toward his pickup.

He didn't bother to answer as he climbed behind the wheel. He had to find out if Abby was still alive. He had to see her. Restraining order be damned.

"Don't go out there," Huck yelled after him as

he took off in a cloud of dust and gravel. He roared out of Whitehorse. Smoke billowed up into Montana's big sky.

LEDGER AND HIS BROTHERS, along with the hired hands, managed to get the horses to safety and save the barns. Now, covered with soot, he stared at the ashes of the house. The firefighters hadn't been able to save it.

Smoke still billowed up, a dark smudge on the skyline.

"At least no one was killed," Cull said as the brothers stood shoulder to shoulder in the front yard. "I talked to Dad. His shoulder is better, but Abby called the doctor anyway."

"How long before we find out what caused it?" Boone asked.

"The fire chief said it should be a few days. Maybe a gas leak." Cull shook his head.

Ledger turned at the sound of a vehicle roaring up the road. "I'll be a son of a…" He stared in disbelief.

"Maybe you better let us handle this," Cull said, grabbing his arm as Ledger started toward the pickup that had just come to a dust-boiling stop in their yard.

He pulled his arm free. "Not a chance. I promised Abby I wouldn't go after him, but I told her all bets were off if he came out here." He stormed over to the pickup as Wade climbed out.

WADE DIDN'T NEED his father to tell him he was a damned fool for coming out here. But he had to know if Abby was all right. Now, though, as he saw the destroyed house, his heart lodged in his throat. If she was in that house when it exploded… His beautiful Abby.

He saw Ledger McGraw, the man he'd hated for years, stalking toward him. Abby had been in love with McGraw from the beginning. She would have married him if Wade's father and her mother hadn't lied to her. Wasn't that what had eaten him up inside for the past three years because he'd suspected it all along? He hadn't gotten Abby fair and square. She'd never wanted him. She'd always wanted McGraw. He'd never felt such pain. And all of it had been for nothing. Especially if Abby was dead.

"Wade? What the hell are you doing here?" Ledger demanded as he advanced on him. The cowboy was covered with soot from fighting the fire and he looked angry enough to kill.

"Is Abby…?"

Ledger kept coming. Wade didn't even bother to throw up an arm as the cowboy punched him. He staggered under the blow but didn't go down. His father had hit him a lot harder than that in his life.

"Just tell me she's alive."

Ledger hit him again, this time driving him back before tackling him to the ground. Wade took another blow before his survival instincts cut in and he started to fight back. This man had been his nemesis for years. He hated him. Hated that Abby loved this man more than him.

But still McGraw was winning this battle.

"That's enough," a male voice ordered as Ledger was pulled off him.

Wade looked from Ledger to his brother Cull. Behind him was the older brother Boone.

"I would have let him beat the hell out of him a little longer, if it had been me," Boone said. All three of them looked like they wanted to kick his ass. He couldn't really blame them.

He wiped the blood from his cut lip with the back of his hand as he sat up. "Abby?"

"She's alive," Ledger said, glaring down at him. "No thanks to you."

Wade covered his face with his hands and, unable to hold back the burst of emotion, began to sob in relief and regret.

Chapter Eighteen

"You want the good news first?" Cull asked. They had all gathered in Cull's cabin, the largest one on the ranch now that the house was gone.

"Huck and Wade have been arrested." He looked at Abby, who was sitting next to Ledger on the couch. "They've both been charged, along with a tech at the lab and our cook. Huck and Wade won't be seeing daylight for many years to come. Vance is going to live—and turned state's evidence against them. He'll get some time, as well, but nothing like he should for his part of the charade."

Ledger saw his father nod solemnly. "I feel sorry for him. I saw something in him…" He shook his head. "I have more good news. While the house is a total loss, insurance will cover rebuilding. I actually think it's a good thing," he said, no doubt seeing that his sons were afraid he was taking it hard. "It's a new beginning. Let's face it, there was a lot of sadness associated with that house."

"It was haunted," Cull said. Ledger knew he was only partially kidding.

His father nodded. "I suppose it was. But my life has changed since I built that house for your mother and our future."

Boone had been looking at his phone. He glanced up suddenly, shock on his face. "Jim Waters has been arrested trying to leave the country with a briefcase full of money." His gaze shot to their father. "Do you know anything about that?"

Travers's smile was almost sad. "Human nature. Jim apparently couldn't overcome his. It's probably just as well since Patricia's trial is coming up. She has implicated him in my poisoning."

Boone swore. "That son of—"

"I have some good news," Ledger interjected. "Wade has agreed to sign the divorce papers when the six months is up. He isn't going to contest it. Also he'll be going to prison and locked up for some time to come."

Travers reached over to squeeze his son's shoulder. "I'm happy for you. I suppose you'll want to start building a house for the two of you on the ranch. Looks like there'll be a lot of construction going on. I like that. I like progress."

"Me too," Ledger said and smiled over at Abby.

"Well," Cull said. "Nikki is going to be back this week. I hate to let my little brother beat me at anything…" He grinned. "I've asked Nikki to marry me. She's said yes!"

There was cheering. Travers suggested a toast.

"There's one more thing," Boone said. "Do you still want me to follow up on that last lead we had about Jesse Rose?"

"I do. But Vance taught me something," their father said. "I need to be more careful. If you don't mind checking it out…"

"Don't worry. If it's not legit, I'll know. Just don't get your hopes up."

"No," Travers said. "I'm going to drive down to the Crandall place. I need to talk to Tough."

"Dad—"

"Cull, I heard him just fine. He isn't interested in being a McGraw. I can live with that. But I believe he's my son. I can hope for some sort of relationship, can't I?"

LEDGER FOUND ABBY standing outside on the cabin porch, looking out at the ranch in the distance. For so long, smoke had curled up from the ruins of the house he almost thought he could still see. He would be glad when the debris was gone and the new house started.

Mostly, he wanted a fresh start with Abby. She'd been through so much. All he wanted to do was make her happy. He knew it couldn't be easy for her hearing about her soon-to-be ex-husband's arrest.

"Are you all right?" he asked as he joined her at the porch railing.

"I've made so many mistakes. If I had just followed my heart…" Abby began to cry.

Ledger pulled her into his arms. "Abby, we've all made mistakes. The moment I heard you married Wade, I should have come to you then. Maybe we could have sorted things out and you could have gotten an annulment since your marriage was based on a lie."

She nodded against his chest. "I should have trusted in our love."

"That's all behind us. I will never give you any reason to doubt it ever again."

"Your home, your beautiful…" She was crying harder. "It's all my fault."

He held her at arm's length. "Abby, it's just a building. No one was hurt. Dad is excited about rebuilding. You heard him. That house had too many ghosts." He wiped a tear from her cheek with his thumb. "I'm just sorry for everything you've had to go through. But that, too, is behind us."

She nodded and gave him a smile through her tears. "I don't know what I would have done without you."

"You'll never have to find out. I love you."

"I love you. My heart would break when you came into the café—and when you didn't."

He smiled at this woman he'd almost lost for good as he got down on one knee.

Abby's eyes widened as he squeezed her hand and

asked, "Abby, will you marry me sometime in the future when you're a free woman?"

ABBY LOOKED DOWN at this man she'd loved for so long. He'd hung in, determined to be there for her even when she'd tried so hard to push him away. If it hadn't been for him, she knew she would be dead.

"Yes!" she said, her voice breaking. She'd never thought she'd see this day. "Oh, Ledger."

She dropped to her knees in front of him, falling into his arms.

He laughed and held her. "Don't you want to see the ring?"

She shook her head. "You can put a piece of string around my finger, for all I care. It doesn't matter. All I care about is being with you always."

"I guess I'll have to take this back," he said after pulling them both to their feet and opening the little black velvet box.

Abby gasped as she looked down at the pear-shaped diamond glittering up at her. "It's beautiful!"

"Just like you." He slipped it on her finger and then met her gaze. "I can wait as long as it takes."

"You've proven that," she said with a laugh.

"You can have any kind of wedding you want."

"I would love to marry you right now, right on this porch with your family as witnesses, if I could."

"I'll call the preacher the moment you're free—if that's what you want," he said, only half joking. "But I think we should do it up proud instead. I want you to have a wedding that you'll always remember." He looked into her eyes. "Meanwhile, I'll start building our house on the ranch. I need you to make it a home. You've seen my cabin."

She smiled. "But I'd still like to keep working at the café—at least until the baby comes."

"The baby?"

"The one you and I are going to make tonight," she said.

"Oh, *that* baby." He kissed her, knowing that things were finally as they should be. Ledger and Abby. Their marriage would be stronger because of the rough road that had gotten them here. And they would get married right here on the ranch.

But tonight they would be together again. He put his arm around her as they went inside and up the stairs to their room.

"ARE YOU ALL RIGHT?" Ledger asked late that night when he found his father standing outside in the moonlight.

"I'm fine," Travers said, wrapping an arm around his son and pulling him over next to him for a moment. "I was just thinking about when your mother and I started this ranch. We had such dreams. I think that was the problem. We didn't want this much. It kind of snowballed as the ranch became so successful. We had no idea that our luck was about to change."

"You can't blame your good fortune on what happened," he said.

"Can't I? Your mother never wanted all of this."

He heard something in his father's voice that sent his pulse pounding. "The twins?"

His father had never looked so old as he did in the moonlight. "You boys were her pride and joy. She was happy with the way things were. I was the one who wanted to give her a girl." He shook his head. "It was all too much for her."

"I'm so sorry."

Travers smiled at him. "How are you, son? I feel as if I haven't paid enough attention to the children I didn't lose."

"We're all fine."

"Your brother Cull is in love. Boone, well, who knows if he will ever find anyone as contrary as he is." He smiled when he said it. "And you and Abby?"

"We're good. We got engaged tonight."

Sadness filled his father's eyes. "Years ago when you came to me—"

"You were right. I was too young to get married."

"But not too young to lose your heart."

"No," he agreed. "I gave it away. There was no getting it back." He smiled. "I've always loved Abby. Nothing changed even when she married Wade."

"Well, that is all behind you now."

"Yes. We all have a chance for a new beginning."

His father sighed. "Let's just hope Boone finds Jesse Rose. Even if it is to know that she's alive and happy. That will be enough."

Epilogue

The sun shone in a cloudless blue sky on Abby and
Ledger's wedding day. Standing with her friends
around her, Abby felt a shiver of excitement. This
was how it was supposed to be, she thought, remembering her other wedding day.

It had been just the four of them, she and Wade,
her mother and Huck. She'd worn a pink dress with
navy flowers. It was one she'd had in her closet, one
that Wade said he liked on her. Huck had gotten her
a rose to hold as they drove to the judge's chambers
to be married.

Afterward, she and Wade had gone back to the
house he had bought. A honeymoon had been out
of the question. "Honeymoons are for people with
money to throw away since they have nothing to do
with marriage," her mother had said.

Abby remembered crying herself to sleep that
night after Wade had dropped off. He'd drunk too
much champagne, some cheap bottles that Huck had
opened on the way from the judge's chambers.

She pushed those memories away like a rainstorm moving on. The sun was out; her friends were all around her. She could feel their excitement.

"You are absolutely glowing," said Sarah, one of the young women she worked with at the café. "I always knew the two of you would get together. The way Ledger always looked at you when he came into the café, it was clear that he loved you."

"It's nice to have you back," another friend said. Abby hugged her. Wade had kept her from her friends, saying they would just put bad ideas into her head.

Ella stuck her head in the door. "You ready?" Her boss looked beautiful in a red velvet dress. It was the first time Abby had seen her in anything other than a white uniform. She'd asked Ella to give her away.

"I'm not even going to ask about your mother," Ella had said. "I'd love to give you away."

Now Abby looked down at the bouquet in her hands. She lifted the flowers and sniffed the tiny white roses. Was this really happening?

She looked up. From the huge terrace behind the new house Travers had built, she could see the Little Rockies in the distance. Horses ran across open foothills, their manes blowing behind them. The day couldn't have been more perfect.

She'd always thought of this ranch as paradise. The times she'd spent here before Ledger went away to college and she married Wade were something she'd hung on to for the past few years.

Now she looked out over the ranch realizing that in a few minutes she would be Mrs. Ledger McGraw. It felt like a fantasy, something she hadn't dared let herself believe was possible.

She thought of Ledger. He'd never lost faith. She felt tears burn her eyes.

"Can you ever forgive me?" she'd asked him that night after they'd made love.

"There is nothing to forgive, Abby. You didn't burn down the house."

"No, Wade and his father did because of me."

"Honey," he'd said, pulling her to him. "Huck Pierce has had it in for my father since they were boys. This has nothing to do with you."

"But I believed their lies. I didn't trust you and I should have."

"Oh, Abby, I knew you'd been lied to but there was nothing I could do. If I'd had my way, I would have ridden into the café and swept you up on my horse and rode out of town with you."

She smiled through her tears. "I dreamed of you doing that."

He laughed. "So did I. But I couldn't. Not until I knew you were ready to leave him. It was the hardest thing I'd ever done, waiting. But now there is nothing keeping us apart. The past is just that." He'd kissed her with such passion she'd let go of the guilt, the grief, the feeling that she could never be happy again.

With Ledger McGraw she could finally know passion, love, tenderness, and happiness.

"I'm ready," she said to Ella. "I've never been more ready."

LEDGER LOOKED UP and saw Abby as the wedding march played. She stepped out in a shaft of sunlight. She wore a string of daisies in her long hair. The dress was a pale yellow that flowed as she moved. She had never looked more beautiful.

His heart soared, making him have trouble catching his breath. He'd dreamed of this day for so long. Now it was finally happening.

"You going to be all right?" his father asked, standing next to him with Cull and Boone.

"I am now," he said.

"Didn't you ever want to give up?" Cull had asked him last night after everyone else had gone to bed. "I think I would have given up."

"You wouldn't have if it had been Nikki. Once you fall in love…nothing can change that."

"I'm happy for you, Ledger," Cull had said and slapped him on the back. "Hope you're as happy as Nikki and I are being married."

"We will be."

As he watched his soon-to-be wife walk toward him, she smiled and their gazes met. He smiled back at her. The future couldn't have looked any brighter on this beautiful Montana summer day. Some things, he thought, were definitely worth waiting for.

* * * * *

The only thing that really mattered was finding Rachel and the rest of the missing women.

Sydney's hand was already on the door handle when Tucker stopped at the gate to the Double K Ranch.

"I've got it," Tucker said. "A real cowboy never lets the bloody wounded do the work."

"More of the cowboy code?"

"If it's not, it should be."

She watched him unlatch the gate and swing it open. It was midmorning now and the sun glistened on his shirtless shoulders and chest. His muscles rippled. Bull-rider muscles, and he'd be back to that soon.

But for now he was making it clear that he was all hers. The shocker was that she was thankful to have him around.

FEARLESS GUNFIGHTER

BY
JOANNA WAYNE

First Published in Great Britain 2017
By Mills & Boon, an imprint of HarperCollins*Publishers*
1 London Bridge Street, London, SE1 9GF

© 2017 Jo Ann Vest

ISBN: 978-0-263-92914-0

46-0917

Our policy is to use papers that are natural, renewable and recyclable products and made from wood grown in sustainable forests. The logging and manufacturing processes conform to the legal environmental regulations of the country of origin.

Printed and bound in Spain
by CPI, Barcelona

Joanna Wayne began her professional writing career in 1994. Now, more than fifty published books later, Joanna has gained a worldwide following with her cutting-edge romantic suspense and Texas family series, such as Sons of Troy Ledger and Big "D" Dads. Joanna currently resides in a small community north of Houston, Texas, with her husband. You may write to Joanna at PO Box 852, Montgomery, TX 77356, USA or connect with her at www.joannawayne.com.

To my wonderful friend and neighbor Zona, the only former rocket scientist I can always count on to have an extra Diet Coke on hand. And in memory of her loving husband, Jim, who actually did help put a man on the moon. Also, a call-out to all my friends who love the rodeo and bull riders as much as I do. Happy reading, all.

Chapter One

Saturday, September 9

Rachel Maxwell opened her eyes. The world remained black. She tried to lift her arms, but blistering pain attacked with the slightest movement. She was alive. That was all she was certain of. Death couldn't hurt this bad.

Her pupils slowly adjusted to the darkness, but the hammering inside her skull was so intense her brain couldn't identify where she was or why. Random thoughts skirted her consciousness.

A faint line of brightness on the other side of the room provided the only illumination. Most likely a space beneath a door, so there must be a light on somewhere. No windows to let in a scant glow of moonlight. No sounds except her own ragged breathing.

She was on her back, stretched out, perhaps in a bed, perhaps not. Her fingers impulsively went to her face. Her cheeks felt swollen, but numb, the only part of her that didn't ache. She struggled to focus.

Fear swelled, crashing through her like ocean waves as scraps of nightmarish images crept through the shadows of her mind. The man dragging her into his truck. His creepy hands all over her.

And then the punishing blows.

Her stomach heaved as the memories grew more distinct. Not a nightmare, but horrifying reality.

She forced her body to move, slid over until her hand touched what felt like rough, splintered wood. She rolled off what must be no more than a pallet of some kind and onto the hard floor. Every joint and muscle cried out for mercy as she forced herself to scoot up on her elbows and crawl toward the light.

When she reached the door, she struggled to stand, her fingers clawing at the door frame until she could wrap them around the doorknob.

She hesitated. If the door opened, it might only lead to more hell. But the faint hint of escape held sway. She turned the knob and shoved her body against it. The door didn't budge.

She beat on the door with her fists. Agony and hopelessness took hold as she slid back to the floor. Tears filled her eyes and sobs shook her pain-racked body. She'd been imprisoned by a monster. The worst was no doubt yet to come.

Chapter Two

Tucker Lawrence braked his mud-encrusted black pickup truck in front of a small stucco-and-wood house on a quiet neighborhood street on the outskirts of Lubbock, Texas.

The home was veiled in darkness. No sounds. No sign of movement, which meant Lauren Hernandez hadn't heard the news yet. The words that would wreak havoc on her life and rip the heart from her chest.

He'd exceeded the speed limits to be the first one here, no easy feat in West Texas, where posted limits were frequently eighty miles per hour with a few stretches at eighty-five. He hadn't wanted Lauren to hear the tragic truth from a stranger.

He'd be letting Rod down if he did.

So now he'd be the one to walk up that sidewalk and ring the bell. He'd tell Lauren that the man she loved with all her heart, the father of their three young children, would never come walking through the front door again.

He wrapped his hand around the truck's door handle, but couldn't bring himself to twist it. Instead he let his head fall to the steering wheel as the heartbreaking images claimed his mind.

Six seconds into the ride on the toughest bull to come out of the chute last night. From the crack of the opening gate, Rod was doing everything right. Great technique. Terrific form. Spurring and staying in control of the bucking, twisting, spinning monster of an animal.

Two seconds to go when the bull went into a spin that threw Rod from the animal's back and drew him into the vortex. All Tucker could see from his position behind the chutes was a tangle of hooves and human body as Rod tried to free himself from impending disaster.

By the time the bull stamped off, Rod wasn't moving. He'd died two hours later from trauma to the brain.

Rod. Laughing, joking, adrenaline running high a few hours ago. Now he was gone. All because he'd lost a battle of wills with a stupid bull acting on instinct.

It wasn't wholly about the money. Nor the glory. Nor the comradery, though all played a part in the rodeo life. It was the thrill of competition, living on the edge, facing death and never believing you wouldn't walk away, sore but breathing.

Tucker opened the door and stepped out of the truck. Dread tore at his heart anew with each clap of his boots along the cement walk. He'd do what he came for, break the news to Lauren as gently as he could.

He wouldn't even try to convince her the risk had been worth it. He wasn't sure he believed that himself now. Bull riding had lost its glory when he'd watched his friend Rod take his final breath.

But where did a man go when he walked away from the only life he knew?

Chapter Three

Monday, September 18

FBI profiler and special agent Sydney Maxwell stepped
into her supervisor's office, nerves taut, geared for a
fight she'd likely lose. Still, it was worth a try. If her
worst fear was realized, she'd need all the inside information she could get.

Roland Farmer stood as she walked in and motioned
toward the seat facing his desk. He smiled. She didn't.
She liked Roland and respected his judgment, but at
this moment none of that mattered to her.

Roland sat down after her, leaned back in his leather
chair and tented his fingers. He stared for a few seconds
before speaking as if he were trying to assess her mood.

He should have no trouble doing that. It was fear,
resolve and urgency. But Roland would quickly pick
up more. He'd see her determination and hear the desperation in her voice.

"Are you all right?" he asked.

She nodded. She was far from all right, but she

couldn't lead off with that, not if she was to have a chance of influencing Roland to listen to reason.

"What's on your mind that's so important it couldn't wait?" he asked.

"I don't know if you're familiar with the situation, but three young women have gone missing over the past six months in the Texas Hill Country under bizarre circumstances. The body of another was found two days ago in a wooded area just outside the small town of Winding Creek."

"Winding Creek, Texas," Roland repeated. "Why does that ring a bell?"

"It was a big story on cable news for months about a year ago. A toddler fell and died from a head trauma while his mother was spaced out on heroin."

"Right," Roland said. "It's coming back to me. It wasn't our case but the mother had the whole town searching for the kid when she claimed he'd been kidnapped.

"A wealthy family, if I remember correctly. One of those ranchers whose cows scratch their backs on oil rigs. But back to the missing women. I take it you think this is a case for the FBI to look into?"

"I do. One of the missing women is from Shreveport, Louisiana, crosses state lines, so it meets our guidelines."

Roland scratched his chin. "You'll be pleased that the powers that be agree with you. It helped that the local Texas law authorities contacted the Bureau last night and requested their help. They are concerned they may have a serial killer on their hands even though only the one body has been found."

"How soon will we be sending an investigative team to the area?"

"I'd guess an assessment team will be in the field within the next forty-eight hours—maybe sooner. Jackson Clark in the Dallas field office will head up the investigation."

A tinge of relief only slightly eased her apprehension. "They'll need a profiler as well as several agents in order to move quickly."

"Are you volunteering to join Jackson's team?"

She nodded. "It makes sense. I went to school at University of Texas, UT, in Austin. I know my way around the area."

"I can put in your request with Jackson. He's aware of your success on the Swamp Strangler case. I'm sure he's impressed enough to consider you."

She'd only met Jackson Clark once when she'd attended a weeklong seminar he'd conducted in Quantico. He was a giant of a man, intimidating, demanding—a brilliant investigator. He was not known for being easily impressed.

There was no one she'd rather see handle this case.

Roland rolled his chair closer to the desk and drummed the eraser end of a pencil against a closed folder. "The only problem I see is that you seem to be taking this case personally, Sydney. If that has anything to do with the woman you couldn't save from the Swamp Strangler, you have to let that go and move on."

"It's not that." She couldn't lie. It was only a matter

of time before the truth would come out and she'd risk losing her job if she didn't level with Roland. "It's even more personal," she admitted.

Roland spread his hands palms down on the table. "Keep talking."

"My sister, Rachel, is missing." The words tore at her heart and her control. She blinked back a tear and stared at the toes of her black pumps.

"I'm so sorry to hear that. Is Rachel the sister who's an attorney in Houston?"

"Yes. She's my only sister." Her only family.

"When did you find out?"

"A few minutes after nine this morning. Connie Ledger, her best friend and a coworker, called when Rachel didn't show up for work this morning and couldn't be reached by phone. Connie tried Rachel's number several times but her attempts resulted in a 'call cannot be completed' message."

Roland's brows arched. "So basically, you're saying she didn't make it into work this morning. There could be a lot of explanations for that."

"And I wouldn't be here if that were the case. Rachel took a week's vacation that started ten days ago on a Friday afternoon. Apparently, no one has heard from her since then."

Roland straightened, his chin jutting as if he was just clueing in to the fact that this was serious. "And you don't know where she was vacationing or whom she was with?"

"I know where she was supposed to be. She called

me the Friday she left and said she was going to a spa resort near Austin for some R & R."

"Alone?"

"Yes, but that's not particularly unusual for Rachel. She's very independent. Her law firm had just successfully wrapped up a case that she'd worked long hours on for weeks before and during the trial. She sounded exhilarated, but exhausted."

"I assume you've contacted the resort."

"Yes. Rachel never showed up, nor did she cancel. They tried to reach her to no avail. When I call her number it just says 'party unavailable.'"

Roland pulled his lips tight across his teeth. "Is she in a relationship?"

"Not currently. She broke up with her boyfriend of four years a little over a month ago. As far as I know, she hasn't dated anyone since then."

"I'm sure you've talked to her ex."

"I called Carl this morning. So far, he hasn't called me back, but Connie reached him earlier. He wasn't aware Rachel was missing, but offered to meet Connie at Rachel's apartment to check things out."

"Did he?"

"No. Connie called the police department instead and an officer met her there. The apartment manager let them in. There was nothing amiss."

Roland leaned in close, propped his elbows and waited for Sydney to meet his scrutinizing gaze. "I know how alarming this is, but try not to jump to any frightening conclusions before you have all the facts."

"I'm not assuming anything. I'm not ruling out anything, either. Taking a vacation alone is very much like Rachel. Not returning to work on time is completely foreign to her modus operandi. She is very serious about her work. She's serious about everything."

He nodded. "Got it. You've got reason to worry. But I'll have to level with Jackson. It can get sticky working a case you're personally involved in."

"I understand, but as part of the investigation team or on my own, I have to get to Texas as soon as possible. I'm prepared to take an emergency leave if necessary and I've booked a flight to Houston that leaves here at one."

"I wouldn't expect you to do anything less." He stood and stepped around the corner of his desk. "Even if you're not officially part of the Bureau's investigation, I expect you to keep me posted. Call if there's anything we can do to help."

"Believe me, I will."

And with or without Roland's permission, she'd call on Lane Foster. Best tech geek in the business. If it was in cyberspace, he could find it. She already had a list of requests for him, some she could have done herself if she'd had the time.

Sydney stood and Roland held out his arms for a sympathetic hug that was appreciated though awkward. Roland was normally the strictly business kind of boss.

She gave a final nod, then hurried from the room, closing the door behind her. If her sister was in any kind of trouble, time was of the essence.

No one knew that better than Sydney.

Chapter Four

It was a few minutes after seven when Sydney finally made it to the front door of Rachel's condo. She'd spent most of the three hours since she'd landed renting a car, filling out a missing person's report at the downtown police precinct and being interviewed by a blunt but hopefully efficient detective. The rest of the time had been spent fighting traffic.

The detective had promised to give the case top priority though she had the distinct impression he wouldn't, at least not yet. Thankfully, she had Lane behind the scenes.

Her nerves tensed as she rummaged in her oversize travel purse for the key. Her sister had moved into the luxurious high-rise with her long-term boyfriend Carl Upton less than a year ago.

Rachel still loved the apartment but her relationship with Carl had withered and died. He'd moved out last month, and according to Rachel, they'd both moved on. He still hadn't returned her call from this morning.

Key in hand, Sydney still hesitated. It wasn't that she was afraid of what she'd find. Connie had assured her that she and the police officer had checked out every square inch of the living quarters.

It was exhaustion, fear and the dread of facing the emptiness that held Sydney back now. She forced herself to turn the key and step inside.

Sydney rolled her luggage out of the doorway and dropped her purse and her briefcase onto the small table in the entryway. The staggering sense of emptiness she'd expected didn't materialize.

Instead, the space overflowed with Rachel's aura of warmth. The scent of the many candles she'd burned whenever she was home lingered in the still air.

Everything was meticulously in order, as always. Sydney had missed out on their father's neat-freak gene but Rachel had it in spades.

Sydney walked through the living area and into the kitchen. Nothing amiss there, either. A check of the refrigerator revealed a few jars of condiments and preserves on the door shelves and very little else.

Anything that would have spoiled while she was at the resort had obviously been tossed. The kitchen trash can was also empty. Rachel was a stickler for details. And the most reliable person Sydney knew.

She would never fail to show up for work without contacting someone.

So where was she now?

Sydney's mind searched desperately as it had all day for explanations that didn't include a conclusion too horrible to imagine. Nonetheless, the serial-killer scenario skulked through her thoughts like a dark shadow, creating a biting chill that reached to the bone.

But that was the worst-case scenario. She had to move past the crippling fear and focus on even the smallest scraps of evidence that could lead her to Rachel.

Was it possible she'd had a nervous breakdown from the pressures she'd put on herself to become the youngest partner at Fitch, Fitch and Baumer?

No. She had too much grit for that. If things had gotten that bad, she'd have told the senior partners off and walked away from the job.

Had she been in a car crash that left her in a coma? Or perhaps had an accident that left her with temporary amnesia?

Only Sydney—with Lane's help—had checked every emergency room and hospital for miles around. No patients fit her description. And her car had not been located.

Sydney's cell phone rang. She checked the caller ID. Lane. She felt anxious and hopeful at the same time. God, did she need some good news.

"What do you have for me?" she asked as soon as they'd exchanged a quick hello.

"Rachel has used two credit cards since the last time she was seen by her coworkers."

"When, where and how much?"

"She used an American Express card on Saturday morning to pay for a room at a bed-and-breakfast in La Grange, Texas."

"Would that be on her route to Austin?"

"It would. I'll send you the rest of the details. Time, name of the B and B, address and phone number."

"Good. What else do you have?"

"She withdrew three hundred dollars cash from an ATM a few minutes after noon that same day in the neighboring town of Winding Creek."

Winding Creek, where the body had been found. The reference rattled her nerves so badly she had to hold on to the back of the nearest chair for support.

"Do we have a photo to prove that it was actually her who withdrew the cash?"

"Working on it," Lane said.

"Were those Rachel's only charges?"

"No. She made a purchase at Dani's Delights, also in Winding Creek, for sixty-five dollars and eighty-nine cents at two eighteen."

"What kind of store is that?"

"A bakery and coffee shop."

"Rachel barely eats. She'd have never paid that much for java and scones. I don't have a map in front of me. Is Winding Creek near Austin?"

"It's south of Austin, closer to San Antonio, but not far out of her way once she left La Grange."

"What's the draw to Winding Creek? Why would she go out of her way to visit that town?"

"I don't have the answer to that."

"We know Rachel was there a little after two on Saturday afternoon and then never made it to her scheduled destination. So somewhere between Winding Creek and the resort, Rachel's plans were ambushed."

"That's the gist of what I've found so far."

Sydney struggled to focus as the fear swelled to near suffocating. "Were you able to locate her phone?"

"Not yet. It's not putting out a signal."

It could be at the bottom of Winding Creek or perhaps hammered to smithereens like the Swamp Strangler destroyed the phones of his victims.

"Thanks for your help, Lane. At least I have a starting point."

If she left now, she could easily make it to Winding Creek tonight. If it was like most small Texas towns, the sidewalk would have already been rolled up by the time she got there, but at least she'd be there when the sun came up tomorrow morning.

Rachel could be most anywhere between here and Austin, but Winding Creek was the next stop for Sydney.

HANK'S HANGOUT WAS the only place within miles of Winding Creek that was still open at eleven thirty on Monday evening. Sydney could thank Siri for finding it.

Not that she wanted a drink or company, but it was a place to start.

She pulled into the almost-empty parking lot and got out of her car. A neon sign touted live music on the weekends and all-night happy-hour prices on Monday.

Merle Haggard's voice greeted her as she stepped inside. Faded publicity posters on the wall dated back to the era of Patsy Cline, Johnny Cash and Willie Nelson during his much-earlier years. Vintage metal plaques cautioned spurs should be removed before dancing on the bar and that horses should remain outside unless they were paying customers.

Hopefully those were in jest, though from looking

at the scratched and marred surface of the bar, it had likely seen some boot scooting.

She considered staking out a bar stool, but that would have left her with her back to the rest of the room. She wasn't sure what she was looking for exactly, but anything would be better than staring at the ceiling of the motel she'd booked when sleep would be almost impossible tonight.

Taking a seat as far away from the loud music as possible, she scanned the room. To her dismay, a lot more eyes were checking her out. Not surprising since she appeared to be the only woman in there sitting alone.

Another time that kind of attention would have made her uneasy. Tonight, her mind was occupied with far more important matters.

Sydney pulled out her cell phone and punched in her instant code for Rachel the way she'd done every hour since Connie had called her that morning. The phone rang only once before a new message started.

"The number of the party you're calling is no longer in service."

She fought back yet another wave of nauseating dread as a young waitress with half-exposed breasts and a pair of butt-hugging denim cutoffs stopped at her table. Her name tag read Betts.

Betts smiled. "The kitchen's closed for the night but the bar is serving until one. What can I get you?"

"A beer, something light." That she probably wouldn't take more than a few sips of.

"I have a good craft beer on tap that would fit that description. Want to give that a try?"

"Sure."

"You've got it. Will someone be joining you?"

Sydney shook her head and went back to scrutinizing the customers. A half dozen or so couples were two-stepping around the dance floor. A few more couples occupied tables, chatting and sipping drinks.

For most, dress was casual, jeans or shorts. Footwear was predominantly Western boots for the men and sandals for the women. No one stood out as suspicious, except for Sydney in her black slacks and tailored white shirt.

A cute cowboy in faded jeans with a nice smile ambled over to her table. "Mind if I join you and buy you a drink?"

"Sorry, but no. I was supposed to meet a friend but I think she may have already left." Sydney unzipped her purse, reached into the side pocket and pulled out a recent photo of Rachel.

She handed it to the cowboy. "Have you seen her?"

He glanced at the photo. "No, but she's a looker. I'm sure I'd remember if I'd ever seen her and I'm in here often."

He stepped back and stared critically. "You're not a cop or something, are you?"

FBI no doubt qualified as his *or something*, but she wasn't ready to reveal that to anyone in Winding Creek just yet.

"I'm not a cop."

He placed the picture on the table. "If you get bored and change your mind about wanting some company tonight, you know where to find me. I guarantee you a good time."

"I'll keep that in mind."

Betts returned with a cold mug of beer and set it and a throwaway coaster on the table next to the picture. She didn't give the photo a second glance.

Sydney decided her questions for Betts could wait. A few customers had left in the short time she'd been here. Time now would be best spent checking out the remaining customers.

Not that she held out any rational hope of just accidentally running into someone who was involved in Rachel's disappearance. Irrationally, she couldn't help but search for someone who triggered suspicion or a situation that piqued her interest.

Fifteen minutes later, she got her wish. She was watching the door when a tall cowboy who looked as if he'd been living on the streets sauntered into the bar. Tall, lean but muscular and with at least two days' growth of whiskers.

Unlike the other customers who seemed to know everyone, he didn't speak to or acknowledge any of the patrons as he walked past the bar and dropped into a chair several tables away from her.

He removed his white Western hat and ran his fingers through short, rumpled brown hair. Betts sashayed over and leaned in so close her nipples were practically looking him in the eye.

He seemed not to notice.

Sydney couldn't hear what he ordered, but Betts returned a minute later with what looked like a glass of whiskey. It was gone in two gulps.

She was still staring at him when he lifted his gaze and looked in her direction. His eyes were mesmerizing even from that distance, bronze colored in the artificial light.

She looked away and tried to make sense of what she was feeling. Her profiler instincts and training checked in. Something about him was affecting her senses. She couldn't just ignore that.

Sydney motioned to Betts.

"Ready for another beer?"

"Haven't started this one yet. I just have a question for you."

"Yeah. What?"

"See the guy sitting at the table by himself?" She nodded toward him.

"Yeah. Quite a hunk, isn't he, but not too friendly."

"So it appears. Is he a regular?"

"Nope. If he was I'd remember him, though he does look a little familiar."

"Are you sure he wasn't in here Saturday night before last?"

"Can't say. I was off that weekend. Went to my sister's wedding over in New Braunfels. I don't think he's local, though. More likely he's renting one of the fishing cabins up near the marina. Looks like a guy on a fishing vacation."

"Are there that many fish to be had from a creek?"

"Oh, yeah, and if you don't want to fish in the creek, there are lakes all around here. They have big fishing rodeos every year in the spring. Man, do we get the fishermen in here then. Tips are great."

"Just one more thing," Sydney said. She picked up the photo of Rachel and handed it to Betts. "Have you ever seen this woman before? She's about five foot six, slender, thirty-two years old?"

Betts studied the photo for a few seconds and then looked back at Sydney. "Nope. Why?"

"She's an old friend of mine who moved to this area a few years ago. I thought I'd look her up while I'm visiting the area, but I'm not sure where she lives."

"Try social media. You can find most everybody on there, even people you don't want to find."

"I'll keep that in mind."

There were fewer couples on the dance floor now and a lot more empty seats at the bar. Evidently the party ended early on Monday evenings. Sydney sipped her beer, stood and walked over to the stranger's table before he decided to cut out, as well.

"Mind if I join you?" she asked, trying for a flirty voice but likely falling short.

"You can sit. It's a waste of time. Whatever you're looking for, you're not going to find it in me."

"What if it's a good time?"

"Then you really need to look elsewhere."

"What if it's only conversation?"

"You can do better talking to yourself."

"You are scraping the bottom of the blues," she said. "Do you live in Winding Creek?"

"Nope."

"Me, either. Where do you live?"

"Wherever I kick off my boots."

Her suspicions surged. "Do you have a name, cowboy?"

"Why do you want to know?"

"If we find ourselves kicking off our boots in the same town one night, I might want to look you up."

"It's Tucker. Tucker Lawrence. But don't bother to look me up. I got nothing going on. Absolutely nothing." He pulled a ten-dollar bill from his wallet and stuck one end of it under his empty glass. "Enjoy your visit to Winding Creek."

Tucker stood, picked up his hat, tipped it and strode out of the bar the way he'd come in, looking straight ahead and not saying a word to anyone.

Sydney walked back to her table, left money for her tab and tip, and then followed Tucker Lawrence out the door. He was already in his truck and pulling away when she jumped into her car and followed him. He might not live in Winding Creek, but if not, he must be staying somewhere nearby.

There was probably at least a 99 percent chance that he was a dead end, but there was always that 1 percent. At least she'd know how to find him again if she needed to and she knew his name unless he'd lied about it.

Sydney followed Tucker down the highway a few miles before turning onto a dark country back road. He took the unfamiliar curves without lowering his speed, making it difficult for her to keep up.

He turned off onto another road, more narrow, hilly and winding than the first. She was almost up with him when she spotted the deer in her peripheral vision.

She threw on her brakes and skidded to a stop just as the animal darted onto the blacktop road. Her heart jumped from her chest at the soft thumping and the jerky movement as the car rolled to a full stop.

She sprang out of the car not thinking that a wounded animal could be dangerous until she got closer to the large buck. The stunned animal stared into her headlights accusingly for a few seconds and then raced to the other side of the road and disappeared into the woods.

No limp. No signs of significant injury. Relief rolled through her. She checked out her car. There were a few stray hairs in her left bumper, but not even a dent. Luckily, she'd seen the deer in time to prevent real damage to it or her or the rental car. She climbed back behind the wheel. Tucker Lawrence was long gone.

By the time Sydney got back to Hank's to question the owner himself, he was gone, as well. Reportedly left early on what he considered a slow night.

There was nothing left for her to do but go check into her motel room and try to get some sleep. Only how could she close her eyes not knowing what Rachel might be facing tonight?

Already missing ten days. The urgency burned like fire deep in Sydney's soul.

THE WOMAN IN Hank's had told it like it was. A man was in damn bad shape when he couldn't shake the blues enough to respond to a stunning woman who'd made the first move.

Tucker had moped around for almost a week, spend-

ing most of that time in cheap motels between here and
Lubbock though he could have afforded first class.

The cheap motels had seemed a better match for his
lower-than-a-snake's-belly mood. He'd stayed in Lubbock just long enough for Lauren's parents to make the
flight from Baton Rouge, Louisiana, to Lubbock to be
with their devastated daughter.

Lauren had taken the news of Rod's death as badly or
worse than Tucker had expected. At one point, Tucker
had to literally hold her up to keep her from hitting the
floor. Only thing that held her even halfway together
until her parents arrived was that the kids needed her.

She was a train wreck, shock and heartbreak reduc-
ing her to a state of helplessness that mimicked that of
her toddler daughter.

Tucker hadn't been in a lot better shape himself, but
watching Lauren face the tragedy rode his nerves even
harder.

Living, breathing, laughing one minute. Brain-dead
six seconds later, though Rod's body had managed to
hold on to life for two more hours.

All for what? That was the question that wouldn't
let go of Tucker.

He should be in Oklahoma this coming weekend,
competing in one of the best-paying rodeos in the September circuit. He'd started in that direction twice, had
even made it to the outskirts of Tulsa once, only to turn
around and head back to Texas.

His life was bull riding. It was all he'd ever known.
All he wanted to know. But that could have just as easily
been his skull the bull was stamping instead of Rod's.

Had watching Rod struggle for that last breath turned Tucker into a coward? Or was he finally developing some brains to go with the testosterone that usually fueled him?

He stopped in front of the gate to the Double K Ranch and left his engine running while he got out, pulled the latch and sent the gate swinging wide.

A few minutes later, he stopped a few yards down from the front of Esther Kavanaugh's sprawling ranch house. He felt years older than he had a couple of months ago when he was here for his brother Riley's wedding.

The house looked the same as it had the first time he'd wound up at Esther's door almost as done in as he felt now. That time it had been his parents who had died unexpectedly.

He started to get out of the truck but reconsidered when he realized there wasn't a light on in the house. Ranchers rose at sunrise. No use to wake everyone in the house this late.

They'd have questions. He was in no mood to answer them tonight. Morning would be soon enough to lay his problems on his two older brothers and Esther.

If anyone could help him come to grips with his twisted emotions, it would be Pierce and Riley. If anyone could figuratively give him a kick in the rear that would get him going again, it would be Esther Kavanaugh.

Come to think of it, the kick might be more than figurative if she felt like he needed it.

He shoved his seat back as far as it would go,

stretched his legs out beneath the dashboard and made himself as comfortable as he could.

Fatigue set in. His eyes grew heavy. His mind took a crazy turn. He fell asleep wondering what the woman from Hank's would have felt like in his arms if he'd asked her to dance.

Tuesday, September 19:

RACHEL SAT HUNCHED in the corner like a guilty child in time-out. The room was still dark but her eyes had adjusted enough to the scant strip of light pushing in from beneath the door that she could make her way around the shadowy environment. Additional light would have made the cramped space even more miserable.

She'd lost count of the days she'd been here. They ran together like drops of spilled coffee. The strong, black brew was delivered every morning, usually accompanied with dry, cold and frequently burned toast.

That was her only way of knowing that a new day had started. The coffee was the bright spot in the vacuous existence devoid of everything except dread and visions of escape.

As much as she craved the coffee, she never finished the full cup. Show that she enjoyed something too much and the monster would stop bringing it.

She never knew what to expect from his visits. Vile language. Threats. Painful slaps to her face or shoves that sent her crashing to the floor.

Bizarrely, there were also times that he showed a

hint of compassion. Like the second time he'd visited her in this hellhole.

She'd been starving. He'd come with a bowl of what tasted like chicken stock. Her pain had been so intense, her joints and muscles so swollen and inflamed she couldn't get the spoon to her mouth.

He'd fed her, slowly, encouraging her to swallow. When she'd had her fill, he wiped her face with a wet cloth and pushed several pills into her mouth. For the pain, he'd said. She didn't trust him, but she swallowed them anyway.

She'd fallen asleep almost instantly. When she woke, the thin sheets on the pallet that were stained with her blood had been changed and her laundered clothes were thrown over the one uncomfortable straight-back chair in the room.

There was also a small heavily stained sink and commode in the back corner, separated from the rest of the space by a dirty strip of printed cotton held by nails in the ceiling.

Who'd have ever believed she'd be thrilled for filthy facilities like that? Hot tears pushed at the backs of her eyelids. Would she ever escape the monster?

The sound of a slamming door cracked through the silence. Rachel's pulse pounded. Her body trembled.

He was coming.

She hunched farther back in the corner, hugging her arms around her knees. The doorknob turned. The door squeaked open. The pungent odor of garlic and sweat swept into the room with the monster.

She studied his face before the door closed behind

him, shutting out the extra light. He smiled as he always did, a big grin that told her just how much he was enjoying this.

He set a tray of food on the floor. "Did you miss me?" His tone was cocky and teasing, as if they were friends or lovers. Her skin crawled at the thought, though blessedly he hadn't touched her sexually—yet.

"Why are you doing this?" she asked. "Why are you keeping me here?"

"I hate coming home to an empty house after a hard day at work." He chuckled at his sick joke.

"I have money," Rachel said. "A lot of money. I can pay you whatever you want if you'll just let me go free."

"If I gave you your freedom, I'd lose mine. Besides, I already have a woman who gives me all the money I ask for."

"I can give you more. I won't go to the police. I promise. I'll stay out of your life forever and never mention this to anyone."

He chuckled again. "Now, why would I let you go now? Your ugly bruises are almost gone. It no longer makes me sick to look at you."

"You'll never get away with this."

"That's where you're wrong, sweet lady. People get away with far worse all the time. No one cares what you do as long as it doesn't affect them. Even murder gets buried in the haystack."

Eventually he'd kill her, but he'd do it slow and torturously, get his rocks off on her fear, revel in her misery as if it were a sexual adventure.

How sick would a man have to be to do that?

If Sydney were here, she'd be able to figure him out. She'd get in his mind, discover the demons that drove him. She'd find his weaknesses and use them against him.

Sydney wasn't here, but she'd know by now that Rachel hadn't come home from her vacation. She'd be certain something was terribly wrong.

She'd found the Swamp Strangler when no one else could. She'd find Cowboy Monster, too.

All Rachel had to do was stay alive and sane until she did.

Chapter Five

Esther Kavanaugh stretched and kicked off the light-weight blanket. The oppressive summer heat and humidity hadn't given in to autumn yet. It seldom did in September, but she had no complaints.

The new cooling and heating system Pierce had installed kept the house as cool and comfortable as she wanted it no matter what the temperature outside. He'd made a dozen other repairs on the old house, as well.

His brother Riley pitched in and helped, even though he was newly married as well and establishing his own ranch right down the road.

That was the kind of young men the Lawrence brothers had grown into. She was thankful for them every day and had loved all three of them since the day she first met them. Now they were literally giving her a reason to keep breathing and getting up every morning to face a new day.

Pierce had been the first to come to her rescue after her husband's death. He'd shown up one morning with his adorable five-year-old daughter, Jaci, just in the nick of time, as the saying went.

Since she was no longer able to pay her bills or take care of the Double K Ranch, he'd offered to buy the ranch from her—house, barns, livestock and all, closed on it days before foreclosure officers at the bank got a chance to get their greedy hands on everything she and Charlie had struggled all those years to build.

Selling the ranch to Pierce wasn't even like losing it. She'd likely have willed it to him anyway since he was the oldest of the brothers she considered her only family.

She'd sold it to Pierce for the price it took to keep it out of foreclosure so he could use the rest of his savings to get the ranch running efficiently again.

She hadn't asked him for a thing in return, but he'd made her a verbal promise that she'd have her house, her garden and her chickens until the day the good Lord called her home.

No reason for a paper contract when you dealt with a man who was as good as his word.

Best part of all was now she had Pierce, his wife, Grace, and Jaci making their home at the ranch. They'd moved into their own cabin two weeks ago, but they were close enough they were in and out of her house every day. And she had Riley, his wife, Dani, and her niece Constance living only a few miles away.

That only left their younger brother, Tucker, for her to worry about.

A world-class bull rider who thrived on the danger and excitement of rodeo life. Followed the circuit, constantly on the move. How was he ever going to meet the right woman when all he had time for was those buckle bunnies out looking for a good time?

He thought he was living the good life but he kept Esther busy just praying he didn't get hurt by one of those kicking, stamping, snorting bulls.

Worries or not, taking in the Lawrence brothers had been one of the smartest things she and Charlie had ever done.

Instinctively her hand reached over and touched the spot where her husband had slept beside her for most of her adult life. The familiar ache grew heavy in her chest. Lord knew she missed that man. Always would.

But lying here getting all pitiful over things she couldn't change wouldn't bring Charlie back. She threw her legs over the side of the bed and wiggled her feet into her slippers before padding to the kitchen.

By the time the coffee was ready, the sun had topped the horizon and the roosters were crowing their welcome to a new day. She filled her favorite mug with the brew, the cup Pierce's daughter, Jaci, had given her that said I "heart" Grandma.

That little girl could sure make Esther's heart smile.

Esther spooned a smidgen of sugar into her coffee. She'd have liked a heaping teaspoonful but Doc Carter kept harping on her to take it easy on her sweets.

Of course, if she listened to everything that old pill pusher said, she might as well be eating cowhide and clover.

Pierce and Riley would be up and hard at work by now—rancher's hours. But one or both would be stopping by later knowing she'd have a hearty breakfast waiting. She'd been cooking big ranch breakfasts for more than half a century and she'd be doing it as long as she was able.

Coffee in hand, she walked through the family room to the front door. Nothing like swaying in her new porch swing and sharing the first light of day with the early birds who'd be flitting around her feeders instead of out searching for worms.

She turned the key in the door only to realize she'd forgotten to lock it again. Years of habit were hard to break although Pierce cautioned her times were changing. They just changed a lot slower around the town of Winding Creek than they did in the big cities.

She opened the door and stepped outside.

"What the dickens?"

She stared at a mud-encrusted truck parked rock-throwing distance from her house. She was about to go get her shotgun and check it out when she saw a hairy-faced man step out of the truck and stretch like he was trying to get the kinks out of his muscles.

Oh m'God. It was Tucker. She set her mug on the porch railing post and raced to greet him.

He opened his arms and she threw herself into them.

"Sorry if I smell as disgusting as I feel," he said.

She stood back and took a gander at him. "You look like you've been sleeping with the cows. How long have you been in that truck?"

"A day or two."

"Without sleep. That's dangerous, Tucker. You could…"

He slipped an arm around her ample waist. "Calm down. I got plenty of sleep, just not in a bed. Lights were all out when I got here and I didn't want to wake up the whole household."

"There's no one here to wake up but me."

"Where's Pierce and his crew?"

"They moved into their own cabin two weeks ago."

"That was fast. All he had was a foundation and a shell when I was here for Riley's wedding. I figured it would be Thanksgiving before he had it livable."

"He had lots of help from Riley and the neighbors, which you'd know if you came around more often. I can't believe your brothers didn't tell me you were coming today."

"They don't know. It was a spur-of-the-moment decision. I had a few days off before I hit the next rodeo and decided to stop by for one of your famous breakfasts. Fresh yard eggs, thick slices of bacon, fluffy biscuits and homemade blackberry jam. My mouth's already watering."

"You came to the right place. First thing you need is to find a razor and I 'spect a shower wouldn't hurt none, either."

He rubbed his heavily whiskered chin. "Right on both counts." He reached back in the truck for a duffel and slung it over his shoulder.

Just having him here lit up her world, but she wasn't quite buying the spur-of-the-moment excuse. Something was bothering him. He was saying the right things, but the words didn't quite ring true. It wasn't just his haggard appearance. She could see trouble in his eyes and hear it in his voice.

She'd pry the truth out of him later. Right now she was going to do what would make them both feel good.

Feed him.

TUCKER KICKED OUT of his boots, stripped out of his clothes and stepped into the shower. Pipes creaked in the old house, but the water was hot and his cramped muscles reveled in the massaging spray.

Crazy that this place had the feel of home though he'd only lived in it for ten months. Painful months of grieving and coming to grips with an existence that would never again include his parents.

He'd been afraid, angry and, most of all, heartbroken. The Kavanaughs had helped him make it through the trauma, especially Esther. Her faith, love and compassion had been his salvation.

He didn't expect that kind of miracle this time. The answers he needed now had to come from inside himself.

By the time he'd showered, shaved and dressed in a pair of his most worn and comfortable jeans, the odors of bacon and coffee were doing a number on his stomach.

He shoved his feet into his boots and started down the hall. Laughter and familiar voices chimed in before he reached the kitchen. Esther had clearly wasted no time in spreading the news that he was here.

"What are you two freeloaders doing here?" he joked as he joined his brothers in the kitchen.

"Checking to see why you came sneaking in like a horse thief in the middle of the night," Pierce said.

"I just figured you stopped by to rub in how much money you're making working eight seconds a night," Riley said, pulling him into a playful neck hold.

"No way. I just came by for Esther's cooking."

"I can buy that," Pierce said. "Let's get to it before the biscuits get cold."

Breakfast turned into a boisterous, laid-back reunion. He needed that more than either of them would guess.

SYDNEY STARED INTO the bathroom mirror, her reflection a haunting image of the agony that had kept her awake most of the night. Her eyelids were puffy, the circles below her eyes dark.

The little sleep she'd gotten had been restless and interrupted by frightening nightmares where Rachel was crying for help or fighting for her life.

The highway noises hadn't helped. Eighteen-wheelers sounded as if they were roaring through her room. Exhaustion would work against her. She needed to be fully alert today, picking up on every clue no matter how small or how well hidden.

She knew from experience and training that it was the seemingly unimportant details that frequently made the difference.

Her sister had spent almost seventy dollars in a bakery. That couldn't have all been for coffee and sweets, but it was a large enough purchase that hopefully whoever had waited on Rachel would remember her. They might recall if she'd been alone or with someone. If she'd seemed distraught or worried. If anyone had harassed her in any way.

Reaching for her brush, Sydney ran it through her layered sandy-blond hair, attempting to force the unruly locks into place. She was only mildly successful.

Her movements on automatic, Sydney applied the basics—moisturizing sunscreen, eyeliner, mascara, a smear of gloss on her lips. The first stop of the morning would be Dani's Delights.

Her phone rang on her way to her car. She fished it from her handbag and checked the caller ID. FBI.

Was it possible Jackson Clark wanted her on the case despite her personal connection?

Her surge of optimism was quickly followed by a sharp pain to her stomach that almost doubled her over.

Please don't let this be bad news about Rachel, she prayed silently as she took the call.

"Is this Agent Sydney Maxwell?"

"Yes."

"Can you hold for a minute? Jackson Clark in the Dallas office of the Bureau would like to speak to you."

"Yes."

She held her breath the few seconds before his booming voice came through. "Thanks for holding, Sydney."

"No problem." No hint in his tone that this was a bad-news call. She breathed easier.

"I don't think we've met but I'm familiar with your work," Jackson said, "especially that amazing job you did on the Swamp Strangler case."

"Thank you. We haven't officially met," she agreed, "but I took one of your classes at Quantico."

"Sorry I don't remember. Those classes are usually

overflowing and I'm busy trying to cover more than the time allows."

"I didn't expect you to remember me."

"I hope I didn't call you at a bad time," he said, "but I just got off the phone with Roland Farmer. He mentioned your sister didn't show up at a resort near Austin a little over a week ago and hasn't been heard from since. I hope you have good news by now."

"No, sir. She's still missing and I'm extremely concerned." Panic verging on hysteria would be more accurate, but a good FBI agent never admitted panic.

"I'm really sorry to hear that," Jackson said. "I'm sure you've talked to local law enforcement."

"Yes, and checked all the hospitals as well as ran a paper trail. The last place we have any record of her whereabouts was a charge she'd made to a credit card in a bakery in Winding Creek, Texas, called Dani's Delights."

"Yes. I also have that information. Does she have relatives or friends in that area?"

"No relatives for certain and no friends that I know of."

"How much do you know about the other women who have gone missing from that area over the past six months?"

"Just the facts that are publicly available. Names. Dates of disappearance. Descriptions. That sort of thing."

"But you think Rachel could be the fourth victim of the perp or perhaps fifth if he killed the girl whose body was found Saturday."

"I think it's possible. Her disappearance fits the pattern. In any case, I think she's met with foul play and is in immediate danger."

"Based on what I've heard, I think you could be right. Bottom line, I'm heading up a team of agents to help the locals investigate."

"When will you start?"

"Is today soon enough for you?"

"Yes. We need to act fast before another body shows up. All of the women are likely in extreme danger."

"I don't know if you've heard but the body has been identified as Sara Goodwin, a sixteen-year-old runaway who was apparently living on the streets in San Antonio. She was never reported as missing, so we have little information on her except what we have from forensics."

"Which is?"

"Preliminary indications are that she was dead for up to a month before they found the body. Cause of death is believed to be by trauma to the head caused by a sharp object."

"Did they find any DNA or other evidence to help identify the perp?"

"Nothing firm at this point. The reason I called is that Roland said you were willing to be assigned to this case."

"More than willing." She needed all the information the FBI could uncover to help her find Rachel.

"In that case, welcome aboard. How soon can you get to Winding Creek, Texas?"

"I'm already here, on my way to Dani's Delights."

"Perfect."

"Then you're not worried about my extremely close relationship with one of the victims?"

"I don't give a damn about protocol when lives are involved. You're a gifted profiler. You proved that on the Swamp Strangler case."

"Thank you."

"I'm leaving my office in about thirty minutes and heading your way. I'll be meeting with Sheriff Cavazos when I get there, but after that I'd like you and the other agents to be available for a full briefing. I'll call you when I have the meeting place verified."

Off and running. She liked Jackson Clark better by the second.

"One other thing," he said. "Don't identify yourself as an FBI agent or as Rachel's sister just yet. I may want you to go undercover on this unless you've already blown that option."

"I showed Rachel's picture to a cowboy and a waitress at a local roadhouse last night and asked if they'd seen her. Neither had. I didn't mention that she was my sister or even that she was missing."

"Can't undo that. If it comes out, so be it, but don't mention Rachel again. Get out there, look over the town and the area, talk to people while we're gathering as much information as we can on the missing girls. You've got a talent for noting what most people miss. Use it."

"I'll need an identity."

"In the works. Lane will be forwarding you a driver's license and establishing the background materials. You're Syd Cotton, a freelance travel/photographer from

New York. It's your first time to this area of Texas, so naturally you'll be asking lots of questions and nosing around."

"I'll stick to that until you tell me differently."

"I'll be in touch around noon and, Sydney, glad to have you aboard. I think you'll be a real asset to our team."

As excited as she was to be on the insider team, the thought of working undercover made her uncomfortable. She'd planned to question the staff in the bakery, see what they remembered about Rachel.

Now the best she could do was look around. She didn't see how much could come of that. It was difficult to imagine a madman choosing his victims as they enjoyed their morning scones and coffee.

But then, stranger things had happened.

THE TOWN OF Winding Creek was like a movie set recreation of the Old West. The low wooden buildings had surely been standing since gambler brawls and gunslingers overflowed from the bars and into the narrow streets.

Only now the stores sold fragrant candles, silver Christmas ornaments, sequined Western shirts and stylish cowboy boots. Main Street, with its brightly painted benches, pots filled with flowers in full bloom and even a few hitching posts along the curb, was so quaint it almost seemed a facade.

A horse trailer pulled by an oversize black pickup truck squeaked to a stop at a traffic light.

Two elderly gentlemen in denim coveralls slouched

on one of the benches, their Western hats pulled low over their foreheads to block the sun. Crumbs from the giant cinnamon rolls they were devouring fell from their mouths to the front of their shirts.

Even more intriguing were the smiles and nods and the tipping of straw Stetsons from strangers. It was easy to see why Rachel had felt it worthwhile to take a side trip to Winding Creek. It was far more difficult to imagine evil lurking among the smiles and welcoming shops.

But somewhere between the bakery and the resort, something had gone terribly wrong. Sydney picked up her pace and hastened the last half block to the bakery.

Her pulse quickened as she stepped inside Dani's Delights. She was struck immediately by the shop's mouthwatering odors and glass cases filled with tempting pastries. The attractive redhead behind the counter was pouring coffee into tall white mugs as she chatted and laughed with her customers.

Sydney sidestepped the line of about a half dozen people waiting for service. The morning rush hour was apparently in full swing with at least half the square metal tables occupied. The noise level was high as the occupants communicated with not only the friends at their table but those sitting several tables away.

The small-town atmosphere registered solidly in Sydney's mind. There seemed to be few strangers in the group, but then, this was half past eight on a weekday morning. The clientele might be vastly different on a Saturday afternoon when Rachel had been here.

Sydney scanned the space. Blue painted shelves filled with inexpensive gift items lined the left wall.

A display of unique pottery pieces filled eye-catching mahogany shelves near a back staircase.

Sydney was immediately drawn to the vases, pitchers and bowls in the pottery area, as she was certain her sister would have been. Sydney picked up and checked the price on the bottom of a small but striking vase glazed in the earthy colors Rachel loved.

Ninety-five dollars. More than the amount Rachel had charged. Sydney checked additional items. There were several bowls and pots in the sixty-to seventy-dollar price range.

"They're made by a local artist."

The voice startled Sydney. She spun around and found herself looking into the expressive eyes of the redhead who'd been serving coffee. A quick glance back at the counter revealed that there was no longer a line.

"The potter does beautiful work," Sydney responded. "I have a sister who'd love the colors and designs."

"You should bring her in or take her to visit the artist's studio. She has a lot more choices than I can display. I can give you her card if you're interested."

"Yes, please do."

"Do you live around here?"

Sydney took a few seconds to compose a response that Jackson would approve. "I live in New York but I'm certainly enjoying your charming town."

"Do you have family in Winding Creek?"

"No. Actually I'm here for work."

"Now you've piqued my curiosity. What kind of work brings you to our small town?"

"I'm a freelancer. I do travel articles for a variety of

magazines and newspapers. I'm thinking this one will feature Winding Creek but include the surrounding area and some interesting anecdotes about the inhabitants."

"You'll meet no shortage of interesting people, that's for sure. Where are you staying?"

"I'm at the motel for now but I hope to find something a little roomier and with some atmosphere."

"There are several popular B and Bs in town that would fit that description."

The bell over the front door dinged as a couple of middle-aged women walked in.

"Best get back to my duties, but if you'll stop by the counter before you go, I'll give you the addresses for the B and Bs and the pottery studio."

"Thanks. I'd appreciate that. And, of course, I want to try your coffee and a pastry before I go."

"Good. I hope you become a regular while you're here."

"I'm sure I will. Do you work every day?"

"Except on rare occasions. I'm Dani, the owner and creator of all the delights. Well, except for the bread. My hubby is fast taking over in that department."

"Sounds like a keeper."

"He definitely is."

Sydney took another look around the shop and then walked to the counter and got in line behind a woman who was choosing an assortment of cupcakes. The bell over the door dinged again and this time it was two extremely good-looking cowboys who sauntered in.

Brothers, she'd bet from their strong resemblance.

One looked a bit familiar. She stared until she realized why.

He was the suspicious stranger she'd tried to follow when he'd left the bar last night.

He looked different all cleaned up, but there wasn't a doubt in her mind that it was the same man. He'd made a point of ignoring her attempts at conversation last night. He might not be that dismissive and rude since he wasn't alone.

She went for her most seductive smile and looked him in the eye as he approached the counter.

"Remember me, Tucker Lawrence?"

Chapter Six

Tucker stared for a second before nodding. "You're the woman from Hank's."

"That's right. Fancy running into you again."

"Wait, you two know each other?" the other cowboy asked.

"We exchanged howdys at Hank's last night."

"That explains why you got to the ranch so late you had to sleep in your truck."

Dani finished serving the customer and stepped from behind the counter.

"Tucker Lawrence. It's about time you paid us poor working relatives a visit." She went in for a hug before turning to Sydney. "Did I just hear that you've already met my amazing brother-in-law?"

"We ran into each other like Tucker said, except that I'm pretty sure *howdy* never came out of my mouth."

Dani laughed. "In that case, we need some real introductions before the next paying customers walk through the door."

She took Riley's arm. "This is my husband, Riley Lawrence, and his brother Tucker."

"And I'm…" Sydney hesitated, but only for a second. "I'm Syd Cotton."

"She's a freelance writer working on an article about our town. Why don't you three find a seat and I'll pour us some coffee," Dani offered.

"I never turn down coffee," Sydney said, "but I don't want to intrude on your family time."

"There will be interruptions whether you're sitting with us or not. Not that I'm complaining. No customers, no income with which to pay the bills.

"Since the guys just had breakfast at Esther's I know they can't hold another bite of food, but can I get you something to eat, Syd? Perhaps a bacon-and-egg croissant."

"They're to die for," Riley said. "You can take my word for it. I sleep with the cook."

Sydney wasn't hungry, but she needed something in her stomach or she'd risk a blistering headache by the time she met with Jackson.

"Sounds wonderful," Sydney agreed.

"I'll get the coffees and the croissant," Riley volunteered. "You two see if you can talk Tucker into staying a few days. I've got a horse barn that needs a roof, so might as well put those muscles of his to work doing something useful."

"My muscles are on break," Tucker quipped, "but my supervisory skills are available to the highest bidder."

"I'm married now," Riley said playfully. "I get supervisory services for free."

"Only when you need them," Dani chimed in as he walked away.

Tucker held their chairs while she and Dani settled into them. Once they were seated Dani reached over and touched Tucker's arm.

"You certainly generated some excitement this morning, showing up without anyone knowing you were coming. Esther was so delighted when she called to tell us, she could barely talk straight."

"Esther gets excited easily."

"She does," Dani agreed. "She's such a dear. If you have time while you're here, I'd like you to meet her, Syd. She's in her early seventies, but she's the quintessential Texas rancher's wife. Good-hearted, hard worker, and she'd do anything for you."

"I'd love to meet her."

"You know, Esther might be willing to rent you a room or two for a few days. She lives in a huge rambling house just a few miles from town on the Double K Ranch. You'd even have Tucker to show you around the ranch and give you an introduction to that lifestyle from an insider's vantage point."

"I'll be leaving tomorrow," Tucker said, putting an end to that possibility before Sydney had a chance to answer.

"Why so soon?" Dani questioned. "You just got here."

"I have obligations elsewhere."

"Esther will be crushed and Riley will be disappointed. I know he wants to personally introduce you to every new Black Angus he's purchased to start his new herd."

"That's next on today's agenda," Tucker said. "We

just drove into town to deliver some supplies he picked up for you."

"I know. He's wonderful, isn't he?"

"If you say so." Tucker stretched his long legs beneath the table.

Riley showed up with a tray of coffees and the croissant just as two middle-aged women with elaborately coiffed hair reminiscent of several decades past entered the shop.

"The Simmons sisters," Dani said. "Two caramel lattes, one with whipped cream, one without, and one chocolate-filled croissant, cut in half and placed on two saucers."

"I'll take care of them," Riley said. "Eleanor Simmons has a secret crush on me. Might as well make her day."

Dani rubbed his back. "Well, who wouldn't have a crush on you, sweetie? But I know exactly how much whipped cream she likes on her coffee, so I'll give you a hand."

They walked away, leaving Sydney and Tucker alone at the small table. A purposeful move, Sydney suspected, since for some strange reason Dani appeared to be playing matchmaker.

The feisty pastry chef would change her mind quickly about that if she realized everything Sydney had just said about herself was a lie.

Sydney sipped her coffee and considered where she should take the conversation. Sitting here in silence was getting her nowhere, but blurting out leading questions would blow her cover before she even got started.

"Did you grow up around here?" she asked.

"Lived here for the first thirteen years of my life."

"Where did you live after that?"

"Kansas."

"Do you still have family here, other than your brother, I mean?"

"I have two brothers, Pierce and Riley. They both live around here. They're the only family I've got."

"Then you're not kin to the woman Dani refers to as Esther?"

"Do you always ask so many questions?"

"I'm just basically a very curious person."

"Sorry. I'm not basically a grouch. I just have a lot on my mind. It doesn't excuse my behavior. No use taking my troubles out on you."

"Apology accepted."

She decided on a different approach. "Life in a close-knit community like Winding Creek is a novel experience for me. It seems like such a safe, friendly area."

"It is."

"But I heard on the news that three women are missing from this area of Texas."

"You got me there. I'm not good about keeping up with the news."

"Not even on social media?"

"Especially not on social media. Cowboys are men of action. We do not chat, eat quiche or drink green smoothies. That's your Texas facts of the day."

"I'll be sure it makes my journal."

By the time the Simmonses had their lattes, there

were another four people in line. Dani was on the phone. Riley was bagging pastries.

Sydney and Tucker stayed silent until both Riley and Dani rejoined them.

Dani shot Riley a conspiratorial look. "I just got off the phone with Esther Kavanaugh. I told her about you needing a place to stay for a few days and she said she'd love to have you as long as you didn't expect anything fancy."

"She hasn't even met me," Sydney said.

"I have, and she knows I'm a great judge of character. Besides, the people at a B and B would never have met you, either."

"It's a tempting offer," Sydney admitted. Exactly what she needed—an opportunity to start insinuating herself into the entwinements of the community. "I'll need to see the place before I make a decision."

"Naturally," Dani said. "Riley and Tucker can drive you out there now. You can see the house and the ranch and Esther will have a chance to meet you."

"I thought Tucker was supposed to be saying 'howdy' to a pasture full of black cows," Sydney said.

"We'll still have time for that," Riley assured her.

"I can't be gone long," Sydney said without giving the reason why.

"You won't have to. Riley will drive you back to town whenever you're ready."

Tucker didn't say a word but he did not look pleased.

Sydney turned back to Dani. "Just one question. You barely know me, so why are you going out of your way to make sure I find the perfect place to stay?"

"I have this sixth sense about people," Dani said. "I know immediately if I like them and if we'll be friends. Trust me, we will be."

Sydney understood the sixth-sense bit. Her intuition about people at first sight was frequently right on target. Right now her intuitions were making her nervous.

She had an inexplicable feeling that if she moved onto the Double K Ranch, she might be putting the three people with her at this table in danger.

But Jackson had told her to get involved. She could at least go see the accommodations.

"You've talked me into it," Sydney said. "Only I'll take my own car and follow Riley. Makes no sense for the men to have to drive me back into town."

"I'll call Esther and let her know you're on your way."

Sydney was not at all sure this was the best way to find Rachel. Perhaps working with Jackson wasn't such a good idea after all.

RILEY DROVE AT a safe speed for following. They stayed to back roads, making a couple of turns before leaving the shops and surrounding neighborhood of homes that looked as if they might date back one hundred years or more.

Sydney studied the passing scenery. Rolling hills of fenced pastureland with cattle grazing or resting beneath the shade of spreading oaks and clusters of towering pines. Ranch homes tucked behind elaborate metal gates that appeared to welcome rather than shut out visitors.

Peaceful. Pastoral. Convivial.

Had Rachel driven down this very road, alone or already in the hands of an abductor? A hunky cowboy, perhaps, who seemed exciting until he'd turned on her.

Last night she'd imagined it might be someone like Tucker, a brooding cowboy sitting alone in a noisy bar, lost in his own troubling world.

Those were not the vibes she'd picked up today. She wondered what part the change in his looks from unkempt to ruggedly virile and handsome had played in her subconscious impressions.

Lean and muscled. Dark hair. Penetrating eyes that communicated what his mouth left unsaid.

It was difficult to imagine the man was an abductor when he seemed to want nothing to do with her. Perhaps because he had a lot on his mind as he'd said. More likely she wasn't his type.

The ringing of her cell phone interrupted her thoughts. A wave of anxiety tensed her muscles. The caller's identity flashed across the car's dashboard display.

Carl Upton.

Guess he'd finally found time to call her back. "Hello, Carl."

"Glad I caught you," he said. "I just saw a news bulletin about Rachel. It asked for anyone who knows her whereabouts to contact the police at once."

"Did they show a picture?"

"Yes, but it was the one that was in the newspaper of her leaving the courthouse with the other winning attorneys last Friday. It's grainy. Hard to make out her delicate features, so I don't know how much good it's going to do."

"I'll get another one to them."

"I can't believe I'm learning about this from a news bulletin."

"You didn't. Connie Ledger called you yesterday morning."

"She said Rachel didn't show up for work that morning. I figured she just got held up in traffic."

"I left you a message to call me back. You didn't."

"I was in a meeting all day. You didn't say it was an emergency."

"Why would I even be calling you if it wasn't an emergency? What else did they say in the news bulletin."

"That it was possibly connected to some lunatic serial kidnapper."

Sydney swallowed hard. She hadn't expected the police to leak that possibility with no hard evidence to support it. "Did they say what brought them to that conclusion?"

"No, but this is starting to freak me out. You don't believe she's been kidnapped, do you?"

"I don't have any idea what's happened to her, Carl."

"C'mon, Sydney. You're FBI. You have the inside scoop. I'm just asking for a little reassurance. You don't believe she's being held captive or..." His voice trailed off.

"I don't have enough facts yet to make that call," Sydney said.

"Have you checked all the hospitals?" Carl asked. "As stressed as she was, she might have collapsed on the street somewhere."

"How would you know that Rachel was stressed? I didn't think you two were still communicating."

"We were together four years, Sydney. You can't just turn off four years of your life like it was water from a spigot."

According to Rachel, they could and had. *I've moved on* had been her exact words.

"When was the last time you talked to Rachel?" she questioned.

"The Friday she left. I called to congratulate her on her win. That was all over the news. She got an offhand mention as being part of the defense team though not the credit I'm sure she deserved."

"I talked to her that night, as well," Sydney said. "She sounded relieved to me. Exhausted but relieved."

"Well, let me know as soon as you hear something."

"Sure. Gotta go now."

Sydney flicked on her blinker and took the same left turn Riley had. She'd go through with the visit to the Double K Ranch, but she'd be counting the minutes until she met with Jackson Clark.

If nothing else, he had an identification on the murdered woman. One piece of the puzzle was better than none.

The fear hit again, knotting in her stomach and hammering at both temples as they reached the gate for the Double K Ranch.

TRAPPED IN THE DARK, dingy dungeon, with nothing new to look at, Rachel was forced to rely on her other senses to remain sane and focused. She knew the monster's footsteps, clunking as if he were stamping around in the Western boots he'd been wearing every time he'd brought her food.

She wasn't sure if he was a real cowboy or just dressed the part. She wasn't sure of anything about him except that he was mentally unstable.

Sometimes he sat down and talked to her like they were old friends, but then out of nowhere, he'd start screaming at her, almost as if there were two men living inside his head.

The dark, dank environment made her surmise she was walled off in a back corner of a basement. The early warning that he was coming was the creaking of the stairs as he descended.

But at times she heard other footsteps and voices. She feared there were other prisoners locked up in this hellhole. She'd tried calling out once, but he'd heard her and punished her with no food until she was so hungry she could barely function.

Rachel rolled off her pallet and pulled herself to a standing position. The aches were not as unbearable as they'd been when she'd first regained consciousness but movement was still painful. The good news was that she'd improved enough that while much of her body was bruised and swollen, she was almost certain there were no broken bones or serious internal injuries.

She held on to the wall as she walked barefoot on the hard cement floor. If she didn't get some exercise her cramped muscles would atrophy.

She'd only made it halfway across the narrow space when she heard the *thump-thump-thump* of approaching footsteps on the stairs. She froze in place. He was coming.

Anxiety swelled in her chest, making it difficult to breathe. She never knew what to expect from his visits and the uncertainty was just another layer of the torture.

Sometimes, he just set her food on the floor and left without even looking at her. Other times, he stared silently at her as if she were a vile, disgusting serpent that had slithered into his space.

This time it sounded as if he were dragging something down the stairs with him. She moved to the door and pressed her right ear against it.

There were shuffling noises and then what sounded like the scrape of a door being opened.

Not her door.

"Help me. Someone, please help me."

The shrill cry was followed by what sounded like something—or someone—being hurled against a wall.

Rachel's hell had apparently gained a new guest. The monster was increasing his menagerie.

Chapter Seven

If Sydney had been telling the truth about wanting to explore the charms of the Texas Hill Country for a travel article, she would have just hit a bases-loaded home run. Riley stopped his truck in front of Esther Kavanaugh's house and she pulled in behind him.

She got out and stood for a moment, absorbing the environment. Esther Kavanaugh's sprawling white clapboard house with its dark green front door and shutters blended in with the pastoral environment. It was neither imposing nor elaborate, but had that lived-in look, warm and welcoming.

A wide porch was accented by two large wooden rockers cozied up to a round wooden table. An inviting porch swing scattered with small, colorful pillows encouraged sitting and staying awhile. Pots of blooming marigolds, vinca and geraniums added color.

A hanging hummingbird feeder was getting lots of use and butterflies fluttered among the lantana that seemed to be taking over the garden that bordered the railed porch.

Both men waited until she joined them. They walked together along the slightly cracked path to the porch.

Tucker opened the unlocked door and held it for her to enter.

"Don't you think you should knock first?" Sydney asked.

"We're family," Riley said. "Well, not biologically, but in all the ways that really matter."

Sydney would have still knocked before just walking in, not that she knew anyone who left their house wide-open.

"You should caution her to leave her door locked," Sydney said. She'd seen too much violence in her job to ever be that trusting.

"She's expecting us," Riley said. "I'm surprised she wasn't on the porch waiting to greet us as much as she loves company."

"I can see how someone could get lonesome out here with no neighbors."

"She's got plenty of neighbors," Tucker said. "They're just not in hollering distance. They're there if you need them."

"Plenty of neighbors and friends," Riley added. "And she has the full lowdown on all of them. There are no secrets in a town the size of Winding Creek."

"I'll be sure to remember that."

Tucker led the way through the house, walking too fast to allow Sydney a good look at the interior. What she saw she liked.

If the comfortable furniture, hooked rugs and col-lection of framed pictures were any indication of Esther's personality, Sydney could see why Dani was so fond of her.

"You've got company, Esther." Tucker's call went unanswered.

"She's probably in the garden or down at the chicken pen," Riley said. "You two can stay out of the heat. I'll go let her know we're here."

He walked out the back door, leaving them alone together again. Tucker stood at the back window that looked out over a pumpkin patch not quite ready for harvest. Not surprisingly ignoring her.

She walked over and stood beside him, aware too quickly of his woodsy, musky scent. His virility gave him a presence that never let her forget he was all man. Strange, since she was used to a testosterone overload in her work environment.

It must be the cowboy mystique or the situation that affected her awareness of him. She had no idea what made him react so negatively toward her.

"If my staying here is going to make you uncomfortable, I'll make other plans."

He turned to face her. "Why do you think you make me uncomfortable?"

"You avoid talking to me."

"I'm not much in the mood for making small talk right now. It has nothing to do with you, so don't take it personally."

"Okay. Does that mean you don't mind my staying here?"

"Not at all. Given a choice, I can't imagine you'd

want to stay anywhere else. I guarantee you'll feel the same once you get to know Esther."

"And yet you're in a huge hurry to cut out again?"

"I have business to take care of."

His phone rang. "Excuse me," he said, answering as he walked out of the room.

"Hello, Lauren."

That was all she heard before he was out of hearing distance, but the strain in his hello was a good indication that Lauren might be part of his problem. Possibly relationship trouble. That would explain a lot.

Not that she knew a lot about that. She'd never been in a serious relationship. She'd tried to convince herself she was serious about a guy a few times, but she'd only been lying to herself.

Apparently, Rachel had done the same with Carl Upton. Gone through the motions of being in love long after she'd realized she wasn't. How else would they have moved on so quickly after living together for four years?

Tucker returned just as Esther and Riley arrived back at the kitchen. Esther's smile lit up the room the second her plump body swayed into the kitchen. She set the basket of late-summer vegetables she was carrying on the counter.

"Sorry I wasn't here when you arrived. It's so hot out there I was afraid these were going to cook on the vines instead of in the pot."

"Please don't apologize," Sydney said. "It's more like I'm busting in on you and disrupting your day."

"Land sakes, honey, I've got nothing but time these days. Even the chickens are getting tired of seeing me."

"I'm sure that's not true."

Esther rubbed the palms of her hands on her jeans and extended the right one to Sydney. "I'm Esther Kavanaugh, queen of the garden and chief cook and bottle washer."

"I'm Syd Cotton. Struggling freelancer and temporarily homeless."

"That's what Dani said. You obviously made an impression on her. She was eager to make sure you have a good stay in Winding Creek."

"For sure I'll be several pounds heavier when I leave here if I spend much time in her bakery."

"Or here," Riley said. "Wait till you taste Esther's biscuits. And her peach cobbler won first place in the town's pie and cobbler making contest last month."

"Yes, but my coconut meringue pie only came in second."

"Biased judges," Tucker teased.

"My house is nothing fancy," Esther said, "but the beds are comfortable and the water's hot. Plenty of space for privacy and spreading out. I've got rooms that have been empty so long the flowers in the wallpaper are starting to droop."

"You two seem to be hitting it off," Riley said. "Syd says she's short on time, so why don't you go ahead and show her around. Pierce needs some mechanical help with his tractor again. I'll hang around with them and watch Tucker get his hands greasy."

"There is one thing," Tucker said. "Since you're a

stranger around here, if you two do come to an agreement, Esther will need references."

"Of course." Syd Cotton would have the best. Lane would see to that.

Esther shook her head. "I'm not selling her the house, Tucker. If I want to have Syd as a houseguest, I guess that's my business."

Now she'd started a disagreement between Tucker and Esther. This wasn't going to work on any level.

"You're right," Tucker said. "Your house, your rules. As it should be."

That didn't mean he and his brothers wouldn't come nosing about to make sure she was acceptable. She'd have limited privacy and that would be a problem.

Once she got into the case, her maps and charts would have to be strung across the walls like huge banners so she could study them. It was the best way to see patterns.

Times and places where Rachel and the others were last seen. Places where they could have come in contact with the perp before the abductions. Any commonly shared links of interest among the women. An extensive study of their social-media habits.

At this point, studying the lifestyles of the missing women was all she'd have to go on.

"Let's start with the bedrooms," Esther suggested. "I have several to choose from, a few with their own bathrooms. And I do have wireless now. Pierce bought me one of those fancy tablets."

"Which she hates," Riley said.

"I don't hate it. Just don't need it. No sense in hanging your wash on someone else's line, and that's exactly what that social-media bologna feels like to me. Now, if you guys will excuse us, we've got business to take care of."

THE HOUSE WAS exactly what Sydney would have needed—if she actually was a freelance writer. The bedrooms were immaculate and, despite Esther's disclaimer, several of them were a bit fancy, at least when compared to the main living areas of the house. One of them even had sliding glass doors leading to a patio, a perfect place for morning coffee.

"This is my favorite of all the guest rooms," Esther said. "It wouldn't give you much room for work, but the room next to it has a writing desk. No reason you couldn't use both."

"I'm sure I could make that work."

Unfortunately, it didn't solve the privacy issue. On the other hand, the old locks on the door had keys in them, so she could keep that room locked at all times.

Even better, Esther was a delight to be around. Outspoken, glaringly honest, upbeat and witty. And a wealth of information about Winding Creek and the surrounding area.

They wound up the tour in the spacious family room. The grouping of pictures on the wall to the left of the stone fireplace captured her attention. Most appeared to be of Riley, Pierce and Tucker.

Sydney walked over for a closer look. She focused on one of the Lawrence brothers when they were much younger. The three of them on horseback, looking at home in their saddles.

"We have such great memories of those boys," Esther said. "They brought so much love into this house. I was proud of them then and even prouder now. They turned into such remarkable young men."

"Exactly how did they come to live with you?"

"Their parents died in a car crash. Tucker was only twelve, just a kid, but he tried so hard to hide all his fears and grief. I just wanted to hold him and let him know it was okay to grieve, but I gave him time to come to me. When he finally did, we cried buckets of tears."

"He was very lucky to have you," Sydney said. "All three of them were."

"I guess so. Social Services couldn't find any foster parents willing to take all three of them, so they were going to split them up. Charlie heard about that, and the next thing I knew, they were living with us. We had them for ten months before a biological uncle they'd never met before showed up."

"So, the boys had to go with him?"

"He had legal rights. We didn't. But Charlie hired a private detective to make sure they were being treated right. Their uncle was a good man."

"Charlie was your husband?"

"For fifty-three years. I loved that man every day of them. I still do. 'Spect I will till they lay me in the ground beside him."

"How long has he been dead—unless you'd rather not talk about it?"

"Oh, I've done plenty of talking about it. Talked so

much people around here are tired of hearing me. They think I don't know what I'm talking about, but I do."

"What don't they believe?"

"That Charlie was murdered. In his own barn. In cold blood. They think Charlie committed suicide. But I know what I know."

A chill washed over Sydney. She didn't know Charlie or anything about him, but she knew Esther was convinced he'd been murdered.

Murdered right here on this ranch in the safe little town of Winding Creek, where even Esther didn't bother with locking her door when she was home alone.

Where Rachel had last been seen. Evil didn't recognize havens.

"How long has he been dead?"

"A year and six months. I remember it like it was yesterday. I was on the porch, waiting on him to come to lunch. There was a big pot of beans on the stove. I'd cooked up some turnip greens from the garden and an iron skillet of corn bread to go with them. And sliced some sweet onions. All Charlie's favorites.

"I waited. He didn't come. He never came."

One huge tear made its way down Esther's right cheek, followed by an avalanche.

Sydney put an arm around her. Esther leaned against her and cried until the shoulder of Sydney's shirt was wet with her tears.

When the last of the sobs played out, Esther pulled away and dabbed at her eyes with her fists.

"I'm sorry. I didn't mean to go there but you're the only one who's given any indication you believe me about Charlie's being murdered. Seemed to tilt me back into the hurt."

"Was his death investigated?"

"Yes, but without my input. My heart couldn't take it when I found the body. By the time I recovered from the heart attack, Sheriff Cavazos had declared the death a suicide."

"And there was no follow-up after your complaints?"

"No. Pierce and Riley both talked to the sheriff but they say there's no evidence to support murder."

Sydney knew that wasn't proof Charlie Kavanaugh hadn't been murdered. Now another young woman had been murdered and four young women were missing in this idyllic rural community.

Coincidence?

Likely, but unusual enough she couldn't ignore it.

They said their goodbyes, forgoing any decision about Syd returning as a paying houseguest.

Sydney literally ran into Tucker as she was leaving. He was coming in the front door as she was going out and they bumped against each other. It was awkward and unnerving, though she didn't know why he had such an unexplainable effect on her. It was time to move past that.

He opened the door for her and moved back. "Sorry. I seem to say that a lot with you."

"Too much," she agreed. "How about we call a truce and start over? See if we can move this into a steadier groove."

"I'm game if you are," he said. He put out his hand. "I'm Tucker Lawrence. Nice to meet you, Syd Cotton."

Her fake name. They'd be starting over with a lie between them, but with this much at stake it couldn't be helped.

She shook his hand, aware of the calluses and the strength in his grip.

"Will you be moving in tonight?" he asked.

"I haven't made any firm decisions, but I definitely won't be leaving Winding Creek for a while."

"Then perhaps you'll let me buy you dinner tonight at the Caffe Grill. Their steaks don't come anywhere near measuring up to the ones I can grill with Kavanaugh beef. However, their burgers are still delicious and their fish tacos go down mighty easy with a beer."

He was serious about starting over. She felt guilty knowing that if she met him in town it would be all business for her. Everything would be until Rachel was safe.

She couldn't think beyond that, but she would like to pick Tucker's brain and see if he and his brothers' take on Charlie's death differed from Esther's.

"I'll be working this afternoon. It might be late before I can get away."

"That's not a problem for me. I'm a night owl myself."

"I thought cowboys got up with the sun."

"Not all of us. I'll give you my phone number. Call me if you want to get together. If you don't, no problem."

"I'll call you by seven," she said. "One way or another, I'll call and let you know."

She put his number into her phone and walked away. Doubt crept into her mind. Was she being totally honest with herself about why she wanted to see Tucker tonight?

Yes, she assured herself. This was all business as long as Rachel and the others were missing and a madman possibly held all their lives in his hands.

IT WAS A quarter past one when Sydney finally got to meet with Jackson and three of the agents she'd be working with. She resented the wasted hours in between, time that she could have been chasing down clues.

But she was not the one in control.

The meeting was in a privately owned fishing cabin overlooking Winding Creek. The creek itself was slow-moving but wide and deep enough that it looked more like a river to her.

Jackson met her at the door. He shook her hand and introduced himself. "Hope you didn't have any trouble finding this place. It's kind of hidden back in here."

"No trouble, thanks to your good directions. I did get a little worried crossing that narrow wooden bridge."

"Know what you mean, but Sheriff Cavazos assured me the bridge was safe."

"Is this his cabin?"

"Belongs to a friend of his but he said we could use it as long as we need. He would have offered us space at his office but they took in water during the spring floods and the back half of the building is undergoing major repair. Could barely hear myself think with all the racket going on."

"Other than that, how did the meeting go?" Sydney asked.

"It went well. Seems like Cavazos's got a good handle on things. At this point, he has no idea if he's dealing with one perp or more. Either way, he fears it's only a matter of time until another woman goes missing."

"Good that he realizes how urgent this is."

"No one knows that better than you. I can only imagine how difficult this is on you. If you want to back out at any time, I'll understand."

"I'm willing to see how it goes," she said. She could make no promises. Sipping coffee and talking to strangers at Dani's wasn't getting the job done.

Three male agents were sitting around a long wooden table when they joined them in the roomy kitchen. They all stood for introductions.

Allan Cullen looked to be in his midforties and explained that he'd been with the Bureau ever since he'd graduated college.

They had that in common. She was twenty-seven and had been with the FBI for six years, having graduated from UT in three.

Second guy was Tim Adams, whom she'd met before but hadn't run into in several years. She knew him better by reputation. He'd helped capture a well-known serial killer in the Northwest a few years back and had been instrumental in cracking several big cases since then.

Rene Foster was the oldest of the bunch, around fifty, she'd guess. His hair was beginning to gray. His hairline was seriously receding, but he'd managed to stay in good physical condition.

That left her. "I'm Sydney Maxwell," she said, "and thrilled to be part of this team."

"You're the profiling queen," Rene said. "You pegged the description of the Swamp Strangler with almost nothing to go on and then tracked him down. Impressed the hell out of us old-timers."

"Thank you," she said.

"Sydney's going to play a slightly different role in this investigation," Jackson said. "She's going to be officially unofficial."

"That's a new one on me," Allan said. "How does that work?"

"She'll be working in the background, using all the information you feed her and giving us the benefit of her expertise but not doing any fieldwork."

"Why is that?" Rene asked.

"Her sister is one of the missing women."

All three of the men turned to stare at Sydney in total silence. Rene finally broke the quiet. "I'm really sorry to hear about your sister. Really sorry."

The others joined in with their condolences, but their expressions revealed more than their concerns about her feelings.

"If any of you have questions about her role, we should clear that up now," Jackson said.

"I would think keeping this objective would be difficult for Sydney," Rene said.

"Sydney, do you want to answer that?" Jackson said.

"I'm not sure I'm ever totally objective when dealing with perps who are abducting and killing women. I don't expect it to affect my judgment."

Not that she could guarantee that.

"If the perp finds out you are the sister to one of his victims, wouldn't that put you in more danger?" Tim asked.

"If danger was an issue, I wouldn't work for the FBI," she assured him. That she was certain of.

"I remember an interview you gave after the Swamp Strangler case," Tim added. "You explained that seemingly casual comments made by the victims' families had given you the most insight into the mind of the killer."

"I can't deny that," she said.

"If that becomes an issue, we can always move her into the field," Jackson said.

In her mind it was already an issue. But how could she turn down access to all of the information the FBI would have at its fingertips?

"Makes sense," Allan said.

Only with everything out in the open, it made even less sense to Sydney. Being officially unofficial sounded more like being close to the loop but not really in it.

"There's bottled water and soft drinks in the fridge, some chips and other snacks on the counter," Jackson told them, "and a fresh pot of coffee. Help yourself at any time. This is going to be a long afternoon."

The guys got coffee. Sydney chose a bottle of water. Her nerves were edgy enough without adding more caffeine to her system.

"Now to get down to a few of the organizational details. This cabin will serve as my living quarters and our joint office while we do the initial investigating. We will be working closely with Sheriff Cavazos and his deputies."

"What do they have for us so far?" Rene asked.

"Computer printouts of all the missing persons reports and information on the recently identified body. Tim is going to fill you in on the latest information not included in the printouts."

Jackson sat down and Tim stood and took the lead. "The body has been identified as Sara Goodwin, a sixteen-year-old runaway last known to be living on the streets of San Antonio. Examination of her body indicated severe trauma with bruises and lacerations around the head and face. Evidence suggested she'd been killed somewhere else and her body taken to the wooded area where she'd been found. Naked. Her head shaved."

The other missing women were between the ages of twenty-two and thirty-two, Rachel being the oldest. They were all from different towns, were not believed to know one another and were all believed to have been abducted within sixty miles of the fishing cabin they occupied right now.

Sydney scribbled a few notes as she listened though she knew they would also get this information in printed form. This meeting was meant to trigger the brainstorming process. Evidence would continue to be gathered and discussed from every angle.

Sydney understood the process but hearing Rachel talked about in the abstract was making her dizzy and nauseous. Not that the others were heartless. Far from it. They just weren't talking about their own flesh and blood.

They spent the next few hours going over the next steps in the investigation process, deciding on priorities, tossing ideas back and forth like rubber balls.

She had no quarrel with Jackson's decisions and leadership, but she was beginning to feel less and less like a full member of the team.

She was on the outside because she was too closely involved. But that was exactly why she couldn't sit back for even a second. She couldn't simply digest and analyze what they shot to her.

Profiling was 10 percent knowledge and practice and 90 percent intuition, at least it was the way she went at it. First impressions, instant reactions to how and what family members and friends reported about the victims, getting a feel that something was off-kilter.

She had to be neck deep in the investigation to trust those.

It was quarter to seven before she had a chance to talk privately with Jackson.

He poured himself another cup of coffee and brought it to the small kitchen table where she was sitting. "I think we're off to a good start," he said. "I know you'll need additional information but that's coming."

"We need it like yesterday," she said.

"Always. Did you pick up anything of interest we should be looking into?"

She explained her meeting with Dani Lawrence and her visit to Esther Kavanaugh's house.

"Interesting," he commented. "Esther's name came

up in my conversation with Sheriff Cavazos this morning. He said she's a good source of information for most everything that goes on in the town and larger community."

"Did he mention that her husband died less than two years ago?"

"No, that didn't come up."

"Esther's convinced he was murdered though the death was ruled a suicide."

"Family members frequently have difficulty accepting a loved one took their own life."

She knew Jackson was right about that, yet Esther had seemed so sure and didn't seem the type who'd spare herself from the truth no matter how painful.

"Esther has offered to rent me a room, or rather, she's offered to rent Syd Cotton a room."

"Are the facilities adequate?"

"More than adequate."

"Then by all means you should take her up on that. Spend time with her. Learn all you can. The Bureau will pick up the tab. Who else lives in the house?"

"No one, although she has a guest now, a man she was foster mother to some years back." Sydney explained the connection to the Lawrence brothers.

"Sounds like you'll be in good hands at the Double K Ranch."

Being in good hands was the last thing she needed now. She had no choice but to level with Jackson Clark.

"I really appreciate the opportunity to work with you and the other members of the team and with the local authorities, but I have to turn you down."

His eyebrows arched. "You asked to be included."

"I thought it was what I wanted, but I understand now why it's a bad idea to have someone personally involved working on a case."

"Care to explain?"

"I have to do this my way, not with my hands tied by the FBI or by local law enforcement."

"Whether you're official or on your own, you can't just go out and ignore the laws," Jackson said. "Do that and you'll never work for the Bureau again."

"If that's what it takes to save my sister's life, so be it. But I do still have all the rights of a private citizen."

"You have more than that," Jackson said. "And you drive a damn hard bargain. I want you on the team. We *need* you on the team. And you need access to our resources."

"I don't want to feel like I'm an outsider looking in," she said. "Rachel's my sister. I need some autonomy."

"You've got it. Now just pretend I'm the boss and let's find this perp and put him away."

"You are the boss," she said. "And thanks."

"If you've got a few more minutes, I'd like to hear even more about your sister, Rachel, and her job as a defense attorney. I don't want to assume she's the victim of a serial abductor and overlook a murderous felon she's come across in her work."

"A very good point," she agreed. Jackson took extensive notes as they talked.

By the time Sydney checked her watch it was a half

hour past seven. She'd missed her deadline for making the call to Tucker. Probably for the best. Just the fact that she wanted to see him proved it was a bad idea.

Chapter Eight

Tucker dropped in Caffe's Bar and Grill a few minutes after six. He took a seat at the bar and ordered a draft beer. He wasn't expecting a call this early from Syd. Actually, he didn't really expect her to call at all.

Worse, he wasn't sure why he cared. Not that she wasn't gorgeous and fascinating, but he didn't know where his life was going in the immediate future. It would be the worst time ever to get involved in a new relationship.

He shifted on his stool to get a better look at the TV off to the left of the bar. The sound was muted but the captions below the picture made it clear they were talking about the body of the murdered girl found practically in the neighborhood.

Then the screen skipped to a shot of Rachel Maxwell, the San Antonio attorney last seen in Winding Creek a little over a week ago.

The peaceful, small town was grabbing headlines again. Which likely explained why the place was full on a Tuesday night. He scanned the room and figured about half of the customers were reporters.

The waitress set his beer in front of him. He took a sip and his mind went back to his own dilemma. Either show up for the competition in Tulsa next Friday or lose his momentum and reduce his chances to make it to the championship rounds in Vegas come December.

Images of Rod's head being repeatedly stamped into the hard dirt floor of the arena darted through his mind. On an incredible high one moment, the cheering crowd, the heightening danger, the thrill of winning against terrific odds.

Seconds later, it was all gone forever.

Tucker struggled to shove the thoughts out of his mind as he finished his beer. By seven o'clock the restaurant section was starting to clear out. The locals ate early.

The bar was more crowded than ever.

He checked his phone to be certain he hadn't missed Sydney's call. He hadn't. He dropped money for his drink and a generous tip on the bar and surrendered his bar stool to the next thirsty customer.

He wasn't even sure why he'd come back to Winding Creek now. He hadn't mentioned Rod's death to his brothers, and apparently, no one else had, either.

Winding Creek had its own hurricane of news hitting right now.

He ended up at Hank's, where he took the same table he'd sat at last night. The bar was jumping tonight. He glanced over to the table where Syd had been sitting last night. Three guys in dark-colored slacks and white shirts unbuttoned at the neck were sipping martinis. Almost certainly not locals.

The same waitress he'd had last night stopped by for his order. "Let's see. Jack Daniel's, wasn't it. Over ice."

"Good memory," he said. "Two shots."

"Do you remember that woman who was in here last night. Sandy-haired blonde. Sitting by herself. Really attractive. She came over and talked to you before she left."

"I remember. What about her?"

"I think she's an undercover cop. She showed me a picture of a woman and asked if I'd seen her in here."

"Had you?" Tucker asked.

"No, but I know who the woman in the picture was now. She's Rachel Maxwell, the attorney from San Antonio who they keep talking about and showing her picture on the news."

"You could be right."

"What's really scary is that if Rachel Maxwell was in here right before she disappeared, the man who kidnapped her might have been in here, too," the waitress said. "He might have abducted her from the parking lot. I mean, if that's the case, it could have just as easily been me."

He couldn't argue that. "You should have the bouncer walk you to your car tonight."

She nodded. "I'm going to do just that. Still, it's super scary."

If Betts was right, it also meant that Syd had been lying to all of them today.

His cell phone vibrated. He pulled it from his pocket and checked the caller ID.

Number Unavailable.

He took it anyway.

"Hello."

"Hi, it's Syd Cotton. I know it's late but I wanted to let you know that I didn't forget. I had to work later than expected. Is it too late to take you up on your dinner invitation?"

"Not at all." He wouldn't miss this conversation for the world.

SYDNEY FRESHENED UP as well as she could in the bathroom at the fishing cabin before driving straight to Caffe's. The area was so crowded tonight she had to park near Dani's bakery and walk around the corner to the restaurant.

As soon as she entered, she spotted Tucker seated alone at a table near the center of the large, open serving area. He waved.

Anxiety balled in her stomach. She had to face him with the truth after feeding him her fake persona. He hadn't trusted her originally; now she'd prove his suspicions true. He'd be angry, and inexplicably that bothered her far more than it should.

If he gave her the opportunity, she'd level with him. And then they'd go their separate ways likely to never see each other again.

Tucker stood and held her chair while she sat down. With Texas men, especially cowboys, manners never went out of vogue.

The waitress appeared almost immediately to take her drink order. She ordered a glass of Chardonnay. Tucker was already half through an icy mug of beer.

He picked up his menu. "Are you hungry?"

"Not particularly," she admitted. The only thing she'd eaten since the breakfast croissant at Dani's Delights was a small pack of chips she'd washed down with a diet soda hours earlier.

That didn't mean her stomach was up to digesting food.

"Can we talk before we order?" she asked.

"Sure." He stared at her, his eyes burning into hers with an intensity that made her hands grow clammy. "Why don't we start with your explaining why you lied about why you're in Winding Creek?"

He knew. She took a deep breath and exhaled slowly. "I'm sorry for the lies. They seemed necessary at the time."

"Right. What's a few lies to a reporter looking for a story?"

Now she was starting to get angry. The anger collided with all the fears, doubts and dread churning inside her. Her nerves were raw. She was losing control of the emotions she'd fought so hard to keep in check.

"I'm an FBI agent, Tucker. I was doing my job. I'll explain if you let me, or I can just go. Whichever works best for you."

"I'd love to hear what you have to say."

His tone had softened as well as his hardened expression. He must sense how frail her control was at this point. She struggled for the most concise way to respond. "I was officially working undercover for the Bureau, investigating the recent murder and the disappearance of women from this area."

"If you're undercover, why are you telling me this now? Why meet me here at all unless… Are you targeting someone in my family?"

"No. This isn't about your family, Tucker. It's about mine." Her voice shook on the admission.

He reached across the table and laid his much-larger hands on top of hers. The kindness was harder to handle than his coldness had been. Never had she felt so vulnerable.

Jumbled words began to tumble from her mouth. "My sister is missing. No one has seen her. They can't find her car. She's held prisoner. Or maybe she's dead."

She'd said it and now she felt as if someone was slashing her heart to shreds.

"Let's get out of here," Tucker said, assuming control as she was losing it.

She nodded, struggling to hold back the tears that were pressing hard against her eyelids. He left some bills on the table and took her arm, maneuvering her through the maze of tables and out the front door.

The tears began to fall as he led her to his truck and opened the passenger door for her. He hurried to the other side, slid under the wheel and snaked his arm around her.

Her head fell against his shoulders as any chance of calmness vanished. Sobs racked her body. She didn't try to fight them now. If she had, the heartbreaking emotions would have exploded inside her chest.

He was still holding her when the tears finally ran out. She pulled away, suddenly embarrassed at her show of weakness.

"Thanks for holding me somewhat together," she murmured. "I don't recall ever being such a train wreck."

"You had that one coming. My attitude certainly didn't help, either."

He started the truck engine.

"Where are we going? My car is just around the corner. I can walk to it."

"Your car is fine where it is for now. We're going to your motel to pick up your things, and then I'm taking you to the Double K Ranch. You need to unwind with some comfort food and a good, strong drink."

"I can get that back inside the Caffe's Grill."

"Too noisy. You also need a comfortable bed in a quiet environment. Have you had an hour of sound sleep since you learned about your sister?"

"Sure. Maybe two hours. But I'm not sure I'm up to going through why I'm really in town with Esther tonight."

"You won't have to. I'll take care of that."

"What makes you think she'd want me there once she finds out I'm on a mission to track a dangerous criminal?"

"You're on a mission to save your sister and others. Esther has the biggest heart in the world. She'll not only empathize, she'll do anything she can to help you." He reached for her hand and squeezed it. "So will I, Sydney. All you have to do is let me."

"You're leaving tomorrow," she reminded him.

"I've had a change of plans."

"Because you think I can't handle this alone?"

"No. You have twice the courage I do. Maybe I'll learn something from you."

She didn't believe that for a moment and it wouldn't change a thing if she did. She had to go this alone. But the meltdown had been real. She had to have at least a few hours' sleep if she was to remain sharp and focused.

Too tired to argue and not sure she wanted to, she was relieved the decision had been made for her. She'd be spending tonight on the Double K Ranch.

SYDNEY EXPLAINED THE full situation to Tucker as he drove her to the ranch. How and when she'd found out her sister was missing. How the last place Rachel had left a paper trail was in Dani's Delights. Why she'd tried to make conversation with him that first night at Hank's.

Tucker was a good listener, quick on the uptake. A nice guy from a great family. More reason why she couldn't drag Esther or any of the Lawrences into this investigation.

Whenever a killer was involved, so was danger that reached out in all directions.

By the time they were approaching the gate to the Double K Ranch, Tucker was concluding a call to Esther to let her know that Syd was with him and would be staying in one of the guest rooms tonight.

He apologized for waking her and encouraged her not to get up. They could talk in the morning.

Sydney couldn't hear the other end of the conversation, but from Tucker's responses, she'd guess that Esther was pleased.

Tucker concluded the call and stopped at the gate.

"That was easy enough," he said. "Esther has already put out clean towels and soaps and turned down the sheets in her patio suite, as she calls it."

"She still thinks I'm doing a travel article. She deserves to know the real reason I'm staying under her roof."

"No point in getting into all of that tonight. She said she'd leave it to me to show you to your room, unless we need her."

"I suppose that is better than confronting her with the details about Rachel tonight. I'm glad she doesn't feel she has to get up and welcome me."

"I suspect there's a bit of deviousness in her decision to leave us on our own."

"Esther, devious? In what way?"

"You'll figure it out. Now, how about jumping out and unlatching the gate for me? Passenger's chore. Part of the cowboy code."

"Yes, sir."

Sydney hopped out of the truck, unlatched the gate and swung it open, stepping carefully across the cattle gap. A slight breeze ruffled her hair, tossing a few strands onto her face. The air smelled of fresh-mowed hay and the honeysuckle that grew in trailing clumps across the barbwire fence.

She breathed deeply, sucking in the fragrances and the sounds that surrounded her. Katydids, the howl of coyotes off in the distance, a horse neighing.

A sudden wave of confidence swept through her. She was a trained FBI agent and woman on a mission.

There was no time for wallowing in fear or dread. All her energy had to be spent on finding Rachel.

Evidently the hard bout of sobs in Tucker's arms had functioned like a release valve, relieving the pressure before she exploded and became useless in the investigation.

Suddenly she was starving.

Tucker drove through the gate and she closed and latched it again before climbing back into the truck with new fervor.

He gunned the engine and they kicked up a cloud of dust as they raced down the dirt road to the house.

Hold on, Rachel. With a little help from Tucker Lawrence, I'm coming as fast as I can.

TUCKER TENDED THE thick slices of bacon, turning them, while Sydney sliced a juicy, ruby-red tomato, no doubt fresh from Esther's summer garden.

He checked the fridge for condiments. "Do you want anything on yours besides the BLT and mayo?"

"Just bread," she said.

"White or wheat?"

"Wheat, if Esther has it."

He checked the bread canister. "You're in luck."

Bringing her here had been the right thing to do. There had been no more tears. The speed with which she'd pulled herself together after her crying frenzy was amazing.

She was a strong woman. It would take that to be in her line of work. But now it was her sister in danger and the strain of that could take down the strongest. He'd seen what emotional strain could do to a man many times on the circuit. A divorce. A family illness. Seeing a rider sustain a serious injury.

Any distraction could rob a man of the competitive edge. A bull rider could hit bottom in a matter of weeks.

His thoughts took a downturn and once again he was back in the hospital, staring into Rod's cold, blank stare as the last of life escaped his jerking body.

Rod, like Tucker, had known his choice of career involved risk, but then, so did many other professions. Just being alive involved risk.

Sydney scooted between him and the range and speared a slice of bacon from the grease and onto a paper-towel-lined plate.

"Falling down on my job," Tucker said. "Sorry about that."

"You looked deep in thought. You're not having regrets, are you?" she asked. "You can always drive me back to the motel, just not before I devour my sandwich."

"I have a world of regrets," Tucker said, "but not about you being here."

"In that case, you keep the bacon from burning and I'll toast the bread."

"You've got a deal." He also opened a couple of beers and set them on the table. "There may be wine if you'd rather have it," he said. "I only like grapes in jelly, so I'm not sure what Esther keeps in the vino department."

"I'm not much of a drinker, but a cold beer sounds good right now."

She was halfway through her sandwich and he was

on his last bite before either of them started a new conversation.

"This may be the best sandwich I've ever had," she said.

"More likely, you were famished."

"That, too. This is the first time I've had any kind of appetite since I got the call that my sister was missing."

"And I've done nothing but eat since getting to the Double K. Cooking is one of Esther's great joys. Fortunately, she's terrific at it."

"I can tell she thinks of you and your brothers as family."

"We all three feel the same about her. She and Charlie didn't just give us a place to live when our parents died. They gave us a home."

"I felt the love in this house the first time I walked through the door."

"My brothers and I were drowning in grief when we arrived for the first time, but I'm guessing we felt the love, too. I have countless great memories from the ten months we were here."

"And now your brothers have come back here to settle down and raise a family. Do you ever think of moving here permanently?"

"I haven't really considered moving anyplace permanently."

"So you just ramble from town to town and ranch to ranch?"

He knew she was only making small talk as an escape from the horrors of her life. No reason to lie about his profession but he wasn't going to pile his problems on top of hers.

"I drive from rodeo to rodeo for most of the year," he said. "I'm on the PBR circuit."

"I have no idea what that means."

"I'm a professional bull rider."

She choked on a sip of beer. "You ride bulls for a living?"

"For a living. Such as it is."

There were years he'd struggled to come up with the entry fees. However, he had no complaints about his earnings this year.

"I've come across bull riding a few times while channel surfing," Sydney admitted. "It looks incredibly dangerous."

"Does that mean you have never been to a rodeo?"

"Afraid so."

"We'll have to change that."

She managed a smile. "Maybe we will."

He'd love to take her to a rodeo, though it might not be him atop the bull.

"Is Charlie Kavanaugh the one who got you interested in bull riding?"

"Charlie introduced my brothers and me to everything there is to know about the cowboy life. How to avoid getting kicked by your horse and to always drink upstream from the herd," he joked.

"And how to ride a bull, at age twelve?"

"The bulls were tamer than the kind of monsters I meet on the circuit, but you gotta start young if you want to be good at it."

"What else did Charlie teach you?"

"How to shoot and handle a gun. Branding. Proper care of our horse. The list goes on and on. Basically, he made damn sure we learned about honor and the cowboy code."

"What's the cowboy code?"

"Basic rules to live by."

"Such as?"

"Never leave spur marks on a horse's flesh. Women should be respected and protected. Put away your horse before you put away your dinner. There were lots of them, but the one at the top of the list was a cowboy always keeps his word."

"Charlie sounds like a man among men."

"Yep. He and Esther. Good folks. That's what they call people like that around here. Charlie was one of the best. He had friends among the richest ranchers in these parts and the poorest. Treated them all the same."

"Who is the richest rancher in this area?"

Her tone grew serious and he knew her focus had moved back to Rachel. Her mind had likely never left there.

"Dudley Miles has the most land and the most cattle. I can't vouch for his bank account, but I hear he burns dollar bills instead of wood in their five fireplaces."

She smiled and took another sip of her beer. "Not only a bull rider, but a BSer, I see."

"Burning bills is a slight exaggeration. The house with five fireplaces is fact."

"Is that the same Dudley Miles who went to prison for the death of his grandson?"

"Yeah. Were you in on that investigation?"

"No. The local police handled that, but it was on cable news 24/7 at the time. Refresh my memory. Exactly how did that go down?"

"Dudley and Millie's bratty, irresponsible daughter, Angela, had a baby. It never came out who the baby's father was, but from all accounts Dudley and Millie were raising the kid. Angela was not big on dependability."

"Spoiled?"

"Totally, and had a drug problem. One weekend Angela was home alone with the two-year-old. She overdosed on cocaine and passed out. When she came to, she found the toddler on the kitchen floor, not breathing."

"Now I remember," Sydney said. "Angela Miles got scared and dumped the kid's body in a wooded area. She told her parents and everyone else he'd been kidnapped."

"Right," Tucker said. "Then when the body was found and the kidnapping lie lost all credibility, Dudley took the blame to protect his daughter, claimed he was totally responsible."

"But now the grandfather is out of prison and Angela is serving time for neglect leading to death and lying to the authorities to cover it up."

"About time. It's a long, tragic story for another night, but there's a reason why I know so much about that event. A few months back, Dani and Riley played an unintended role in Angela's finally going to prison. In the process, Dani was almost killed. Get her to tell you that story someday."

"I will." Sydney stared at the half-empty beer bottle

she was rocking back and forth. The remaining fourth of her sandwich apparently forgotten.

"Where was the boy's body found?" she asked.

"A few miles from Dudley's spread, probably not far from where the news reporter said Sara Goodwin's body was found."

"Who owns that land?"

"An investor out of Los Angeles owns the land where Dudley's grandson was found. He's not from around here, and if I've ever heard his name, I don't remember it. I only know that much because Dudley has been trying to buy it from him for years. It borders the west side of Dudley's spread."

"Do you think he also owns the land where Sara Goodwin's body was found?"

"I'm not sure if his land extends that far west or not."

Syndey stood and carried their plates to the kitchen. "I want to see the area where both their bodies were found. Do you think you can locate those spots?"

"I can take you right to the area where Dudley's grandson's body was found. I only have a general idea of the other crime scene, but we can probably find it. I'm sure it's roped off with police tape."

Tucker wiped down the range and counter while Sydney rinsed the dishes and slid them into the dishwasher. "I'd like to be there by daybreak," she said, "before either area is barraged with reporters."

"That's manageable."

"I don't expect you to get involved, Tucker. You can drive me into town to pick up my car, and then I'll follow you to the locations. You can stay in your truck while I look around."

"What do you expect to find?"

"Whatever's there to be found."

He suspected that would be deer, rabbits and possibly a rattlesnake or two. But intensity burned in Sydney's eyes again, the urgency to find her sister riding her nerves.

"You need to get some sleep," he said. "Dawn comes early. Come on. I'll walk you back to your bedroom."

She didn't put up an argument.

She stopped at the door to the guest room and turned to look up at him. Her bluish-green eyes glowed from the emotional fire that blazed inside her. Her full sensuous mouth opened in a slight smile.

"Thanks for helping me make it through the meltdown," she whispered.

"My pleasure."

She trailed the fingers of her right hand down his arm. Her touch released a stampede of desires, all hitting him right between the thighs.

He'd never wanted to take a woman in his arms more.

He held back, knowing the timing was probably all wrong for her.

"See you at sunrise," she whispered. And then she opened her door and disappeared behind it.

"It should be light enough to see by the time we get to the first spot," Tucker said. "If not, I have a superbright flashlight in my truck bed with all my other gear."

"Which one do we hit first?" she asked.

"The spot where Dudley's grandson's body was discovered, if that works for you. We'll come to it first."

"Okay." She sipped from the travel cup filled with strong black coffee Tucker had handed her on their way to the truck.

"It may be a waste of time," she admitted. "There's no reason to think there's any connection between where Angela Miles dumped a body and the current crimes."

"For what it's worth, I concur with you on that."

"Still, it's hard to ignore the strange coincidence of two bodies from unrelated crimes turning up in such close proximity, especially on the outskirts of such a quiet, safe town like Winding Creek."

Trust your instincts. Always pay attention to anything that just doesn't feel right.

She'd learned that early in her FBI career and found it to be true more often than not.

"I know you've considered all the odds and know far more about this than I do," Tucker said. "But isn't there a strong chance that Rachel's disappearance isn't connected to any of this? A chance that she might not have been abducted at all? I mean, you read books where people have a minor stroke or fall and hit their head and get amnesia."

"Anything is possible." Her heart and her brain were convinced otherwise. Besides, the FBI would continue to explore those options for all four of the missing women.

It was the chance that Rachel and the others were in

immediate and deadly danger that drove Sydney. That wouldn't abate until the missing were found.

They drove the next few miles in silence. Tucker was still basically a stranger, but she was glad he hadn't let her talk him out of coming with her.

The blacktop road took a sharp curve and then began a steady incline. Tucker slowed and turned right onto a rutted dirt road that quickly disappeared into a heavily wooded area. The canopy of leaves and lush pine needles shut out the dawn's light, turning everything the dark purplish color of an ugly bruise.

The road began to disintegrate, becoming more rock than dirt. Eventually, it vanished completely in front of a crumbling chimney where a house had once been. .

"This is the end of the line," Tucker said as he killed the engine. "The body was found somewhere between here and the waterfall."

Sydney didn't see a waterfall, but as she climbed out of the truck she heard the splash and gurgle of moving water.

Tucker retrieved the flashlight and a machete from the back of the truck. He handed her the flashlight. "I'll walk ahead of you and try to clear you a path through the worst of the undergrowth."

"Is it this dense all the way to the waterfall?"

"No, but don't expect too much from the waterfall. It may not be much more than a trickle at the end of a scorching summer."

"I didn't realize you were that familiar with the area."

"I'm not, but it's starting to come back to me now

that we're here. Charlie brought us deer hunting in here a couple of times. Pierce got his first buck here."

"Shooting and riding bulls as a boy of twelve. I'm starting to see how you chose such a dangerous way to make a living."

She aimed the flashlight's beam at the ground in front of her as she maneuvered over and between clumps of prickly brush, snakelike vines and fallen limbs. Without Tucker wielding the machete, the old path would be almost impossible to navigate.

She felt something crawling on her arm. She shivered and looked down at the biggest spider she'd ever seen. Her heart seemed to stop as she knocked the dark, hairy monster off her arm and into the thick brush at her feet.

She hadn't expected anything this creepy. The howling of coyotes and the husky croaks of bullfrogs provided the soundtrack for what felt like a scene from a B-rated horror movie.

Yet a young mother had chosen this spot to dump the body of her toddler son, and then let her own father go to jail for her callous crime.

When Rachel was safe again, Sydney would make a trip to the prison to visit Angela Miles. She'd be an interesting and no doubt informative case study for profiling.

The trees thinned out and the sky lightened to a pale gray. Sydney turned off the flashlight and picked up her pace.

"Watch for loose rocks," Tucker cautioned. "There's a sharp drop-off just before you reach the waterfall."

"I will."

She reached the falls before him. She looked back to see what was keeping him.

He held up the machete. A headless rattlesnake dangled from the blade. "Watch out for these, too," he said. "Fortunately, my machete found it before it found me."

She heeded his advice, holding tight to the slim trunk of a leaning mulberry tree as she stretched over for a better look at the tumbling stream of water and the rocky area just beyond it where the body had been found.

Two deer stepped out of the trees and into the pool beneath the waterfall for a cool drink. And just past them at the edge of the woods was what looked like a scrap of red cloth, possibly an item of clothing.

"Tucker, come take a look at this."

"Be right there."

She let go of the tree trunk and took a step toward the edge. The ground shifted, tipping her off balance. She grabbed for a limb that was just above her head.

Her hand scraped the spiny wood as the branch splintered and split. She fell on her backside and went sliding across the surface of the hard, angled rocks, finally landing in the mud at the edge of the falling water.

Blood dripped from her skinned elbows and her back felt like she'd been sleeping on hot coals.

But from this vantage point she saw far more than the red scrap.

Her blood ran icy cold.

Chapter Nine

Tucker half crawled, half tumbled down the rocky ravine in his haste to get to Sydney. He'd seen the large, angular stone shift. In a split second he'd dropped the machete and reached for Sydney, but it had been too late.

His hand missed her arm and the soft fabric of her blouse slipped right through his fingers.

By the time he reached her, blood dripped from her elbows and her left hand.

He stooped down beside her and turned her hand palm up so he could judge the depth of the scratches. "We have to get you to a doctor."

"I don't need a doctor. Help me up," she ordered.

"You may have broken a bone or two."

"I don't think so. My rear hurts more than anything else. Just give me a hand or move so I can get up by myself."

He ignored her demands and instead ripped off his shirt. He grabbed a bottle of water from his backpack and poured about half of it over his shirt.

"Let me have that hand again. I can at least try to

clean the worst of the wounds. You've got blood running down your arm from cuts on your elbows, too." She finally cooperated and he slowly poured the remaining water over her hand and arms.

Blood still oozed from a couple of jagged scratches on her hand. He fashioned a makeshift bandage with his shirt and wrapped it around her hand, leaving the thumb free.

"Thanks," she murmured.

"This doesn't eliminate seeing a doctor."

"All it needs is some antibiotic ointment. We're staying on a ranch. Esther is bound to have a first-aid kit around there somewhere."

"You may need a tetanus shot."

"I had a booster two months ago. The FBI sees to things like that." She scooted away from him and tried to get up without putting pressure on her hand.

He took her right hand and helped her to a standing position. "What was it you wanted me to see before you fell?"

She brushed off the seat of her jeans and pointed to a scrap of red that seemed to be caught in the low branches of a persimmon tree.

"Stay here, and I'll go check it out," he said.

Unsurprisingly, she didn't stay but followed him as he splashed through the shallow water to the other side of the ravine.

She pulled the material from the tree and held it up in front of her. "It's a women's blouse. It hasn't been here long enough to turn black from the elements."

"It's summer," he reminded her. "It could have been

left here by teenagers having a little summer fun beneath the falls."

"It could be," she said. She folded it and handed it to him. "Put it in your backpack for now in case the blood seeps through my fancy bandage."

"Are you ready to tackle the trek back to the truck?"

"Not yet."

She scanned the area around the falls and then started walking away from the side where she'd fallen. The gorge was not as steep on that side but the trees were and the underbrush was thicker. Worse, his machete was at the top of the other side of the ravine.

She swatted at a mosquito around her face.

"As soon as we leave this clearing the mosquitoes will get much worse," he cautioned.

"Mosquitoes, spiders, snakes. I can't believe anyone would come here for afternoon delight."

She stamped a few feet farther. He hurried to catch up with her before she disappeared into the thick foliage.

"Oh, no!"

He raced to her side. "What is it?"

She pointed to a spot a few feet in front of her. "What does that look like to you?"

"The first rays of morning sun glinting off fancy taillights." He swallowed the curse that flew to mind. "How in the hell did someone get a vehicle down here?"

"And why?" Sydney added.

It was easy to tell it was dread and not curiosity that edged her voice.

The incline grew steeper and he took her arm to

steady her as they approached the wreckage. The body of the car was almost invisible until they were close enough to touch it, hidden by the branches and the trunks of young trees it had knocked down as it plummeted.

He lifted a large limb off the roof. "A late-model SUV," he noted.

She trembled. "That's Rachel's car."

"Are you sure?"

She didn't answer but pushed past him and tried to open the dented driver's-side door. When it wouldn't budge, she peered through the dirty windows.

"I must have dropped the flashlight when I fell. I need it. I can't see inside."

"Let me try the door," he said.

She moved away. He tried the back door and it opened easily.

"Careful what you touch," she cautioned. "There could be fingerprints inside where it's dry and not exposed to the elements."

As apprehensive as she was, she was on top of her game. Tucker took a quick look inside.

No body. No obvious bloodstains. He breathed easier and stepped back while she crawled inside the back seat. When she got out, she leaned against the car with her good hand and took a few deep breaths before speaking.

"Do you have your phone with you?"

He reached in his pocket and handed it to her.

Seconds later, she had Jackson Clark on the phone and she was back in control. Nothing wimpy about FBI agent Sydney Maxwell.

"As soon as I get cleaned up and properly bandaged, I want to pay a visit to Dudley Miles," Sydney announced.

"Fine by me. I like the man, but I don't see what you're going to get out of it."

"Hopefully the same kind of confidence in him you have. I'm not accusing him of anything, but the strange coincidences are becoming a frightening pattern. How do you explain Rachel's wrecked car being found in almost the same spot as his grandson's body was found?"

"Dudley had nothing to do with his grandson's death or the disposal of his body. The woman who did is in prison."

True, if all the suppositions in that case were true. But what if they weren't? What if someone else was involved? What if the guilty person had never been arrested or even accused?

She and Tucker had spent an hour at the waterfall discussing the case with Jackson, Agent Rene and Sheriff Cavazos. Jackson had called Cavazos in an effort to keep local law enforcement involved. Cavazos was as insistent as Tucker that Dudley Miles was spotlessly clean.

Her conscience wouldn't let it go.

"It's also urgent I talk to Dani," Sydney said. "She may have been the last person to see Rachel before she disappeared."

"What about stopping at an emergency care clinic? There's one on the highway just past where they put in the new dollar store."

"I'm not running to a clinic for a few scratches. Like I said, I'm sure Esther has first-aid supplies. You'd have to living on a ranch, wouldn't you?"

"Yep. And if that doesn't do the trick, I can call a vet. They make house calls."

"Ha. Ha."

She shifted in the seat and put her hand to the small of her back.

"You must be sore after that fall," Tucker said.

"Nothing an aspirin or two can't fix."

And a week in a back brace. But she'd worked hurt plenty of times when there was not nearly as much at stake.

Her next hurdle would be explaining everything to Esther. Not only was Sydney not a sweet and harmless travel writer, she might bleed all over her sheets.

All small stuff. The only thing that really mattered was finding Rachel and the rest of the missing. Her hand was already on the door handle when Tucker stopped at the gate to the Double K Ranch.

"I've got it," Tucker said. "A real cowboy never lets the bloody wounded do the work."

"More of the cowboy code?"

"If it's not, it should be."

She watched him unlatch the gate and swing it open. It was midmorning now and the sun glistened on his shirtless shoulders and chest. His muscles rippled. Bull-rider muscles, and he'd be back to that soon.

But for now, he was making it clear he was all hers. The shocker was that she was thankful to have him around.

TUCKER PLOPPED DOWN on the top slat of the corral and hooked the heels of his boots on the bottom slat. He'd left Sydney back at the house getting her wounds cared for by Esther and Pierce's wife, Grace. No doubt, she was going through the same grilling he'd just endured with his brothers.

"Now you know as much as I do about the investigation," Tucker said.

Pierce pushed his straw work hat to the back of his head. "Sydney sounds like one smart, tough woman, but this has got to be really rough on her. Glad she finally confided in you."

"Amazing that she and Dani connected so fast," Riley said, "or was that more than coincidental?"

"The scant paper trail Sydney has on Rachel indicates that that the bakery is the last place she used her credit card."

"Does Dani know that?" Riley asked.

"Not yet. She will soon. We're heading that way soon. Sydney is hoping Dani remembers her and might know if she was alone or with someone. Any clue would be helpful."

"Film from the security camera might show that, even if Dani doesn't remember," Riley said.

"This is really starting to hit close to home," Pierce said. "I'm not sure I want Grace running the roads by herself or just with Jaci until the freaky lunatic is caught."

"And I may hang around the bakery a little later in the morning," Riley said. "Keep my eye on things until the customers start piling in and Constance leaves for school."

Tucker jumped off the fence, his boots digging into

the carpet of grass as he landed. "It's guaranteed I won't be telling Sydney what she can and can't do."

"She's FBI," Riley said. "What do you expect?"

"Exactly what is going on between you two?" Pierce asked.

"Basically, what I've already told you. I forced my way into her life and she hasn't kicked me out yet."

"It's a little more than that," Pierce said. "You arrived here in a serious funk."

"Was it that obvious?"

Riley socked him in the arm. "Was it ever, bro? You weren't yourself at all. We figured it had to be woman problems to bring you that low."

He'd come here for his brothers' feedback on the indecision that plagued him. Now was probably as good a time as any to talk about it.

"You remember me talking about my rodeo buddy Rod the last time I was here?"

"Yeah," Pierce said. "You said he was one of the best bull riders on the circuit this year and a really great guy. Said he was giving you your roughest competition this year."

"He was. He died last week."

Riley dropped his favorite curse word when not in mixed company. "Was it work related?"

"Yeah. Six seconds into the ride on the meanest and biggest bull in the night's contest. His form was perfect. The crowd was on its feet. This might have been the closest any of them had ever come to seeing a perfect score."

"Man, that had to be tough to watch."

"The worst."

"At least he died doing something he loved," Riley said.

"He died leaving a wife with no husband and three young children with no father. After watching Rod take his last breath, I had to drive to their house in Lubbock and give them the tragic news."

"That explains and justifies the funk you were in," Pierce said. "Wouldn't be much of a man if that didn't get to you."

"Then I must be a hell of a man."

Riley put his arm around Tucker's shoulders. "I've never doubted that."

"Watching Rod die has made me rethink a lot of my life choices."

"Does that mean you're thinking of giving up bull riding?" Pierce asked.

"I'm considering it. I haven't made a decision."

"That's a big one," Riley said. "I was worried if I could give up my rambling ways when I met Dani. It didn't take her long to convince me she was the one thing I'd always been searching for."

"If I had a woman like Dani who loved me, I might feel the same." Or maybe not. Bull riding had been his life for years.

"You might have to give yourself a chance to fall in love," Pierce said.

"Maybe I will." He couldn't deny that Sydney was getting to him, but she was firmly planted in her career. He couldn't see her giving that up to follow a bull rider from town to town.

"I better get back to the house," he said. "Sydney will be ready to roll again. It almost killed her to take time out from the investigation long enough to change out of her bloody clothes."

"Understandable and admirable," Pierce said. He clapped Tucker between the shoulders—a man's hug when they were afraid a real hug would let too many of those pesky emotions escape.

"I'm available to talk about anything if you want to toss possibilities around. I can't tell you what to do, though. That has to come from inside yourself."

"Same here," Pierce said. "Whatever you decide, I'll back you fully and put you to work on the ranch while you're deciding what to do next."

Both were as supportive as Tucker had expected. He was as undecided as ever, but being with Sydney and seeing what she was up against had left him with no time or energy for courting the blues.

"We'll talk more later," he said, turning to go.

"Do you mind if I call Dani and give her a heads-up on why Sydney is really in town?"

"No. It's out in the open now. If you miss anything, Sydney will fill her in when we get there."

"Be careful out there, bro," Pierce called.

That was number two on his agenda. Number one was keeping Sydney safe.

THE BELL ABOVE the door tinkled as Sydney and Tucker stepped inside Dani's Delights. The place was far more crowded than it had been yesterday. Tables had been pushed together on the left side of the room, accommodating at least a dozen women.

Most looked to be in their fifties and sixties and they were all talking and laughing at once and sipping whipped-cream-topped iced lattes. The rest of the crowd was a mixed bag of people—all ages, both genders, most in shorts or jeans, a few in suits.

When Dani spotted Sydney and Tucker, she untied her ruffled white apron and waved them to the counter where she was finishing up with a customer.

"I have everything you ordered, Mrs. Miles, and tell your husband I put a complimentary oatmeal-raisin cookie right out of the oven in there for him."

"Thank you. That's Dudley's favorite."

"I know. He checks in to see if I have them a couple of times a week."

Sydney stared at the rail-thin woman Dani was talking to. That had to be Angela Miles's mother. Only with her pale complexion and the deep wrinkles around her mouth and eyes, she looked years older than Sydney would have expected.

She took her package of pastries from Dani and walked out of the shop looking straight ahead as if avoiding eye contact with anyone in the crowded shop.

Sydney couldn't help but feel sorry for her. It surely broke her heart to lose her grandson so tragically, and then lose her daughter to the bars of a prison cell.

Tucker sidled up to the counter. "Hate to interrupt business, Dani, but can you spare a few minutes to talk? It's important."

"I'll make time. Tammy can handle things for me."

The young woman who was boxing giant cinnamon rolls dripping with creamy frosting assured her she could.

"We can talk in my office behind the kitchen," Dani said. "It's small but a little quieter than it is in here. Plus we'll have some privacy."

"Perfect." Sydney joined Dani behind the counter. It was obvious Dani had talked to Riley, which meant one less painful explanation Sydney would have to give concerning Rachel and the investigation.

They followed Dani through the spacious kitchen with its giant ovens and long, wide counters for rolling out dough and mixing batter. The equipment and tools of the trade that were in plain sight were all shiny and sparkling clean.

Dani perched on the corner of her desk. Sydney and Tucker took the two metal folding chairs.

"Can I get you guys some coffee? Or food?"

"We've been at Esther's," Sydney said.

Dani laughed. "Enough said. No one ever leaves there hungry."

"I suppose Riley told you my real name is Sydney Maxwell."

"He did. In fact, he did a good job of catching me up on the situation."

"I should apologize for lying to you when we met."

"No need to apologize. You had good reason. Besides, the instant bond I felt with you had nothing to do with your name. I still expect us to be friends."

"I appreciate that."

Dani stared at Sydney's bandaged hand. "Could I get

you some ice or lotion or some antibiotic cream before we get started? Or something for pain? Riley said you took a bad fall this morning."

"My elbows got the worst of it. Hence the long-sleeved blouse in ninety-five-degree weather. But none of the cuts are deep. No stitches needed and Esther and Grace gave me the full first-aid treatment. I'm fine."

"If you change your mind, I have some Tylenol. I can't tell you how sorry I am to hear about your sister. I became positively ill when Riley told me."

"It's not been easy," Sydney admitted. "I just have to think positive and stay focused on finding her. That's the reason I stopped by your bakery yesterday."

"So," Riley said, "do you have a photo?"

"I do." Sydney slipped Rachel's photograph from the inside pocket of her handbag and handed it to Dani. "Do you remember seeing her? She was in here on Saturday, September 14, around two fifteen."

Dani scrutinized the picture for several seconds before responding. "She was in here. I remember because she was interested in the same pottery collection you asked about. She bought one of my favorite pieces, an odd-shaped bowl in a terra-cotta glaze."

"Was she with anyone?"

"Not that I remember, but I can't say for sure. I don't even remember if she sat down or if she picked up something to go. We were particularly busy that Saturday. Several of the stores had sidewalk sales to get rid of their summer items."

"Do you remember if Rachel mentioned anything about going to a resort in Austin?"

Dani shook her head. "I'm drawing a blank. If she mentioned it, I don't remember."

Frustration swelled again. Sydney couldn't bear another dead end.

"What about film from your security camera?" Tucker asked. "How long do you keep that?"

"At least a month or two."

"Then you must have it for September 14."

"I had it until this morning when Sheriff Cavazos came in and asked for all my tapes. I gave them to him. I had no idea at the time that you needed them."

"Not a problem," Sydney assured her. "If there's anything of use in them, I'm sure I can get access." Through proper channels or around them.

"If it matters, he didn't just request mine," Dani said. "One of the women who works part-time at the candle shop came in for a scone right after the sheriff left here and she said he'd requested theirs, as well."

"Even better. Did Riley mention that the fall that led to my discovering Rachel's car this morning was in the same area where Angela Miles's son's body was found?"

"He did. That's bizarre but I can't imagine the two can be connected in any way. You know, I moved here and bought this bakery to have a safe place to raise my niece. I'm beginning to have doubts about the safety factor."

"Was that Angela Miles's mother you were waiting on when we came in?"

"Yes, it was. Poor woman. She's become a shadow of the woman she was before her grandson died. She used to come in and talk to everybody. Now she barely speaks to me."

"I'm sure she's heartbroken," Sydney said.

"I'm sure, but her daughter is a very sick young woman. I just hope she's finally getting the psychiatric help she needs."

Sydney and Tucker had thanked Dani for her help and had just stepped out of the shop and back into the blistering sun when Sydney's phone rang.

"Hello, Jackson."

"I'm glad I caught you," he said. "Are you by yourself?"

"No. Tucker is with me."

"Glad to hear that. I have bad news."

Chapter Ten

Sydney's fingers tightened around the phone, bracing herself as best she could for Jackson's news.

"What is it?"

"We weren't able to get any usable fingerprints from the exterior of Rachel's car."

Sydney exhaled sharply, releasing the breath she hadn't realized she was holding. A fingerprint report was the least of what she'd been dreading, but she knew from his tone there was more.

"And inside the SUV?" she asked.

"We retrieved several different fingerprints. I'm sorry to have to hit you with this, but the prints of one of the missing women was found inside the car."

The ray of hope she'd held on to that Rachel might not be one of the serial abductor's victims disintegrated. She was disheartened, but not surprised. On some level of consciousness, she'd known that all along.

"Whose prints were they?"

"Michelle Dickens."

Sydney had always had a keen short-term memory for relevant facts. She reviewed in her mind what she'd learned about Michelle at her meeting with Jackson's team yesterday. Age twenty-five. Disappeared after leaving a friend's parent's vacation cabin near Winding Creek.

Michelle had spent two days there reuniting with a group of sorority friends from University of Texas. Attractive. Brunette as all the missing women were. Had no police record. Currently working as a petroleum engineer.

"Are you okay?" Jackson asked.

"I'm getting there. I was just trying to remember what I know about Michelle."

"We have more information on her today than yesterday—on Michelle and the others. What's the chance you can come by the cabin today?"

"Chances are always excellent if you have relevant facts. What time?"

"I'm available now, but I can make an appointment for later if that suits your schedule better."

"Now works."

"Will you be bringing Tucker Lawrence with you?"

"Will it be a problem if I do?"

"No. In fact, I'd welcome him."

She hadn't been expecting that response though the two men had seemed to bond at the wrecked car scene that morning.

"Any particular reason why you want him there?" she asked.

"He knows his way around the back roads and the rural areas and he has excellent connections in his brothers, who live here, his sister-in-law who owns the bakery and Esther Kavanaugh, who, according to Sheriff Cavazos, knows everyone around these parts. And except for a few speeding tickets, he's whistle clean. And I'm assuming he told you he's a championship bull rider. How's that for tough?"

Tough and thoughtful. Those two didn't always come in the same package. "Sounds like you ran a background check on him?"

"Of course. Don't worry. He checked out. Plus we won't be discussing anything that's classified. Did Dani remember seeing Rachel in the bakery?"

"She did, even remembered selling her a piece of pottery. She didn't remember if Rachel had been alone."

"I expect that information to be forthcoming. We'll talk more when you get here."

"Thanks for calling," she said. "One or both of us will see you in a few minutes."

"Who are we going to see in a few minutes?" Tucker asked when she broke the connection.

"Jackson Clark, but you don't have to go. I can handle this and I'm sure your brothers and Esther would enjoy some time with you."

"There you go, trying to get rid of me again."

"You're a glutton for punishment."

"Right. Ask any bull who's ever sent me flying into the dirt. You mentioned fingerprints and someone named Michelle. What's that about?"

"Michelle Dickens. She's one of the women who went missing a couple of months before Rachel did. They found her fingerprints inside Rachel's car."

"Son of a bitch." Tucker took her arm. "Excuse the

outburst, but I know that finding out for certain she was abducted wasn't the news you were hoping for. Not the news I was hoping for, either. But in a way it's good news. It means the abductor kept Michelle alive for at least two months."

"Yes, but living under the control of a madman."

Tucker put an arm around her waist and started to his truck.

She stopped walking. "I need to take my own car this time before it gets labeled abandoned and towed to the pound."

"I'm not even sure they have a lot for impounding cars in Winding Creek. But even if they do, you don't have to worry. By nightfall, everyone in Winding Creek will know it's your car if they don't know it already."

"I don't see how."

"The small-town grapevine. Rumors fly at the speed of light. But if you want to take your car, I'll leave my truck here and ride with you."

"I find it hard to believe you're volunteering to become even further involved with me in this investigation."

"I'll be as involved as you'll let me be."

She should ask why, but she wasn't certain she wanted to go there again just yet. His answer might be as ambiguous as hers would be if asked why she liked having him around. All she knew was it felt right and that was good enough for now.

"We can go in your truck," she said. "My rental car is not a four-wheel drive made for back roads like the one to Jackson's cabin or whatever shortcuts you may take to Dudley Miles's ranch."

"Are you certain that's how you want to spend a chunk of your afternoon? Dudley's one of the good guys. Always has been."

"That doesn't mean all his friends, employees and acquaintances are. He may know something and not even realize he knows it."

"Do you want me to call and make sure he'll be home?"

"No. I prefer the element of surprise."

"Your game. Your call."

"Then let's go," she said. Her game was deadly, and the clock might be running out.

Jackson was the only one present when Sydney and Tucker arrived at the cabin. He wasted no time in getting down to business, leading them back to the kitchen after a quick greeting.

Sydney knew he was well aware that finding Michelle Dickens's fingerprints in Rachel's car had shot the urgency level to the moon. The women might all be saved if they could track down the kidnapper fast enough. Every second counted.

"I see your left hand is bandaged. Did you get those wounds on your elbow taken care of, too?" Jackson asked.

"They're fine. Just scratches. Esther and Dani's sister-in-law, Grace, took good care of me."

"Nice to have in-house medical care, but you need to watch for infection."

"I will. No time for complications."

"Soft drinks in the fridge, coffee in the pot," Jackson said. "Unhealthy snacks on the counter. Help yourself."

Sydney went to the fridge for a diet soda. The fridge's contents consisted of Cokes, beer and a jar of salsa. "Is this what you're living on?" Sydney asked.

"Not entirely. Rene picked up some greasy burgers and brought them over for dinner last night, and I stopped for tacos at a drive-through after we finally finished at the car scene this morning."

Sydney sat down between the two men. Pens, note-pads, files, a laptop and a portable printer had been shoved to the other end of the table, no doubt to make room for Sydney and Tucker.

"I also stopped by Dani's Delights," Jackson said.

"That's odd. Tucker and I just left there and Dani didn't mention meeting you."

"I didn't introduce myself. I wanted to be sure you'd had a chance to explain about Rachel first. And I wanted to get a feel for the place before anyone realized I was FBI."

"What did you think?"

"Busy. Lots of local people who knew each other. Not a place I'd expect a serial abductor to pick out his victims, but you never know. Some of the worst have proved to be a Prince Charming until the full truth came out."

"An abductor and likely a killer," Sydney corrected.

"Alleged killer," Jackson said. "The deeper I get into this, the less convinced I am that Sara Goodwin's killing is related to the disappearance of the others. She doesn't seem to match the pattern."

"In what way?" Tucker asked.

"She was sixteen and homeless. Didn't have a car. The only tie to Winding Creek is that her body was found near here. The others were between the ages of twenty-five and thirty-two and all appeared to be in this area by choice. And at this point, they are only missing."

"Has at least one of our agents interviewed the friends and/or relatives of all the missing women?"

"No, but we're making progress. Rene's at the airport now, taking the short flight to Shreveport to meet with Alice Baker's roommate. He won't be back until late tonight. I'll shoot that report to you as soon as he gets it to me."

"Thanks. Do you have any additional information from the Shreveport Police Department?"

"I just got off the phone with a detective who has talked to the roommate twice. He says her story hasn't changed, so he has nothing new to add to his report."

"Then the printouts and digital files you gave me yesterday are up to date on Alice Baker?"

"It's all I have until we hear from Rene. Tim did an in-depth interview with Michelle Dickens's parents this morning, but he's driving back to San Antonio to give them the latest news in person."

"What about Karen Murphy?" Sydney prodded.

"Next on the list. Her truck-driver husband will be home from his cross-country run later tonight, and Tim and I will be interviewing him first thing in the morning at their home in New Braunfels. That is unless a more pressing matter takes precedence, such as we had when you discovered Rachel's car this morning."

Jackson picked up a folder filled with handwritten notes torn from small notebooks. He shoved it across the table to Sydney. "These are copies of the notes the guys scribbled down yesterday during their research and interviews. I'd like you to do the same with your impressions from visiting the crime scene this morning. I want to keep us all on the same page."

"Sometimes hastily scribbled notes are more useful than the formal reports," Sydney said. "Off-the-cuff comments cut to the chase." Sydney opened the folder. There were two sets of notes, carefully stapled together.

She picked up the top one. Michelle Dickens, age 25, missing since August 20.

Michelle was a kindergarten teacher in Kerrville, Texas, who was engaged to be married the first week in October. Got along with everyone. Athletic. Loved hiking, biking, rock climbing and snow skiing.

She was last seen at her parents' house before driving back to Kerrville after spending the weekend shopping for a wedding dress. She didn't buy one. Paper trail ended with a charge made at an Exxon station on the highway about ten miles from Winding Creek. Parents in state of almost-crippling panic.

Sydney understood that completely. She looked through the next set of notes. Alice Baker. Lived in Shreveport, Louisiana, with her roommate. An unemployed petroleum engineer, she had been traveling to San Antonio on March 9 for a job interview. She'd never kept the appointment.

She had charged a pair of Western boots at a boutique in Winding Creek and food and drinks at Caffe's Bar and Grill.

Her roommate insisted she was extremely cautious, not the kind to even talk to strangers, much less get in the car with one. Alice was licensed to carry and always packed a small pistol when she traveled alone.

Obviously, she hadn't seen trouble coming in time to use her weapon. Or if she'd hesitated to pull the trigger, the perp might have wrestled it away from her. That happened far too often with inexperienced shooters.

"Our perp is definitely not straying far from his community playground," Sydney commented. "He doesn't necessarily live here, but he spends a lot of time here."

"If he sticks this close to home, he's either extremely brazen or thinks he's too smart to get caught," Jackson said.

"Or he wants to get caught," Sydney said.

"I plan to oblige him," Jackson said. "I'm still puzzled by how and why he drove the car into the ravine. I can't imagine he trusted Michelle to drive Rachel's car while he followed her in his. Too much opportunity for her to escape."

"Unless she's experiencing the Stockholm syndrome and has bonded with the kidnapper," Sydney said. "If that's the situation, she might be helping him kidnap the others."

Sydney was almost certain that Rachel would never let herself be brainwashed by her kidnapper. But she couldn't be positive of that.

"You're in cowboy country," Tucker said. "First thing

I thought of was horses. The second was four-wheelers. Almost every ranch has those."

"If he had someone follow them on horseback, that would mean he has an accomplice."

"Not necessarily," Tucker said. "Based on the assumption he is local and holding the women nearby, he could have hauled a couple of horses up in a trailer. Same with an ATV. I noticed the SUV had a trailer hitch."

"I missed that," Sydney said, hating to admit she'd overlooked any detail. "But I would have seen a trailer if there had been one."

"He could have come back for that later, in his car or whatever he drives."

"Just thinking," Jackson said, "but why bring the girl along at all if she wasn't driving the SUV for him?"

"Maybe he was afraid she'd escape if he left her behind," Tucker said.

"No, if he's holding her prisoner, he has a way to keep her imprisoned," Sydney said. "But maybe he wanted her to think he was taking her out to kill her and leave her body to rot in the woods."

Or maybe he had done exactly that and the body hadn't been found yet. Her insides quaked at that possibility.

"Dani said Sheriff Cavazos requested film from her security cameras this morning. Were you aware of that?"

"I am. He'd already pulled several places in town as part of his ongoing investigation. He's sending us copies of those as well as film from several other shops, restaurants and bars that he's collecting today. The locals trust him, so they're cooperating fully. They also want that perp found. The natives are definitely getting restless and with good reason."

"When will you get the film?" Sydney asked.

"Cavazos said by late afternoon. Then I'll shoot it to Lane and have him work his analysis magic."

"Let me know when you get that."

"Believe me, I will. And if you come up with any kind of theory as to the identity of the perp, you are to get back to me at once. No going after him alone. Get that?"

"Of course."

"*Not* the way you did with the Swamp Strangler."

"Trust me. I will never make that mistake again."

She finished her drink and carried the empty can to the trash basket.

"Where do you go from here?" Jackson asked.

"To pay a call on Dudley and Millie Miles. You must agree with me that it's extremely coincidental that Rachel's car was dumped in almost the exact spot where the Mileses' grandson's body was dumped."

"I agree, but I talked to the sheriff and one of his deputies about Dudley Miles. Neither of them could say enough good things about the man. His daughter was another story—narcissistic with no sense of decency—but she's in prison."

"I told her the same thing," Tucker said.

"I believe both of you. I just want to talk to the man. He must have a lot of cowboys running the ranch. He can talk to them and see if any of them came into contact with Rachel. The perp we're looking for might even be one of his workers. We have no reason to weed out that possibility."

"You're right. Go with your instincts. Just get me a profile on the perp that leads us to him before he strikes again."

"I plan to do just that."

Hopefully talking to Dudley Miles would help that along.

Chapter Eleven

They stopped for a late lunch at Hank's. The smell of hot grease, onions and spices made her nauseous. She knew it was more nerves than odors, but the only remedy she knew for that was to keep at it.

She spent most of her time there showing Rachel's photograph to the few waitresses she'd missed the last time she was here and to some of the customers Hank pointed out as regulars who might have seen Rachel either in his place or around town.

People were sympathetic and took a good look at the picture. Again, no luck.

They left as soon as Tucker finished his burger. Her grilled chicken salad was untouched except for moving a few greens around with her fork.

She fought to keep the dark and frightening thoughts at bay. All her energy was needed to keep her focus sharp and driving. They were ten minutes into the drive before she noticed that Tucker was wearing the now-familiar brooding expression of a troubled man.

As depressing as the situation was that she'd dragged him into, she knew that was not the only thing he was dealing with. She'd noticed that the first night they'd talked, even before she'd interrupted his whiskey and gloom.

"I get the feeling you have something other than this investigation on your mind. Do you want to talk about it?"

"Am I that obvious?"

"No, I'm that intuitive."

"Which is no doubt why you're a great profiler. I have some decisions I need to make. Nothing nearly as critical or urgent as what you're dealing with, so let's not get into it today."

His phone rang before she had time to delve deeper. He punched the answer button on his dashboard. A second later, Esther's voice filled the car.

"I hope I didn't catch you at a bad time. Are you still with Sydney?"

"I am. We're in my truck and my phone is on Speaker. What's on your mind?"

"I know how important it is for you to be with Sydney right now, but I just got off the phone with Dani. She says Constance wants to know when she's going to see her uncle Tucker."

"I'd like to spend some time with her and Jaci. Maybe tonight."

"That's why I'm calling. We're talking about having a family dinner tonight. Nothing fancy, just a few of your favorites. Fried chicken. Fresh peas from the garden."

"You do know how to lure me in. Throw in a banana pudding and I'm there."

"Banana pudding is a given when you're in town."

"I'm not exactly sure what time we'll get back there, so don't make it before seven."

"You'll come, too, won't you, Sydney?" Esther asked.

"I think it's best if I don't. I would only be a drag on the party atmosphere."

"Everyone understands what you're going through, so they won't be expecting frivolity or bubbly from you. And you can meet my two adorable granddaughters."

"I'd love to meet them."

"And you have to eat to keep up your energy. So it's settled?"

"Settled," she agreed. "I have to work tonight, but I'll make time for dinner."

A boisterous, loving family was probably not what she needed right now. But they had all done so much for Sydney, she could hardly say no, especially knowing it would mean so much to Esther.

After Tucker broke the connection, he reached for her hand and gave it a squeeze. "I won't let them hold you to the dinner promise if you're not up to it."

She hadn't stopped to think that he might not want her there, throwing a damper on the gathering with his family. He was giving her his days. He might well want his nights to himself. She wondered again about the decisions he was making and if they involved a woman.

"When you said work, you didn't mean you're planning to go out trolling for the perp alone, did you?" Tucker asked. "Because if you are, I need to call Esther right now and cancel my dinner plans."

"No," she said. "I'll be working at the ranch, but you

can't follow me around forever, Tucker. You must have bulls waiting."

"The bulls and I are taking a break."

She wasn't sure what that meant, but she went back to watching the pastoral scenes fly by as the road became hillier. She was certain she'd never seen this many cows, bulls and horses in her life.

They passed a huge red barn on the east side of the road that she was certain she'd seen before. The land to the west of them was fenced with barbwire but heavily wooded. "Is this where we were this morning?"

"If we turned down the next dirt imitation of a road we come to and followed to the top of the waterfall we'd end up in the same exact spot. Another mile down this road and we'll arrive at Dudley's spread."

"Then it would be possible for the perp and Michelle to have driven the car to the waterfall and then ridden horses or an all-terrain vehicle back to land belonging to Dudley Miles without ever getting on anything except dirt roads."

"It's possible," Tucker admitted. "It's also possible they rode west into an area of dozens of small farms and weekend ranches owned by people who like to get out of town and experience the country lifestyle when they can."

"I strongly suspect Sheriff Cavazos checked all those out before he requested help from the FBI."

"He's likely checked out Dudley's wranglers, as well."

"I'll still feel better after I meet Dudley Miles for myself."

The wooded area gave way to lush green rolling hills

and a seemingly unending strand of white-painted farm fencing that had cost someone a small fortune.

Tucker pulled up and stopped in front of a magnificent double-arched black iron gate. Two huge black ironwork stallions were built into the fence, their front feet reared up as if they were about to attack each other. Their heads and long necks extended over the top edge of the gate. Two brick columns supported the gate.

"I don't think I've ever seen a gate that impressive," Sydney said. "It's like a piece of expensive art."

"I'm sure it cost like one, too." Tucker lowered his window, reached out and punched a button on the brick support post. The gate swung open.

"I'm surprised it wasn't locked," Sydney said.

"No one does a lot of locking gates around here. Never needed to until now. I suspect that might change if an arrest is not made soon."

Once the gate had closed behind them, Tucker made a call to Dudley to let him know he had company.

"Tucker Lawrence. I heard you were in town. Glad you found time to stop by and see me. I'm out checking on the hay baling, so you'll have to give me a few minutes to get back to the house."

"No problem."

"Wait on the porch if you don't mind. Millie's usually napping this time of day. Better not to wake her."

Tucker made a couple of turns on a winding road before the house came into view. It was a far cry from what she'd expected. "Wow! We're not in Kansas anymore. I'm not even sure we're in Texas. Who knew ranchers lived like this?"

"I CAN ASSURE you that most don't," Tucker said as he climbed from the truck and hurried over to open her door. "The most popular rumor is that Millie Miles got stuck in the pages of *Gone with the Wind* and never escaped."

"She has all the antebellum trappings. Second-and third-floor wraparound verandas. Wide, winding staircase. Huge white columns. Beautiful garden. All she needs is Rhett Butler."

"She doesn't need him. She has a cowboy," Tucker teased. "To set the record straight, that is never settling for less."

"You could be biased. I'll reserve judgment until I've met the man," Sydney said.

They took the paved walk to the steps. He put a hand to the small of her back as they climbed the stairs to the shaded veranda. Once there, Sydney settled into a cushioned rocker. Tucker propped against one of the support columns.

It had been several years since Tucker had been to the Eagle's Nest Ranch and he'd forgotten how pretentious and out of place the house was among the rolling pastures of the Texas Hill Country.

"The first time I visited this ranch was years before I went to live with Esther and Charlie," he said, sliding far back into his past. "I was in the first or possibly the second grade. My class made a field trip out here so that us 'town' kids could get a taste of life on a working ranch."

"Is that trip what inspired you to become a bull rider?"

"No, that came years later, when I didn't get a contract from the NFL and realized I might have to take a real job. But I had been competing in bull-riding events for years by then."

"But even as a kid, you must have been impressed with all this."

"You got it. I went home and told my mother we'd been to the White House and met the president. When she stopped laughing, she tried to convince me differently. It took a lot of explaining to persuade me I was wrong."

Sydney laughed. The sound caught him by surprise. It was the first time he'd enlisted more than a tentative smile from her. He loved hearing it, but the joy was immediately choked off by a knot of revulsion and bitterness.

His muscles bunched. If he could get to the monster who was putting Sydney, Rachel and so many others through this hell, he'd swear he could kill the man with his bare hands. It was a brand of hatred he'd never experienced before.

Tucker heard the clopping of approaching hooves and looked up to see Dudley riding toward them on a splendid black steed. He climbed out of the saddle and tethered the animal to a low branch of a young oak tree several feet away from the porch.

Dudley grinned broadly as he climbed the stairs. His shoulders were stooped and the hair that had been almost black a few years back was almost completely gray. His ruddy, wrinkled flesh might pass for leather.

The years since his grandson's tragic death had clearly not been kind to him.

Dudley extended a weathered, callused hand. "Great to see you, Tucker. You look fit, as always." The two of them shook hands before Dudley turned toward Sydney.

"And this is Sydney Maxwell. You must have heard of her by now."

"Yes. News does travel fast in Winding Creek."

Sydney extended her hand. "Nice to meet you, Mr. Miles."

He shook her hand. "Just call me Dudley. Everyone does."

"Have you talked to the sheriff lately?" Tucker asked.

"Yep. He was out earlier today, doing what he called routine questioning of some of my wranglers. It was a waste of time and I told him so. I know my men. They may not be sophisticated but they're hard workers and they're honest. Otherwise, they don't last past their first payday."

"Sometimes people can fool you," Sydney said.

"Sometimes," Dudley agreed. "But I can still assure you I don't have any perverted, murderous kidnappers working for me. Anyway, Cavazos mentioned that one of the FBI agents on this case was a sister to one of the victims and staying with Esther Kavanaugh. I reckon that's you."

"Yes. I'm hoping to find someone who might have seen my sister, Rachel, while she was in Winding Creek. Someone who would know if she was alone or seemed to be in distress. I know they're familiar with a few details of the other missing women by now, but no one has likely heard of Rachel."

"Good idea. It's nice Tucker is here to show you around the town. We don't see much of him. I suppose he told you he's a big-time bull-riding champion."

"I didn't tell it nearly as well as you just did," Tucker said.

"All you Lawrence brothers are much too modest. But to get back to the crisis at hand. Does the FBI have any suspects?"

"Not that I know of," Sydney said. "Hopefully that will change soon."

"I'd like to do something to help before you leave. What about my offering a reward for information leading to the women's rescue?"

"That's a generous offer," Tucker acknowledged.

"I like to help in cases like this when I can. Give it some thought," he added when Sydney didn't jump on the offer. "Just tell me how much you think would be appropriate and I'll write you a check."

Dudley pulled a key from his pocket, unlocked the front door and pushed it open. "C'mon in. I'm already as hot and sweaty as I can get, but no reason for the two of you to stand out here in the heat."

They followed him through the house and onto a glassed-in porch that ran the length of the back of the house. The room overlooked a kidney-shaped pool surrounded by chic outdoor furniture and huge pots of blooming plants. No beach towels in sight. No floats. Every lounge chair was perfectly straight.

Tucker wondered how long it had been since anyone

had actually swum in the pool. Even the room they were in now seemed more for show than relaxing. Sydney chose a straight-back love seat. He sat down beside her.

"If you two will excuse me for a minute, I need to call Becker to come get my mount and see that he's put away properly. Then I'm going to grab myself a tall glass of iced tea. What can I bring you to drink? A beer? Cocktail? It's five o'clock somewhere."

"Iced tea sounds good," Sydney said.

"Nothing for me," Tucker said.

As soon as Dudley left the room, Sydney leaned in close. "Do you think he really meant the offer of a reward?"

"I'm sure he did. Charlie always said that if your mule was in a ditch, his best friend Dudley would be along with a tractor to pull you out, and then offer you a new mule to go with the one he'd rescued."

"He and Charlie must have been very close."

"They were. Friends from back in their high school years. They were always there for each other."

Except Dudley obviously hadn't come rushing in with a check when Charlie was drowning in debt and about to lose the ranch and the house. Of course, Charlie was so damned independent, he'd probably never let Dudley know how bad things were.

Dudley rejoined them with the two glasses of tea in hand. He set one atop a coaster on a small mahogany table next to Sydney and took a chair opposite them.

Dudley leaned back and crossed a foot over the opposite knee. "How's the bull-riding business going, Tucker?" he asked, casually changing the subject from

Rachel's disappearance as if they were here to shoot the bull.

"I've had a good year." Good enough that he could be headed to a national championship win if he could get his head on straight.

"Glad to hear that. I've caught your performances a few times on TV this year. Not often since I tend to fall asleep in my chair about ten minutes after I turn on the TV at night. The announcers can't say enough good things about you."

"I've been lucky."

"Some, but mostly you've worked hard at it. Plus you're a natural. Charlie was so proud of you and your brothers. I couldn't believe the change that came over him and Esther when you three boys moved in with them. It's a shame they couldn't have kids of their own."

"Were you and Charlie close friends?" Sydney asked.

Tucker had already had this conversation with Sydney and had no idea where she was going now.

"We didn't see that much of each other over the last few years. I wish I'd kept up with him better, but we still got together occasionally to go hunting or fishing. He was a good man. It took the heart and soul right out of Esther when he committed suicide. Only thing that saved her was having Riley and Pierce and their families move in around her."

"She believes he was murdered," Sydney said.

That explained where this was heading, but surely she didn't think there was a link between Charlie's death and Rachel's abduction.

"When I first heard the news, I thought suicide didn't

seem at all like Charlie," Dudley said. "He was a man of faith and conviction and I couldn't see him leaving Esther for any reason. But he was shot with his own gun. No other fingerprints on it. No evidence that anyone had been anywhere near the barn that day but him. Sheriff Cavazos said it was obvious suicide and I had no reason to doubt him."

"Cavazos told Riley and Pierce the same thing," Tucker said. "He assured them the investigation had been thorough and there was no evidence of foul play."

Dudley sipped his tea and then licked moisture from his bottom lip. "You know, I don't think I ever told anyone this, but Charlie paid me a visit a few days before he took his life."

"Did he talk about his debt problems?"

"No. If he had I would have bailed him out. You know that. He came because he was worried about me, though he must have been horrified of losing his ranch and the only life he and Esther had ever known."

Sydney uncrossed her legs and leaned forward. "What did he tell you?"

"That he knew I was lying to protect Angela and that I would never have gotten drunk when I was supposed to be tending my grandson, that I would never have dumped his small body in the woods."

"Shows how well he knew you," Tucker said.

"He said he had proof and that if I didn't tell the truth in court, he was going to take his proof to the sheriff. Looking back, I 'spect he might have done just that if he'd stayed alive awhile longer."

"And you wouldn't have gone to prison for Angela's

crime," Sydney said. "You're certain you never told anyone about this?"

"Nope. Probably shouldn't have mentioned it to you now. God knows I don't want anything said that will upset my wife any more than she already is."

"How is Millie?" Tucker asked.

"She goes through some of the motions of living, but it's like there's no heart left in her. She goes into town a couple of days a week, runs a few errands, goes to church, sometimes even has lunch with old friends.

"Crazy thing is she can't stay in the house all day yet can't stand driving. Sometimes she insists she needs one of my wranglers to drive her where she wants to go."

"Good thing you have one to spare," Tucker said. "Pierce says good help is getting hard to find."

"True. That's one reason I've never moved any of my livestock over to that strip of land I bought from Mike Kurlacky when he got the gout so bad he couldn't take care of himself, much less his cattle."

"Is that land lying idle?"

"More or less. Millie gave one of my wranglers, Roy Sales, use of it to raise some hogs while I was in prison. He's living there now, but I'd take it back if you ever decide to settle down back here in Winding Creek and want to buy it. Plenty of room to raise some rodeo stock."

"That day might not be too far away."

"Roy did all the repairs on the house while I was in prison. Millie said she wanted to do something to pay him back. But enough of that. I know you came here to talk about more urgent stuff than hogs and cattle."

Sydney reached into her handbag and took out the photo of Rachel. "I'd appreciate it if you'd take a look at my sister's photo and tell me if you remember ever seeing her in Winding Creek."

Dudley studied the photo. "She doesn't look familiar. Unless she was hanging out at the hardware store, the feed and tack store or the saddle repair shop, it's not likely I'd have run into her."

"What I'm really hoping for is to find out who she might have been seen with before she disappeared."

"Makes sense. The abductor has to be hooking up with his victims somewhere."

"I have extra copies of the photo. I'll leave that one with you. Perhaps your wife or some of your wranglers may have seen her."

"That's a damn good idea. I'll post the photo in the bunkhouse and tell them to check it out. Now back to my offer of a reward. How about twenty-five thousand dollars for anyone who gives information that leads to the rescue of the four missing women?"

"That's extremely generous," Sydney said. "If you're serious I'll talk to my supervisor at the FBI and see how he wants to handle this."

"I'm serious as the business end of a .45."

"If that's settled, we should probably be going and let you get back to work," Tucker said.

"You're right. A rancher can't afford to be burning daylight these days." Dudley gulped down the last of his iced tea and stood.

Sydney thanked Dudley again for his cooperation

and reward offer as he walked them to the front door. There was no sign of Millie.

"If you're this way in the fall, let's do some hunting, Tucker."

"I'll hold you to that if I get back this way," Tucker said. "Can't make any promises. The fall rodeo circuit doesn't allow for much time off."

But if he didn't get back to bull riding soon, he may as well spend the fall hunting. He still needed to accumulate points and earnings to get to the championship round.

They'd climbed back in his truck and were still buckling their seat belts when Sydney hit him with the next humdinger.

"I think there's a good chance Charlie Kavanaugh was murdered and that someone in the Miles family is responsible."

Chapter Twelve

"Don't look so shocked," Sydney said. "I didn't pull this out of the clouds. Dudley himself offered the motive. Charlie wasn't going to go along with his lying to the court."

"Dudley just offered you twenty-five thousand dollars. He's been a philanthropist all his life, has helped fund every charity event that takes place in this part of Texas. He'd been a friend to Charlie for years. I find it hard to see him as Charlie's killer."

"I didn't say Dudley killed him. It may have been Millie or their daughter, Angela. They wouldn't have had to do the deed themselves. They could have paid someone else. Believe me, that happens far more than most people realize."

"I wouldn't put anything past Angela, but Dudley just admitted we were the first ones he'd ever talked to about Charlie's threat."

"His life was in a state of heartbreaking turmoil at the time. He may have forgotten or Charlie may have mentioned it to someone and it got back to Angela."

"You could be right," Tucker admitted. "But I think

we're jumping tracks here. Are you trying to tie what happened to Dudley's grandson to Sara Goodwin or to Rachel's and the other women's disappearance?"

"No. Not at this point, but I can't ignore the facts. I have a sworn duty to turn this information over to someone in authority. I just wanted to alert you first."

"You do what you have to do," Tucker said. "If Charlie was murdered, the last thing I want is to see his killer go free."

"Then we're on the same page."

She breathed easier. Nothing Tucker said would keep her from following her conscience but she didn't want him to feel as if she were turning on him.

She benefited from bouncing ideas off him, respected his opinion. She liked riding with him in his truck. Liked the sound of his voice and the saunter when he walked.

Sydney took a deep breath. There was no denying the swelling attraction but she couldn't deal with any of that right now. There was far too much at stake.

She was making a phone call to Jackson when they passed a lopsided gate with a crooked sign that said Kurlacky's Acres. She wondered if Tucker was serious about buying that land. From bull riding to raising bulls. Somehow she couldn't see that happening any more than she could see herself walking away from the FBI. One day maybe, but not anytime soon.

When Jackson answered, she explained Dudley's offer of the reward. As expected, he was all for it.

He had good news, as well. One of Cavazos's deputies would be dropping off a thumb drive for her at the ranch. The material would include a copy of relevant footage from Dani's Delights security camera.

She broke the connection and twisted in her seat so that she could face Tucker while she caught him up to date. He was staring straight ahead, his hands wrapped tight around the steering wheel. His brows furrowed into deep wrinkles.

"You're doing it again," she said.

"Doing what?"

"Shutting me out of what's bothering you."

"What's bothering me is that we haven't located your sister or apprehended the kidnapper from hell."

"You mentioned before that you were dealing with troubling decisions."

"It's nothing."

She didn't believe him, but then, she knew so little about him that she could be reading this all wrong. "I'm a good listener, but if you really want me to butt out, just say so and I won't mention it again."

"Is that straight from the 'good cop' manual?"

"I'll take that comment to mean you don't need my input."

They rode in silence until he turned onto Main Street for Sydney to get her car.

"I have to pick up some supplies at the drugstore before I drive back to the ranch," she said.

He nodded but didn't turn to face her until he pulled up next to her car. "Sorry for the bite of sarcasm back there. That was my macho defenses kicking in."

"Apology accepted."

"If you're still game to have me unload on you, I have a proposition for you."

He sounded so serious she was almost afraid to answer. "Let's hear it."

"Go horseback riding with me when we get back to the ranch. I know the perfect spot for you to unwind and me to spout my problems. It comes with a sunset and a fabulous view."

"Okay, cowboy. You've got yourself a deal."

IT HAD BEEN several years since Sydney had been on a horse but it took only a few minutes for her to feel at home in the saddle again. Her mount was a gentle black quarter horse named Beauty, said to be one of Constance's favorites.

Beauty needed little guidance from Sydney but easily kept up with the much-larger sorrel that Tucker rode. They started out at a walk.

"You look like you've been riding all your life," Tucker said. "You didn't mention you were such an experienced horsewoman."

"Beauty is making this easy. I dated a guy whose father owned a ranch back in college but I haven't done much riding since."

"He taught you well. Are you more comfortable at a walk or are you ready to pick up the pace a bit?"

She wanted to race like the wind, wanted to feel the wind in her face and feel as free as she had before her sister had been swallowed up by evil.

That wasn't going to happen, but losing control and being thrown by Beauty was a distinct possibility if she became too carried away. She'd already had one fall today and lucked out with only minor injuries. No reason to push her good fortune.

"Let me get used to the walk for a few more minutes. If Beauty hasn't turned on me by then, we can move up to an easy lope."

"A lope. You're starting to sound like a cowgirl."

"You know the old saying. Love a horse before you fall in love with a man."

"And did you?"

"Fall in love with the horse or a man?"

"Either."

"Not yet, but I could quickly grow fond of a sweet little filly like Beauty."

Tucker picked up the pace and she followed a few paces behind. He sat straight in the saddle, his long legs a perfect fit in the stirrups, his Stetson making the definitive statement. This was his world. Livestock, horses, bull riding. He was the real deal.

Tucker slowed until they were riding side by side. He looked at her and tipped his hat. Something bubbled inside her like fine champagne. Her pulse quickened.

"You're smiling," he said. "Does that mean you're up for a longer ride?"

"Sure. My overwrought nerves are even starting to unknot a bit." At least for the moment.

"Then let's take the horses to a gallop and see if the ranching spirit can refresh your soul."

She experienced a full five minutes of exhilaration before a new wave of anxiety and guilt hit with the force of exploding dynamite. Her fingers tangled in Beauty's reins as horrifying images swept through her mind.

Rachel, enduring the touch of a monster. Rachel, starving and begging for food. Rachel, cowering in fear while she prayed and waited in vain for her FBI agent sister to come to her rescue.

It took all Sydney's mental strength to keep the images from sinking into the blackest pit of all.

She took deep breaths, fighting to return to full mental control. Guilt and panic were two of the worst possible emotions for her in this situation. *Undue stress leads to poor decision-making.* She'd heard that countless times since coming to work for the Bureau.

She wasn't in this alone. Jackson and three of the top agents in the FBI were working this case. Local law enforcement with all their manpower were out there hitting the streets day and night.

An hour's time spent with Tucker after a day that started at daybreak would only make her more alert, more focused and better able to give Jackson what he needed from her.

An accurate profile of the perp so that they could narrow their parameters and track him down before he struck again or a new body was discovered.

She straightened in the saddle and took a deep breath. In minutes, she'd talked herself through the panic attack. Her nerves settled enough that she could appreciate the serenity of the environment.

They had obviously been steadily climbing while she'd been overcome with her bout of needless guilt. They were at the crest of a hill. Acres and acres of rolling pastures crisscrossed by barbwire and dotted with clusters of towering pines and ancient oaks stretched out in all directions.

The sky above was painted in streams of gold as the sun began its descent to the distant horizon. She reined in Beauty to a slow walk and let the tranquility seep bone-deep.

Tucker came back to join her. "This is the best view on the ranch."

"It's amazing, like a painting springing to life as I watch."

"When I was twelve, I used to ride up here and pretend I was the king and all the land I could see was my kingdom."

"I suppose it is someone's kingdom. Is this all part of the Double K?"

"Not all, but a good bit of it. Charlie bought it when land was cheap. A spread like this today would cost like it was a rich kingdom. Esther sold it to Pierce for a fraction of its true worth."

"Did it upset you and Riley that she chose to sell it to Pierce?"

"Not in the least. A ranch this size is an enormous amount of work and responsibility. Riley and I weren't ready to take that on and likely never will be. It all worked out great. Pierce is a born rancher. Esther will always have her home. It's a win-win."

Tucker dismounted and then helped her from the saddle. He tethered their horses to a tree branch near a shallow creek. Both horses quickly waded in and lowered their necks for a long drink.

"There's more to see," Tucker said, "though you might prefer to miss it."

"Why would I?"

"It's another rocky gorge, steeper than this morning but with far less water rushing over the edge to the rocky creek below."

"Since we've already proved I'm about as graceful and sure-footed as a drunk chimp on skates, how about we save that for next time?"

"The next time it is."

Tucker took a small Mexican blanket from his saddlebag and tossed it over his shoulder. They walked upstream a few yards before he spread the blanket over a thick carpet of grass and pine straw.

Sydney knelt and then settled herself cross-legged.

Tucker joined her on the blanket except that he stretched out on his back and tugged his Stetson low on his forehead to protect from the glare of the low-riding sun.

A honeyed warmth crept through her. Wrong time. Wrong place. But being with Tucker felt so right.

"I can tell you're good at it, but what made you choose a career with the FBI?" Tucker asked.

"My dad was a homicide detective. He was the most amazing and bravest man I knew and I always wanted to follow in his footsteps. He raised Rachel and me pretty much single-handedly after my mother died from complications from what was supposed to be routine removal of a benign tumor."

"Where is your dad now?"

"He died of a bullet wound to the head trying to intervene and save a kid who'd gotten caught up in gang warfare. He had one more year until he retired."

"How old were you then?"

"It was my first year in college. When I graduated, I was hired by the FBI and knew from day one it was where I belonged."

"You picked a dangerous career."

"I try not to think too much about that. I know it involves risk, but I'm doing what I love. What's life if you lose your passion?"

"I suppose that's a question everyone has to answer at one time or another."

She untwisted her legs and lay back on her side facing him, suddenly craving the extra closeness. "Most of the time I think I have it all figured out. This week I'm hanging on by a thread that's on the verge of splitting in two. Any bravado I manage to exhibit is fake."

"That's why I'm hanging around," Tucker said. He propped himself up on his elbow so that they were inches apart and facing each other. "I'll be there to catch you if the thread snaps."

"I appreciate that, but you know that if we compared job risks, you'd win by a landslide. Bull riding has to be the most dangerous sport in the world."

"Most bull riders would agree with you on that."

"How often do you get hurt?"

"Every time I get thrown, but there are lots of different degrees of hurt. Mostly it's lumps and bruises that a six-pack of beer and a few painkillers can handle. But I've broken a few bones. Had a couple of concussions. Wounded my pride more times than I can count."

"And yet you still do it?"

"Yeah. Like you said. It's the passion. And it's my life."

"We came up here to talk about you," she said. "Lest we get sidetracked, what kind of decisions are you struggling with?"

"None," he said. "The decisions have all been made. Passion wins."

His voice grew husky. She met his gaze and felt as if she was drowning in the depths of his sun-kissed eyes.

She should move away. She should get up.

She did neither.

Tucker slipped his arms around her and pulled her close. His raw strength made her feel weak and empowered at the same time. An unfamiliar hunger raged inside her.

His lips found hers and she melted into his kiss. The world tilted out of focus, releasing a rush of mystifying emotions that created a need she couldn't fight.

Out of breath and with tears spilling from her eyes, she finally pulled away.

Tucker wiped a tear from her cheek with the back of his hand. "I'm so sorry, Sydney. I don't know what came over me. It just happened and then…"

"Please don't be sorry. I'm not crying because you kissed me. I don't even know why I'm crying. It's just that I'm an emotional wreck and I just can't do this right now."

"I understand. Just know that I never meant to hurt you or take advantage of your vulnerability. That's the last thing I'd willingly do."

He stood and then took her outstretched hands and pulled her to her feet.

The strength in his arms and hands almost sent her into tears again. He was her haven in the storm, but was it only safety she'd been thinking about when she got lost in his kiss?

"Promise me something," she said as they walked back to the horses.

"Anything."

"When this is over and Rachel and the others are safe, promise me we'll get together and finish that kiss."

"You've got yourself a deal."

RACHEL HEARD THE approaching footsteps but didn't cower in fear. The monster was like an attack dog. If he sensed fear, he became even more abusive and punishing.

She was experimenting with a new defense theory, a version of reverse Stockholm syndrome. Play with his mind. Give him reasons to think she understood him and enjoyed his horrid visits to her private hellhole.

The door opened. She forced a smile so fake it made her sick to her stomach. "You're here," she murmured. "I was afraid something had happened to you."

"You needn't worry about that. I'm in complete control and I have a nice surprise for you."

"I hope it's that you'll take me out of this room. I can cook dinner for you while you relax."

"No—guess again. Wait. Don't bother. I'll tell you." He smiled, showing his snuff-stained teeth, and walked nearer.

"I saw your sister today."

Chapter Thirteen

There was no way of knowing if the monster was lying or telling the truth. Sometimes she wasn't even sure he knew, but there was a good chance he'd run into Sydney.

Rachel had known all along that Sydney would come looking for her as soon as she realized Rachel was missing. With FBI capabilities on her side, she'd have had no trouble following the paper trail to Winding Creek.

The monster set the plate of beans he was holding on the floor by the door. "Why so quiet? I know you're not surprised. You must be as excited as I am about having FBI Sydney join us here in our cozy home."

Say the right thing. Don't give up the game. Stay alive until Sydney and the rest of the FBI agents come storming in.

"You'd like Sydney. She's smart like you are. She figures things out that no one else can."

"If she were smart, she wouldn't be strutting around town drawing so much attention to herself. She's making this so easy on me. So ridiculously easy."

"How is she drawing attention?"

"Showing your picture to everyone she sees. Asking

about you everywhere she goes. Big FBI star, coming to save you." He laughed as if that were a marvelous joke.

"Maybe you should give yourself up to Sydney and the FBI. I'll tell her you didn't really hold me captive, swear my stay here was voluntary. They couldn't do anything to you if I did that. You could go back to your life. I could go back to mine."

"You don't know what's going on here, Rachel. For an attorney, you can't figure anything out. I'll save myself. I'm the smart one."

"Don't make Sydney come after you. She never loses. Do you know what she did to the Swamp Strangler?"

"This ain't no swamp, and if I were you, I wouldn't be holding my breath waiting on her to ride to the rescue. She's picked up a cowboy to keep her company. Moved in with him, so I understand."

Rachel was certain he was lying about that. If Sydney was with a cowboy, it was because he fit into her investigation.

"Have you ever watched someone die, Rachel?"

Once again the monster's mood had changed in an instant, as if he'd traveled to some dark, Satan-held corner of his mind.

"Yes," she said honestly.

She'd arrived at the hospital just in time to see her father draw his last breath after being shot in the line of duty. Shot by someone as evil as the monster.

"One minute you're laughing while they beg you not to hurt them. The next they're choking on their own blood, terror swimming in their eyes."

He was totally in the dark zone now, making no sense, his eyes glazed over.

"How many people have you killed?" she asked softly.

"Only the ones Mommy tells me to. I'm a good boy."

A sickening terror crawled inside her. He was stark, raving mad.

Sydney was the only hope for her and for others who might be imprisoned with her. But the monster had obviously crossed the line to total insanity. At any moment, it could be too late.

ONE OF PIERCE'S newly hired wranglers was in the horse barn pitching fresh hay into the stalls when Sydney and Tucker returned. While Tucker unsaddled their mounts, she'd made a quick call to Esther. The package containing the USB thumb drive was yet to arrive, but most of the family was already there.

The wrangler had offered to take care of Beauty and the sorrel so they could meet the others at the house.

"I'm not going to dinner looking like this," Sydney said, as they walked back to the house.

"You look damned cute to me and there's definitely no dress code on the Double K."

"I smell like horseflesh."

"You'll fit right in."

"I'm sure my hair is going in a hundred different directions."

"More like fifty." Tucker reached down and tucked loose locks behind her ear.

"I promise I'll make it a quick shower and change. Your family is probably already tired of waiting on us."

"We're not late, but you'd best go in by way of your patio or you'll get ambushed on your way there and never get to the shower."

"Good idea."

"Do you need me to go through the house and unlock it for you or did you leave it open?"

"It's locked, but the key's in my pocket."

He walked her to the door and lingered just long enough to make the moment awkward. The kiss was between them now and that changed everything no matter what they told each other.

Another time, another place and things might have been different, but all her focus had to be on rescuing Rachel. A mistake in judgment could be fatal. That bit of wisdom was forever seared into her mind.

She stripped from her clothes, dropping them on the vanity before stepping into the shower. As she lathered the shampoo into her short hair, unbidden memories rushed into her mind. The body of the beautiful college coed, naked, facedown in the murky bayou, waiting to be the next meal of a hungry alligator.

The Strangler's hands around Sydney's neck, a second away from death. A lifetime of experiences hadn't raced through her mind as people often said. The past hadn't given her the strength to keep fighting. It was the dreams of the future that had made her keep fighting.

Those dreams were forever lost to Sara Goodwin. Sydney couldn't let them be lost for Rachel and the other captives.

She finished her shower and pulled a blue sundress from the small guest room closet. Casual, not too revealing, not too slouchy.

Now, if she could just ready her mind for family time. A very *brief* family time before she went back to the work of analyzing what they had so far, hopefully with new data from Dani's security film.

One solid clue. That might be all it took, but she needed it now.

SYDNEY HAD ZERO appetite when she joined the women and girls in the busy kitchen. The smell of frying chicken quickly took care of that.

"You made it," Esther said. "I was worried that horse-riding adventure might have left you plumb tuckered out what with you being up since dawn."

"I'm fine, just needed a quick shower."

"I love that dress," Dani said.

"Thank you. It's the only dress I brought with me. Everything else is business skirts and slacks and two pair of jeans. I wasn't expecting to do any socializing."

"I'm glad we thought of your moving in here," Dani said. "You need real meals. Mental work needs as much fuel as physical tasks. Plus you got a little physical exertion in today, too."

"It's all part of the process," Sydney said. "I go wherever the investigation takes me."

"Just stay safe," Esther cautioned. "Let your gun do your talking."

"Grandma," Constance said. "You want her to shoot people?"

"If they need it."

"Perhaps we should change the subject," Dani said. "Anyone have good news?"

"Well, I was planning to wear a sundress myself tonight," Grace said. "It's one I bought just two months ago, but when I put it on, it was a little too snug." She smiled conspiratorially, pulled her loose blouse tight and patted a small bulge in her stomach.

"Lord a mercy!" Esther squealed. "You're pregnant! I knew it when you turned that ugly shade of green and rushed from the breakfast table last week."

"You were right. But it's official now. Saw the doctor again and I'm in my second trimester."

The room erupted into hugs and congratulations.

Jaci started dancing around the room and singing at the top of her very healthy lungs. "I already knew it. I already knew it. I'm going to be a big sister. I already knew."

"You are so lucky," Constance said.

"I guess that means Pierce knows, too," Dani said.

"Yes. He's had as hard a time keeping it a secret this long as I have. He might be a teensy bit upset that I didn't wait until he was here to make the announcement. But I couldn't keep it in a second longer. It just bubbled right out of me."

"We're gonna have a baby around here," Esther said. "I just wish my Charlie was here to see it." She hummed a lullaby as she went back to transferring pieces of golden fried chicken from a deep fryer to an already-overflowing platter.

Sydney thought about the troubling statement Dudley had made that afternoon. If Dudley didn't tell the truth in court, Charlie would. He was not willing to see Dudley in prison for his spoiled and irresponsible daughter's crime.

It was the mark of a good friend. But had it cost Charlie his life? If so, knowing the facts wouldn't bring Charlie back. But would it ease Esther's mind or just bring all the pain and grief to the surface again?

Either way, if Charlie Kavanaugh had been murdered, he deserved justice. She'd look more into that later.

"Sydney, would you mind getting the butter from the fridge? I think these potatoes need a bit more."

"Sure. How much do you want? I'll cut it for you."

"Another fourth of a stick." Dani continued beating a huge bowl of potatoes with a hand mixer.

Grace stepped around Sydney and pulled a pan of fluffy biscuits from the oven. It defied logic that this many women could be cooking in one kitchen and making it seem more like a party than work.

Even the youngsters were busy. Constance sliced bananas with a table knife and Jaci layered a glass baking dish with vanilla wafers, all but the one she'd just slipped between her lips.

"How can I help?" Sydney asked.

"You just sit down and keep us company," Esther said. "You don't want to hurt the hand or get the bandage soiled."

"I'll change it anyway before I go to bed and the hand doesn't hurt unless I hit it against something or try to make a fist."

"You can oversee Jaci and Constance's project," Grace said. "The custard is in the saucepan on the front left burner, slightly cooled and ready to pour as soon as the girls have their first layer in place."

"I think I can handle that."

Sydney felt at home almost immediately. She'd come from a small family, just her, Rachel and their dad. This was her first experience being even a temporary part of a family this big, boisterous and caring.

Even more amazing, they weren't your typical family. Esther was clearly loved by everyone but actually kin to none. Jaci was Grace's stepdaughter. Constance was Dani's niece.

All held together by love, laughter and no doubt a few tears. She wondered how she'd fit into a family like this when so much of her time was spent dealing with the uglier side of life.

Definitely not something she needed to be concerned about tonight. One banana did not make a pudding. One horseback ride did not make her a cowgirl. One kiss did not equate with forever.

AN HOUR AND a half later, dinner was reduced to a few leftovers, the kitchen was clean with much help from the men and the film had still not arrived.

Stuffed and ready to relax, the whole family settled in the family den.

Uncle Tucker was clearly the star of the evening. Jaci climbed into his lap. Constance snuggled next to him on the wide leather sofa.

"Uncle Tucker, can you please stay until Saturday afternoon so you can watch me barrel race in our weekly rodeo? Please." Constance put her hands together in prayer form as she pleaded.

"I'll do my best," Tucker said. "Riley told me how good you are."

"She's already accumulated more points than some of the seventh graders," Riley said.

"And I've only lost my hat a couple of times all summer."

"Style is very important in barrel racing," Tucker said.

"I know. One time the wind blew it off, so you can't really count that."

"Absolutely not."

"And you can watch me do the mutton busting," Jaci said. "You can watch me, too, Sydney. I think I might win."

"I hope you win," Sydney said. "What is mutton busting?"

Jaci's eyes grew wide and she slapped her hand over her mouth to demonstrate her total shock. "You are a full-grown woman and you've never heard of mutton busting?"

"No. It's a good thing I have you to explain it to me."

"Well, you better come and watch so you'll know everything about it. First they put a helmet on my head, and then they sit me on the back of a sheep. When they let go, the sheep starts running as fast as it can. I just hang on until I tumble off."

"Does that hurt?"

"No. Sheep are little. They just like to run fast. It's fun, especially if you win."

"Right on," Tucker said. "Hanging on is the most important part."

"Speaking of holding on, let's check out the PBR network and see what the bull riders are doing," Riley said. He picked up the remote, turned on the TV and switched to the bull-riding channel.

The volume was too low to hear what the announcer on screen was saying, but the caption running below the picture said it all.

Rodeos have moment of silence in memory of Rod Hernandez.

Esther planted her feet and stopped the movement of her rocking chair. "Oh, no. Did you hear that, Tucker? Rod Hernandez. Dead. Wasn't he a friend of yours?"

"We were close."

"Did you know about this?"

"I did."

"Was he killed by the bull?" Esther asked. Her fears for Tucker shook her voice.

Riley turned off the TV. "Maybe we should table this conversation until later."

"I really need to be going," Grace said. "Jaci has school tomorrow."

"Same here," Dani added.

Tucker said nothing. This was clearly why he'd seemed so distant at times. He'd been grieving the death of his friend and hadn't wanted to upset her with his problems. Nor had he wanted to give Esther reason to worry about him.

The doorbell rang while they were gathering their things.

"I'll get it," Tucker volunteered. Sydney followed him to the door.

The visitor had a star pinned to the breast of his khaki uniform.

The security film had arrived.

Chapter Fourteen

Tucker handled the quick introductions between Sydney and the sheriff and then left them alone.

The sheriff peeked inside the open door. "Sounds like a party going on inside."

"Esther hosted a family dinner in honor of Tucker's visit."

"I don't want to interrupt your meal."

"You're not. We've finished and most are in the process of leaving."

"Good. I need to talk to you about something in private."

"I have a room of my own. We can talk there."

"If it's all the same with you, can we just take a short walk lest the mosquitoes get too bad to stay outside? I've been sitting at my desk for the last two hours finishing up some dadburn paperwork the county requires. Too much sittin' and my arthritis starts acting out."

"A walk would be fine."

Once they were down the steps, he took a worn path that trailed around the side of the house. "Jackson Clark speaks mighty highly of you," Cavazos said.

"I'm glad to hear that. I have great respect for him."

"He seems like a good man. Reasonable about most things. Here's the problem I'm having with all this. You FBI people come in here with lots of good ideas and every resource imaginable."

"It can be very effective," Sydney answered. Wherever this was going, she doubted she was going to like it.

"You got the know-how, but I know my folks. I know who to push for information, who to back away from. When and where to tread lightly."

Now she knew exactly where he was going. "Is this about Tucker and my visit to Dudley Miles this afternoon?"

"You might say that. It's about his wife, Millie. She's a good woman but she's had a hard go of it these last two years. Family problems that just tore her apart."

"I realize that," Sydney assured him. "What's your point?"

"Dudley says she got awfully upset when you were there today. She's scared you're trying to drag up the past and she just can't take no more trouble."

"We didn't even see her. She was supposedly in her room napping. How did she know we were there?"

"I reckon she caught a glimpse of you from her window when you were coming or going."

"I can understand how she knew Tucker. He's an old family friend. She's never met me. How could she know I'm an FBI agent?"

"She's seen you in town. Everyone has. You've been in most every store at least once and were even out at

Hank's a couple of times. Winding Creek's a mind-everybody's-business kind of town."

"And yet no one seems to know anything about the four women who disappeared from this area."

"Yep. That's a strange one, which leads me to think that the perp is not from around here. My hunch is that it's someone who makes deliveries or travels through here for some other reason on a regular basis."

"We can't rule out that he is from around here. For one thing, how would he happen to pick all nonlocals for his victims if he didn't know the area?"

"You've got me there. All I'm saying for sure is if you need to see Dudley again, I'd appreciate it if you'd go through me. I can ask the questions for you or he said he'd meet you at my office anytime. He just don't want to get Millie all riled up."

"He offered me twenty-five thousand dollars in reward money."

"He's bringing the check by my office in the morning. I'll leave it to you and Jackson to decide how to get the word out."

"Fair enough. Have you seen any of the security film yet?"

"Not yet, but one of my deputies looked over the portion of the tape I brought you. It covers a two-hour time slot that includes the time period before Rachel entered Dani's Delights until well after she leaves. He didn't spot anything out of the ordinary, though he did mention it would be nice to be able to hear instead of just see what was going on. Still, he figured the film was as useless as a knot in a stake rope."

Whatever that meant, she prayed it proved not to be true.

"One of my night clerks is copying all the tapes we confiscated today. That way I can get them to Jackson first thing in the morning."

"That will be a big help."

"Something better help soon. Whole county's chewing their bit—men scared to let their wives and daughters out of the house by themselves. That's why I wanted to be sure and get this to you tonight."

Nor did he want to miss warning her not to upset Millie Miles.

"Guess that about does it for now," Cavazos said. "I'll let you get inside and get some rest."

"I'll be burning the midnight oil tonight," she said, "starting with the security tape."

"If you're half as good as Jackson claims, you might have this all figured out by morning."

"I know Jackson didn't promise you that."

"'Bout damn near it." He handed her the small brown envelope that held the thumb drive. "A change of subject, but do you reckon Esther's got some of that dinner left?"

"I'm sure she does."

They'd reached the back of the sprawling house. From this point the path they'd taken meandered past a nearby woodshed. Sydney's small patio was a few yards to the right.

"When you see her, tell her that you walked me to my patio door and I went in to get some work done."

"Will do. And thanks for understanding about Millie."

She understood, but that didn't mean she'd grant his request. Lives were on the line.

SYDNEY KICKED OFF her white sandals and switched on her laptop. Anxiety rode her nerves again. Four women's lives might be riding on what she did or didn't discover.

If the deputy didn't see anything that looked suspicious, then Rachel must have been alone. Best scenario now was to spot someone or something that raised questions in her mind.

She took her computer, small notebook and a pen to an upholstered chair tucked away in the corner of the room. She missed her office with its large desk and work area and a huge wall for charting her findings.

She was fifteen minutes into the digital recording when she got her first glimpse of Rachel entering the shop. Her breath caught. Her sweet sister, relaxed, stunning in a flowing, summery dress.

She was immediately struck by the desire to stop the frame and let that image soak in, but her mind overrode her emotions. She needed to see everything that transpired exactly as she would have seen it if she'd been there the first time.

She would replay it many times before the night was over.

Rachel was alone. She stopped momentarily before getting in a line that stretched almost to the door. Two teenage girls were in front of her, both on their cell phones. An elderly couple with two preteen boys—likely their grandsons—were behind her.

No doubt bored from the inactivity, the boys started some horseplay. One shoved playfully; the other fell into Rachel. She laughed it off, though it was evident the gentleman was scolding the boys. After that, Rachel and the grandmother got into what was obviously a friendly conversation.

That was the extent of Rachel's involvement with strangers until she reached the counter. Dani greeted her with a smile and then bagged Rachel's pastry while the same cute teenage girl who'd been helping out today served as barista.

Instead of taking a seat, Rachel perused the gift items while she sipped her coffee, the pastry still in its bag. At one point, she picked up a colorful coffee mug, checked the price and returned it to the shelf.

She didn't speak to anyone until she reached the pottery display. Two men who appeared to be in their midtwenties seemed to be comparing two tall vases.

A minute later they engaged in an animated conversation with Rachel. No sign of confrontation or disagreement. Eventually, Rachel decided on a bowl and went back to the counter to pay for it.

She talked with Dani as she completed the credit-card transaction and carefully bound the bowl in protective wrap. Rachel returned the wallet to her handbag, took her package and left, balancing her bowl, pastry and coffee.

A man who was coming in as she was leaving held the door for her.

That was it.

Rachel hadn't pulled out a roll of cash at the register, hadn't engaged with any men except the two extremely unlikely suspects at the pottery display, and her only run-in had been with a mischievous kid who accidentally bumped into her.

Worthless as a knot in a stake. She had to ask Tucker what that meant.

She was glad Tucker was giving her this time alone to work but she wondered if she'd see him again tonight. If he did come in to say good-night, then what?

The kiss was still on her mind, just tangled with the ever-increasing urgency of finding Rachel. The intensity of her attraction toward him had accelerated so fast she was afraid to trust her emotions.

One thing was for certain: she'd never let any other man into her life so quickly. Had never once been blown away by a kiss.

She rewound the tape and started it over at the point just before Rachel entered the store.

She paused the play immediately. She'd been so intent on Rachel's movements that she hadn't noticed the woman who'd been leaving the bakery as Rachel entered.

Even now she couldn't be certain, as much of the woman's face was blocked by the door, but it looked like Millie Miles. Sydney quickly zoomed in on the image.

She was almost sure it was Millie. Not that her being at the bakery at the same time as Rachel carried any suspicious connotations, but the Miles family were popping into this investigation on a regular basis.

Other than Millie catching Sydney's attention, the second viewing gave her nothing. Neither did the third.

Disappointment had reached new levels, but she was nowhere near ready to give it up for the night. She'd brush her teeth, wash her face and change her bandage before she started charting everything she knew about every element of this investigation.

Few serial perps had ever chosen their victims strictly at random. Something triggered their acts.

Unless the perp was completely mad.

TUCKER HESITATED AT the closed door to Sydney's room. He didn't want to make her think he was being pushy by interrupting her while she was working. Yet he couldn't just ignore the fact that she might need his company after viewing the film.

He tapped softly.

"Who is it?"

"Tucker."

"Come in if you dare."

Neither the words nor the tone were welcoming. He opened the door and peeked inside. The floor was littered with markers, tiny stick-on stars, tape and white poster board. Presumably, the supplies she'd picked up in town earlier today.

"An art project?"

"If it is, I'm failing badly. Take a seat if you can find one."

He dropped to the edge of the bed. Sydney was sitting cross-legged on the floor, sticking stars on a detailed map of Winding Creek and the surrounding area that had been taped to a large square of poster board.

"How did your talk with Esther go?" Sydney asked.

"She thinks I'm a hardheaded, macho imbecile who thinks it's cool to try and get myself killed just for the fun of it. Other than that, she loves me."

"You can't blame her for worrying."

"I don't blame her. I'm not even sure she's wrong. That's an interesting map," Tucker said, ready to change the subject. "Where did you get it?"

"It was in the folder Jackson passed out at the first meeting along with the personal data of the women who'd been reported missing. All except for Rachel's. I had to fill everyone in on her."

"What do the stars represent?"

"The blue stars show the last place the women were known to be before they disappeared."

"What do the numbered stars next to the blue stars represent?"

"The order in which they went missing. The time of day they were last seen is printed on the white strip stickers."

Tucker stooped on his haunches to get a better look.

"I'm looking for a pattern," Sydney explained. "The pictured representations tend to make them pop out at you better than a table of printed facts."

"Just like on the cop shows on TV."

"Yes, except I tend to go overboard with all the facts I like to include. I'm a visual learner."

"Makes it easy to see how fast the frequency of the abduction is escalating," Tucker said. "One six months ago. One three months ago. And now two in the past six weeks."

"And then he's likely responsible for Sara Goodwin's death and no one knows for sure yet when she went missing."

"Guy is definitely brazen."

"Or he has mental problems that are worsening," Sydney said. "Here's what we know so far. The missing women are all attractive brunettes who were traveling alone. Since they were all last seen in this area, I assume he hooked up with them at some spot in or around Winding Creek."

"Except for Rachel's car, none of the women's vehicles have been found," Tucker added. "It could be that he has a place to dump them where they haven't been found and he ran out of space."

"Good point. But he has to make sure no one sees him driving their car."

"Maybe he forces them to drive him somewhere, and then he k..." Tucker stopped short. Sydney knew as well as he did that there was a chance all the missing women were dead, but she'd avoided saying it out loud.

He got that. Positive thoughts were far more productive.

"I think the perp either lives in Winding Creek or near here," Sydney said. "He's somewhat of a loner. For some reason, he spends a lot of time in town. When forced to interact, he holds it together so that people may think he's odd, but don't realize how mentally unbalanced he is.

"He may not be actively looking for victims, but

something he sees in a woman triggers the violent nature he may have kept in check for years until something happened to change that."

"You are good at this," Tucker said.

"I could be way off track," she admitted, "but I don't think so. What I can't figure out is how he gets the women to go with him. Is it willingly? Or does he overpower them? If so, how does he do that over and over without being seen? And where are they now? Prisoners in his house or some isolated location where no one goes except him?"

"Most every ranch except the very smallest has old, dilapidated structures somewhere on their land. Barns that haven't been used in years. Rotting sheds filled with nothing but spiders, snakes and rusting tools. The problem is it would take weeks or maybe months to search them all."

"That's why we have to keep narrowing this down."

"And cover this town and surrounding areas with posters offering that reward Dudley promised," Tucker said. "That would get everyone looking for this guy on their own land, doing your work for you."

"Or getting themselves killed trying to apprehend him. We have to stress that all we want is information. No one is to go after this man on his own."

"Lot of luck with getting that message across," Tucker said. "This is rural Texas. I'd wager most cowboys or ranchers carry a gun in their vehicle or have one with them when they're out working. For protection from snakes, not people. But they know how to shoot."

"Still, we have to stress the perp is dangerous. I'll work on designing the poster tonight."

"Did you get anything enlightening from Dani's security film?"

"No. It seemed like business as usual. Rachel was alone. She talked to several people, but nothing that looked the least bit threatening. She did talk to two men about pottery. I'll ask Dani about them, but I didn't get any bad vibes."

"Rotten news."

"Yeah. That's why I'm back to the drawing board. Millie Miles made an appearance, but she was leaving as Rachel was arriving. I don't know if the sheriff mentioned it to you, but he said my visit upset Millie and that Dudley doesn't want me on the ranch again."

"He mentioned it. I told him to stuff it—in a gentlemanly way, of course."

"Of course."

Sydney picked up the markers and loose stars and dropped them into plastic bags.

"Through working for tonight?"

"Through with the art part, not nearly through with the thinking and searching for any pattern that could lead us to the freak."

Tucker helped her pick up the rest of her supplies. When he finished, he went back to his perch on the edge of the bed. To his surprise, she walked over and sat down beside him.

Their thighs touched. Inconspicuously. Unintentionally, he was sure. His chest tightened and his manly urges checked in as if on autopilot. She put her hand on his arm, and when he met her gaze, he felt the heat deep inside him.

"Is something wrong?" she asked. "Why are you looking at me that way?"

"I don't think you really want me to answer that question."

"I wouldn't have asked if I didn't want to know."

"I'm thinking how gorgeous you look tonight. I love you in jeans. But you look delectable in that dress. To be honest, it's all I can do not to take you in my arms right now."

Her lips on his was her unexpected response. Passion exploded like fireworks. He kissed her lips, the tip of her nose, her eyelids and then back to her lips again. He couldn't get enough of her. Every part of his body craved more.

Yet when she pulled away, he forced himself to let her go.

"I know I started this but I can't keep doing this, Tucker. It's not you. You do everything right. It's just that my emotions are so raw and unprotected right now."

"You don't have to say more. I'll never push you into anything you're not ready for. When the time is right, we'll both know."

"Thanks. I'm going to the bathroom to get ready for bed," she said, "but only because I'll fall asleep working. You should probably be gone when I come back."

His mouth didn't argue the point. His body did. It was hell watching her walk away.

SYDNEY CLOSED THE bathroom door and leaned against it, struggling to put everything in some kind of perspective that made sense. Her concern for Rachel was ripping her heart from her chest.

How could she feel this level of attraction for a man she'd just met?

The only explanation was that the heart-wrenching feeling of helplessness was making her emotionally vulnerable. Tucker wasn't just an incredibly virile hunk. He was smart, thoughtful, protective.

It would be only natural that he'd stir strong feelings inside her. When this was over, when Rachel and the others were safe and the world tilted back on its axis, she'd figure this out.

Until then, she couldn't let anyone affect her focus— not even Tucker Lawrence.

She pulled a pair of pink flowered shorty pajamas from the drawer beneath the dressing table. Simple, comfortable and unsexy pajamas just in case Tucker came back.

She took her time washing and creaming her face while struggling to regain her proper focus, though her energy was beginning to falter.

It was at least five minutes later when she opened the door and stepped back into the bedroom.

Tucker had not left. He was stretched out on her bed on top of the covers, fully clothed except for his boots. His head rested on her pillow. His eyes were closed.

He was snoring, not the house-shaking racket her dad used to make, but nonetheless loud enough there was no doubt that he was sound asleep.

Temptation took an unbidden turn, and she experienced an almost-overwhelming desire to crawl into bed beside him. Not to make love, just to feel her body lying next to his for a few brief moments.

Instead she went back to her computer and spent the next few hours going over every tidbit of information she had yet again.

Eventually, the words began to blur and her thoughts got lost in a fog. She glanced at the clock. It was 2:00 a.m. Tucker was still asleep. She suspected he hadn't been sleeping well after watching his good friend die so tragically. Either that or *not* making love had worn him out.

Her mind was muddled from exhaustion. She didn't have the energy or the inclination to wake him up. She stepped out of her slippers, flicked off the light and crawled into bed beside him. Caught somewhere between levels of consciousness, she cuddled against him.

He made her feel safe.

Chapter Fifteen

Thursday, September 21

Tucker woke to a sharp blow to his stomach and low growling and moaning sounds in his ear. He realized where he was and what was going on just in time to avoid another jab to his body, not from a fist but Sydney's elbow.

He pulled her into his arms and rocked her against him. "I've got you, baby. You're safe. It's all good, just a nightmare."

She jerked away from him and sat up in bed.

"Tucker?"

"It's me." He didn't remember falling asleep in this bed, but obviously he had.

"You're still here?"

"Looks that way. Not intentionally," he assured her. "I've been sound asleep. Bed is too damn comfortable." He'd only planned to stay in her room long enough to make sure she was okay after her abrupt escape to the bathroom.

That was the last thing he remembered.

She lay back down, her hands cradling her head as she stared at the ceiling. "It's fine. Again, not your fault. I could have sent you away at any time, but I just crawled into bed with you."

She rolled over to face him. "You're safe. I was too tired to jump your bones."

Moonlight and shadows played on her face, just enough light to see the fear that still gripped her, the fear she was trying to cover up with a light banter he wasn't buying.

"Must have been a tough nightmare," he said. "Want to talk about it?"

"It was bizarre," she said. "Things were twisted. The Swamp Strangler was chasing me through the swamp but Rachel was with him and I didn't know if she was trying to help me or kill me. There were dead bodies all around us. Only their eyes were open and they were looking at me."

The nightmare still held sway over her emotions. He could hear the torment in her voice. He ached to hold her tight and comfort her, but that could be the worst move he could make. He basically understood nothing about women.

"I'm fighting the Swamp Strangler all over again," she murmured. "I think that's all in the past, and then he invades my thoughts and dreams. What if he's affecting my ability to do my job?"

He remembered hearing about the Swamp Strangler, a south Louisiana serial killer who raped his victims and then left their bodies in murky waters of a bayou to be eaten by the alligators. He didn't remember exactly how he was captured.

"Were you in on that case?" he asked.

"Yes. I profiled him, and then realized who his next victim would be and where he would be taking her. When I couldn't reach her by phone, I knew if someone didn't stop him immediately, it would be too late."

He could see where this was going and sense how upset she was getting just talking about it. "You don't have to go there now, Sydney. He's dead. He's done with."

"I was too late," she said. "Minutes too late. I saw the body facedown in the water and knew it was too late. I went after him, chasing him through bog so damp and spongy I was afraid I'd get sucked into it too deep to ever escape."

Her body trembled and he could stand it no longer. Tucker pulled her back into his arms. "It's over, baby."

"But it wasn't over. This was his world and he used his mastery of the environment to capture me. I felt his fingers tightening on my throat. I felt life ebbing away. And I knew I wasn't ready to die.

"Somehow I got to the tiny gun hidden inside my wristband and put six bullets into his body before he lost his grip on my throat."

He held her, not saying a word while the strain and tension slowly let go of her body. He knew the grief and mental upheaval of watching a close friend die. It might totally destroy Sydney to find that she'd failed in saving her sister's life.

Yet all he could think of was keeping Sydney safe.

"Don't take chances this time, Sydney. Promise me you won't go after this lunatic alone."

"I promise."

He wasn't convinced. She burrowed her head under his chin and scrunched against him.

Damn. The urges hit again, his whole body aching to make love with her.

"I need to go back to my room and let you get some sleep," he whispered.

"You can stay," she whispered.

The invitation was clear. He wanted to accept so badly that walking away would just about kill him. But sometimes a man just had to do what a man had to do.

"Not tonight, Sydney. I can't stay and not make love with you, and I don't want our first time to be tainted by anguish. I want it to be a night you remember forever because I know I will."

He kissed her lightly and then got up quickly. He had to get the hell out of here while he still could.

SYDNEY OPENED HER EYES. Sunshine flooded the bedroom. She rolled over quickly and checked her phone. Eight o'clock. She never slept this late when she was working. How had she let this happen? Exhaustion was no excuse.

She kicked off the sheet but made the mistake of glancing across the bed to the spot where she'd lain in Tucker's arms during the wee hours of the morning.

She let her hand slide to the pillow, still wrinkled from the weight of his head. His musky scent filled her senses.

At this moment she felt closer to him than she'd ever felt to any other man. She'd shared more of her fears, let him see deep inside the part of herself she normally kept secret, and she'd only known him since Monday.

Enough. She'd have to figure out any relationship that might or might not happen when her mind was clear and her emotions weren't in free fall. When the current madness was over and the relentless abductor was behind bars.

She dressed hurriedly, slipping into a pair of white capris and a pale blue pullover shirt. She didn't bother with makeup but calmed her mussed hair with a brush before heading toward the kitchen.

The house was unusually quiet, though odors of bacon, cinnamon and coffee hung heavy in the air. When she reached the kitchen, it was clear that breakfast was over and done with. The table had been cleared. The dishwasher was running.

She lifted the coffeepot. It was full. Evidently Esther had made a fresh pot before they'd all left to go about their lives. As it should be. Her life had been consuming theirs.

She poured a cup of coffee and was about to call and check in with Jackson when she heard the back door open. Esther was singing an old Frank Sinatra standard when she stepped into the kitchen with a basket of fresh hen's eggs over one arm and a basket of yellow squash over the other.

"Good morning," Esther said. "Sorry I wasn't here when you got up, but I have to get outside and do a little gathering and harvesting before it gets too hot. If we don't get a break in this heat soon, I may have to go on one of those Alaskan cruises my friends keep talking about."

"You should," Sydney said.

"Have you ever been there?"

"No, but I've always wanted to. Maybe next summer the two of us can go up there and explore the glaciers."

"I'd like that."

As strange as it was to admit it, Sydney would like that, too. Three days and she was already feeling part of the family. There was probably a hidden meaning there that she wasn't going to get caught up in this morning.

"The guys finished up breakfast early today," Esther said. "Price of beef is up right now and they're helping Pierce check his livestock, deciding which ones to take to market this month and how many to feed and fatten awhile longer."

"Before this week, I had no idea how complicated or how time-consuming ranching is. Nor would I have guessed how dedicated these Texas cowboys are to their lifestyles."

"Cowgirls, too," Esther said. "Once it gets in your blood, there's no getting it out."

"What about your friend Millie Miles? Is she one of those rancher's wives who would hate living anywhere except on the ranch?"

Esther shook her head and started putting away the eggs. "That Millie is a horse of a different color. She's one of those heiresses, spoiled by all that fancy stuff from the day she was born. Her father died in his fifties and all the money from his software fortune fell into her bank account like manna from heaven."

"Really. She seems quite a bit younger than Dudley. I assumed she'd married him for his money."

"Nope. Not that Dudley was poor, mind you. His daddy left him that huge stretch of land he lives on and one of the most prosperous cattle operations in this part of Texas. I reckon they fell in love either with each other or the idea of being in love. I was never sure which."

"Then you don't think they're happily married now?"

"I think she went off the deep end the day her grandson's body was found, and then fell to rock bottom when her daughter went to prison. Looks worse every time I see her, like a woman on her way to meet the devil who knows there's no turning back."

An odd analogy. Esther, with all her Texas roots, had a way of saying things that cut right through to the truth.

Sydney's cell phone rang. It was Jackson.

She excused herself and walked into the hall to take the call in private.

"Did you get a chance to look at the film that Cavazos dropped off?"

"I did. It led nowhere."

"Then let's move on. Lane just sent me a digital composition that combines and frames photos from seven different security cameras around Winding Creek. We can analyze who was in what store at what time on what day and compare it with what we know about where the victims were last seen."

"God bless Lane and his willingness to give up sleep for work."

"You must be doing some of the same," Jackson said. "The file you sent with the design for the award poster was dated in the wee hours."

"When I was brain-dead," she said. "I hope it makes sense."

"Looked good to me. I've passed it on to the sheriff. His people will post it immediately on a Winding Creek website and also post paper copies of it all over town."

"That's a start. When do I get Lane's file?"

"That's why I'm calling. Head over this way now. The rest of the team is on the way. Let's brainstorm our way through this and figure it out. I have a strong hunch that our depraved perp is about to make his next move."

Jackson was known for the accuracy of his hunches.

Chapter Sixteen

Sydney pulled into the drive at Jackson's temporary office setup as Rene, Allan and Tim were climbing out of Rene's personal SUV. Tim carried a large white bag with the top folded over several times. Allan carried a box of doughnuts.

Tim waited until she caught up with them and held the door for her.

"I hope there's something healthy to eat in the bag," she said.

"*Delicioso* tacos," Tim said. "With jalapeños and extra hot sauce. You're gonna love them."

"And for your information, these doughnuts are super nutritious," Allan informed her. "Grease, flour, sugar. All the main food groups."

"Not to worry," Rene said. "The boss specifically ordered a non-spicy breakfast taco for you. He has high hopes for you breaking the secret code to help find the Lone Star Snatcher."

Sydney hurried to catch up with Rene. "What did you call him?"

"Damn it. Sorry, Sydney. I didn't mean to let that slip in front of you."

"Let that slip? Does that mean you guys have been referring to the perp that way all week and keeping it from me?"

"It just slipped out of my mouth one day when we were talking," Tim said. "You know it's not that we're not taking this case dead serious. It's just force of habit to give worthless scum like our perp a nickname."

"Never meant to offend you," Rene added as they walked back toward the kitchen.

Another of the problems with her being personally involved in the case. They were worried about her sensitivities when they needed to all be talking freely.

"I'm not offended," she assured them. "I know how serious you all are about apprehending the perp and saving Rachel and the others. Rest assured, that is nowhere near as repulsive as what I've been calling him in my mind."

"You're seriously okay with it?" Allan asked.

"Seriously. I don't care what you call him. Let's just bring him down."

They were all in favor of that.

Eager to get started, they passed out the food and poured the coffee in no time flat. After a few more minutes to adjust the equipment delivered from Jackson's Dallas office that morning, the spliced and edited version of the film was showing on a large portable screen.

"If you see anything you want to comment on, let me know and I'll pause the frame," Tim said.

The film started on March 9 at 2:45 p.m. and had

been taken from the Chic Cowgirl Boutique, where Alice Baker from Shreveport, Louisiana, charged a pair of expensive boots at 3:30 p.m.

"She looks relaxed," Tim commented.

"Definitely alone."

"Pause," Allan said. "Not a clear image, but check out the tall cowboy with the sexy young blonde. I'm almost sure I saw him in the drugstore last night with a different blonde, also very attractive. He was picking up a prescription while I was buying shaving cream."

"Probably just a playboy but keep an eye out for him moving forward," Jackson said.

"Notice the older guy looking at the boots on the sale rack," Tim said. "He keeps turning around to look at Alice while she's admiring her boots in the mirror."

From the boot shop the film composite progressed to other Winding Creek locations, same day, both before and after her trip to the boutique. Alice wasn't seen again.

Shopping for boots might have been her fatal mistake.

This continued for what seemed like forever until they finally hit a speck of pay dirt. The last record for Michelle Dickens was a charge at an Exxon station just out of San Antonio. Nothing had placed her in or within forty miles of Winding Creek.

But there she was, perusing the local candle shop on August 20, the day she disappeared.

The shop was almost empty and the only person in there who looked even vaguely familiar to Sydney was the woman in charge of the shop.

And Millie Miles. For a woman who didn't even have the energy to drive anymore, she sure made it into town often enough.

"Whoa. Hold it right there," Sydney said. "The woman in the white pantsuit is Millie Miles. It probably means nothing but I also saw her leaving Dani's Delights just as Rachel was walking in."

"We may see several people more than once," Jackson said, "but still worth noting. It definitely appears that all roads lead to and leave from Winding Creek."

They finished the morning with the tape at Dani's Delights that Sydney had looked at over and over last night. She wasn't up to seeing it again.

She slipped out of the kitchen and onto the back porch. The day was already sweltering. Her spirits were scraping bottom. She checked her phone for missed messages and found one from Tucker.

She called him back immediately. His voice didn't cheer her, but all the same it felt good to hear him say hello.

"Sorry I missed you this morning," he said. "Pierce wanted some other opinions and I didn't want to wake you."

"That's fine. Jackson wouldn't have approved your attending this meeting anyway."

"You sound down," he said. "I hope it's not from bad news."

"No. It's from having no news. Nothing to jump-start the search or even nudge it forward."

"Hate to hear that. I'm back at Esther's. Do you want

to meet for lunch? All I have to do is grab a quick shower."

"I'll need to call you back and let you know. This is Jackson's meeting and I'm not sure what he has in mind next."

"No worries. Just give me a call. I'm easy."

"The faces are all starting to run together," Rene was saying as she rejoined them in the kitchen. "It's nearly one. I say we break for lunch."

"Just one quick follow-up question before we scatter," Tim said. "You may be the one to answer this one, Sydney. Are the Houston detectives still questioning your sister's ex-boyfriend?"

"He's been cleared," Jackson said. "Airtight alibi. Water-skiing up at Lake Conroe with friends from work all afternoon that Saturday."

"I never really considered him a suspect," Sydney said, "but glad they checked him out."

"I'll bet ninety to nothing the Snatcher drives a pickup truck," Tim said. "I've never seen so many in one small town. I'm starting to feel like a wimp in my sedan."

"And most of them black," Rene said.

"Agreed," Tim added. "With numerous scratches to the paint and a few layers of red Texas clay splattered around the tires to prove they don't belong to sissy city dwellers."

Sydney excused herself and went to the bathroom for relief and to freshen up. When she returned to the kitchen, Jackson was the only one in sight and he was on the phone.

"Whatever you do, don't let her out of your sight. I'll be right there.

"Grab your handbag, Sydney. The perp has struck again. Only this time the victim got away."

SHERIFF CAVAZOS MET them at the door to the County Sheriff's Office. "She's not hurt physically but she's an emotional wreck. She gave us a little information but then clammed up. Says she only wants to talk to a woman. I figure you're the best one for the job, Sydney."

"What's her name?"

"Joy White. She fits the same pattern as the other victims. Attractive. Brunette. Thirty-one years old. She's not from Winding Creek."

"Where is she from?" Sydney asked.

"I don't know. She teared up and started crying before we could find out where she was from or why she was here in Winding Creek today."

"Where was she when she was attacked?" Jackson asked.

"About ten miles out of town on the blacktop, what we natives refer to as the scenic drive back to the main highway. I've got a crime-scene team out there now, but feel free to send your guys out there, too, if it would make you feel better. I can give them directions."

"Thanks. I'll get hold of Allan and Rene and have them call you. I'll wait here to see what Sydney learns."

"Lead the way," Sydney said.

"Joy's in my office. I figured it would be less frightening for her than the cold, sterile interrogation areas."

"Good thinking."

The sheriff left Sydney at his office door. She tapped softly. When no one answered, she opened the door and slipped inside.

She kept her voice low and calming. "My name is Sydney Maxwell, Joy. I'm with the FBI. I heard you had a close call this morning."

"He tried to kill me. I didn't do anything. He didn't know me. He just wanted to kill me." The words were broken, fighting their way out between short gasps of breath.

"I believe you and I know how scary that must have been."

"Why? Why me?"

"We think he may be the man responsible for the women who've gone missing from the Winding Creek area over the last few months. We need to stop him before he hurts someone else."

"He's crazy. I could see it in his eyes." She closed her eyes tight for a few moments before opening them again.

"Can you tell me what happened?" Sydney asked.

"How do I know he won't come after me again if I do? Are you going to protect me?"

"If you need protection, I'll see that you get it. I know how afraid you are, Joy, but you got away. You're one of the lucky ones."

Joy covered her face with her hands. Sydney pulled up a chair so that they were facing each other, so close that their knees brushed when Joy shifted in her chair.

"My sister is one of the missing women, Joy. I don't

know if she's dead or alive. I only know that she and at least three other women might still be his captives."

Dead or alive. The words were difficult to utter, but the truth refused to be silenced this time.

Joy uncovered her face and clasped her hands tightly in her lap. "Heaven help them." She wiped a tear from her cheek with the back of her hand. "What is it you want to know?"

"Everything, just the way it happened. Take your time. Don't leave anything out. I'll be right here with you. There are law-enforcement personnel all around. He can't hurt you now."

Finally, Joy opened up and the words tumbled from her lips, mostly coherent, sometimes stifled by a shudder.

Joy was a romance writer from Gruene, Texas, who'd driven to Winding Creek that morning to speak to a county-wide book-club meeting.

The library had a parking lot but it was full when Joy got there and she had to park two blocks away near the pharmacy on Main Street.

The only place she went after the meeting was to Dani's Delights to get an iced latte to drink on her way home. She hadn't seen her accoster at the library or in the bakery and hadn't realized he was following her until he drove up even with her on a two-lane road.

"He started waving his arms and yelling hysterically for me to pull over to the shoulder and stop the car. I tried to wave him off, but he looked so upset, I rolled down my window. He pointed to the back of my car and told me I was leaking gas and sparks were flying.

"I didn't see any smoke and I was afraid to stop. There were no other cars in sight and there were wooded areas on both sides of the blacktop."

"What made you stop?"

"He slowed and dropped behind me, still waving for me to pull over. Then I heard an explosion that sounded like it came from my trunk. I thought the car might be about to blow up."

"I can see why you would."

"I threw on my brakes as I pulled to the shoulder and jumped out of the car. There were no flames, no smoke, only this wild cowboy running toward me."

"What did you do then?"

"I panicked, jumped back in the car and grabbed my revolver from beneath the seat. Before I could lock the door, he yanked it open and was coming at me, both hands fisted.

"I shot and the bullet hit him in the right leg. Blood spurted everywhere. I didn't care. I kicked him away from my car and left him bleeding in the middle of the road. I drove all the way to the highway before I felt safe enough to pull over and call 911."

Tears started to flow down Joy's cheeks. "It's not my gun. My husband made me bring it because of all the trouble we've been hearing about. I've never shot a man before."

"You did the right thing, Joy. The brave thing. You may have saved the lives of many other women."

Now all Sydney needed from Joy was an extremely accurate description, but the urgency had soared to its highest level yet.

The Lone Star Snatcher would be running scared and a psycho running scared was dangerously unpredictable.

Roy Sales put the whiskey bottle to his lips and gulped it down as if it were water. His leg hurt something fierce and whiskey was the only painkiller he had.

He was in big trouble now. The whole town would be talking about the attack. The sheriff, the FBI, even the Texas Rangers would be out to get him now.

They'd be looking for a man with a bullet wound in his right leg. They'd have his DNA and his description.

He couldn't even show his face at the big house to force Millie to give him more money. His sweet little blackmail deal was over. He'd done what she asked, killed on demand. Blew poor old Charlie Kavanaugh's brains out with him begging for mercy.

He didn't like to kill. He hadn't wanted to kill Charlie. He hadn't wanted to kill sweet little Sara Goodwin, but she'd called him a monster. A monster, after he'd picked her up off the street and taken her in.

She'd said he was crazy. He wasn't crazy. He did what he was told. Mommy didn't like it when he disobeyed. She didn't like to have to lock him in the cold, dark basement. She just wanted him to learn to be a good boy.

Mommy was yelling in his brain now. He put his hands over his ears and tried to shut her out, but she wouldn't stop. She never stopped. Even after he'd pushed her off the ladder and killed her, she wouldn't stop tormenting him.

Kill your prisoners. Kill your prisoners. Kill your prisoners and run for your life. Run, Roy. Run and never stop.

They weren't prisoners. They were his guests. He didn't want to kill them. He didn't like being alone at night when the voices came at him from all directions.

But he couldn't just leave the women here to tell all kinds of lies about him.

He'd burn the shack to the ground. That was it. There would be nothing but ashes. They might even think he'd burned with his guests and then they'd never come after him.

All except Rachel. He couldn't kill Rachel. She was starting to understand him. They were friends. His mother hated her, but that was too bad. This time he wouldn't listen to her no matter how loudly she screamed into his mind.

Rachel would be going with him.

It was time to start the fire.

Chapter Seventeen

They had their description. They knew how the kidnapper operated. Rene had even found a huge firecracker casing at the crime scene to explain the explosion.

It was progress. It just wasn't enough progress.

Sydney called Tucker as she left the sheriff's office and asked him to meet her at Dani's Delights so that she could explain the latest developments. The way he'd stood by her this week, he deserved to be kept in the loop.

And she wanted to see him. No use in hiding from the truth any longer. It didn't change anything at this point, but she was tired of fighting the unalterable fact. She was falling hard for the bull rider.

She drove the few blocks to Main Street and pulled into the angled parking spot between two black pickup trucks that had both edged over the white line and into her space.

Wide, long-bed, black pickup trucks. Her FBI team was right. The town was overrun with them. What did the cowboys have against magenta or deep burgundy?

Millie Miles stepped out of the passenger-side door

of the truck to Sydney's right just as Sydney was stepping out of her car. This was obviously one of those days she hadn't wanted to drive. Why should she when she could just have one of her many wranglers to serve as chauffeur.

Or maybe she had the same chauffeur every day. Driving Mrs. Millie.

In town—on a regular basis like the day Rachel had been walking into Dani's Delights when Millie was walking out. Had Millie been in Winding Creek but perhaps in different shops whenever all of the victims had last been seen in Winding Creek?

It was a long shot but the best thing she had going now.

Sydney walked over to the truck, stopped beside the driver's open window and introduced herself.

"Hi, I'm Sydney Maxwell with the FBI." She flashed her badge. "May I ask you a few questions?"

"Am I in trouble?"

"Not unless you've broken the law."

"I had a speeding ticket last year."

"I'll let you pass on that. I just noticed Millie Miles getting out of your truck. That's so nice of you to drive her around. Do you do that every day?"

"No. That's usually Roy Sales's job."

"Where is Roy today?"

"He was here earlier. He dropped the boss lady off at the library for some kind of meeting. He was supposed to come back and pick up her and a friend at Caffe's after lunch. He never showed. The friend got a ride home and I drew the flunky card. Don't tell the boss lady I put it that way."

"Never. What do you think happened to Roy Sales?"

"Who knows. He's like a blister. Annoying as hell and doesn't show up until the work is done, if you get my drift."

"I do. I think I may have met Roy before. Does he have greasy brown hair that crawls into his shirt collar? A slight build. Short—only a few inches taller than me." As per Joy White's description except for leaving out the crazy look in his eyes.

"Yep. You've met him. That's him to a T."

Her heart burst into overdrive. This was the way it felt when all the pieces fell into place.

She thanked the driver for his trouble, rushed back to her car and put in a call to Jackson. She got his answering machine, which meant he was likely talking to someone else. He didn't like to be out of touch with his agents.

She left a message.

"I think we've got our man. Name's Roy Sales. Works for Dudley and Millie Miles. I'm headed out to Kurlacky Acres Ranch, where he lives now. Meet me there. Call Tucker for directions. And hurry."

Excitement and adrenaline rushed through her, but even that couldn't bury the surging fear. She had no idea what she'd find when she got to Roy's place.

She prayed as she pushed the accelerator nearly to the floor.

Please let Rachel be alive and well. Let all the Snatcher's prisoners, however many there are, be safe.

SYDNEY ALMOST PASSED the rickety gate before she saw it. She slammed on her brakes and swerved into the dirt and grass of the drive.

It occurred to her that she didn't know where to go once she was through the gate. Tucker had said there were shacks, sheds and dilapidated barns scattered all over some of the ranches.

The smart thing to do would be to pull her small rental car into one of the wooded areas she could see from here and wait for Jackson. She couldn't afford any stupid mistakes this time.

With luck, Roy would be working at Dudley's ranch. They'd be able to search the premises for Rachel and the others before dealing with him. Once they encountered him, he'd know this was the end of the road for him. She didn't expect him to go down easy.

She got out of her car to open the rickety gate.

She smelled smoke before she saw the black furls sweeping above the treetops. It could be just a trash fire.

It could be Roy Sales's last hurrah.

Panic jolted her into action. The latch on the gate was locked. She ran back to the car and barged through the gate, knocking one side completely off its rusty hinges.

Her plan to wait for Jackson to arrive was canceled. She followed the smoke until she was close enough to see brilliant gold and yellow blazes shooting toward the sky.

By the time she reached what was left of the house, timbers were falling and most of the roof was gone.

She jumped out of her car and heard women screaming for help, their voices almost drowned out completely by the roar of the flames.

"I'm coming, Rachel. I'm coming," she screamed. She rushed toward the fire. The heat and smoke stole her breath but she kept pushing on.

Her eyes poured water. Her lungs burned. Coughing spells tore from her dry throat. The fiery blazes were lapping at everything around her. Struggling to stay conscious, she fell to her knees. Then she looked up and saw three women stumbling hand in hand from the blaze. Coughing and fighting for breath, they fell to the ground in a huddle the second they were out of harm's way.

Sydney crawled toward them, her heart beating so fast it pushed her along. Finally, she escaped the worst of the fire and called out for Rachel.

The women turned toward her. None of the three were Rachel. Dizzy and nauseous, Sydney stumbled back toward the flames. She could swear she heard Rachel calling her name. She fell to her knees as the heat overtook her.

She tried to get up, but her legs wouldn't move. She was so hot, so very, very hot. Someone picked her up in his arms as a huge timber crashed around her. Or maybe it was death calling her home.

Blinded by smoke and tears, she looked up and had to blink repeatedly before she realized it was Tucker who had saved her from the flames.

"How did you get here? Where did you come from?"

"Jackson called and said you were here waiting on backup."

"I didn't save Rachel."

"I know. I'm so sorry, baby. So very sorry. God knows you tried."

Reality merged with grief. She wiggled out of his arms but held to Tucker to keep her balance even after her feet were planted on solid ground. "We have to help the women who just escaped that literal hell."

When she turned to find them, they were no longer there.

"There were three women who walked out of the fire. I didn't dream them, did I?"

"The only person I saw was you," Tucker said.

"I know they were here. Everyone except Rachel was right here a few minutes ago. The fire must have burned the locked doors that held them."

"Jackson's on his way here. If they're here, he'll find them. Let's get you to my truck."

"I'm not leaving here until we find them." She rushed off into the woods to look for them.

"Sydney, over here."

The voice was the quietest of whispers but Sydney was certain it was Rachel calling to her. Rachel. Alive.

"I'm coming," she called through sobs of pure joy and thankful release. "Oh, Rachel, I'm coming."

Finally, she caught a glimpse of her sister motioning to her from behind a thick tree trunk.

Moving as quickly as she could, she made her way to Rachel. She collapsed into Rachel's arms, holding on tight, afraid to believe Rachel was really alive and safe.

"Don't make a sound," Rachel whispered. "The monster is out there somewhere, Sydney. He's always there."

"No, you're safe," Sydney whispered. Safe. Her sister was safe and alive. Relief surged through her as she let the feeling sink deep into her heart.

"My friend Tucker is waiting for us. The FBI is on the way. The monster is history."

"No. You'll see. He's never going to let me go. He'll kill us both."

"Why do you think that?"

"Because he always does what he says."

This time the voice was gruff and Sydney felt the barrel of a gun pressed against her temple. Rachel was right. The monster had been there all along.

"So this is the way you want it, Rachel? You'd rather run away from me and burn to death than stay with me. In that case, who wants to die first? Oh, that's right. I promised Rachel she could watch her sister die. Or was it the other way around?"

Sydney took a deep breath. She'd been here before. That time the Strangler had the upper hand. This time it was the Lone Star Snatcher, but the situation was the same.

Take control or die. If she was going to die anyway, what did she have to lose?

The gun was at her head. A quick pull of the trigger and it would all be over and the Snatcher would win. She and Rachel would be the monster's last victims.

She was not ready to die. She had a bull rider waiting for her and a whole marvelous life to live.

She tripped intentionally and fell backward, maneuvering her body so she'd fall against Roy Sales's injured leg. Roy yelled out in pain and then raised his pistol to slam it into her head.

Instead it went flying through the woods.

"Sorry, Roy. Not my first rodeo and you just bought yourself lifetime accommodations in the state pen. Now, would one of you ladies mind picking up Roy's gun and handing it to me? I hated to get it dirty but he wasn't playing nice with it."

"Tucker." Sydney turned to find the situation reversed. Tucker was a step behind Roy with his gun pointed at Roy's head.

No one had ever looked that good to her in all her life.

A symphony of sirens signaled the approach of the sheriff, Jackson and hopefully a fire truck or two.

Alice, Michelle and Karen joined them at the edge of the woods. All the women ended up crying thankful tears in each other's arms.

Each of the women would go back to their lives a different person than they were before this horrible experience, but they were going back alive. Sydney would be there to help Rachel through her adjustment every step of the way.

The reign of the Lone Star Snatcher was over, but that wouldn't end the evil in this world. That was why Sydney would be staying with the FBI. Somebody had to fight for right. She loved the job, so it might as well be her.

Unless that meant giving up Tucker. In which case she might have to reexamine her whole life to this point.

Rachel and Sydney met briefly with Jackson. A more

detailed meeting was set for first thing the following morning, after both of them had some rest and recovery time.

Rachel went back to Esther's with Sydney and Tucker, and his marvelous family welcomed her with warm, embracing arms.

It was hours later before Sydney and Tucker finally made it to her bed. This time Tucker got to stay all night and they finally made love.

Three times.

Epilogue

Three weeks later:

Tucker had returned to the rodeo. He loved it as much as ever and was thankful he hadn't walked away from it. But rodeo wasn't all he loved.

He was head over heels crazy about Sydney but the relationship seemed to be stalling out at the commitment stage. He'd always heard it was men who were afraid of commitment, but he couldn't wait to promise forever. Sydney wouldn't even mention the *c* word.

The ring was in his pocket, but what would he do if she said no? Beg? Not his style.

Riding bulls had never been this scary. He walked out to the porch to wait for Sydney. She was driving in from Dallas, where she said she had an important meeting with Jackson today.

He'd driven in from Waco, where he'd just come in first in the bull-riding competition.

He and Sydney had to do a lot of planning to get time together, but it was always worth the trouble. Not just making love with her, as fantastic and exciting as that was. He loved every second he spent with her.

Esther joined him, a glass of tea in hand. She sat down in her porch swing and watched him pace.

"What's gotten into you tonight? You're as wired as an electric line."

"I'm just looking forward to seeing Sydney."

"You two aren't having problems, are you?"

"Not that I know of."

"Don't you mess it up with her, Tucker. She's smart, sweet and fun. You're not going to run into many women like that in a lifetime of looking."

"I agree."

"I sure do appreciate her getting me some closure on my Charlie's death. I knew he didn't commit suicide. We loved each other too much for him to just check out on me like that. It didn't make me miss him any less, but all the same it was salve for my grief."

"Good to finally get justice for Charlie," Tucker said. "I'm not surprised to find out Millie was behind the killing or that Roy Sales could be lured into the murderous scheme with her money. I am shocked Millie finally admitted her part in that. She'll be behind bars for a long, long time."

"My Charlie was just so honest," Esther said. "He knew his friend Dudley wasn't guilty and that Millie was always letting Angela get by with anything. When Charlie went to her and threatened to tell the truth, she just up and had him killed."

"Charlie is just another trial Roy Sales will be facing. He also confessed to the murder of Sara Goodwin."

"Do they have any idea why he killed her?" Esther asked.

"The theory that's being tossed around is her murder is what triggered his going over the edge. He thought she wanted to be with him and then she started calling him the same sort of names his mother used to call him."

"The dark-haired mother who looked a lot like Rachel and his other victims," Esther said. "They say his mother used to lock him up in the basement for days if he just spilled his milk or got his clothes dirty playing outside. What kind of momma would do a thing like that?"

"One that shouldn't have had children," Tucker said. "Sales had his problems. That didn't give him the right to kill and torture others."

"What he done was bad and that's for sure," Esther said. "But even though he killed Charlie, I'm glad they put him in that mental hospital to see if he's fit to stand trial. The psychologist said Roy Sales even believed he'd killed his mother because he wished she was dead when she tortured him. Truth was she just accidentally fell from a ladder."

"I suppose the defense will claim the torture he went through as a child was what caused him to lock Rachel and the others up in that crowded storm shelter," Tucker said. "Too bad he didn't get help before he caused so much hurt to so many people."

A car pulled up in front of the house and stopped. When Sydney stepped out, Tucker hurried to meet her.

She fell into his open arms and they stayed that way for long minutes.

"How did your meeting go?" he asked.

"Great. I can't wait to tell you about it."

"Then don't." He opened the trunk to get her luggage. "Let's hear it."

"It's not something I want to just blurt out."

He wasn't sure he was going to like this. "Want to take a walk before we go inside?"

"I do."

This was starting to sound like a breakup moment. He stuck his hand deep in his pocket and worried the engagement ring he'd hoped to put on her finger tonight.

They walked awhile in silence before Sydney broke her news. "I've been offered a really nice promotion but it will require moving to Dallas."

"Are you going to take it?"

"That all depends on you."

"I'm not sure what you mean."

"I love you, Tucker. I love you so much that I can't even imagine living without you. But I love my job, too. And you love bull riding. Living in Texas instead of Nashville would make it easier for us to get together, but I'm still not sure we would ever have enough time for us."

"We'll make time. It will take effort but we can do it. Vacations. Days I'm not in competition, I'll spend with you. Weekends you can fly to meet me wherever I'm competing."

"Will you settle for that?"

"I guess the real question is, will either of us settle for less? We don't fit into the one-size-fits-all mold, Sydney. We take risks. We go for the passion, at least that's what a wise woman once told me."

"What if she was wrong?"

"I know her well. She meant every word of it and she's almost never wrong. As brave as you are, don't tell me you're afraid to take a chance on us."

He curled his fingers around the ring in his pocket and then fell to one knee.

"I love you, Sydney Maxwell. I have since the first day I met you. I don't want you to give up something you love for me. That would only diminish both of us."

"And you can be happy with my continuing to work for the FBI?" she asked.

"I certainly can't be happy if you're not happy. We'll go through lots of changes in our life. My body definitely won't hold up to bull riding forever. You might want a family one day. But we'll change on our terms when we're good and ready."

He took her hand. "Will you marry me and join me in the best damn love affair in the history of all mankind? All it has to last is forever."

"You're sure."

"I've never been more sure of anything in my life."

"Then the answer is yes. I love you, Tucker, and I have no doubts that marriage to you will be the most exciting adventure of my life."

He slipped the ring on her finger, stood and took her in his arms. They sealed their promises with a kiss that took his breath away.

A thrill a minute with Sydney for as long as they lived. It couldn't get any better than that.

* * * * *

MILLS & BOON®

INTRIGUE
Romantic Suspense

A SEDUCTIVE COMBINATION OF DANGER AND DESIRE

A sneak peek at next month's titles...

In stores from 7th September 2017:

Just can't wait?
Buy our books online before they hit the shops!
www.millsandboon.co.uk

Also available as eBooks.

MILLS & BOON®

Why shop at millsandboon.co.uk?

Each year, thousands of romance readers find their perfect read at millsandboon.co.uk. That's because we're passionate about bringing you the very best romantic fiction. Here are some of the advantages of shopping at www.millsandboon.co.uk:

* **Get new books first**—you'll be able to buy your favourite books one month before they hit the shops

* **Get exclusive discounts**—you'll also be able to buy our specially created monthly collections, with up to 50% off the RRP

* **Find your favourite authors**—latest news, interviews and new releases for all your favourite authors and series on our website, plus ideas for what to try next

* **Join in**—once you've bought your favourite books, don't forget to register with us to rate, review and join in the discussions

Visit **www.millsandboon.co.uk**
for all this and more today!